"Gardiner skillfully builds tension as the pace accelerates toward the most dramatic, exhausting, and satisfying ending I've read in quite some time. Woman power, y'all."
—*Lone Star Literary Life*

"Gardiner, who has thirteen well-received titles to her name, including Edgar Award–winner *China Lake*, has turned in another winner with *Into the Black Nowhere*. Crime-thriller fans appreciate her compelling, well-developed characters—both good and bad—her sense of plot, her master of heart-stopping twists, and her pace, which is TV-ready, as her recent accomplishment shows, combine to create a roller-coaster of a reading ride."
—*The Florida Times-Union*

"Robust character study mixed with an engrossing police procedural . . . Gardiner knows how to push the terrifying envelope."
—Oline Cogdill, *Sun-Sentinel* (South Florida)

ALSO BY MEG GARDINER

Phantom Instinct
The Shadow Tracer
Ransom River

UNSUB NOVELS

UNSUB

JO BECKETT NOVELS

The Nightmare Thief
The Liar's Lullaby
The Memory Collector
The Dirty Secrets Club

EVAN DELANEY NOVELS

China Lake
Mission Canyon
Jericho Point
Crosscut
Kill Chain

INTO THE BLACK NOWHERE

AN UNSUB NOVEL

MEG GARDINER

DUTTON

DUTTON

An imprint of Penguin Random House LLC
penguinrandomhouse.com

Previously published as a Dutton hardcover

First Dutton premium mass market printing, 2019

Copyright © 2018 by Meg Gardiner

Penguin supports copyright. Copyright fuels creativity, encourages diverse voices, promotes free speech, and creates a vibrant culture. Thank you for buying an authorized edition of this book and for complying with copyright laws by not reproducing, scanning, or distributing any part of it in any form without permission. You are supporting writers and allowing Penguin to continue to publish books for every reader.

DUTTON and the D colophon are registered trademarks of
Penguin Random House LLC.

ISBN 9781101985571

Printed in the United States of America
10 9 8 7 6 5 4 3 2 1

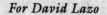

For David Lazo

We serial killers are your sons, we are your husbands, we are everywhere.

—*Ted Bundy*

INTO THE
BLACK
NOWHERE

1

The cry pierced the walls, ringing through the darkness. Shana Kerber roused and squinted at the clock. Twelve forty-five A.M.

Her voice came as a sigh. "Already?"

Shana huddled for a minute under the comforter, clinging wishfully to warmth and sleep. *Hush yourself, Jaydee. Please.* But the baby's crying intensified. It was her strong, wide-awake, *I'm hungry* cry.

The night was bitter. Early February, the north wind scouring Texas. It whistled through the cracks in the farmhouse, rattling the doors in their frames. Shana rolled over. The other side of the bed was cool. Brandon wasn't home yet.

For a few more seconds Shana lay still, aching with fatigue, hoping Jaydee would quiet. But she was crying to beat the band. Ten months old and still up twice a night. Shana's mom swore things would get easier. She'd been swearing so for months. *When, Mom? Please, when?*

"Coming, baby," Shana murmured.

She tossed back the covers, brushed her sleep-tangled

hair from her face, and slogged out of the bedroom. The hardwood floor creaked beneath her bare feet. Jaydee's cries grew clearer.

Six feet down the hall, she slowed. The crying wasn't coming from the nursery.

The house was completely dark. Jaydee was too little to climb out of her crib.

Shana turned on the hall light. The nursery door was open.

A sliver of ice seemed to slide through her chest. At the far end of the hall she could see into the living room. On the sofa, half lit by the hall light, a stranger sat holding her little girl on his lap.

The icy sliver sank through Shana. "What are you doing here?"

"Don't worry. I'm a friend of your husband." The man's face was in shadow. His voice was soothing—almost warm. "She was crying. Didn't want to wake you."

He seemed completely relaxed. Shana walked slowly to the living room. She glanced out the front window. The moon was full. An SUV was parked outside. A placard hung from the rearview mirror.

"Is that . . ." She looked him up and down. "Army? Are you . . ."

The baby twisted in the man's arms. He bounced her. "She's quite the little doll."

He tickled Jaydee and made baby talk. Shana tried harder to see his face. His eyes remained in shadow. Something stopped her from turning on the table lamp.

Is he a friend of Brandon's?

Shana extended her hands. "I'll take her."

The wind battered the windows. The man's smile persisted. Though she couldn't see his eyes, Shana had a gut certainty that he was watching her.

She edged forward. She was eight feet from him. Out of his reach. "Give Jaydee to me."

He didn't.

Her hands were open. "Please."

Jaydee twisted in the man's arms. Her chubby legs pumped like pistons. Shana's heart thundered. She saw the power in the man's hands and knew she couldn't simply charge at him.

The shotgun was under her bed. Five seconds was what it would take to run to the bedroom, grab it, and rush back down the hall. It was a twelve gauge. It was loaded.

And it was useless, because this man was holding her child to his chest. Her breathing caught, like a cloth snagging on a nail.

She inched forward. "Give her here."

For a few seconds, he continued bouncing Jaydee. Crying, the little girl reached starfish fingers toward Shana.

"She wants her mama," the man said. "Aww, come here."

Shana held still, her own arms outstretched. "Give me my baby."

The smile stiffened. The man set Jaydee gently beside him on the sofa.

Before Shana could inhale, he lowered his shoulders,

gathering himself. He was in motion when the light finally hit his eyes.

The dashboard clock read one thirty A.M. when Brandon Kerber turned onto the gravel driveway. The truck bounced over the ruts, stereo blasting Chris Stapleton. Brandon whistled along. His rare Saturday night out had been golden—a Spurs game in San Antonio with friends from his army days. He curved past the stand of cedars and the house came into view.

"What . . ."

The front door was open.

Brandon gunned the F-150 up to the house. The windows reflected the truck's headlights like wild eyes. He jumped out. In the wind, the door was banging back against the wall. An acid taste burned his throat. Banging that loud should have woken Shana up. Inside the darkened house, he heard a mournful sound.

Crying.

Brandon rushed in. The living room was cold. The headlights threw his shadow ahead of him on the floor like a blade. The crying kept up. It was the baby.

Jaydee lay huddled on the floor. He scooped her up. "Shana?"

He hit a light switch. The living room lit up, neat, clean, and empty.

Jaydee's eyes were red-rimmed. She was exhausted from sobbing. He pulled her to his chest. Her cries diminished to pathetic hiccups.

"*Shana*."

Brandon ran to the bedroom with the baby and flipped on the light. He spun and strode down the hall, looking in the nursery. In the kitchen. The garage. The back porch.

Nothing. Shana was gone.

He stood in the living room, clutching Jaydee, telling himself, *She's here. I just can't see her.*

But the truth closed in on him. Shana had vanished. She was the fifth.

2

Early-morning shadows slashed the road. The sun blazed gold through the pines. Caitlin Hendrix accelerated and swung her Highlander into the grounds of the FBI Academy in Quantico.

Beneath her black winter coat, her credentials were clipped to the left side of her belt. Her Glock 19M was holstered on the right. The text on her phone read Solace, Texas.

Caitlin got out, and the freezing wind lifted her auburn hair off her shoulders. The Virginia winter constantly reminded her she was an outsider here. She liked it that way. It kept her on her toes.

She buzzed through the door and headed for the Behavioral Analysis Unit.

Suspected serial abductions, the text read.

The people Caitlin passed walked faster than the detectives she'd worked with back at the Alameda Sheriff's Office. They turned corners more crisply. She missed her Bay Area colleagues—missed their pride and camaraderie. But she loved seeing *FBI* on her creds, with the words *Special Agent* beneath her name.

Phones rang. Beyond the windows, the blue glass walls of the FBI Laboratory complex reflected the rising sun.

Caitlin approached her desk in BAU-4, where she was currently one of eight agents and analysts assigned to Crimes Against Adults. She said good morning to her colleagues as they arrived. Everyone had received the same text.

The Behavioral Analysis Unit was a department of the FBI's National Center for the Analysis of Violent Crime— a branch of the Critical Incident Response Group. Its mission involved investigating unusual or repetitive violent crimes. *Critical incident response* meant that when a hot case came to the BAU, it acted, and fast, because time was limited and people were in danger.

Like today.

She barely had time to take off her coat before an office door opened at the far end of the room.

"Don't get comfortable."

People looked over. Special Agent in Charge C.J. Emmerich strode toward them.

"Five women have disappeared from Gideon County, Texas, in the last six months. The latest was two nights ago," he said. "The victims have all vanished on a Saturday night. And the period between abductions is diminishing."

Emmerich's gaze swept the room and landed on Caitlin.

"Escalation," she said.

His nod was brief. "Commonalities between the abductions indicate that we're dealing with a single offender. Someone who's growing bolder, more confident."

Emmerich was her official mentor as an agent-in-training. A legendary profiler, he radiated such self-discipline that it unsettled her. Solemn, intense, he attacked cases like a hawk attacks prey. When he swooped in for a kill, his talons were sharp.

"The Gideon County Sheriff's Office has requested our assistance," he said.

His assistant stood and passed out file folders. Caitlin flipped through hers.

Escalation. She scanned the pages in the file, looking for exactly what that word meant in this case.

She was no longer a raw rookie but was still finding her feet as a criminal profiler. She had a cop's experience and instincts; she was learning to interpret crime scene evidence, forensics, and victimology to build a picture of a perpetrator. Profiling was based on the insight that everything at a crime scene tells a story and reveals something about the criminal. The BAU studied offender behavior to uncover how they thought, predict how they would escalate—and apprehend them before they could put any others in danger.

"The victims have been taken from public places and their own homes," Emmerich said. "No witnesses, and so far, no probative forensic evidence. As the sheriff put it, they simply vanished."

Vanished. Caitlin's eye was drawn to the composite sketch pinned above her desk.

White male, late twenties. The sketch caught his slit-eyed stare and casual menace. He had walked past her in a California biker bar. Later, in a dark tunnel, he'd crucified her hand with a nail gun.

The Bureau's facial recognition software couldn't identify him. He was the Ghost: a killer, a betrayer, a hiss in the wiring. He had helped the serial killer known as the Prophet murder seven people, including her father.

He'd promised they would meet again. She was waiting for his call.

But that couldn't rate her attention this morning.

She turned a page in the file folder and saw a photo: a woman in her midtwenties, only a few years younger than she was. Lively eyes, a self-assured smile, halo-gold hair.

Shana Kerber. Caitlin lingered on the photo, wishing she could tell her, *Hold on. People are searching for you.*

"It's been twenty-nine hours since the latest abduction," Emmerich said. "The locals need us on scene while there's still a significant chance to find this victim alive. And if we can find her, maybe there's a chance to save the others."

He pointed at Caitlin and another agent. Caitlin's pulse kicked up a beat.

"Grab your go bags. Flight leaves Dulles for Austin at ten thirty."

3

Solace sat halfway between Austin and San Antonio at the foot of the Texas Hill Country, sliced down its eastern edge by Interstate 35. Caitlin and the team rolled in under a white winter sun.

Caitlin had been to Texas only once, as a child. She recalled hours spent driving through vast empty spaces. Since then, the I-35 corridor had become a hundred-mile strip of outlet malls, car dealerships, and condo developments. But when they pulled off the freeway, the fast-food world receded and the landscape opened up: oaks and cedars, dirt roads, cattle grazing behind barbed-wire fences.

"Heavy foliage, few streetlights. Solace is what, four thousand people?" she said.

At the wheel of a Suburban borrowed from the local FBI office, Special Agent Brianne Rainey looked chill behind her sunglasses. "Forty-three hundred."

In the back seat, Emmerich had his head bent to a file folder. "Gideon County is sparsely populated. But San Antonio's the seventh-largest city in the US." He glanced at the countryside. "Doesn't look like it, but Solace is considered part of an urban megaregion."

Rainey eyed him in the mirror. "The Texas Triangle. San Antonio, Houston, Dallas–Fort Worth."

He nodded. "Massive cities mixed with rural expanses."

He meant: tens of thousands of potential suspects, and millions of acres where they could hide. They passed a water tower painted with SOLACE, HOME OF THE BLACK KNIGHTS. Mailboxes built in the shape of Texas.

"The stars at night are big and bright," Caitlin said.

Rainey smiled, briefly. "The coyotes wail along the trail." Her Air Force Academy ring flashed in the sun. Her face returned to its impassive reserve.

Rainey wore her cool poise so expertly that Caitlin didn't know if it was an innate gift or a carefully honed mask. She was thirty-nine, African American, married with ten-year-old twins. Her long braids were pulled back into a high ponytail. She was thoughtful and frank— Caitlin was learning that if Rainey challenged her, it was usually with good reason. She'd been with the FBI for ten years, the BAU for three. Rainey owned every crime scene she walked onto. It was an intimidating skill. One Caitlin wanted to learn.

Solace High School went past out the windows. Playing fields, stadium lights. The gym was painted with a twenty-foot-tall knight on a rearing warhorse.

Emmerich flipped through the file. "Town's economic base is agricultural. Three banks, twelve churches. The high school educates seventy percent of school-age students."

"The other thirty percent?" Caitlin said.

"Homeschooled," he said. "Shana Kerber graduated from the high school, as did two other victims. Most people in Solace know these women. The offender may too."

On Main Street, the sidewalk was empty. The Red Dog Café went past. Solace Hardware. Betty's Pets. Life at the speed of molasses.

"Plenty of places for the abductor to hide his victims," Rainey said.

Telephone poles flashed by, covered with fluttering flyers. It had now been thirty-six hours since Shana Kerber was taken. With every hour that passed, the likelihood of finding her alive plunged.

"Streets are too quiet," Caitlin said.

"Small town," Rainey said.

"Fearful town."

They pulled into the Gideon County Sheriff's Office.

The sheriff's station was the size of a McDonald's. Outside, the Lone Star flag whipped in the wind beneath the Stars and Stripes. With Caitlin's coat unbuttoned, the chill pierced her thin black sweater. Inside, the scuffed linoleum and bulletin board featuring Ten Most Wanted photos felt comfortably familiar to her. The clerk behind the counter appraised the three of them astringently.

Emmerich raised his credentials. "SAC Emmerich for Chief Morales."

Morales emerged from an office down the hall. "Special Agents. Appreciate your coming. We're all hands on deck."

Morales had an oil-drum chest that filled his brown

uniform shirt. Chief undersheriff for Solace, he wore jeans and old cowboy boots. Behind his rimless glasses, his brown eyes were sharp. He led them to a back room, crowded with desks, that served as the station's Investigations Section. On one wall, corkboards were covered with eight-by-ten photos.

They were the same photos Caitlin had glimpsed on the drive into Solace—stapled to telephone poles and taped inside the window at the Red Dog Café and laminated to the cyclone fence outside the high school.

Blond young women with cheerleader physiques. The missing five.

She approached the board. "No question he has a type."

"Yeah," Rainey said. "Texan."

Morales rubbed the side of his nose, seemingly annoyed. Rainey raised a mollifying hand.

"I went to Randolph High in San Antonio," she said. "My father was stationed at the base."

Caitlin walked along the board.

> **Kayley Fallows, 21.** August 25. 11:45 P.M. Red Dog Café.
>
> **Heather Gooden, 19.** November 17. 11:10 P.M. Gideon Western College campus.
>
> **Veronica Lees, 26.** December 29. 10:15 P.M. Gideon Gateway 16 Cinema.
>
> **Phoebe Canova, 22.** January 19. 12:15 A.M. Main Street, Solace.
>
> **Shana Kerber, 24.** February 2. 1:00 A.M. (approx.) Residence.

Emmerich turned to the chief. "We've read the files. Tell us what else you know."

Morales approached the corkboard. "One minute they were there. The next, gone. Starting with Kayley Fallows."

The girl in the photo had sunlit hair and a coquettish smile.

"She walked out the kitchen door at the end of her shift at the Red Dog Café. Cook having a smoke watched her walk away. Cracked a joke, saw her wave over her shoulder. Or maybe shoot him the bird. She was kind of a saucy kid. Is." He straightened. "She cut across the parking lot behind the café, walked out from under the lights, and that was it. We've investigated the cook. Everyone on staff. All the customers we could identify."

He tapped the next photo—Heather Gooden, pictured in a Solace High cheerleader's uniform.

"Heather stepped out the front door of her dorm to walk fifty yards across a quad to the college coffeehouse." His voice roughened. "Never made it."

"You sound like you know Heather," Emmerich said.

"She's been friends with my daughter since kindergarten. It's a blow."

Morales cleared his throat and continued. "Veronica Lees. Went to the movies at the multiplex with a girlfriend. Halfway through the film she went to the concession stand—and never came back."

The young woman had a big smile, big hair, and a big cross on a chain on her neck, gold against her pink blouse.

"The file indicates there's CCTV," Emmerich said.

Morales sat at a desk and teed up a video. In low-resolution color, they watched Veronica Lees appear, wallet in hand, walking briskly through the crowded lobby to the counter. She bought a box of Junior Mints, then worked her way back through the crowd. She turned a corner into a hallway.

Morales stopped the video. "That's it. She never returned to her seat."

It was spooky. Simple. There, then not.

"Can you play it again?" Caitlin said.

This time, Caitlin watched the crowd in the lobby, assessing whether anybody paid obvious attention to Veronica Lees. Nothing jumped out at her. But there were dozens of people on-screen. She needed to take the time to watch it analytically.

"Can you send that to me?"

He nodded.

Rainey said, "Exterior video footage?"

"'Fraid not," Morales said.

Emmerich examined Lees's photo. "Personal issues?"

"We looked," Morales said. "But she hasn't contacted a single friend or relative. Credit and ATM cards haven't been used since that night. Veronica left her purse on her seat when she went to the concession stand. And her husband didn't concoct a story that she took off with a lover, like that ass in Austin a couple years back." He tossed his head in the direction of the state capital to the north.

Emmerich, pacing near the corkboard, crossed his arms. "George de la Cruz."

Morales nodded. "He was convicted of murder, even though his wife has never been found."

A man came through the door like a fullback, bulling toward them. He shook hands. "Detective Art Berg. You're the profilers."

Emmerich turned back to the corkboard. He tapped the photo of the fourth victim. It showed a thin young woman with a stringy blond dye job. Black roots. A choker with a heart, wearing a dingy tank top. It was a mug shot.

"Tell me about Phoebe Canova's experience in the system," he said.

"Arrests for prostitution and possession of methamphetamine. The two were related," Berg said. "She stopped her car at a railroad crossing. When the train passed, her car was empty." His lips thinned. "She has an eighteen-month-old. Little boy named Levi."

"Pimp?" Rainey said. "Johns?"

"Working on both," Berg said. "But in those circles, people refuse to talk."

"They think she did something that got her killed. And that if they talk to the cops, they'll put a target on their own backs."

"Basically," Berg said. "Fear of retaliation."

"Have other women involved in prostitution disappeared?"

"Over the last two years, in San Antonio, definitely. But not like this."

Rainey said, "Were any of the victims besides Phoebe Canova known drug users?"

Berg shook his head. "Phoebe's life was spiraling

around the drain. Sad case." He folded his arms. "But I don't want to take her off the board. Don't want to blame the victim. What was she wearing? Why was she out so late? Nope."

Emmerich turned, tightly. "Nor do we. But we need to investigate the UNSUB's victimology."

UNSUB was the FBI's term for the unknown subject of a criminal investigation. Emmerich nodded at the photos. "Why did the abductor choose these women? Understanding that will help us narrow the search for the offender."

Chief Morales nodded. His shoulders dropped a short inch. Caitlin thought she knew why: because Emmerich had said *the* offender. *The* UNSUB. He'd validated Morales's conviction that these disappearances were related.

Detective Berg looked at them with weary eyes. "Now Shana."

"Connections between the victims?" Caitlin said.

Morales rocked on the heels of his boots. "Three of them graduated from Solace High but didn't know each other. Aside from that, what connects them is getting grabbed late on a Saturday night."

Emmerich looked at the chief. "The decreasing interval between disappearances is a dangerous sign."

Morales ran a hand through his hair. "This has the whole town on edge. Talk's going round, people think the occult is involved."

"As in satanic panic?" Caitlin said.

"Solace is a religious town. The idea somebody's taking women for a ritual purpose . . ."

"But you've seen no evidence of that."

Morales shook his head. "Zip."

She didn't doubt him. Satanic ritual killings were an urban legend, not an epidemic.

Berg said, "The problem is, they're just gone. We have no evidence."

Emmerich turned. "That's inaccurate. We have the victims' entire lives to examine. And we have the things they left behind." He tapped the board.

"Phoebe's car," Berg said.

"And Shana's baby." Emmerich turned to Caitlin and Rainey. "You go to the Kerber house. Then the scene where Canova's car was found."

"Yes, sir," Caitlin said.

Morales told Berg to go with them. "Examine everything that's been left behind, down to molecules of air. I know you've looked at it all, thoroughly, but do it again. Shana's out there, and we're running out of time to bring her home."

4

In the afternoon light, the farmhouse where Shana and Brandon Kerber lived looked quaint. A porch swing hung outside the main window. Beyond the cedars and lantana along the edge of their property, a new condo complex was visible. When Caitlin and Rainey got out of the Bureau Suburban, they heard distant traffic on I-35.

Detective Berg climbed out of a years-old Caprice. "Brandon's staying at his folks' house with the baby."

"We'd like to talk to him. It will help develop the victimology," Rainey said.

"You know, that sounds like a fancy word for prying into Shana's life."

"Figuring out why the missing women were chosen will help us understand the UNSUB's psychology. That'll allow us to build a profile," she said. "Does Shana have any enemies? Anybody who might want to harm her?"

"Nobody. I already asked."

"Did she mention anybody watching her or following her in the past few months? Anybody who made her feel uncomfortable?"

"Brandon says no. So do Shana's parents."

Caitlin felt the wind on her back. "What do they say about Brandon?"

Berg's glance was sharp. "They love him. And he has a rock-solid alibi. He was on the jumbotron at the basketball arena in San Antonio when Shana disappeared." He led them to the porch. "They're all torn up pretty bad."

Caitlin hadn't intended her question to sound cold—just thorough. Investigators needed to evaluate situations analytically. They couldn't let sympathy cloud their judgment. But equally, they had to guard against becoming jaded. When Caitlin had been a street cop, she had to remind herself not to become so cynical and suspicious that she started eyeing everyone as a potential offender—even off duty, at kids' birthday parties. People who became police officers tended to rank high on belief in authority. Some officers struggled to separate the power of the badge from their yearning for control.

Intimidation was a drug. But control was an illusion.

And right now, Caitlin didn't feel they had any kind of grip on this case, or even a clear view of what was happening. She felt like there was a tiger slinking through the tall grass, camouflaged by its stripes.

Yellow crime scene tape strapped the Kerbers' front door. Berg slit it open with a penknife. Inside, the heat was off, the light jaundiced, slanting through blinds onto the dark wood floor. The place already felt sadly empty.

Caitlin examined the door. "Signs of forced entry?"

Berg shook his head. "Brandon insists that Shana always locked the door, but who knows?"

She studied the latch bolt and strike plate. "This lock is so flimsy, a credit card could jimmy it."

Rainey said, "Maybe Shana opened it."

"When Brandon got home, only the hall light was on," Berg said. "If Shana had opened the door, I think she would have turned on a light in the living room."

Caitlin slowly circled the room. "Something woke her."

"The baby." Rainey's gaze swept the view. "The Kerbers keep firearms in the house?"

"Shotgun," Berg said. "It was found under her bed."

"Loaded?" Caitlin said.

He nodded.

Rainey scowled. "That little girl crawling yet?"

Berg said nothing. Caitlin would never leave a loaded weapon unsecured, much less within even a crawling child's reach. From the disapproving way Rainey shook her head, she wouldn't either.

"Prints on the shotgun?" Caitlin said.

"Brandon's and Shana's," Berg said. "Nobody else's."

Rainey stepped toward the hall. "Shana had no warning of danger."

"None," Caitlin said. "Or she would have come out of that bedroom holding the shotgun, and barred the way to the nursery." She glanced at the master bedroom. "Whatever got Shana out of bed, it literally disarmed her."

"This guy was slick, and quiet, and *fast*." Rainey turned. "And he left only one thing in the house out of place."

The wind rattled the door and crept around the eaves. Caitlin recalled the written statement given by Brandon

Kerber, describing the scene he found when he arrived home. She felt a chill.

"The baby," she said.

Rainey nodded. "He had a plan, and it used a ten-month-old. As bait, or a bargaining chip, or a way to overpower Shana. He is one calculating, remorseless predator."

5

In Solace, at the railroad crossing where Phoebe Canova had disappeared, Caitlin and Rainey parked and walked toward the tracks.

Under the white sun, the crossing looked ordinary and, perhaps because of that, strangely ominous. *It was spooky. Simple. There, then not.* The tracks cut across Main Street and ran south into scrubland. Vehicle traffic was sporadic. A brown pickup truck pulling a horse trailer clattered across the tracks. As it passed, the driver slowed and eyed them through the window before pulling away.

"We're going to be news soon," Caitlin said. "Word spreads in a small town."

"Believe me, some guy on Reddit is already speculating about this from his cubicle in New Jersey. There'll be twenty-five theories on this case by the time school lets out."

They crossed the tracks, stood in the road, and looked back.

Another pickup, older, red, cruised to a stop behind

their SUV. A man in his fifties got out. He hitched up his belt and walked toward them.

"Heard the FBI was in town. Would that be you?" he called.

Two women in black suits, surveying a crime scene. Good odds on that guess.

Caitlin nodded. "Yes, sir. You are?"

"Darley French. I was in my truck, right where you're standing, when she disappeared."

Rainey's eyebrows rose. "You witnessed the abduction?"

He had a wad in his cheek. "No, ma'am. The crossing arm came down just before I pulled up. That Phoebe gal hadn't arrived yet. I was the only one on the road."

"You've given a statement to the sheriff's office?" Caitlin said.

She knew he had. She wanted to hear what he had to say now.

"You bet." He turned to the tracks. "Freight train come along, and when it finally passed and the crossing barrier went back up, saw her car across the tracks. Just sitting there, headlights shining, exhaust blowing from the tailpipe. Driver's door was open." He spat. "I pulled forward. Dome light inside her car was lit. Purse was on the passenger seat. Car was empty."

Rainey said, "That must have spooked you."

"Felt like a beetle was ticking up my spine. No other cars on the road—not even taillights."

"You saw nobody else on the street? On foot?" Caitlin said.

He shook his head. "Car was here. Girl was gone. I called the sheriff."

Caitlin gestured at the asphalt where she stood. "This is where you were stopped."

"It was."

"How long did it take the train to pass?" Rainey said.

"Few minutes. Leon Russell song played almost all the way through," French said.

Caitlin pulled the file folder from her shoulder bag and flipped through it. "It was a freight train a mile long. Traveling at thirty-one miles per hour." She ran her finger down the page. "Train that length, traveling at that speed, it would have taken one hundred twenty-five seconds to clear the crossing."

Rainey stared at the spot where Phoebe Canova had parked.

"She was abducted during a two-minute window." She raised her arm. "Freight cars coupled in a train are separated by roughly three feet. Mr. French, you would have seen headlights between them as the train passed."

"I was vaguely aware. Not paying attention. Turning up the radio."

Rainey set her hands on her hips. "Two minutes."

Caitlin nodded. "From initial approach to abduction to escape without a trace." She looked around. "It was midnight."

Rainey nodded slowly. "Most businesses shut down. Still."

They walked across the tracks to the spot where Phoebe

Canova's car had been found. The exact location was marked with spray paint on the asphalt. Four corners, neatly lined up.

"She was well back from the crossing barrier, and stopped square," Rainey said.

"Didn't swerve. No sign that somebody was pursuing her."

Darley French sauntered up to them. "You have a theory, ladies?"

"Do you?" Rainey said.

"Customer didn't like the service she provided him. Decided he wanted the next session free."

Caitlin and Rainey mulled that, expressionless. After a minute, French handed them his business card. "I'm around."

He meandered back to his truck and drove off.

Caitlin watched the pickup pull away. "As witnesses go . . ."

"He's a dandy." Rainey put on her shades.

Phoebe Canova's red Nissan Altima sat in a shed at the sheriff's impound yard near the station. Detective Berg met them there.

Caitlin circled the vehicle. It had a ding on the right rear panel, but the damage was edged with rust.

"No evidence that another vehicle collided with this car the night of the abduction," she said.

"No," Berg said.

In the shed, out of the wind, their words felt close. Caitlin pulled on latex gloves. The car had already been processed, the vehicle was dirty with fingerprint powder, but it was procedure for her, and habit.

Rainey said, "Any hits on prints?"

"Phoebe's prints on the driver's door and interior. Her younger brother's on the passenger-side door. He's sixteen." Berg caught Caitlin's curious glance. "Anybody with a driver's license or state-issued ID in Texas has a print on file."

"Gotcha," Caitlin said.

The interior had been vacuumed for trace. Berg said that the vacuum evidence had been sent to the county crime lab but nothing useful had turned up.

Caitlin said, "The car was found with the driver's window down? It hasn't been lowered or adjusted since then?"

"Deputy who responded to the nine-one-one call found it exactly like this."

"Driver's door was open," Rainey said.

"Wide-open."

Caitlin opened the driver's door and crouched down. A red fir-tree-shaped air freshener hung from the rearview mirror. The interior of the car smelled like wild cherry.

She said, "Was it this cold that Saturday night?"

Berg said, "Colder. Near freezing."

She stood. "Why did Phoebe lower the window?" She looked at Berg. "What was the condition of the interior when you first saw the car? Neat? Messy?"

"Purse wide-open on the seat. Whataburger wrappers in the passenger-side foot well." He rubbed his chin. "Bunch of receipts in the cup holders."

"Loose papers. But they hadn't been blown around

the interior. Suggests she didn't lower the window while she was moving, but only after she stopped at the railroad crossing."

Berg grunted.

"Why'd she put it down?" Caitlin said. "To toss a cigarette butt?"

"She didn't smoke," Berg said. "At least, there's zero evidence of that. No cigarettes in her purse. The auxiliary power unit in the dash here has a phone charger plugged in, not a cigarette lighter."

Caitlin nodded. "The air freshener doesn't seem to be covering up any lingering tobacco smells."

Rainey leaned in. "Or weed."

"So why'd she roll down the window when she stopped for the train?" Caitlin said. "To call to someone on the street?"

"It was past midnight." Rainey crossed her arms. "You get much foot traffic that time of night?"

"No," Berg said. "Everything on that block was closed up tight, and we haven't had any witnesses come forward."

Caitlin thought about her next words. "To speak to a cop who pulled her over?"

Berg shifted. Caitlin became newly aware of the chill in the air.

Berg stuck his thumbs under his belt buckle. "It wasn't one of our officers who did this."

He couldn't have looked more chapped if he'd actually adjusted his tighty-whities.

But he spoke. "GPS in the department's cars shows that none came within three miles of the railroad crossing in the twenty minutes before the nine-one-one call came in," he said. "When Darley French phoned, the nearest unit was across I-35. Yeah. All our vehicles have GPS. You can download it and see for yourself."

Caitlin nodded. She was sure that Emmerich was doing exactly that.

"Solace sheriff's substation has four patrol cars," Berg said. "Plus the unmarked pool vehicle for detectives. None of them was anywhere near the railroad crossing when Phoebe vanished."

Caitlin and Rainey exchanged a glance. The Solace sheriff's substation had five vehicles. How many did surrounding cities have? Austin? San Antonio? The broader county sheriff's fleet? The state troopers and the Texas Rangers?

"You jump to conclusions awfully fast, Agent Hendrix."

"I'm not concluding anything. Perhaps Ms. Canova lowered her window to speak to somebody she *thought* was a police officer."

Berg didn't look placated. "You're saying we've got nothing."

"That tells us something."

"Anything worthwhile?"

"Don't know yet."

But Berg wasn't far wrong. They had no witnesses. No forensics. No apparent connection between the women who had disappeared. Just a black hole into which they'd seemingly fallen. Caitlin quietly closed the door of Phoebe Canova's car.

6

When Caitlin and Rainey returned to the sheriff's station, Emmerich stood at a new corkboard in the detectives' room. He had tacked up a large map of Texas. He was sticking pushpins into it.

"Results?" he said.

"Plenty." Rainey walked over to the board, hands in the pockets of her slacks. "The UNSUB left no prints on Phoebe Canova's car. He either wore gloves or never touched the vehicle."

"If he didn't touch it . . ."

"He persuaded her to get out."

Caitlin approached. "He didn't touch the car."

Emmerich raised an eyebrow. "That a hunch?"

"Deduction. The car was found with its engine running. And the transmission in park."

"Maybe Phoebe put it in park because she stopped for the train."

"The train took two minutes to pass—same time as some stoplights. And at a stoplight, if you're driving an automatic, you don't shift gears. You sit on the brake," she said. "Phoebe put it in park when she decided to open the door and get out, so the car wouldn't roll forward."

Berg and Chief Morales came in. The map drew their curiosity.

Emmerich nodded at it. "These are the locations where each of the five missing women was last sighted."

Laid out visually, the implications were painfully obvious. The Red Dog Café. The college quad. The multiplex cinema. The railroad crossing. The Kerber home.

"They range north to south across almost fifty miles," Emmerich said. "But—"

"But they're all within two miles of I-35," Morales said.

The red pushpins looked like a set of buttons running up the front of a shirt.

"More than that. They're never more than two hundred meters from a road that feeds directly into a freeway on-ramp." Emmerich took a red marker and connected the abduction sites in a fat line that ran down the page like a vein. "It's a feeding ground."

Morales turned to him. "What do we do about that?"

"We construct a profile of the UNSUB. So we can start hunting him."

The team checked into a Holiday Inn Express, hard by an exit on I-35. Caitlin changed into jeans. Across the street was a taco stand. She texted the others, asking if they wanted her to pick them up anything.

Rainey replied, Bring the fire. Emmerich texted, Street food?

Caitlin replied, TEXAS street food. Bigger, better. And it's the law.

She jogged across the road, feeling tired but wired. Working for the BAU carried serious responsibilities, and could drain her. She'd seen it in the eyes of the Solace officers today. *Tell us we really do have an UNSUB at work. Tell us who this SOB is.*

And do it now, because Shana's out there.

To the east, empty hills rolled toward the horizon. The interstate kept up its asphalt drone. At the taco stand a few pickups were parked, and people at picnic tables waited for their orders, huddled into jackets, texting.

They looked relaxed. But female customers stayed near the light from the stand's interior.

When Caitlin worked a case somewhere she'd never been before, she always found a cheap, busy, local place to eat. It was a way to judge the temperature on the ground. Getting dinner from a local dive meant more than merely recouping your per diem. You learned about a place by walking it, and talking to people, and listening with your ears and your inner tuning fork.

Here, she sensed that the taco stand was someplace construction workers and college students and soccer moms all felt welcome. Behind the order window, mariachi music blared from a boom box. She heard English and Spanish and maybe Hindi. The place felt friendly and seemed safe. But people were keeping their eyes on their surroundings. Women were avoiding the shadows. Solace was jittery.

The young man working the counter said, "What'll you have?"

She read the menu board behind his head. She counted twenty-five different tacos, ranging from pulled pork to Jamaican jerk chicken to sriracha shredded lamb with Cotija cheese and cranberry habanero jam.

"Yeah. All of them." She laughed.

She returned to the hotel with two bulging bags of hot food. Rainey came down to the lounge area off the lobby. Caitlin handed her a fat handful of napkins.

Rainey unwrapped a taco and took a healthy bite. "Goddamn."

Caitlin ate relentlessly. "I may put in for a transfer to the local field office."

Restored, she checked her watch. The team was going to meet in an hour to analyze the results of the day's investigation. She had time. She cleared up, headed outside, and called Sean Rawlins.

"Babe," she said.

"Howdy."

His voice had a smile. She warmed, even as the chill evening turned her breath to frost.

"They speak American here. You don't have to translate," she said.

"You buy cowboy boots yet?"

"Black with skulls and red roses." She was wearing Doc Martens. She would rather pour hot sauce in her eyes than shop. "You on the road?"

"Crawling across the Bay Bridge."

She felt a pang, a deep wish for the bay, the soaring towers of the bridge, the sunlight skipping across ten thousand whitecaps between the Golden Gate and Alcatraz. She wanted the scent of the Pacific, and the beauty of the cities and the mountains, and her man. She closed her eyes.

She opened them and felt small, surrounded by the sweep of the continent. The sky was vast. It was glorious and terrifying.

"Brief me on Texas," Sean said.

His abruptness made her laugh. Sean sounded strong. His energy was everything she had barely dared hope for a year back. Sean had been gravely wounded by the Ghost, the UNSUB who'd nail-gunned Caitlin, during the confrontation that killed her father. For excruciating days, Sean had hovered near death. She had never felt so powerless. And, as he fought for life, she had grasped how completely she loved him. It had shocked her into an electric understanding that *here and now* is everything.

"Cat?" he said.

The sky had turned cobalt. A full moon was rising. The horizon was chalky pink.

"Here," she said.

"This investigation going to turn into something?"

"It has. Something serious."

She told him about the case. The breeze scudded past, but she didn't go back inside the hotel. Out here, she felt a connection with Sean—as though, if she could only see over the western horizon, she would spot him in his Tundra pickup, one arm hung on the windowsill, the other draped across the top of the steering wheel, dark hair windblown. He was an ATF agent, a certified explosive specialist. And he was fifteen hundred damned miles away.

She had taken the FBI job with almost no hesitation. Sean had encouraged her. He told her she would kick herself if she passed it up.

She had no regrets. But now, while she was working from Virginia, he was three thousand miles away in Berkeley.

"How's Sadie?" she said.

"She's perfect. She spilled a bottle of glitter in the truck the other day. By the time I got to the field office I looked like a disco ball."

Caitlin smiled. Sadie was four.

Sean shared custody of the little girl with his ex-wife. Their divorce was amicable, but everything hinged on the fragile construct of "co-parenting." Michele had a good job as an ER nurse that she had no wish to leave. She would never agree to Sean moving to the East Coast with Sadie. And Sean would never move to Virginia without his daughter.

Caitlin and Sean had said, *We'll work it out.* Two feds. How hard could it be?

She stood under the sunset. "Kiss Sadie for me. I'll talk to you tomorrow."

She hung up. The air had turned cold. But the sunset raged on. The western horizon was an acrylic red, spreading, never ending, deepening to purple.

When she finally headed inside, the clerk at the front desk smiled.

"Bet they don't have sunsets like this where you come from," he said.

"Never seen anything like it."

"Austin was originally named the City of the Violet Crown. Because of sunsets like this."

"That's lovely." She tucked her cold fingers into her coat pockets. "Originally? They decide it was too romantic for the Old West?"

"City fathers changed it to 'the City of Eternal Moonlight' after they built giant arc lamp towers to light the streets. Because of a serial killer in the 1880s," he said. "The Servant Girl Annihilator."

"Really."

"Killed a dozen people. Two women on Christmas Eve. Chopped them in the head with an ax."

She stood immobile.

He stapled some paperwork. "You and the others are from the FBI, aren't you?"

"Yes."

He nodded to himself, eyes bright. "Cool."

She watched him.

Finally, he said, "Anything else, ma'am?"

"No. Thanks."

Copies of the local paper were stacked on the desk. The *Gideon County Star* had a splash headline: WHERE ARE THEY? The missing women's photos ran beneath it.

In her room, Caitlin turned on the television and pulled out her laptop and her field notes. As the computer booted, a local news report came on the TV.

A brunette in a red suit looked at the camera with an *it's bad* expression. "Police in Solace believe the disappearances of five women are the work of a serial abductor and have called in the FBI. Our Andrea Andrade reports."

Oh.

The screen switched to a report filmed in Solace. The reporter, a younger brunette in a different red suit, walked along the railroad tracks. She spoke of the terror in Solace and the vanishing of young mother Shana Kerber. Shana's tearful parents appeared.

"Bring our baby back," her mother pleaded. "Our girl is precious to us."

Caitlin's throat tightened. She breathed out. *Empathize, but maintain your distance.*

She wished Shana's parents had spoken to her team before going on camera. Emmerich would have coached them to mention Shana by name. To humanize her, turn her into a real person in the eyes of the UNSUB.

The report shifted to a local firing range. A firearms instructor put five rounds through a paper target at ten yards. He had big shoulders and a bigger belt buckle. His holster was tied around the leg of his jeans with a cord, Wyatt Earp style.

"There's evil in this town," he said. "Satan is loose among us. If you don't protect yourself, you're probably going to become a victim of it."

The film cut to citizens blazing away at more paper targets. Caitlin shook her head. Even in the worst situations, when an apex predator was killing in a town, most people didn't become victims. But that's not how fear worked.

The report cut again. On Main Street, the reporter was speaking to Darley French.

"Yeah, the FBI is in town," French said. "Two women agents interviewed me about that girl I saw go missing from her car."

Caitlin tossed her laptop aside.

"Profilers," French said. "That means a serial killer. But they have no more clue who it is than I do."

The report cut back to the studio. "We're seeking confirmation that the FBI's Behavioral Analysis Unit is in Solace. We'll keep you updated on this worrying development."

Caitlin stood. If this story erupted into the national media, the heat could inflate it to a wildfire. A mythology and narrative would take hold. It would be hard to dislodge. And potentially dangerous.

She didn't wait for the scheduled team meeting. She picked up the phone and called Emmerich. "We're on the news."

Madison Mays pulled into the parking lot at her apartment complex as the last light of sunset faded to gray. She hoisted her backpack over her shoulder and shut the car door with her hip. She was dog tired from a full day of classes at Gideon Western College, followed by her shift as a barista at the outlet mall near campus.

From apartments came music and conversations and

Wheel of Fortune. Beyond the parking lot, traffic droned along I-35. Madison climbed the stairs, reached into her pocket for her keys, and stopped.

"Shit."

She'd left the keys in the ignition. She rushed back down the stairs to the car.

She grabbed the keys, locked up, and headed back toward the building. As she reached the sidewalk, a car cruised across the parking lot. The headlights swung by, illuminating the breezeway that led to the far side of the building.

In the shadows, a man stood watching her. She jumped.

He was tall and dressed like a banker who'd taken off his tie now that the office day was done. His dress shirt was a crisp white. He was holding a phone.

She pressed a hand to her chest. "Jesus."

She couldn't see much of his face. He touched the phone to his forehead like a gentleman tipping his hat. The headlights swept past and he returned to darkness.

A flutter went through her stomach, like moths beating their wings. She needed to get past him to reach the stairs. She sensed that he was still looking at her.

"Apartment four ninety-two," he said.

She nearly ignored him, but his voice had a note of authority. Like, legal authority.

She frowned. "I don't think the units in this building go up to four ninety-two."

He blinked. His eyes looked silvery in the moonlight. "You're mistaken."

He raised his phone, giving her a glimpse of the screen. There was a text, yes, but she couldn't read it. The moths in her belly beat their wings.

She looked him in the eye. There was something. A note of . . .

Want.

Upstairs on the second-floor walkway, an apartment door opened. "Madison?"

Patty Mays filled the doorway, cutting off most of the light. Her voice was iron.

Madison said, "Mom, he's looking for apartment—"

"Get inside."

The man walked briskly away.

Madison hurried up the stairs. Patty waited on the walkway, one side of her lit by the living room lights, feet planted wide, watching the man cross the parking lot. Madison ducked into the apartment. Patty followed and closed the door. Locked it. Dead bolted it.

She stared at Madison. "What were you thinking?"

"He was lost. I think he was a cop." But her stomach fluttered.

"I don't care if you think he's Dirty Harry come down from heaven. Devils walk in disguise."

Patty reached behind her back and pulled the Smith and Wesson .40 caliber revolver from the waistband of her yoga pants.

Madison peered through the curtains. In the parking lot, the man passed beneath a streetlight and again faded into the shadows.

The moths didn't stop fluttering until his taillights disappeared down the road.

Probably nothing, she thought.

But another part of her said, *Pay attention to the moths.*

7

The morning broke cold and misty. At eight A.M., when the team rolled up to the Solace sheriff's station, three news vans sat out front. In the station lobby, the first thing Caitlin saw were camera spotlights, bright on Chief Morales's careworn face. He stood surrounded by reporters. Microphones jutted toward him.

"We strongly suspect that the women who have disappeared since August were abducted by a single individual," Morales said. "We want to assure the public that we're taking every step possible to apprehend the perpetrator, to ascertain the whereabouts of the missing women, and return them to their families."

He didn't say *alive*.

"We ask women to take sensible precautions to guard their safety. Buddy up. Maintain awareness of your surroundings," he said. "If something feels wrong, pay attention. That little voice, telling you that you're in danger—listen to it. The life you save may be your own."

Morales didn't suggest the women of Gideon County arm themselves. He didn't have to.

A reporter caught sight of Caitlin and her colleagues. It was the brunette in the red suit. She abandoned the chief and approached Rainey.

"You're the FBI?" she said.

Rainey remained impassive. "We're from the FBI's Behavioral Analysis Unit, here to assist the Sheriff's Office. Chief Morales will answer further questions."

But the microphones and cameras pivoted.

A male reporter raised his hand. "Do you have any suspects?"

"Does the FBI hold out any hope of finding the missing women alive?"

The red suit raised her voice. "Is a serial killer committing these crimes?"

Behind his rimless glasses, the expression on Chief Morales's face was relieved but despondent. He gestured to Rainey: *Your turn.*

Brittany Leakins turned away from the television and bit her thumbnail. Not the kind of lunchtime news she wanted to hear. The light in her kitchen was pale and sharp. In the high chair, Tanner fussed.

"Hush, little dude."

Brittany grabbed a damp dish towel and wiped baby carrots from Tanner's face. He squirmed and kicked the footrest. She found his pacifier on the floor, fuzzy with crumbs and lint. She considered walking the six steps to rinse it under the kitchen faucet, then put it in her mouth, sucked it clean, and shoved it between Tanner's lips. She hoisted him from the high chair and set him on her hip.

"Come on, champ. Sleepy time."

Brittany figured if he went down, she'd have a good forty-five minutes to nap—maybe enough to return from the land of the zombies. Tanner was her beautiful little man, but if she didn't get some sleep, she was going to end up crawling across the kitchen, barking like a dog.

Speaking of which, where was Shiner?

The television burbled, the news still talking about the missing women. Brittany's stomach churned. This place was isolated—like Shana Kerber's house. Twenty miles outside Solace, a spread Kevin had inherited from his grandparents. It sat on a hundred acres, land that was supposed to tide her young marriage through the years and decades to come. But those acres didn't look like money to her right now. They looked bleak, and rife with secret places where kidnappers could hide.

She pulled aside the curtains. On the yellow grass in the backyard sat a rusting swing set that wouldn't do for Tanner, no sir. She looked at the split rail fence and the fields beyond it, and at the woods that ran to the horizon. *Dark and deep*, that line from the Robert Frost poem they'd read in high school. Oaks and chaparral, Texas lilac and those endless tangled grasping branches of the cedars that covered the hills.

She had let the dog out half an hour ago. He was nowhere to be seen.

She opened the back door, and the chill caught her. The sky was pearly. She whistled.

"Shiner."

On the television, a reporter stuck a microphone in the face of a black woman wearing a suit. Good Lord. The FBI was here.

"*Shiner.*"

The golden retriever could get through the split rail fence. They'd installed an electronic fence, but the shock it gave didn't always stop him. He was a determined dog and couldn't seem to comprehend cause and effect.

She whistled again, and he loped happily out of the woods.

She stepped onto the porch. "Shiner. Come here, you jailbreaker."

The dog crossed the field and clambered between the rails of the fence. He was muddy. And he'd picked up something on his travels. Retrievers—they brought stuff home. But this wasn't a bird. It looked like a soggy newspaper. Maybe a fast-food bag.

"You better not have been eating a moldy hamburger." She shook her head. "Drop it."

The dog didn't. Shiner trotted across the yard, tail wagging. He smelled like a pond. Brittany heard the television inside, the FBI woman. Something colder than the winter air fell through her.

The thing in Shiner's mouth was white, soaked through with red. But it wasn't a fast-food bag.

It was an old piece of cloth. Maybe an oil rag. A dishrag. Maybe that was red wine. Except she knew it wasn't. Inside, the TV blared. The FBI woman looked severe, like she was warning them of the end of the world.

"If you spot anything out of the ordinary, something

that seems wrong, I urge you to contact the sheriff's department. Anything that could relate to the missing victims. Discarded items of clothing. Shoes, purses . . ."

Brittany took a step back and snapped her fingers. "Shiner. Drop it."

The dog let the cloth fall to the porch.

Brittany swallowed and clutched Tanner tight. "Shiner. Inside."

The dog ran into the kitchen. Brittany followed, bolted the door, and found her phone. In the background, the FBI agent's voice cut the air. With shaky fingers, Brittany called 911.

"I need the police. My dog just brought home half a shirt. And it's covered in blood."

The FBI Suburban swooped into the driveway at Brittany Leakins's home like a fighter jet diving to the deck for a strafing run. At the wheel, Emmerich's eyes had a hard gleam. He skidded to a stop behind two sheriff's office SUVs and leaped out into blowing dust. Caitlin and Rainey followed. Outside the house, Detective Berg was pacing. A K-9 unit was unloading their dogs into the waning pink afternoon.

Emmerich strode up to Berg. "Your dogs lead, we'll follow."

Inside the house, a young woman rested a toddler on her jutting hip. Her lips were pressed white. Beyond the house were woods so dark they looked black.

A K-9 officer clipped fifteen-foot leads to the harnesses of two bloodhounds. "Go find."

Without a sound, the bloodhounds turned, put their noses to the ground, and began hunting a scent trail. They zigzagged across the backyard, then took off toward the fence. Their handlers jogged behind, uniform jackets zipped to the throat, sunglasses reflecting the hard light.

Heads low, the dogs clambered between the rails of the fence and cut a line across the field toward the trees. Berg and the FBI team followed.

Caitlin had changed into brown combat trousers and Doc Martens. Her black Nike running jacket was zipped to the throat beneath an FBI windbreaker. Yellowed grass rustled beneath her feet as she crossed the field.

From the photo she'd seen, the scrap of bloody white fabric the Leakins dog had dragged home was eighteen inches long by nine inches wide. The lab hadn't yet analyzed the blood to determine whether it was human, but from the design and stitching, the fabric had undoubtedly been torn from a garment.

A nightgown.

When they entered the tree line, the temperature dropped. Caitlin and the others followed the K-9 officers in single file. The ground was rocky, the scrub and trees thick. Emmerich pushed branches aside without slowing. He glanced over his shoulder once. His expression said both *Keep up* and *Everybody okay back there?*

They were a mile deep in the trees when the bloodhounds topped a hill and raced down the far side. Boots digging into dry soil, Caitlin sidestepped down the slope behind the K-9 officers. For a minute, she lost sight of the dogs. Then a mournful baying rolled across the woods.

Caitlin emerged from the trees to the sound of rippling water. Beside the bank of a creek, the bloodhounds had stopped, tongues lolling. The K-9 officers commanded them to sit. One of the officers petted the dogs and said, "Good girls."

Caitlin stopped. They all did.

Berg's shoulders dropped.

Emmerich blew out a breath. "I know you were hoping this wouldn't be at the end of the trail. So were we."

They stood at the sandy edge of the creek. In front of them lay Shana Kerber.

She was laid out on the soft earth, on her back, parallel to the stream. Her eyes were closed beneath gray-white lids. Her arms were crossed on her chest. She looked like Snow White awaiting the prince's kiss.

She was wearing a bloodstained white baby doll nightie. She lay in a circle of red-black dirt. Her jugular had been slashed.

8

The K-9 officers pulled the dogs back. Brusquely, Detective Berg told a uniformed deputy to set up a perimeter and control access to the hillside. The sun had fallen into the branches of the trees to the west, and shadows grayed the landscape. Standing back for the moment so as not to contaminate the scene or trample possible evidence, Caitlin and her team surveyed the tableau at the edge of the creek.

"He took care to lay her out," Rainey said. Her voice was calm, but when she wiped trail dust from her face, her hand was a fist. "He didn't dump her."

Emmerich's arms hung at his sides. "Posing a body as if at rest usually indicates undoing. But I don't think that's what we're looking at here."

Undoing meant attempting to symbolically reverse a crime. A killer might cover a victim's face. Wash the body. Tuck a blanket around the victim. It often indicated remorse.

Caitlin said, "This wasn't regret."

"It's a display. A loving display," Emmerich said.

Berg snapped on a pair of latex gloves, descended to the bank of the creek, and knelt by Shana Kerber's side to examine her body. He lifted her right hand from her chest.

"Rigor's passed already." He set her hand back down, gently. "She's been dead more than twenty-four hours. I'd say two days at least. Maybe longer if she's been out in this cold the whole time."

Caitlin felt deflated. Shana had been killed before the FBI had hit the ground in Texas.

Emmerich joined Berg beside the body. "That neck wound severed her carotid and windpipe. She was unconscious within seconds."

The water sighed through the creek. Berg carefully pulled back the woman's blood-matted hair.

"I'm not a forensic pathologist, but it looks to me like she also has a depressed skull fracture," he said.

Rainey scanned the creek side. Her gaze narrowed. "Emmerich. Detective."

Six feet upstream from the victim's body, a photograph was stuck upright in the soft dirt of the bank.

It was a Polaroid. Rainey and Caitlin descended the hill to get a better look.

It was a photo of the victim—a close-up of her dead face. It had been snapped where she lay on the bank. The photo was positioned in line with her body, as if it were the prayer card of a grisly saint, watching over her.

Noise roiled the hillside above them. An officer distantly shouted, "Stop!"

A young man came charging down the hill. His eyes were bulging, his mouth wide.

"*Shana!*"

Berg jumped to his feet. "Brandon, no."

He ran toward the young man, arms spread, like he was going to corral a horse.

Brandon Kerber barreled forward. "Shana—"

Emmerich sprang after Berg toward the young man. Emmerich was deceptively lean—built like a wrestler, with muscles strung like wire. Together, he and Berg roped Brandon to a halt.

The young man fought. He caught sight of the bank of the creek and went rigid. "No. No, no."

Berg turned him away from Shana's body. "I'm sorry, son."

He nudged Brandon back up the slope, pressing him into the screen of the trees, where his wife's corpse wouldn't be visible. Caitlin clenched her jaw.

Berg put a hand on Brandon's shoulder and spoke in a low tone. "How'd you know where to find us?"

"Brittany Leakins called. I didn't believe it was true."

His shoulders were shaking, his breathing labored. Caitlin's throat tightened.

Emmerich, standing a foot from the young man, observed him without expression. But Caitlin knew that Emmerich was slamming down emotional shutters on Brandon's pain. His dispassion wasn't exactly a mask. But it was both protective and distancing, so he could continue doing his job clear-eyed. A skill she was still trying to master.

Brandon shook his head. "It's not her."

Berg pressed a hand to the young man's chest. "Son, I'm sorry. It is. I recognize her."

"No." Brandon tried to juke and slide around Berg.

Emmerich blocked him. "Under extreme stress, our perceptions can go awry. Our minds protect us from what we're seeing. Mr. Kerber. Sir. I'm sorry."

Brandon's face and neck had flared crimson. "That's not my wife. I can *see* that thing there. It's wearing a white nightgown."

Berg raised a placating hand. "Brandon . . ."

"She wore pink flannel pajamas," Brandon said. "She doesn't *own* a white nightgown." He pointed at the body. "That's not her."

9

For a pleading, desperate moment, Brandon Kerber pointed at the body. "It's not Shana."

"You positive?" Berg said.

"Thousand percent."

Berg turned to the creek, consternated. Caitlin crouched to get a fresh view of the body.

She wasn't inured to violent death. Like most Americans, she had reached adulthood without ever seeing a corpse. But in her first week as an Alameda sheriff's deputy, she'd rushed to a car crash, primed to aid the injured driver, only to find him halfway through the windshield.

That's what dead looks like, a ghostly voice had hissed. She called the meat wagon, set out flares, worked the scene, went home, and cried under the shower. After that, she learned to separate herself from the dead. She didn't cry again.

But she wasn't hardened. Looking at the shell of a young life, she always felt a stab in the heart. And in this job, grief didn't lurk—it swarmed. She now tried to dodge the creeping pain and analyze the scene with fresh eyes.

On the bank of the creek, the dead woman's face was aimed skyward. Her eyes were closed. Her lips were blue. But her blond hair, her features, her frame—and the fact that the trailing dogs had followed Shana's scent straight to this creek—told Caitlin that Brandon was mistaken.

He had stopped trying to force his way past Berg and Emmerich. He was waiting for them to agree with him. He pinned his gaze on the creek side. On the nightgown. He began to blink. Maybe at the sight of the wedding ring the dead woman wore, or her toenails, painted midnight blue.

His voice rose half an octave. "No. It doesn't look like her. And . . . it doesn't have her tattoo." He tapped his chest.

Emmerich returned to the body. He bent and delicately pulled back the shoulder of the nightgown.

Her skin was gray. The shadows were gray. The dirty four-inch strip of duct tape applied to her chest was gray. Exposed to the elements, and to wildlife predation, it had slipped. The tattoo was visible. The ink was black. Above the woman's heart, in Celtic lettering, it read, *Brandon*.

Brandon's momentary triumph, the holding-on-by-his-fingernails hope, drained away. Howling, he threw his head back and sank to his knees.

Berg and a deputy managed to get him to his feet and walk him up the slope. Emmerich remained at Shana's side.

Rainey said, "The skin isn't reddened where the tape was stuck?"

Emmerich shook his head. "Applied post-mortem."

His face was stark. He was considering the implications. "She's *his*. The UNSUB wanted to make that absolutely clear. He—"

He stopped. Touched the fabric of the nightgown. "Wait."

Caitlin and Rainey drew closer to get a better look.

It took only a few seconds, now that Caitlin focused on it. Filmy, sheer, the nightie draped Shana from shoulders to midthigh. It was creamy white, and the fabric was microfiber. *Shit.*

She straightened. "It's different from the fabric Brittany Leakins's dog dragged home."

"Two nighties," Emmerich said.

"But the trailing dogs led us straight to her."

Emmerich looked lost in thought, then turned sharply. "The scent item the K-9 officers used. We missed it."

"They didn't use the torn strip of fabric the retriever brought home?"

"That went straight to the crime lab. It's evidence. They were smart enough not to contaminate it further."

"We got to the Leakins home after they gave the bloodhounds a scent article."

Emmerich shouted up the hill. "Berg."

The detective was out of earshot. Emmerich got on his phone.

A minute later, cell to his ear, he eyed Caitlin and Rainey. "They were looking for Shana Kerber, so they used a sweatshirt that belonged to her. They got it from her house this afternoon."

Caitlin said, "But if the first strip of fabric was from a different article of clothing . . ."

Into the phone, Emmerich said, "Get the K-9 unit back to the Leakins house." His voice was urgent. "There's another woman out there."

10

They reached the Leakins house as the last violet glow of sunset was ghosting to indigo. Jupiter stabbed the horizon in the west. This time, the K-9 unit waited for Detective Berg to bring a sealed brown paper evidence bag from his car. The dogs circled, anxious to work. Berg slit the seal and with gloved hands removed the bloody strip of white fabric Shiner had brought home. A dog handler presented it to the bloodhounds. The dogs sniffed, alert and straining.

The K-9 officer said, "Get it, girls."

The bloodhounds lowered their noses to the ground. Within seconds they caught the scent. They took off across the yard, through the split rail fence, aiming for the woods.

Berg returned the torn fabric to the evidence bag, re-sealed it, signed it, and locked it in his car. He wordlessly approached the FBI team.

They turned on their flashlights and followed the dogs across the field into the trees.

The bloodhounds had a strong scent and moved in

tandem, quickly, the clasps of their leads clicking against their harnesses. The oaks gave way to cedars—gnarled and dark, a blackening thicket. Branches clawed at Caitlin's hair and sleeves. The light overhead turned to a scrim of gray seen through jet-dark greenery. She swept the beam of her flashlight across the ground. The cold was penetrating.

They were far past the spot where Shana had lain, deep in a tangled cedar forest, when the dogs slowed and disappeared over a ridge.

When the team climbed over the tangled roots of a dead tree and emerged in a clearing, Caitlin stopped. The bloodhounds were silently circling something, but at a distance.

Just beyond the dogs she saw it. They all saw it. A form on the ground, in a soft depression in the earth. She was dressed in white.

She was struggling to crawl.

Caitlin's heart jacked into overdrive. "Jesus."

She burst past Berg and the dog handlers, throat tight, running. Under the swinging beam of her flashlight, the girl juddered helplessly.

"Come on. She needs—"

A thick smell hit her, gamey and putrid. A low grunting came from the darkness. Caitlin stopped, horrified.

The girl was dead. In the shadows, a feral hog was gnashing her with its tusks.

Mouth dry, Caitlin ran at it, yelling and waving her arms. The pig looked at her with tiny black eyes, then spun and dashed into the undergrowth. She pressed the back of her hand to her mouth.

The dog handlers and Berg looked at her like she was crazy.

One of the K-9 officers shook his head. "Them things are mean."

She was breathing hard. "It was disturbing the scene."

And chewing on the body. A sick shiver ran through her.

The clearing abruptly fell silent, as if all life within the forest had emptied away. Caitlin looked down at the disturbed ground before her.

The body was garbed in a white nightgown. When they turned their flashlights on it, Caitlin immediately saw that it was the nightgown from which the torn fabric had been taken by the golden retriever. She stilled, trying to take in the whole scene. Her field of vision, which had been narrowed to tunnel focus by adrenaline, slowly expanded.

The young woman's wrists were viciously slashed. The cuts ran diagonally up the inside of her forearms, along the line of the radial artery. Maybe ten centimeters—four inches. The cuts had severed arteries, veins, muscle, and tendon, exposing the interior of her arms like cuts in raw steak. To the victim, it would have been excruciating. But she would have lost consciousness in under a minute.

Caitlin's hands went to the scars on her own forearms. They weren't as deep, but they were plentiful. Like the victim's, they'd been made with a razor blade. Unlike the victim, she'd made them herself. A lifetime ago.

The beam of the flashlight caught the redness around the victim's wrists, about three inches wide. Her skin was dusty and had marbled from the breakdown of red blood cells staining the walls of her vascular system. But the signs were clear.

"Ligature marks," she said. "Skin irritation. Duct tape."

Detective Berg knelt beside the body. "It's Phoebe Canova."

Caitlin stepped back mentally, seeing the victim's body in its entirety. Her field of vision continued to expand.

Then goose bumps rose. Around Phoebe's body, maybe six feet away, photos were stuck in the ground like headstones. They were Polaroids.

Caitlin stepped back physically. The photos showed women in white nightgowns. They were blond. Some were alive and terrified. Most were dead.

Rainey spoke in a low voice. "Holy Jesus. How long has this guy been killing?"

Caitlin counted the photos. There were twelve.

11

The harsh fluorescent lights were buzzing when Caitlin and Emmerich arrived back at the Solace sheriff's station. Rainey remained at the crime scene with Detective Berg. The station, after business hours, was nearly empty. Emmerich pinned fresh crime scene photos to the boards.

He loosened his tie. "Let's develop the profile."

The photos were clear, sharp, and grim. Phoebe Canova's wilted body, tossed by the feral hog, lay splayed on the ground. Under the camera flash, the baby doll nightie bloomed a shocking, otherworldly white. The nightgown, and Phoebe's skin and hair, were streaked with dirt and blood. But beneath the grime, Phoebe's cheap blond dye job had been washed and brushed. And makeup had been applied to her now green-gray skin. Her lipstick was ruby red.

The UNSUB—one calculating, remorseless predator—had done this. Then he had left Phoebe in the forest for animals to savage.

The sight of the hog seemed to fill Caitlin's head. She

saw again its tiny gleaming eyes, its tusks gnashing Phoebe's body. What was the Bible story about Jesus casting demons into a herd of swine?

A bone-cold ache sank into her. A devastating serial killer was at work. What kind of man could *do* this?

"Hendrix."

She looked at Emmerich. "Yes, sir."

"Raise the shutters."

For a moment, she thought he meant the windows.

"These crime scenes have given us a wealth of information. We need to mine it," he said.

"I'm assimilating it."

Emmerich quieted until she gave him her full attention.

"You're standing halfway across the room from the evidence."

Caitlin fought, constantly, to keep emotional distance from the cases she worked. And Emmerich knew why. Her father, Mack, had been a homicide detective—the original investigator on the serial killings committed by the Prophet. The case had bled into his off-duty hours, his home life, and his tormented mind. It shattered him and tore his family apart.

As a teenager, it had led Caitlin to despair and self-harm.

In her wallet, she carried a scrap of paper on which she'd written her goals before she pinned on a sheriff's star. *Dedication. Persistence. Job stays at the station.*

She worked, every day, to brand those words on her

heart. Because when she ignored them, she slipped from relentless pursuit into dangerous obsession.

She stood rigidly still.

"The only way to find the line is to approach it," Emmerich said. "And we need a deep dive here."

To track the UNSUB, she had to get inside his mind and understand his methods. How was he selecting and hunting these women? What was driving him to kill?

Emmerich wanted her to open up. To let the UNSUB in.

She nearly let out a hysterical laugh. When she opened up, she knew, she bled.

His expression was calm and patient, but charged with expectation.

She knew little about Emmerich's personal life. He was divorced, with two teenage daughters whose photos filled his office. He enjoyed fly fishing. He was an Eagle Scout. In his twenties, he had hiked the Appalachian Trail. He'd been with the FBI for eighteen years, plunging headfirst into the dankest, most violent cases in the country.

His back was straight, his shoulders level. The lights cast his shadow in multiples across the floor.

Caitlin sometimes wondered if Emmerich was the man her father could have been. Investigating the Prophet slayings had poisoned Mack Hendrix, literally and emotionally, and broken their family. If it hadn't . . .

"These crime scenes reveal the killer's signature and indicate his paraphilia," Emmerich said. "We start there and work outward to connect it to his identity."

His hands, as often, hung at his sides, as if he were a gunslinger ready to draw. His stern countenance was underlain with compassion. His empathy was genuine, and it warmed her. And she knew he hoped to draw out her own empathy in return—to get her to understand and share the feelings of the UNSUB.

She approached the board. "You mean we have to search for a homology."

In biology, a *homology* meant that different creatures had a similar structure because of shared ancestry. In archaeology, it referred to beliefs or practices that shared similarities due to historical or ancestral connections.

In criminal profiling, it was the elusive point where character and action came together.

With this offender, character and action had come together at least twelve times. And the results had been put on display in the cedar forest. Caitlin stared at the crime scene photos of Shana Kerber and Phoebe Canova, laid out in white, surrounded by Polaroids.

"Paraphilia hardly covers it," she said. "He's trying to perfect a hell of a fantasy."

She walked slowly along the board, taking in the full flow of the information. The missing women's photos. The map of Texas with I-35 highlighted in red. The abduction sites.

"The forest displays are the climax of the killer's sexual psychodrama." *Cherry on the UNSUB sundae.* "Before he ever spots a potential victim, he has his script worked out."

"He's meticulous," Emmerich said. "And confident."

"He maintains control throughout his crimes." *Movie theater. Main Street. Farmhouse.* "There's no sign of struggle at any abduction site. He gets victims to lower their guard or go with him willingly."

He started to take shape in her mind. "He has a well-honed facade of sincerity and the ability to manipulate women." She tapped a photo of Phoebe Canova's car at the railroad crossing. "The open driver's window suggests he uses a con to gain the victims' confidence, then overpowers and takes them in plain sight."

Emmerich crossed his arms. "Agreed. What does he do when he's not committing murder?"

"Stays clean. He's good at not getting caught." She thought for a second. "He won't have a criminal record."

"Unfortunately for us."

"The fact that the killings occur on weekends suggests he has a nine-to-five job." She turned it over in her head. *The empty car. The movie theater. An undisturbed house.* "He's persuasive and gregarious. The job may involve sales."

"He compartmentalizes."

"Yes. He keeps up a seemingly normal life. He'll have a wife or girlfriend."

Down the hall, the back door of the station buzzed open. Rainey came in.

Emmerich said, "Status?"

"Forensic unit arrived. They'll be working those scenes at least twenty-four hours." She noted the new crime scene photos. "Signature, clearly. Elaborate and specific."

Caitlin said, "Staged by a man who looks like Mr.

Ordinary. Somebody who keeps the monster in a mental cage."

"And when he unlocks it, he kills," Emmerich said. "Viciously. He's a grandiose narcissist. His rage and sense of entitlement drive him to destroy the happiness of others."

Caitlin stuck her hands in her back pockets. "He's got to have burning memories of rejection that stoke him. Convince him his actions are justified. Women hurt him, so he hurts women."

Rainey shook her head. "You're suggesting he's an anger-retaliation rapist, motivated by a desire to humiliate the victim. But these attacks go beyond revenge." Her cool facade flickered, and for a second, revulsion edged in. "He's an anger-excitation rapist and killer."

Caitlin considered it. "A sexual sadist. Asserting power and instilling fear are what excite him."

Emmerich began to pace. "Anger-excitation rapists stalk victims by car and range outside their own neighborhoods. His vehicle will have a kidnapping kit. Duct tape, zip ties, box cutter, ski mask or panty hose."

Caitlin examined the crime scene photos. Slashed wrists. Heavy cosmetics, almost Kabuki. Pristine nighties.

"All his victims bled copiously, but half the nightgowns have no blood on them. The cosmetics are slathered on. He dressed them and made them up *after* death." She turned. "He reduces them to objects in a twisted fantasy. Nothing more than dolls for him to possess, control, and ultimately destroy."

Rainey drew nearer to the board and examined the

copies of the Polaroids. "I expect he takes multiple photos and keeps some as trophies. These, at the scene, they're calling cards. Planting the photos—he's staking his claim to being the creator of these objects. Declaring ownership, as author of the fantasy."

Caitlin frowned at the photos.

"What?"

"The slashing of Phoebe's wrists disturbs me."

"It disturbs all of us."

"The killer prepares these women like a sacrifice. It's suicidal ideation, forced upon the unwilling." She paused. "Phoebe Canova had been missing for almost three weeks."

Emmerich continued to pace. "But the ME estimates she's been dead two weeks."

"He kept her alive. He tortures his victims both physically and mentally."

"What reaction does he want from them?"

"Terror. Surrender. Despair. Submission." Caitlin shook her head. "Destroy them emotionally, and he takes their souls as well as their bodies."

"Why does he attack on Saturday nights?"

"Busy during the week?" Caitlin said.

"Maybe." Emmerich crossed his arms. "This started in August. What triggered it?"

Rainey shook her head. "No way to know, yet."

"And why is he accelerating his kills?"

Rainey looked thoughtful. Caitlin stepped into the silence.

"He got a taste for it."

Emmerich raised an eyebrow. "Judging from the Polaroids he planted around Phoebe Canova's body, he's had a taste for some time."

Rainey said, "I get what Caitlin's saying. He's becoming brazen."

"He's succeeding at abducting and killing these women without getting caught," Caitlin said. "And success breeds confidence."

Emmerich nodded. "He has a compulsion. And once he gave in to it, he couldn't stop. Killing has become more than a need or pleasure. It's become a habit."

"And with every murder, he becomes more adept. More self-assured. And more convinced that he's . . . invisible."

Emmerich, already somber, seemed to draw in on himself. "Finding the bodies tonight blows that out of the water."

"No," Caitlin said.

She flushed, realizing she'd contradicted the boss. But Emmerich merely looked at her with curiosity—and maybe a hint of amusement.

"Finding the bodies spoils the killer's dollhouse game, with *these victims*," she said. "But it doesn't lead back to him. Not yet. Given his ego, he's still going to think that when it comes to grabbing victims, he's invulnerable."

"You don't think he's going to back off?"

"Discovering the bodies, by itself, won't do it. And Saturday night is coming fast. We should presume we have only days to stop him."

Emmerich considered it. "Write it up for presentation."

"Yes, sir." She took a beat. "His narcissism convinces him he's superior to the world. If we tell him we're on his trail, we might puncture his sense of invincibility. *That* might spook him into backing off."

Emmerich nodded. "And we may shake loose some leads. Time to get proactive."

12

At eight A.M., the detectives' room filled with uniformed deputies and detectives in jeans and polo shirts. A weak sun slatted through the venetian blinds. On the board, the Polaroids of women in white looked like a congress of the dead.

Chief Morales swept in. "Listen up. These FBI agents have information on who we're dealing with."

Emmerich thanked him. His white shirt was crisp and starched, his cheeks pink from a fresh shave. He looked focused, as though he planned to waste not one syllable.

"A single perpetrator abducted the missing women and killed the two victims who were found yesterday," he said.

A deputy blurted, "A serial killer."

"Yes."

The collective intake of breath sucked air from the room. Emmerich gave Caitlin a nod. She passed out copies of the two-page profile of the UNSUB she'd written up overnight.

White male, early-to-late thirties. Some college education.

Employed at a white-collar job, possibly in sales. Will have a wife or girlfriend.

She walked to the front of the room. It was her presentation. She took a breath.

"He lives within fifty miles of Solace," she said, "in a detached house with landscaping or trees that provide privacy. He drives a vehicle that's large but won't stand out. He needs it to transport his victims but doesn't want it to be memorable. It's probably an American make, muted in color, and may have tinted windows."

She told them about the kidnapping kit he would likely keep in the vehicle. Officers flipped through the profile. Some took notes. Caitlin felt caffeine and nerves kicking in.

"The UNSUB hunts between ten P.M. and one A.M. Darkness allows him to slip nearly unnoticed into neighborhoods and position himself at vantage points where he can observe and select his victims. Unlit side roads, tree-covered plazas, hallways, and even rooms that are dark in contrast to the victims' location."

Tight faces turned to her.

"He's taking risks. Abducting women in public places. Darkness negates some of that risk, but not all." She turned to the map of Texas tacked to the board and tapped the I-35 on-ramps that the UNSUB had used to fade away with his victims. "His ability to gain control over victims without drawing attention to himself, and the way he escapes the crime scene so quickly, indicate planning and composure."

A detective at the back said, "Does this mean he's an organized killer?"

"It indicates a methodical approach." She paused and considered her words. "The FBI has backed away from classifying offenders as 'organized' or 'disorganized.' Those terms describe an UNSUB's psychological makeup and the way they commit their crimes. 'Organized' implies offenders who are socially adept, often have above-average intelligence, and show indications of order before, during, and after a crime. They often conceal victims' bodies. They're calm and relaxed after committing murder. And their victims are most often strangers—targeted because they're in a particular place or have certain characteristics."

She glanced at the photos of blond women on the board. Everybody did.

"'Disorganized' implies offenders who are socially inadequate and sexually incompetent. Who kill when they're distressed and confused—acting suddenly, with no plan to evade detection. Leaving victims where they're killed. Not attempting to conceal the body," she said. "But the categories aren't mutually exclusive. It's not a dichotomy—more a continuum. So we don't classify this UNSUB as organized." She took a beat. "But he certainly shows signs of order and control."

"So, this guy is Mr. Chill?" Detective Berg said.

"He kills out of rage, displacing his anger onto proxies for someone who injured him emotionally. Killing provides him with emotional and sexual gratification," she said. "He takes possession of his victims. These women are objects to him. Not fully human. In his mind, in fact, he's the only human being on the planet."

"Gratification," a deputy said.

She nodded. They'd received the autopsy results on Shana and Phoebe.

"He sexually assaults his victims, then kills them. Then he lays the bodies out in a way that suggests he revisits them after death." She looked at her notes instead of the deputies. "I'm not saying that he's a necrophile. But dressing and grooming the bodies provides satisfaction. He wants to prolong the excitement of the kill. He's not dumping them. He's preserving them. As *his*."

A sick silence hung in the air.

"Why the nighties?" Chief Morales finally asked.

"A fetish, a memory—something makes him associate the negligees with sexual desire." She looked at the photo of Phoebe Canova's body. "The makeup—he's probably attempting to restore a semblance of life and obscure signs of decay. Again, trying to extend the illusion as long as possible. And maybe making them up to resemble a particular woman."

Morales began to pace at the back of the room.

The deputy shook his head. "Psycho."

Caitlin turned to the photos on the board. "The killer is increasingly confident. The first victim, Kayley Fallows, left the Red Dog Café and walked down a dark street. The UNSUB had copious cover from which to observe and attack her without the risk of being seen."

She pointed at subsequent photos. "Heather Gooden disappeared while walking fifty yards between her college dorm and a coffeehouse. He had a narrower window of opportunity and acted with increased boldness. Then he took Veronica Lees from the movie theater. Still greater confidence and sophistication—multiple opportunities for customers and staff to see and remember him. Video cameras. A narrower window of time to gain the victim's trust and gain control over her."

"And all in plain view," Berg said. "Was he showing off?"

"No. But his previous successes gave him the assurance that he could succeed. That he could act with impunity."

"I think he's on the theater's CCTV," Berg said.

"There's a high probability he was captured on video—*if* he entered the multiplex through the front entrance. Presuming none of the emergency exits were propped open or the alarms disabled," she said. "We're working on it."

Berg nodded and pointed at the photo of Phoebe Canova. "An even higher-risk abduction. Main Street, in plain view, while a pickup idled forty feet away. *Now* he's showing off."

"Agreed."

Caitlin moved on to Shana Kerber. She tapped the young mother's photo. "This is the boldest abduction yet. Entering the victim's home, where he would normally be at a disadvantage and more likely to leave forensic evidence. But he got away."

A deputy in the back said, "So what's he look like?"

"Ordinary. Well dressed, in clean, neat clothes. Maybe attractive. He blends in."

"No facial tattoos."

"No. This UNSUB appears deliberately nonthreatening." She straightened. "But he has a predator's instinct for people who are vulnerable. He catches women when they're distracted, or in a rush, or half asleep. He's skilled at seizing opportune moments to take advantage of others." She paused a second. "Think about people you know who have that skill."

"You think we know this guy?" a deputy said.

"Lots of people do."

The deputies shifted, disconcerted.

Emmerich spoke up. "This UNSUB is mobile, he's confident, and from the Polaroids, we know the murders in Solace aren't his first killings. You should investigate other disappearances along the I-35 corridor. It's his hunting ground."

Berg nodded at the map. "I-35 runs near five hundred miles through Texas."

"And another thousand miles north to Duluth, Minnesota. But Texas is a place to start."

Caitlin panned the room. "This man is dangerous and driven, and unless we stop him, he's going to kill again."

Berg's frown was challenging. "What are you going to do?"

Emmerich said, "We're going to hold a press conference with the chief. And see if anybody out there has any information."

Morales raised his chin. "Somebody knows this son of a bitch. We're going to find him."

13

Television news crews crowded the sidewalk in front of the sheriff's station. They came from Austin and San Antonio, along with print reporters and photographers, a stringer from AP, local bloggers, and two dozen Solace citizens. Grim and purposeful, Chief Morales spoke into a thicket of microphones. He confirmed the deaths of Shana Kerber and Phoebe Canova and emphasized that the department was urgently seeking the suspect, probably a white man in his thirties. Behind him, Caitlin stood beside assembled deputies, detectives, and the FBI team.

Morales finished speaking. "I'm going to turn the microphone over to Special Agent Brianne Rainey of the FBI, who has more information."

Rainey stepped up. Her black coat was sleek, her braids swept back into a chignon. She looked as sharp as an arrow. "We believe the man who has committed these murders lives along the I-35 corridor between Austin and San Antonio. He's part of the community. People know him. They work with him." She scanned the assembled media. "There will be signs that he's committing these crimes. He may go out unexpectedly on Saturday nights. He may leave and return without explanation, or with an implausible explanation. If you recognize a man who fits this description, please contact the sheriff's department."

She made eye contact with every journalist, then looked into the cameras. "This offender scouts potential victims ahead of time. He watches women at home and at work before choosing an opportune moment to attack. If you've seen anybody in your neighborhood or on the street who seems out of place—somebody watching a house, or a business, somebody who doesn't belong— please contact law enforcement."

Reporters scribbled. The TV people held out their microphones.

"If you feel like *you've* been watched, or if you've been approached by a man seeking assistance or asking you to accompany him somewhere, call the sheriff's office. Your vigilance can help apprehend this killer."

Morales handed Rainey several eight-by-ten photos. They were photocopies of Polaroids found around Phoebe Canova's body in the forest. Jane Does. Rainey held them up.

"We're appealing for your help to identify these three women."

A deputy passed out copies. Behind him, Caitlin and Emmerich stood silently, props for the press.

"Questions?" Morales said.

Caitlin, without moving her lips, whispered, "Here we go."

The Austin TV brunette said, "The Saturday Night

Killer. He takes women and makes them dress up in white nightgowns?"

"Yes," Morales said.

The Saturday Night Killer. Caitlin kept a poker face. The BAU never gave an UNSUB a nickname. They avoided mythologizing serial killers. She was afraid that these photos would give tabloids a hard-on to come up with more piquant names for the murderer. *The White Nightie Killer* came to mind.

"Will you institute a Saturday curfew?"

"Are you going to shut down schools?"

"Why has it taken so long to bring in the FBI?"

Caitlin stood behind her shades. She and Emmerich scanned the crowd, memorizing faces, analyzing body language. Some offenders injected themselves into the investigation of their own crimes despite knowing the cops watched for it. The station's CCTV camera was capturing everybody there.

Morales said, "That's all. Thank you."

He headed into the station with reporters shouting questions at his back. Rainey followed him.

As she passed, Caitlin said, "Let's hope this works."

Rainey opened the door. "Hope is for church on Sunday. Let's flush this snake from its den."

14

In downtown Dallas, Saturday night was popping. Skyscrapers were brightly lit. The broad downtown streets were a river of headlights. Despite the cold, the North Point Plaza mall in Uptown, near the tangle of expressways that spaghettied through the city center, was packed. The upscale shopping center's garage was one hundred fifty yards from an on-ramp to I-35, the Stemmons Freeway.

Teri Drinkall stepped out of the elevator on garage level five, holding a shopping bag from Neiman Marcus and another from an independent bookstore and a third from California Pizza Kitchen, containing her shrimp pesto pizza. The clack of her stack-heel boots echoed from the concrete floor. When she'd arrived three hours earlier the garage had been packed, but it was almost empty now. Her Ford Escape was parked at the far end of the floor. A gust lifted her blond hair from her shoulders.

She rounded a pillar near the fire stairs and heard a man's voice.

"Excuse me."

She jumped and spun, bags swinging. Her key ring was in her right hand, her keys jammed between her fingers like talons.

The man stood near the stairs, half shadowed. "Sorry, didn't mean to startle you."

He was stylishly dressed, with a warm voice. He looked abashed. He was pressing a hand to the wall, apparently for balance.

"I hate to bother you. But I need a hand getting to my car."

On the concrete in front of him were shopping bags from a toy store. A Paddington Bear peeped out of one.

Teri smiled.

The man smiled back.

Sunday afternoon light fell through the sheers on the bedroom windows, dappled with shadow from the backyard oaks. Standing beside the bed, the man eagerly examined the new Polaroid. It was so fresh. The details were vivid. The light captured detail, every swell of her body, the gleam in her eyes.

Dallas women had an extra measure of polish. A little cowboy kick.

She'd been worth the drive.

He'd been beyond angry when the Gideon sheriffs and the FBI found the women in the cedar woods. They'd ruined his work. Brought dogs. Taken his prizes. He'd been *furious*. Then, when they held the press conference, he'd become alarmed.

He had considered holding off. The girl he had in

mind, the barista named Madison, had seen him scoping her apartment complex. She was baby blond, saucy, with an insincere, *May I take your order* smile. Young and blank-eyed. But she'd seen him, if just for a few seconds. Taking her, with the FBI goddamn shouting *watch out* from the rooftops, was too risky this weekend.

And the old rage—the awful, righteous craving to *show* them, to make these women *see,* to quench his want before he exploded—had risen and coursed through him. It had thundered beneath his temples, telling him: *Nobody can take this from me. It's* mine.

And Dallas was two hundred miles up the interstate.

He admired the photo for another minute, then added it to the display. His exhibit was secret—he kept it stashed behind a false wall in his closet. He pinned Debbie Does Dallas to the board. She added a gleam to the assemblage. He ran his fingers across the collection. *So many white negligees, so carefully chosen . . .*

He untacked a photo of a teenage platinum blond. The photo was old. He cared for it diligently, keeping it out of the light so it wouldn't fade, using the same pinpoint hole every time he tacked it to the board, but after all this time, the white border betrayed greasy gray smears. He loved caressing it but now tried to keep his fingers above the surface.

Not today. She had started it.

He had tried to forget, and forgive, and ignore, and pretend that it didn't matter, but everywhere he went, the world teemed with others like her. The dismissive. The selfish. The ones who threw him aside like a gum wrapper. The beautiful, the superficial, the emotionally juvenile. The ones who failed to care. Who didn't comprehend that if you stomped on a man's spirit, there was no coming back. The ones blind to the depths.

He pressed the photo to his lips and bared his teeth, as if he was going to bite it.

The doorbell rang.

Heart pounding, he pinned the photo back in place. He reluctantly locked away his stash and checked himself in the mirror. His color was high, his eyes bright. He looked like he'd been working out.

He had been.

As he strolled down the hall, the images from the corkboard sent a stimulating prickle along his skin. He allowed himself a single smile, broad and hungry, then smoothed his expression and opened the front door.

"Central Market was out of jalapeños. I'll substitute serranos." In swept Emma, bubbly as always, with two grocery bags in her arms. "The corn bread muffins will have a kick, but hey, we can live it up. I'll get the soup on."

"You'll work your magic. It's no problem," he said.

She blew him a kiss and headed toward the kitchen, her Bambi-brown hair soft in the light, her floral perfume reminding him of schoolteachers and maiden aunts.

"And you're the kick," he called after her.

Over her shoulder, she gave him a bashful smile.

He turned to the door. "Well. Hello."

The six-year-old girl stood on the porch, holding a DVD of *Frozen*.

"Is that what we're watching today, Miss Ashley?" he said.

She giggled and hopped up and down. "You silly. You know it is."

"Come in. Your mom's getting lunch on."

She skipped past him. It was Disney movie day. Smiling, he closed the door.

15

Monday morning, Caitlin walked toward the hotel checkout desk, pulling her roller suitcase. Solace had escaped the weekend unscathed. The BAU team was returning to DC on an eleven A.M. flight.

Rainey was already there. The clerk had stepped into a back office. Caitlin said good morning and set her key on the counter.

Behind her, Emmerich's voice echoed across the lobby. "Hang on to that."

She and Rainey turned.

"Disappearance Saturday night. Dallas," Emmerich said.

Rainey's eyes widened. "That's significantly beyond the UNSUB's previous hunting zone."

"The Dallas police think it's linked to the murders here in Solace. They're sending everything to the sheriff's office." His hair was damp from a shower, white shirt blinding in the morning light. "There's video."

A sharp buzz ran up Caitlin's spine.

At the sheriff's station, Detective Berg handed Emmerich an eight-by-ten blowup of a driver's license photo. A young vanilla blond.

"Teri Drinkall. Twenty-five. Paralegal at a downtown Dallas law firm. She never came home from a Saturday shopping trip. Her boyfriend and roommate have alibis."

Caitlin gathered with the others at Berg's desk. The detective cued up the CCTV video from the garage. His face was morose.

"It's not helpful. You'll see." He hit PLAY.

The video was silent black-and-white. The camera was mounted in the ceiling near a bank of elevators in a multi-story parking garage. Three seconds of nothing rolled by. Then the missing woman crossed in front of the camera.

Teri Drinkall was petite and had an energetic stride. She carried two shopping bags in her left hand and had a third draped over her right forearm. Her purse was slung over her shoulder, keys in her right hand. She looked like she was heading directly toward her car. She passed beneath the camera and walked toward the far end of the garage, providing a view of her back.

She jumped, startled.

She turned her head sharply, her attention caught by something unexpected. Something offscreen.

Caitlin shifted, itching for more. Beside her, Emmerich stood with his arms crossed, fingers drumming.

On video, Teri turned to her right. Her back remained to the lens. She tilted her head and spoke.

Caitlin desperately wanted to know what she was saying, but they couldn't see enough even to attempt to read her lips.

Teri nodded and walked out of frame. Her shadow trailed her and disappeared.

Berg stopped the playback. "That's it."

Emmerich said, "Play it again."

They watched, focusing, two more times. Berg looked frustrated. Emmerich pulled out his laptop and set it on a conference table.

"Send it to me," he said.

"You think you can get anything out of that?"

"Our technical analyst at Quantico might."

Berg forwarded the video. "What could they find?"

Emmerich leaned over the computer, typing. "Shadows, artifacts, reflections—anything that might provide information about the person the victim spoke to."

Caitlin touched Berg's arm. "Can you play it one more time, please?"

He cued it up again. She watched.

It was clear to her that Teri had jumped because somebody had spoken to her. Otherwise she wouldn't have turned and spoken in response. Teri's head remained level as she spoke. That indicated she was talking to somebody of roughly similar height—an adult. Caitlin focused on the screen. This time as she watched, she tried to read the missing woman's body language.

Teri went toward the unseen speaker willingly. Why did she nod and agree to the UNSUB's request? What ruse did the killer use to lure her away?

By the time Teri walked out of the frame, her posture indicated complete disarmament. When she'd first walked on-screen, it was different. She had her car keys out and raised—ready to hit the alarm if anything seemed sketchy. She was prepared to respond to sudden threats—like any self-aware big-city woman.

She still had the keys raised, and *between her fingers,* like claws, when she first turned. Then she lowered them. She showed . . . concern. And . . . emotional discomfort?

Caitlin watched again. Between the time Teri was first startled and the time she lowered the keys, her shoulders dropped. Her head tilted to one side, in an attitude people frequently adopted when speaking to small children or whimpering animals. It was more than mere concern. It was . . . pity?

"The ruse he used convinced her he was more than just harmless. It convinced her he was damaged," Caitlin said. "In some way. She wanted to help him. He turned her completely around emotionally, in less than four seconds."

Berg said, "He played injured?"

"Possibly. I'd add that to the profile."

"It's our guy?"

"Maybe." Caitlin felt queasy.

Emmerich forwarded the video to Quantico. He didn't look up. "If it is, releasing the Polaroids didn't spook him into backing off."

Berg looked at Caitlin. "It sent him up the interstate."

At noon, the stockbrokers at Crandall McGill were busy under the bright Phoenix sun. Phones rang. Televisions were quietly tuned to financial and news channels, tickers crawling across the bottom of various screens.

At the reception desk in the lobby, Lia Fox transferred a call and signed for a stack of FedEx envelopes. The deliveryman gave her a nice, appraising look. She was thirty-six, sleek and petite, and knew she looked good in the pencil skirt and stilettos. Her dark hair was cropped short for the heat. It made her face look severe, but she'd decided she liked it that way. Fierceness was something she wanted to try.

She waved good-bye to the delivery guy, slurped the dregs from a cold brew, and scrolled through texts on her phone, swiveling back and forth on her desk chair. Tizzy's sick *again*, her mom wrote, about her dog. Scored a try! her sis squealed, about sports, or a test, or sex. Lia replied to both with a thumbs-up. She gathered the FedEx envelopes and headed back into the office to deliver them.

As she passed the traders' desks, a wall-mounted television caught her eye. It ticked something in the back of her skull, but she continued walking. Around the corner, another TV was tuned to the same news channel. The chyron read, TEXAS POLICE, FBI SEEK KILLER.

She saw the Polaroids and stopped.

A broker came out of her office. "Lia?"

Lia stared at the television.

"Lia. Is that for me?"

The broker had her hand out. Head pinging, Lia handed her an envelope.

"What's wrong?" the woman said.

Lia shook her head, eyes pinned on the television screen. "Nothing."

The broker looked up at the screen. "Good God. How horrible."

Lia tried to breathe but her chest seemed locked. The broker was speaking to her but all she could hear was the pinging tone in her head.

The broker waved a hand in front of her face. "You look freaked-out. What's wrong?"

Lia turned to her. "Nothing."

She spun on her sharp heels and sped back along the carpeted hallway. Before she got to the front desk, she turned into the ladies' room. She locked herself in a bathroom stall and leaned back against the wall, trembling.

She whispered, "It can't be."

When she returned to the front desk, she managed to ignore the plasma screen in the lobby waiting area. But eventually, like poison ivy, the itch became overwhelming. At the top of the hour she walked over, unmuted the TV, and flipped through news channels until she found breaking news.

"A sixth Texas woman has disappeared, this time in Dallas."

Lia's hands fell to her sides. Like the other women who'd disappeared, Teri Drinkall was blond, and young, and slim, and gone. Gone, gone, gone. Their photos flashed on the screen. One after the next, like Barbies on a shelf at the toy store.

And the Polaroids. So many blonds, so much terror. Baby doll nighties.

A tremor started in her leg. It crawled up her belly and settled in her chest.

"The Dallas police have no suspects in the disappear-ance," the anchor said, "but are in contact with authori-ties in Gideon County, where five other women have disappeared. Two of those women were found murdered last week. The FBI is assisting with the investigation but has provided no further comment on the case."

The anchor looked austere, and worried. A list of tele-phone numbers flashed on the screen—tip lines.

Lia paused the TV. For a whole minute, then two, she stared out the front doors into the stinging Arizona sun-shine, until tears rose in her eyes.

With shaking fingers, she raised her phone. Reading off the television screen, she dialed.

When the call was answered, she closed her eyes. "I need to speak to the agents working on the Texas murder case. I know who the killer is."

16

The phones in the Solace sheriff's station were ringing nonstop. Every line was lit up with worried calls and wild tips.

The Saturday Night Killer is my neighbor.

It's the guy at the gas station who looked at me funny.

It's my mother-in-law.

The killer got into my trash. It's a garbage man.

I'm the killer.

I smothered them with a dry-cleaning bag.

I ran over them with a lawn mower.

At the front counter, a blond teenager dressed in a barista's black outfit spoke breakneck quick, describing a man she'd seen, holding her hand up to indicate his height. Chief Morales looked like his blood pressure had risen high enough to jet-wash a bus. Detective Berg's tie seemed close to strangling him. Outside, the white sun fell on a near-empty Main Street. A subaural pulse of panic seemed to fill the air.

At the conference table in the detectives' room, Caitlin

leaned toward her laptop, earbuds in. She was videoconferencing with the unit's technical analyst in Quantico, Nicholas Keyes.

"I know you're data mining the Dallas parking garage CCTV footage," Caitlin said. "But there's another video, of the third victim. I'd bet hard money the UNSUB is on it."

Veronica Lees's disappearance at the multiplex cinema played in a window on her screen.

"What I need is motion analysis," Caitlin said. "A way to pair the victim with the other people in the theater lobby, individually, then determine whether one of them watches, touches, or follows her."

"I count a hundred twenty-five people in that lobby. Rough estimate," Keyes said.

He was staring at his own screen rather than at Caitlin. The computer's glow reflected from his horn-rims. At twenty-eight, he had a nimble mind and a depth of knowledge that seemed ancient.

"I know that's a lot of work," Caitlin said.

"Not if I apply the correct model." Keyes's fingers ran fluidly across his keyboard. A pencil was jammed behind his ear. "Couple ways I can attack this."

Emmerich strode into the room and approached the conference table.

"Keyes, hang on." Caitlin pulled out one earbud.

"Caller says she knows who the killer is." Emmerich handed Caitlin a message slip. "Preliminary screening indicates her claim may have credibility. This woman will take a video call. Get a look at her face, listen to her, and determine whether *credible* is the right word."

"Right away."

With a crisp nod, Emmerich left.

Caitlin swiveled back to Keyes. "I gotta—"

"Heard. Go." His eyes darted, scanning his screen. "I have an idea."

"Involving?"

"Slant routes and interceptions."

He clicked off before Caitlin could ask him more. She set the message slip on the table and put through a video call. It was answered almost instantly.

"Ms. Fox."

Lia Fox was hunched toward the screen, licking her lips, nervous. She had close-cropped black hair and a hard jaw but looked as frightened as a fawn.

"Agent Hendrix?" Fox said. "You're in Texas? You're investigating these murders?"

"Yes. What information do you have for us?"

"You have to promise." Fox steepled her hands in front of her lips and closed her eyes briefly before staring intensely at Caitlin. "My name stays out of this. I'm anonymous."

"I'll keep your name confidential," Caitlin said. "You believe you can identify the killer?"

Lia's eye twitched. "My ex-boyfriend. His name is Aaron Gage."

She exhaled as though speaking those words had drained every ounce of her energy.

Caitlin wrote the name down. "Tell me about Gage. Why do you think he's the man we're looking for?"

"He stalked me. He . . ." Lia pressed a hand over her mouth.

"Take your time. Just tell me what happened."

Lia took a few seconds, seeming to work up her courage. She clenched her jaw. It made her look worn-down.

"I was a freshman in college. Rampart College, outside Houston. I was eighteen and . . ." A shrug. "Aaron was hot. Rugged, a whole Clint-Eastwood-on-a-horse vibe."

Caitlin nodded, encouraging her.

"But he liked to party," Lia said. "He drank. Things got dark."

"What makes you think he's the suspect in these killings, Ms. Fox?"

"I was kind of a mess," Lia said. "Skating on all my classes. Just wandering, you know? I stayed with him longer than I should have. He was my first boyfriend and . . ."

Her cheeks were blazing. She looked like she'd been holding this in since freshman year.

Caitlin softened her voice. "It's okay. I'm listening. Keep going."

Lia nodded tightly. "One night at his apartment, he— we—got wasted. Got into a screaming match. I stormed into the bedroom and locked the door. Shoved a chair under the knob. Aaron pounded on it, called me names, yelled that I was worthless . . ."

Caitlin continued to nod. "And?"

"And I cried myself to sleep. Aaron kept drinking and burned the apartment down."

That woke Caitlin up. "He deliberately set the apartment on fire?"

Lia flinched. "I don't know. Maybe he passed out. The fire department labeled the cause of the fire 'undetermined.'"

Caitlin asked her for the address of the apartment and date of the fire.

"When I woke up, the bedroom was smoky and Aaron's roommate was pounding on the door, begging me to get out." Lia's eyes were growing bright. "I opened the door and flames were burning on the living room ceiling. Front door was wide-open, neighbors in the hall, yelling for me to run."

"It sounds terrifying."

"It still makes me sick." Lia's voice quavered. "And I know you're thinking, 'So what?'"

Caitlin saw genuine fear on the woman's face, but Lia was correct: She'd heard nothing so far to link Gage to their UNSUB.

"I'm listening."

"I never spoke to Aaron again. I broke it off. Boom, over." Lia leaned toward the screen. "And that's when things got creepy."

"Describe 'creepy.'"

"I started getting cards in the mail. Never signed. 'Stop ignoring me,' 'You're making a mistake,' 'What's wrong with you?' Then gifts started showing up on the porch," Lia said. "At first, sweet things. A charm bracelet. A music box. But when I didn't respond, he started leaving Barbies. They were . . . damaged."

A soft chill descended on Caitlin's shoulders.

"Arms torn out of their sockets. Neck broken. Face burned with a cigarette lighter. Legs . . ." She looked away, then fiercely back at the screen. "Legs spread. One was placed on top of a dead rat, like—the doll was screwing it. It scared the shit out of me."

"Did you tell anyone?" Caitlin said.

"My roommates. I couldn't tell my parents—they would have known I had . . . I'd had *relations* with a boy, and would have gone ballistic."

"Anybody at the college? The police?"

Lia scoffed. "Campus public safety? They busted kids for violating curfew and playing hip-hop 'too loud.'" She made air quotes. "Rampart's a small Christian college. The administration didn't want to know about students having—sex."

Lia looked down and lowered her voice. "They would have hauled me up on disciplinary charges. Demanded repentance and maybe expelled me."

Caitlin thought, *Glad I didn't go to Rampart.* But she was sadly unsurprised to hear how the college would have responded to a student being stalked.

"What else?" Caitlin said.

Lia's voice strengthened. Now that she was rolling, she was getting more emphatic with every word.

"Late at night he would stand across the street in the dark, watching my place."

"You're positive it was Aaron Gage?"

"He stayed out of the light, but same build, same

height. My roommates saw him too, and were freaked-out." Her eyes shimmered. "Then he killed my cat."

The chill blew across Caitlin's shoulders.

"Slit its throat and left it in the backyard, surrounded by photos of me," Lia said. "The photos were taken at Aaron's apartment, of me, asleep. In a *fucking* white nightie."

Tears brimmed. Lia swiped them angrily away.

Caitlin was still. "Did you tell the authorities about the cat?"

Lia shook her head. "But I took a picture. I wanted it as evidence if things got bad."

Caitlin held back: Fire setting and animal torture were already very damn bad. Even a puritanical college administration would take such evidence of stalking seriously. The police would have immediately considered Lia's life to be under threat.

"I have to ask—at that point, what kept you from calling the cops?" Caitlin said.

Lia's cheeks flamed red. She began blinking and licking her lips. "Just . . . it was a bad time. Can we leave it at that? It *happened*."

She held up a photo. Caitlin's stomach tightened.

The cat lay small and lifeless, blood caked in the fur around its throat. The photos were stuck in wet grass around it. In all of them, Lia lay unaware, asleep in a simple and revealing nightgown. A repeated witness to death.

"Aaron did this," Lia said. "That's what counts. You have to believe me."

"Please scan and send that to me." Caitlin's heart was

beating like a drum. "I also need to examine the original. I'm going to have an agent from the Phoenix FBI office contact you."

"Yeah, I get that."

Caitlin clicked her pen. "I need all the information you have on Aaron Gage. Full name, date of birth, place of birth. Any photos you can send me."

Lia rattled off the pertinent information but said, "I tore up all my photos and flushed them. I wanted any memory of him *gone*."

"Do you know where Gage is?"

"No. Don't want to. Want *not* to know. I left Rampart. I transferred, and you better believe that this freaky shithead Aaron Gage is a major reason why."

"Who might know?" Caitlin said.

"I cut off contact with most people at Rampart. I couldn't tell you." Her gaze shifted to the side.

Caitlin didn't doubt that Lia was convinced of Gage's guilt. And that she was terrified. And that she was withholding something.

"Do you have any idea where I could start looking?" Caitlin said.

"Last I heard, he joined the army." Lia turned back to the screen. "It's *him*. He's not just a drunk-ass stalker anymore. He's a full-on killer." She leaned in. "Find him. 'Cause I'm putting myself out here, way past the line."

Lia ended the call. The screen went black.

Caitlin strode down the hall, searching the station, until she found Emmerich. Rapid-fire, she filled him in.

"We need to find Gage. He was controlling and angry. Plus the fire setting, killing the cat—that's as clear a set of behavioral indicators for psychopathic sexual sadism as it gets."

Emmerich said, "Fox had no prompting from you before bringing any of this up."

Caitlin felt affronted. "Absolutely not."

She knew better than to lead a witness, or to shape the information she drew out of a witness in questioning.

"The sheriffs have withheld the fact that Shana Kerber's throat was slit and that the Polaroids found in the forest were stuck in the ground around the body," Caitlin said. "It's the killer's signature. That doesn't strike me as coincidence."

Emmerich's gaze sharpened. "Me neither."

17

Working with Nicholas Keyes at Quantico, Tuesday morning Caitlin tracked down Aaron Gage. He was alive. He had an address across the Red River in Rincon, Oklahoma.

"Oklahoma," she said. "Way beyond the current kill zone. That fits the profile of an anger-excitation killer who hunts outside his own neighborhood."

"I-35 runs through Rincon," Keyes said, on speaker. "Gideon County is a straight shot, due south."

Rainey came in. Hearing the conversation, her eyes went to the wall map of Texas.

Keyes said, "And I can confirm one part of Lia Fox's story. Gage served in the army. Military records coming to you now."

"Thank you," Caitlin said.

Rainey tapped her knuckles on the conference table. "Copy me."

Caitlin felt a surge of excitement. But five minutes later, Rainey read through the records and shook her head.

"Eight years' active duty, multiple deployments, Purple Heart, honorable discharge—he's not the UNSUB."

"Why not?" Caitlin said. "The UNSUB loves violence. Multiple deployments to active war zones would give him cover to commit atrocities."

"Our UNSUB loves violence he can *control*. And war is never controllable." Rainey's voice had a harsh edge. "He loves violence he can *inflict*, against people who are in no position to fight back. The United States has a volunteer army—people join knowing they might go into harm's way. The UNSUB wouldn't touch that with a tent pole."

Caitlin felt a pinprick of doubt, and resentment that she immediately tried to squelch. *Listen to the experienced agent.*

"Acknowledged," she said. "But there's something in this story that needs investigating. We won't know what it is until we talk to Gage."

Across the room, Emmerich and Detective Berg leaned over a list—names that had come in via the tip line. Emmerich listened to Berg, underlined several names, and looked up. His gaze caught Caitlin's. His question was wordless.

"Located him. We're on it," she said.

Caitlin held out her hand to Rainey for the car keys.

"It's going to take us hours to drive to Oklahoma," she said.

Rainey handed over the keys. She knew that Emmerich was the one who had agreed to this. But Caitlin

didn't know how Rainey felt about that. She recognized
that her own position in the unit was unusual. She'd been
recruited straight out of an Alameda County Sheriff's Office homicide unit. She didn't have the years of investigative experience most FBI agents accumulated within the
Bureau before they joined the BAU. She sometimes felt
like the teacher's pet. She knew she had to earn her
stripes.

Oklahoma was going to take the rest of the day. She
couldn't afford for this trip to be a snipe hunt.

"There's a real lead here. It's important," she said.

Rainey nodded. "Then we should get going."

Rainey headed for the door. As she walked, she scrolled
on her phone, searching the military records they'd received from the DOD. Outside, she hopped in the SUV
and made a call, trying to reach Aaron Gage's former
commanding officer. Caitlin got in the driver's seat.

"Please tell Colonel Marthinsen to return this call as
soon as possible," Rainey said, buckling her seat belt.

Caitlin fired up the engine. Two minutes later, she hit
the on-ramp for I-35 North.

The hills of southern Oklahoma slow-rolled across the
winter-gold prairie, dipping to rivers and creeks, thick
with leafless trees. The road curved through farmland
and past a Chickasaw resort and casino. Caitlin drove
silently behind her sunglasses. Rainey worked on her laptop until they pulled off the interstate in Rincon and
headed into the countryside. Shutting down her computer, she pulled up a map on her phone.

"Judging by satellite imagery, Gage's cabin is smack in the middle of the woods." Her face was grave, but her tone was sardonic.

"As in teen-slasher-movie woods?"

"As in black girls and geeks die first." The edge left her voice. "It does match the profile."

They pulled off a twisting country road and bumped along a rutted gravel driveway. Rocky promontories barred their view until they topped a rise and found a half-acre property where the cabin faced south, toward the red clay river that lazed across the horizon. Caitlin pulled up in front and stopped.

"Well."

The cabin was rustic, with a broad porch and wide windows. Across the driveway sat an old red barn. It was sun bleached and listing. The door was open.

Inside, in the slatted light, sharp farm implements dangled from the rafters, jangling in the breeze like sinister chimes. Caitlin and Rainey exchanged a look.

They climbed from the Suburban. Scanning the barn, the drive, the trees, the shadows, they approached the cabin.

Caitlin had her coat unbuttoned, right hand low, not touching her weapon but making sure she had free access to it. No cars in the driveway or barn. No animals. No sound.

She climbed to the porch, sweeping the view, and knocked on the door. As she did, Rainey's phone rang.

Caitlin glanced through the front window. Saw no sign of movement inside. The lights were off.

Rainey answered the phone. "Colonel Marthinsen. Thank you for returning my call so promptly."

She listened, her face intent. From the phone, Caitlin could hear the man's baritone voice.

She knocked again.

Rainey said, "I understand, Colonel. Yes. His final deployment . . ."

From the back of the cabin came a man's voice. "Coming."

Caitlin stepped back and turned sideways to the door.

"Thank you, Colonel." Rainey hung up. Her face was unreadable. "Gage's former CO. He filled me in on how Master Sergeant Gage got his Purple Heart."

Her expression hinted at irony. Inside the house came footsteps. A man's—and a dog's paws ticking on a wooden floor.

The door opened. Aaron Gage stood shadowed in the doorway.

"Yes?" He wore dark glasses. He turned his head slightly, as if judging who was at the door by the way their bodies blocked the breeze.

At his side was a black Labrador. A guide dog. Gage held his harness.

18

FBI? What's going on?"

Aaron Gage was red bearded, lean, fit, like a kick-boxer. His dog stood patiently at his side as he gestured Caitlin and Rainey into the house.

He closed the door. "Did I hear you mention Colonel Marthinsen?"

"You did," Rainey said.

"What kind of questions required a call from my former commanding officer?"

He stood by the door, now unwilling to welcome them further. His posture, Caitlin observed, was army straight.

"We needed to know what *wasn't* in your official records, Sergeant." Rainey's voice was velvet and matter-of-fact. "Colonel Marthinsen told me how you lost your sight."

"It wasn't a covert op," Gage said. "Afghanistan's on the map. And an IED is only secret until your Humvee drives over it. Why are two feds at my door?"

Caitlin felt the flush on her cheeks. *Good question.*

They'd driven two hundred fifty miles to interrogate a man who could not be the killer.

Rainey's lips were pressed tight. She was biting back *I knew it.*

For a few seconds, Caitlin felt the brackish wash of failure. *Snipe hunt.* It had been too good to be true. Rainey had told her so.

Yet she couldn't shake the feeling that this lead had a legitimate basis.

She had run background on Lia Fox. On the long drive, Rainey had spelled her at the wheel, which had given her time to send requests and get the information. Lia was who she said she was. No criminal record. No history of filing false police reports. She'd never been sectioned. And the Houston Fire Department had confirmed the time and location of the apartment fire. They'd forwarded their call logs and the department's fire incident report. Gage's apartment had been gutted. The source of the blaze was a lit cigarette. The manner of combustion was, as Lia had claimed, undetermined. Evidence at the scene suggested an accident—that Gage had passed out while smoking. But arson could not be ruled out.

Caitlin had checked the date of the fire. It was a Saturday night.

The FBI's Phoenix Division had spoken to Lia and obtained the original photo of the dead cat surrounded by snapshots. The photo was digitally dated, and the date appeared to be genuine.

And, more than eighteen years later, Lia Fox remained

terrified about the fire, the aftermath, and the man standing before Caitlin.

Caitlin saw no evidence that Lia was a fabulist. To the contrary. If Lia had jumped to conclusions about Gage, she had cause. Real events had shaped her fears.

Rainey was radiating impatience. But Caitlin's gut told her not to let go of this. Not yet.

"We're investigating the serial disappearances and murders in Solace and Dallas," she said to Gage. "You may be able to help us."

"Me?" His mouth hung open. "Those women they found in the woods? Jesus. What do you think *I* can tell you?"

"You attended Rampart College."

He went silent. Eventually, he said, "That was a long time ago. What's the connection?"

"Your apartment was gutted by a fire," Caitlin said. "What can you tell us about that?"

"Nothing," Gage said.

"Sir?"

He stood like he was at parade rest, holding the guide dog's harness. "I can't tell you anything, because I have no memory of the fire."

Rainey gave Caitlin a plain look now, not worrying that Gage would catch her side eye or other visual cues.

"Why not?" Caitlin said.

Gage paused, seeming to read the mood in the air, deciding whether to continue talking.

"Back then I was pretty fucked up," he said.

"How so?"

"Booze. I'm from a family of alcoholics and when I started college I set out to continue the family tradition." He tilted his head. "Who told you about the fire—Dahli?"

"Sir?"

"Who told you? My ex-girlfriend, Dahli—Dahlia Hart?"

Caitlin declined to say. "There was talk that you harassed your girlfriend after the fire."

He recoiled. "What? Absolutely not. Harassed her? One hundred percent no. I never even saw her again. Jesus, who told you that?"

Caitlin felt a dropping sensation in her gut. "You wouldn't have needed to see her to harass her, Mr. Gage."

"Goddammit. She was . . ."

He stopped himself. For a second, he seemed on the verge of an outburst. Then he pulled back.

Caitlin pressed further. "Somebody killed her cat and left it for her to find."

Gage's mouth opened. "Somebody killed Slinky? Are you serious?"

He seemed horrified, but Caitlin was intrigued that he remembered the name of the cat.

"Mr. Gage? We have concerns that you may have been the one who did that."

"You didn't know, did you?" His voice was as dry as sand. "About what happened to me in Kandahar. That's why you're here. You thought I was killing people in Solace. What, because I grew up in Texas? Because of Dahli?"

Rainey said, "Sir—"

"Listen. After I burned down my own crib, I got clean

and sober. Enlisted. Served six tours, until I was wounded. I never saw Dahlia again. I never *spoke* to her again. I never *contacted* her again. I didn't harass her. I sure as hell didn't kill her cat." He shook his head. "Really? You think I would bash some kitten's head in because a girl broke up with me?"

His face was flushed. He was breathing hard.

The cat's head hadn't been bashed in.

"So I was a mess. I was a drunk at twenty. But I was *never* violent with women. Or animals. I got eight years' active duty under my belt, honorable discharge, got my degree. I work for a local nonprofit now, finding jobs for other vets. I have a family. None of this is me. It never was. It never will be."

Family. Rainey was perusing the living room. The plaid sofa had a plush toy on it. There weren't many photos on the walls, but the ones on the windowsill portrayed Gage and a petite strawberry blond. A set of building blocks was scattered in the corner.

Rainey slowly shook her head. She mouthed, "Dead end."

Caitlin drew her aside. Quietly, she said, "We've eliminated Gage. But not the *incident*. It matches the UNSUB's profile exactly. *That's* the homology—where the killer's character and action first came together."

Rainey's mouth drew to one side. She arched an eyebrow.

"We're missing something," Caitlin said.

She returned to Gage. "We didn't mean to cast undue suspicion on you. But this investigation is urgent. We're after a murderer who has killed at least two women and abducted four others since last summer. We need all the help we can get."

Gage's shoulders and jaw relaxed perhaps a millimeter. "Understood."

At his side, the dog yawned. Gage said, "Chevy, sit." The Lab promptly did.

Caitlin said, "Something happened back in college that may be pertinent to our investigation. Memories fade, or become twisted—especially those formed under life-and-death circumstances. But we have to either get to the bottom of this or eliminate it completely." She thought for a second. "Do you have any photos from that time?"

Rainey frowned, maybe thinking, *Why would a blind guy hang on to photos?* But Caitlin was thinking, *Why would he purge?*

"Yeah," he said. "A few things that didn't get burned up in the fire."

He pointed them at a closet near the front door. Inside it was a cardboard box of college memorabilia.

In a photo album Caitlin found Dahlia Hart—Lia Fox—in a group shot at a picnic. She ran her fingers over the photo, stunned. Lia's long hair was dyed platinum blond. She would fit right in among the Polaroid dead.

Rainey looked over Caitlin's shoulder. She was thoughtful.

There were a dozen college kids in the photo, haphazardly gathered for the shot. The girls looked experienced at posing for the camera. The boys looked like they could barely stop goofing around long enough to snap the photo. Gage stood in the center of the shot. His bright blue eyes and slightly boozy smile seemed warm and easygoing. Lia sat at the picnic table. Her smile was photogenic but somehow glum.

Immediately behind her stood a dark-haired, good-looking young man. His gaze was fixed on her.

Caitlin turned to Gage.

"There's a photo taken at a picnic." She described it to him. "One of the men is white, has dark brown hair, light eyes, he's roughly your height."

Gage slowly shook his head. "I vaguely remember the picnic. That could be a number of guys."

"He's wearing a diver's watch. And a New Found Glory T-shirt."

Gage thought for a moment. "WWJD bracelet?"

The young man in the photo wore a black wristband with four white letters. "Yes."

"Sounds like Kyle. My roommate. Kyle Detrick."

Caitlin reexamined the photo. Kyle Detrick stood close to Lia, and there was no question in her mind that he wished he could stand closer. Beside him, Aaron Gage, gripping a bottle of Lone Star, seemed oblivious to the passion pouring from his friend.

"Tell me about him," Caitlin said.

Gage held back a moment, seemingly analyzing the motive behind the question. When he spoke again, it was with a knowing reserve.

"He was a psychology major. From back east—Florida. We roomed together for a semester. Until the fire."

"How'd you meet?"

"I posted an ad for a roommate."

Rainey was shifting in her stylish boots, arms crossed. FBI agents never crossed their arms unless they had covering fire or were one hundred percent positive that the person they were talking to presented no threat. Or, Caitlin thought, when they were trying not to throttle a colleague. But she let Rainey stew. A new idea was taking form in her mind.

"What was he like?" Caitlin said.

Gage's expression remained remote. "Normal guy. Bought beer for the apartment."

"Did you become friends?"

The pause was more deliberate this time. "We got along. Hung out."

Outside, a pickup truck pulled up next to the Suburban.

"That'll be Ann and Maggie," Gage said.

The strawberry blond from the photo on the windowsill climbed out, hoisting a toddler on her hip.

She set the child down, and the little girl ran after a bird. Ann Gage stared through the wide front window at the scene in the living room. She was small but looked strong. She looked ready to defend her husband and home against whatever intrusion was taking place.

"Mr. Gage," Caitlin said, "how did your roommate get along with Dahlia?"

Gage paused a long time. He turned his head toward the sound of his daughter's voice. He seemed torn between wanting the FBI gone and doing what it would take to get them to go.

In a faraway tone, he said, "He liked to watch her."

Caitlin blinked to make sure she'd heard him correctly. "Surreptitiously?"

Gage nodded. "This one time, I found the bathroom door partway open while she was taking a shower. I closed it, then noticed Kyle's door was open too. He had a direct line of sight to the shower. I said, 'What the hell?' Kyle pretended it was coincidence, that he hadn't seen anything. But . . ."

Rainey dropped her arms to her sides. "Sergeant?"

He ran a hand over his short hair. "I caught him another time, sniffing her nightgown."

Caitlin let the word hang in the air a second. "Can you describe it?"

"The nightgown? Short. Low-cut. A sexy thing I gave Dahli. I was a dumb sophomore who wanted a sexy girlfriend. I think Kyle was too. But the sexy girlfriend he wanted was mine."

Ann Gage opened the door and came in. Her boots scuffed against the hardwood. Her glare was challenging.

"Ladies." She raised her chin. "I presume you're not the IRS, here to personally deliver our tax refund."

Rainey said, "Mrs. Gage."

Aaron held out his hand to his wife. "Babe. The FBI is investigating those murders down in Solace."

"You thought it was Aaron?" Ann said.

Their little girl, Maggie, popped through the door and skipped up to Gage. "Daddy!"

He crouched and picked her up. "How's my Tigger?"

She giggled and began telling him about her trip to town. Ann stared at Caitlin and Rainey.

Caitlin said, "Mr. Gage, may we take this photo with us?"

Ann approached. "What's that?"

"Old news," Gage said. "It's all right. It may factor into their investigation." He sensed his wife's unease. "It could be important."

Caitlin removed the photo from the album. "Thank you, Mr. Gage. If we need anything else, we'll be in touch."

She and Rainey headed out the door. Ann Gage shut it sharply behind them.

19

They barreled back down the interstate under a deepening blue twilight, with Rainey at the wheel. Before they hit the Red River, Caitlin got on the phone with Nicholas Keyes.

"Detrick. *D-E-T-R-I-C-K*." Caitlin had no middle name, no date of birth, no Social Security number or address, but Keyes would dig.

"Got it," Keyes said. "Full shopping list. Any extras?"

"Rampart College records if you can get them." Caitlin snapped a copy of the picnic photo and forwarded it. "Start by confirming whether Mr. Eyes-On is actually this guy."

Rainey pegged the speedometer at the limit. She drove with the calm sharpness honed by tactical driver training. Caitlin could imagine her porting her twins to tae kwon do. Rainey, she was sure, would never swerve to avoid a squirrel. But she would explain that small furry creatures could never outweigh children's safety, and tell them she was sorry they'd had to hear that thump.

"I'll hit you back ASAP," Keyes said.

He ended the call. Caitlin phoned Emmerich.

"Hendrix," he said. "The interview?"

Be candid. No point in hedging. And Emmerich, she'd learned, appreciated subtlety but hated weaseling.

"Gage isn't the UNSUB."

"That's conclusive?" he said.

"Yes. But we have a new lead."

She summarized the visit with Gage. "I think Lia Fox was stalked, but she's mistaken about the stalker's identity. I think it may have been this man Detrick. The cards she received were unsigned. Lia never saw who left the gifts on her porch, never saw the face of the stalker in the shadows across the street," she said. "If Gage's account is accurate, Detrick was at minimum a voyeur."

"Interesting," Emmerich said. "Find him."

Sunset had come on. Trees flashed past, skeletal, branches fingering the orange horizon in the west. Caitlin ended the call and sat, thinking, as Rainey raced from the hills and across the muddy river into Texas, onto a windswept, endless plain.

The headlights ate the concrete. The dashboard lights turned the SUV into a stark cavern, Rainey's eyes shining as she stared through the windshield. Everything Caitlin had known—San Francisco, Berkeley, her little rented house in Rockridge, her friends and life—felt immensely distant.

She picked up her phone again and placed a video call. When Sean answered, she said, "Hey, G-man."

Sean beamed. "Hey, G-woman. Why so serious?"

Caitlin straightened and smiled but felt caught out.

Sean turned his phone to give her a view of his surroundings. "Look who's here."

He was at the front door of a cheery town house. The daylight was still golden in the East Bay. He was dropping off his young daughter, Sadie, at the home of his ex-wife, Michele Ferreira. The little girl hopped into view, dark hair in pigtails, brown eyes lively. She wore a Wonder Woman T-shirt and tiny tennis shoes with daisies on them.

"Cat!" she squealed.

"Hey, Roo."

Michele strolled along the hall, waving. Her hair was cut shorter than usual, spiked into a fauxhawk. She had on her raspberry-colored nurse's scrubs.

"Woman," Michele said. "You look like you're calling from a cave. Tell me Texas hasn't retreated to the dark ages."

"It's ahead of California, if you ask the sun, and everybody in the state," Caitlin said.

"Missed you at the hash on Sunday."

Michele and Caitlin were members of a running club, the Rockridge Ragers. They ran 5K twice a week. Caitlin knew it was surprising, and strange, that she and Sean's ex had hit it off. She didn't care. Not when she'd come so close to losing Sean at the hands of a killer. Not when Sadie had come so close to losing her father. What mattered was that Sean was breathing, laughing, *here*. She couldn't worry about any potential awkwardness with Michele.

And running was a salve for whatever ached in Caitlin's

life. She missed those hours. Missed Michele's openness and sense of humor.

"We got half the group lost in the Berkeley Hills," Michele said. "Only the smell of beer lured them out in the end."

Caitlin smiled but felt melancholy that she and Sean couldn't talk privately. She cooed at Sadie's teddy bear and blew Michele a kiss.

Sean took the phone back. His face was a welcome sight. "You on the road?"

"I-35, forty miles north of DFW."

He scanned her face, his smile tempered with concern. "We gotta get you out of those dark Bureau SUVs."

"It's why I joined the FBI," she said. "I won't keep you. I'll let you get back to Sadie."

"How about I come to Virginia in a couple of weeks?"

"Yes."

She said it so eagerly that Sean laughed.

"I'll book flights tonight," he said.

"I love you."

"You should." He smiled, comically, and said good-bye.

She lowered her phone to her lap. It was warm in her hand. Outside, the night had deepened, but now she was humming. She became aware of Rainey beside her at the wheel. Her colleague was deadpan.

"Out with it," Caitlin said.

Rainey continued staring at the road. Her eyes were large, observant, bright—as always. Her braids were drawn back into a twist. In profile, she looked like Lady

Liberty on the hundred-dollar gold coin. If Lady Liberty kept a Glock in a Gore-Tex webbed holster on her hip.

"Come on," Caitlin said.

Rainey took her time. "I know you went through hell with the Prophet."

Oh boy, Caitlin thought. *Here we go.*

"Did you join the Bureau to get as far from that case as possible?" Rainey said.

"I took this job to make a difference."

"Honey." The tires rang on the concrete. "Course you did. We all did. You can say you love it. You're scared of it. You're proud. You're a badass bitch. Girl Scout with a twelve gauge. Reading psychopaths' minds is your superpower." She cut a glance Caitlin's way. "You can dig it."

For a second, Caitlin gaped. Her mouth hung open.

"But you did take a job three thousand miles from your boyfriend," Rainey said. "It's clear you have avoidance issues."

Caitlin pulled her coat tight around her. "I wish I did. I wouldn't have encouraged you to start this conversation."

"You have a family history of estrangement from—"

"Don't say Daddy."

Rainey took a long bend at speed. "You've been sighing and staring out the window. That's not just because of this case. Or job anxiety. And by the way, you're doing fine."

Caitlin turned. Rainey glanced at her.

"Kid, you're solid," she said.

A knot loosened in Caitlin's chest.

"But don't tell me you're not lonely." She nodded at Caitlin's phone. "Your boyfriend heard it. Hell, that stuffed bear heard it."

"My mom probably heard it, so she'll be calling any minute," Caitlin said.

"Just don't put up more walls than necessary."

"Compartmentalizing—"

"Is necessary," Rainey said. "But if you barricade yourself against the people you love, you lose."

"I know that."

"Yeah? You're best friends with your boyfriend's ex. Tell me you haven't hammered up some boards to keep both those relationships intact."

The road straightened. Caitlin said nothing.

"Don't isolate yourself. You'll drive away your friends and lovers, and blunt your effectiveness in the field. Lose-lose."

"Did Emmerich tell you to work me over? Remind me to tap into my empathy?"

"He's not wrong. You have an uncanny sense of when people are lying, and what motivates them. You should develop that, not suppress it."

"Were you a shrink before you joined the Bureau?"

"Air Force Psy Ops."

Caitlin laughed, hard and brief. "It all makes sense now."

Rainey didn't smile, but lifted an eyebrow. She looked wry. "I like to know about the people I ride with." She set her right hand on the gearshift. "Tell me about the round you took a few years back."

Caitlin couldn't help giving her a look.

"I saw the scar. Gym at the hotel," Rainey said. "Left shoulder."

Caitlin hadn't talked about it in years. "Bank robbery. My second year as an Alameda patrol officer. I got hit as I ran from my car to a staging point." She flexed her shoulder. It felt fine. "The round missed my ballistic vest. But it also missed nerve bundles and the brachial artery. I was unlucky, but very lucky."

"No shit."

"It felt like a sting. Hot. I only realized I'd been hit when I reached the staging point."

Rainey looked thoughtful. "I know the feeling."

Now it was Caitlin's turn to wonder whom she was riding with.

"You were young," Rainey said. "Of course you expected to escape. That kind of luck can convince you you're immortal."

Caitlin touched her right arm, where the tattoo read, *the whole sky*. Rainey didn't know about its meaning to her. It was a line from Rita Dove's poem "Dawn Revisited."

> *The whole sky is yours*
> *to write on, blown open*

The phrase symbolized second chances—and the opportunity she had been given to choose life, after nearly killing herself at fifteen. The tattoo ran across the scars ridging her forearm, the ones she had etched over and over with a razor blade. A snake circled the scars on her left.

She said, "Immortality's a dangerous idea. I believe in the here and now."

Rainey's lips pursed. A mile passed, the big American engine humming in the cold night. Rainey's voice lightened.

"Make some friends in Virginia. Get a hobby. Scrapbooking, or mixed martial arts."

"Needlepoint. I can embroider a pillow with *badass bitch*."

Rainey smiled, just a wisp. "Find time with your man, ASAP."

"On it."

"And you were right about this trip being a legitimate lead. Next stop, Kyle Detrick."

She put on music, *Madama Butterfly,* and turned it up. Opera flooded the car. She accelerated to seventy-five and drove into the night.

20

I found him."

Nicholas Keyes sounded like a hammer hitting a nail. On video, he stalked back and forth behind his Quantico desk. He was wired, his hair standing up like he'd stuck his finger in a socket. His skinny tie was askew, his sleeves unevenly rolled up. In the Virginia morning sun, his eyes looked like shiny marbles.

"Detrick?" Caitlin said. "Where?"

His smile was beyond electric. He pointed at the screen. "There. In Texas."

He sat down at his desk. "Kyle Alan Detrick, born Tallahassee, Florida, currently lives and works thirty miles up the interstate in Austin."

He sent photos. Caitlin's nerves lit up.

The first photo was a student ID from Rampart College. Detrick was indeed the man in Aaron Gage's picnic snapshot, the guy wearing the New Found Glory T-shirt. The second photo was Detrick's current Texas driver's license. He was older by eighteen years, and, if anything, better-looking.

Caitlin didn't put much store in deciphering personality by driver's license photos. But Kyle Detrick had a presence. His chin was up, his gray eyes vivid—yet opaque. She couldn't tell whether he was trying to seduce the camera or express disdain at having to visit the DMV. He was tan and sleek. His dark hair was cut just short of edgy. His dress shirt was as white as meringue.

Keyes scrolled down his computer screen. "Age thirty-eight. He studied psychology at Rampart College but left without getting a degree."

"How long after the apartment fire?" Caitlin asked.

"A few months."

Rainey walked up behind her. Keyes clicked to a new document.

"No outstanding warrants, no arrest record in Gideon County, Travis County, Austin, Tallahassee, Harris County, Houston, nothing on ViCAP or NCIC," he said.

"He's clean."

"And he works at Castle Bay Realty."

"He sells houses." Caitlin stood. "We need to tell Emmerich."

Rainey headed for the door. "He went to the county medical examiner's office. Call him. I'll drive."

The trip to Austin took them along a bruising section of I-35, under a pale skillet of sky. They passed beneath gigantic interchanges, five levels tall, where semis took turns at sixty miles per hour a hundred feet above them.

"There aren't this many freeway interchanges in Los

Angeles, and LA is ten times the size of Austin," Caitlin said. "Who got the concrete concession from the state?"

"Austin's one of the fastest-growing cities in the country," Rainey said. "More than a million people in the metro. Named the best American city to live in by *U.S. News & World Report,* if you ever get a hankering for Longhorns football and Texas politics."

"I try not to hanker."

To the west, the forest-green outcroppings of the Hill Country came into view. Ten miles from downtown they got their first glimpse of the skyline. It was mostly new, mostly striving, bright and glassy and angular, clogged with cranes putting up even more skyscrapers.

They crossed Lady Bird Lake and headed into the city center on Cesar Chavez. They passed sparkling high-end hotels and a tin-roofed barbecue shack and old bungalows repurposed into neon hipster bars. A billboard advertised: AUSTIN—THE LIVE MUSIC CAPITAL OF THE WORLD.

"True," Rainey said. "You can't enter a single building in the city without hearing a guitar. I went into the women's room at McDonald's and a Texas swing band was playing Willie Nelson."

Up Congress Avenue, the state capitol dominated the end of the street. They rolled past restaurants, food trucks, and parks. In the distance, Caitlin spotted the tower on the University of Texas campus. At night, after a Longhorns victory, it would be lit orange. The sunlight pulled her eye to the railing around the observation deck.

Rainey followed her gaze. "Sixteen dead after Whitman opened fire back in 1966. Thirty-one injured."

"I remember hearing unarmed students rescued a wounded teenager under sniper fire. Two outgunned cops and a citizen made it to the observation deck to take him on. Braver than hell."

They pulled into a parking lot behind a brick office building. The air was crisp, the sunlight silvery in Caitlin's eyes, when they got out and walked to the offices of Castle Bay Realty.

In the lobby, beyond potted palms, the blond at the desk wore hairspray and Miss America–caliber cosmetics. A sapphire-colored cross hung from a chain around her neck. It dipped deep into her cleavage, like a meat thermometer.

Her desk plate said BRANDI CHILDERS. She sized up Rainey and Caitlin as an ill-matched couple here to ruin their lives by jointly purchasing a starter home. "How may I help y'all?"

"Kyle Detrick, please," Rainey said.

They held out their credentials.

"One moment."

Brandi picked up the phone. Her smile didn't waver. She could have aced the pageant question about world peace.

She made a call and replaced the receiver. "He'll be right out."

A minute later, the door to the back of the office opened.

For the briefest of moments, Kyle Detrick paused in the doorway, taking them in with a gaze that seemed both voracious and analytical. Just as quickly, the look was replaced by a welcoming, gregarious bonhomie.

He strode up to Rainey, hand extended. "Kyle Detrick. How can I help the FBI?"

He was smooth, but Caitlin got the sense that seeing female agents had surprised him.

"We're investigating the murders in Solace," she said.

Detrick turned to her. "Wow. Horrible business."

He was taller than she was, which was saying something, because she was five-ten and wearing two-inch heels. His wardrobe was Brooks Brothers on the range—tailored wool blazer, button-down shirt, pressed jeans, mahogany cowboy boots. His baritone voice was rich. His cologne was obvious. His eyes were pale gray and startlingly clear.

He gestured toward the door. "My office."

Brandi looked dismayed. Maybe that she wasn't going to get to hear the juicy stuff.

Down the hall, beyond the chatter of phone conversations and a printer spewing title documents, Detrick closed his office door and stood with his arms akimbo.

"I know the FBI doesn't pay courtesy visits. What do you think I can contribute to your investigation?"

Deciding when to approach a suspect was a strategic decision, and a tricky one. Caitlin and Rainey had conferred with Emmerich while driving to Austin. The killings were headline news. No matter how oblique their questions, meeting Detrick would alert him that he was on their radar as a suspect. If he was the UNSUB, that could induce him to get rid of any souvenirs he'd kept—such as photos and the clothing worn by Shana Kerber and Phoebe Canova.

But the joint FBI-sheriff's press conference hadn't stopped the UNSUB from abducting Teri Drinkall in Dallas. They had to take bolder steps.

Emmerich had said, *Rattle him.*

Rainey strolled to a corner where she could survey the office and observe Detrick's demeanor. Caitlin stood in front of the window, making sure that from Detrick's perspective, she was backlit. It would make him squint uncomfortably and find it hard to read her expression.

"Do you do business in Solace?" she said.

He shook his head. "Austin and Lakeway. I'm so busy, I turn away potential listings every day. Don't have to bigfoot the Realtors in Gideon County." His gaze was probing. "Why?"

Rainey pointed outside, at an SUV in the parking lot. "That brown Buick Envision. Is it yours?"

Detrick stepped toward the window. "My company car, yes."

He had a leonine build, strong through the shoulders, with a lazy stride, a slow way of turning—like a big cat that would enjoy rolling over in an equatorial sun. Beneath his crisp dress shirt, he was built. Caitlin got the impression that should he decide to, he could launch with ferocious speed and strength.

He looked back and forth between them. His gray eyes had a pewter glint. "Don't keep me in suspense. What's this about?"

"We're looking for a similar vehicle," Caitlin said. "And its driver."

"A brown SUV? Because mine is Bronze Metallic."

Rainey peered at the Envision. "That shade actually skews toward 'burro' on the Pantone color scale."

Detrick frowned at her, nonplussed.

Caitlin said, "When was the last time you were in Solace?"

"You think the driver saw something?" Detrick said. "It couldn't be me. I haven't been to Gideon County in . . ." He looked at the ceiling. "I don't know how long."

"Shana Kerber was abducted the night of the second. Will you check?" Caitlin said.

He strode around to his desk and leaned over his computer. He shook his head. "I went to a UT basketball game that night."

She opened a pocket notebook. "How about these dates?"

She read off the dates the other women had vanished. More slowly, he perused the calendar. He had alibis for every night.

"Real estate seminar."

"Concert."

"Driving range."

He straightened, looking concerned. "Who told you I drove the Envision?"

Nobody had told them. They didn't know until just now. *The UNSUB will drive a large vehicle that won't stand out. Probably an American make, muted in color.* Caitlin merely looked him up and down.

"Right," he said. "How many Envision drivers are you talking to?"

Caitlin took in the office. Everywhere, she saw Kyle

Detrick, All-American Poster Boy. One wall was dominated by photos that featured him. On a bookshelf was a
framed Salesman of the Month certificate. Plus a football, signed *Earl Campbell*. And a plaque with a Bible
verse: *He who sows bountifully will also reap bountifully.*
Each one must do just as he has purposed in his heart. 2
Cor. 9:6–7.

"Are you talking to all of them?" Detrick said. "I
mean, is this a reverse Cinderella story—the girl drives
around questioning guys, and if the car fits, he loses?"

Caitlin turned, slowly, and gave him a stare as cold as
sleet.

He raised his hands and looked at the floor. "Sorry. I
don't mean to sound flip. This case is tragic, and I know
you're working hard to solve it." He sighed. "But if
you're searching for a witness, I can't help you there. I
wish I could."

On his desk was a photo of him with a dainty brunette. The woman was looking at him adoringly. At her
side was a little girl, perhaps seven years old, likewise
beaming at Detrick.

"Wife and daughter?" Caitlin said.

"Good friend." He smiled.

Another picture showed him at a church potluck, surrounded by laughing men. The same woman and little
girl were off to the side.

"Church friend?" Caitlin said.

"We met at Chapel of the Hills." His smile remained.
His gaze was charismatic. "It's a welcoming place. Great
people." His face turned thoughtful, and he crossed his

arms. "A few of us men have been talking about organizing neighborhood watches. These murders—it's terrible. Maybe you could come to the church, give a safety talk."

"Some Saturday night? Would you be there?"

He paused, for just an instant, like he'd spotted a glitch in the Matrix. Then he glided on. "It would reassure people. And you'd pack the place. Woman agent, with your sass and that gun? You'd rock it. Girls would listen."

"Talk to your pastor."

"Soon as I get a free minute."

His charm was effortless. But beneath it, she heard a hiss. It was minimal, almost inaudible, and it set her on high alert.

He was too smooth. He hadn't asked the question that anxious citizens often blurted out. *You don't think I had something to do with it, do you?* Aaron Gage had practically spat the question. But Detrick hadn't acted like an anxious citizen at all.

A paperweight sat on his desk: *Westside Crisis Hotline.* She picked it up.

He took it from her, gently. "I volunteer there."

Rainey sauntered closer. "How did that come about?"

"Because people need help." Detrick sounded surprised by the question. "The hotline saves lives. Desperate people phone in—suicidal people." Emotion colored his voice. "My church urges members to give back to the community. This is my way. I studied psychology in college. I have the knowledge and skills that can make a difference."

"Answering crisis calls can be a tough volunteering experience," Rainey said.

"But incredibly worthwhile."

Detrick stared at Rainey, pained and seemingly sincere. His phone rang. He took the call, then said, "I have a closing. The documents need to be filed within the hour. You'll have to excuse me."

They left their cards on his desk. Detrick gave his card to Caitlin, placing it carefully in her fingers. He wrapped his hand around hers, enfolding the card in her palm.

"Call me if I can help. Day or night," he said.

"You'll hear from me."

He squeezed her hand. His smile was dazzling. When he let go, the imprint of his fingers remained on the back of her hand.

In the lobby, as she and Rainey headed for the door, Brandi stood up.

"Excuse me."

They stopped. Brandi cast a furtive look toward the interior of the office.

She spoke sotto voce. "What's going on? Why were you talking to Mr. Detrick?"

"Is there something you want to tell us?" Caitlin said.

Brandi pressed her lips tight. The crucifix rose and fell between her breasts as she breathed. Behind her desk, on a credenza, a framed photo showed her dressed in camo, kneeling beside a five-point buck she'd brought down with a crossbow.

"Yeah," she said. "He's amazing. I don't know who

sent you here to pester him about this awful thing in Solace, but leave him alone."

Outside, they climbed into the Suburban and Rainey fired up the engine.

She cruised past Detrick's Envision SUV. "Get photos of the rear end."

Caitlin raised her phone. Rainey looked like a fox tracking a rabbit in the brush. Caitlin glanced back at the building. At his office window, Detrick stood watching them.

"We're not going to leave him alone," Caitlin said.

Rainey pulled out. "Not for one second."

21

"No." Detective Art Berg pulled documents off the printer and walked away from Rainey. "He doesn't sound like he fits the profile. At all."

Berg seemed to fill the cramped hallway at the Gideon County Sheriff's Office. He bowled into the detectives' room. Caitlin looked up from the conference table where she was working.

"We have seventy-five plausible suspects to check out," Berg said. "Thanks in part to the press conference your boss urged us to hold."

He slapped the printout onto his desk, atop a pile already an inch tall. He stabbed it with his finger. "Men seen in the vicinity the nights of more than one attack. Men who knew more than one victim. Men who—despite your profile—have criminal records for sexual assault. These are the people we need to investigate before looking at your Salesman of the Month."

Rainey's silver earrings flashed in the sun. "Kyle Detrick fits—"

"The profile, I know."

"He owns a two-year-old Dodge Charger. But for work, he has access to a company vehicle—the bronze Buick Envision that Agent Hendrix and I saw parked at his office. That vehicle is leased by Castle Bay Realty. I just got off the phone with the insurer that issued Castle Bay's fleet policy. They have GPS histories for all insured vehicles."

She handed Berg a sheaf of paper and glanced at Caitlin. Caitlin stood and walked over.

"The insurer gave me the last six months of GPS records for Castle Bay's fleet vehicles, downloaded *this afternoon*," Rainey said. "Nineteen out of twenty vehicles have intact records. One has been erased."

Berg flipped through the papers. "Bronze Envision."

"The vehicle assigned to Kyle Detrick. To which he has access seven days a week, because he holds open houses on weekends."

Berg frowned. "The GPS information wasn't automatically forwarded to the insurer?"

"No. It's held in the vehicle's onboard system unless the insured party needs to transmit it—generally in case of accident or theft."

"Huh."

"The GPS system is integrated into the vehicle's control center. The driver can't simply press reset and delete the data. It requires a hard reset, using an exterior monitor plugged into the car's system via a USB bus."

"And Detrick's GPS has been erased."

"Reset to factory settings."

Caitlin tucked her hair behind her ear. "Going to such lengths, right after we paid him a visit?"

Rainey's look was arch. "Bingo. And Castle Bay wouldn't want employees to delete their travel records. They need mileage for tax purposes."

Berg said, "What if the GPS simply fried itself? You know that's what this guy will say."

"There's more. Hendrix, can you get Keyes on video?"

Caitlin grabbed her laptop and connected to their analyst at Quantico. Keyes came on-screen, looking like he'd been chewing espresso beans. Caitlin spun the computer so Berg could view the monitor.

Keyes gave a chin-up hello. "I've rendered the CCTV from the Dallas garage with forensic video software. Sharpened the images, reduced motion blur, and adjusted the exposure."

He brought up the edited version. They saw Teri Drinkall walk into the frame. In the original, she had looked like she was walking through Vaseline. Augmented, her black-and-white image was crisper. Again they watched her jump in surprise, and turn, and speak to somebody off-camera.

Berg tapped his fingers against the desk, a parody of impatience. "What am I supposed to see this time?"

The video ran for two more seconds, and Keyes hit PAUSE. "That."

In the left half of the screen, a black Dodge Ram pickup was parked beneath a fluorescent light strip, backed into an angled space. Teri Drinkall had walked directly past the truck before disappearing from view.

"The windshield of the truck," Keyes said.

Under the fluorescent lights, it gleamed. In the original version, the reflection had been overwhelmed by glare.

"When you're trying to read a license plate, or identify a face, certain details have to be isolated."

"Don't tell me you can actually enhance videos like they do on TV," Berg said. "Instant prom photos."

"Nowhere close," Keyes said. "Our software defines object edges, maximizes variances in shadows, and predictively enriches imagery." He smiled. "Though I do want the bad guys wondering whether the Bureau can yell, 'Enhance!' and see what's in their jockey shorts. I may have secretly encouraged that Internet meme." He nodded at the screen. "In this video, the problem isn't just the quality of the camera. It's the windshield of that truck—a convex surface, angled fifty-five degrees from the vertical. But . . ."

He hit PLAY. In the windshield, fuzzy and indistinct, was a reflected image of what was happening around the corner from the camera.

It looked like a foggy Salvador Dalí painting, but they could see Teri Drinkall continuing to walk away from her own car. Once again, her back was to the camera. She was side by side with a figure who had dark hair.

"That's the man she went with," Keyes said.

Caitlin exhaled.

"Extrapolating from Teri's known height, the man is 1.85 meters tall. Six foot one," he said. "Same as Kyle Detrick."

Berg looked thoughtful but was subtly shaking his head.

"That's not all," Keyes said. "They're only in view in the reflection for two-tenths of a second. But when they pass beyond view again, there's this."

A dim geometric shape was warped in the windshield view.

"That's a vehicle," Keyes said. "That's the vehicle the UNSUB led Teri to."

Caitlin leaned toward the screen. "It's the back end of an SUV."

She pulled out her phone and opened the photos she'd snapped in the parking lot at Castle Bay Realty.

She turned the screen to Berg. "Looks like a Buick Envision."

Berg's frown deepened. "No year, no plate number, no verification that it's actually bronze, and not beige or gray or blue, much less a Buick." He took Caitlin's phone and compared her photos to the rendering on the screen. "I'll concede that this is circumstantial evidence. But it's hardly enough. And the parking garage video provides no evidence that the SUV in Dallas belonged to the UNSUB. Much less that he put Ms. Drinkall into it."

Rainey said, "Is it enough to move Detrick up your list of suspects?"

Berg shook his head. "This guy Detrick is a member of the men's group at his church. Maybe he joined the congregation to meet women, or whip up his potential sales base. Maybe someday we'll find out he's skimming commissions from the brokerage for selling high-end condos to tech 'influencers' moving into Austin." Berg's face was turning the maroon of his shirt. "He's not our most viable suspect. He goes to the back of the line."

He lifted the stack of papers on his desk. "If you could help us evaluate these leads, *that* would advance the investigation. Because Saturday is coming up sooner than any of us would like."

He tossed Caitlin her phone and walked away. Caitlin and Rainey felt the air rush out of the room with him.

"The guy's frustrated," Caitlin said.

"I'll give you that." Rainey turned back to the computer screen. "Dallas PD?"

Keyes nodded. "Already sent it to them." He clicked off.

Still staring at the screen, Caitlin rewound the video two seconds, to the moment when the reflections of Teri and the UNSUB flashed on the pickup's windshield.

She touched the screen. "What's that?"

She pointed at a bright streak that ran vertically along the UNSUB's side.

"That whitish stripe? It looks metallic," Rainey said.

"Something he was carrying? Weapon?"

"Good question." She scanned the screen. "You still think he was playing injured?"

Caitlin nodded. "A crutch?"

They zoomed in and out but could draw no inferences.

Caitlin shook her head. "Can't believe Keyes got this much out of it. He's a sorcerer."

Rainey glanced up. "Keyes came to the Bureau from NASA. The Planetary Science Section at the Jet Propulsion Laboratory." She sounded admiring. "A lot of our video software was developed for the space program. When you're looking at 2-D photos of the moon or a comet, you need heavy-duty math to determine an object's size and distance. How do you think the Apollo program surveyed the Sea of Tranquility? They needed to know, 'How deep is that crater at our landing site, *really*?' We use that capability to deal with angled reflections and convex surfaces."

"Thank you, Isaac Newton. And Nicholas Keyes."

In the hallway, Emmerich walked past. He looked solemn.

Rainey said, "Print a high-res copy of that parking garage image."

22

Caitlin found Emmerich in Chief Morales's office. He was on the phone, holding a manila folder labeled GIDEON COUNTY MEDICAL EXAMINER. She rapped on the open door and he nodded her in.

Into the phone, he said, "I spoke personally to Ms. Canova's mother. I told her she can expect the body to be released this afternoon."

The chief's space was spare, except for a topographical wall map of Texas and a Mexican saddle on a pommel in the corner. The saddle's silver rowels were shot through with light. Outside the window, a freight train rattled toward the railroad crossing where Phoebe Canova had disappeared. Bells rang and the crossing arm descended.

"Yes," Emmerich said. "Thank you, Doctor."

He ended the call and set the folder on the desk. "ME's preliminary report on Phoebe Canova. Cause of death is exsanguination, due to dissection of the right and left radial arteries. External exam found trace—two short, dark hairs that could belong to the UNSUB. Non-follicular."

No DNA, he meant.

"Next of kin confirms that the cosmetics applied to Phoebe's face didn't come from her personal supply."

Caitlin realized why he had looked so somber when he came in: He'd paid a visit to Phoebe's mother.

Emmerich closed the manila folder. Seemed to push a restart button on his emotions. He turned his attention to Caitlin.

She handed him the still image from the Dallas garage video—Teri Drinkall and the UNSUB, passing the SUV.

"Detective Berg discounts Detrick as a suspect, but we shouldn't," she said.

Emmerich examined the photo. "This definitely does *not* exclude him. But it doesn't implicate him, either. What does?"

Rainey appeared in the doorway. Caitlin took a second to put her thoughts in order.

"To start with, he's *off.*"

Emmerich's expression didn't change.

Reset. "He lives at the geographic center of the disappearances and murders." She turned to the wall map of Texas. "Detrick's Austin home is here." She tapped a point south of town, a sparsely populated area a mile off the interstate. "We've profiled an anger-excitation rapist and killer who prefers to hunt beyond his immediate environment. Which fits Detrick exactly, while still putting him in the center of the overall hunting grounds."

The train's caboose clattered by outside.

"I've checked his alibis for the nights in question. They're uselessly vague," Caitlin said. "And I took photos of his SUV. It's freshly washed. You can see from the photos that the dashboard is gleaming—it's been dusted and cleaned with polishing spray. Which suggests that the entire interior has been wiped down and vacuumed. And," she said, "its GPS history has been wiped."

"Wiped."

Rainey approached the desk. "Electronically jet-washed almost as soon as Hendrix and I left Castle Bay."

Caitlin said, "When we were at Detrick's office, he stepped too close to me. He . . ." *Just say it.* "He seemed attracted to me. He pressed his card into my hand like he was handing me his hotel key."

She waited for pushback. Got none. "Detrick acted like we were engaging in flirty banter, not discussing serial murder."

Emmerich shook his head. "That's not enough."

She reached deeper. "He fits the profile. Narcissist. Hyperconfident. Salesman. And he's intensely interested in *suicide.* That's at the heart of the UNSUB's fantasy."

Outside the window, the freight train rumbled away and the crossing arm lifted.

"Agreed." Emmerich stared at the CCTV still image. "He's worth a further look. What do you propose?"

She tried not to let her excitement show. "Let me dig."

"Where?"

"The Westside Crisis Hotline."

23

The Westside Crisis Center occupied the second floor of a renovated nineteenth-century house in downtown Austin. Shaded by ash and lacebark elms, it sat behind a white picket fence a few blocks from the university.

It was late afternoon when Caitlin arrived. The day had warmed from near freezing to the high seventies. Her black V-neck sweater and pegged slacks absorbed the heat, and the fabric hummed against her skin. The offices were old, a warren. The wood floor creaked when she came through the door.

The man who emerged from the director's office to greet her looked like an English professor. He was gray-bearded, African American, and thumped across the room like a benevolent bear in a checked shirt and Dockers.

He shook her hand. "Darian Cobb." His expression was warm but wary. "I've never spoken to an FBI agent before."

She had thought out her approach to this meeting. Before she brought Detrick's name into the conversation, she needed to gather as much information about the hotline's operations as possible. Cobb ran a service that depended on building trust between counselors and callers. She didn't want to mislead him, but she didn't want him to clam up and show her the door either.

"We think the man who's committing these crimes may have a familiarity with crisis counseling," she said.

"What kind of familiarity?"

"I can't go into detail."

"As a caller? Counselor? Social worker? Psychiatrist?" Cobb looked increasingly guarded. "All calls to this hotline are confidential. I won't release callers' phone numbers. You'd have to get a court order."

"I don't want you to breach your callers' confidentiality. I would like you to tell me how crisis phone counseling works."

He looked quizzical. "Behavioral analysis. You're profiling the killer?"

"Yes."

He digested that. "Do you think the killer is familiar with *this* hotline?"

"I can't rule it out."

He took a pensive second. "We get thirty calls a night. Fifty to sixty on weekends. We staff the phones twenty-four hours a day."

"Callers always phone the landlines here at the center?"

"Always. Volunteers aren't permitted to give out their personal numbers. If they ever need to push an incident to critical status—say, if a caller threatened to commit an atrocity—volunteers call nine-one-one on a separate line and contact a supervisor."

She looked through a door into an interior room where tables were set up with phones. Under the white afternoon sun, a young woman was bent over a thick textbook, twiddling a highlighter in her fingers. Another volunteer was organizing files.

"What's the procedure when the phone rings?" Caitlin said.

"Calls are answered in the order they come in, and taken by the next volunteer who's free. Callers can remain anonymous, but volunteers encourage them to give at least a first name," Cobb said. "Volunteers are trained to handle a variety of situations—depression, suicidal thoughts, drug and alcohol abuse, domestic violence."

"Do they work from a script?"

"They're trained on a series of steps to take," Cobb said. "Number one, determine whether the caller is in acute crisis. Is their life in danger *right now*? Are they at risk of dying in the next ten minutes?"

Caitlin nodded.

"Volunteers must be clear. Don't guess—*ask*. 'Are you safe?' If the caller says no, immediately move to solve the problem. Call nine-one-one, police, ambulance, get first responders to the caller's location. The Austin Police Department has officers trained in crisis response, and we liaise with them. If there's an external danger, work to get the caller to a safe place." Cobb's voice was calm but insistent. "If the caller isn't in imminent danger, the volunteer can take a breath and prepare to stay on the line for as long as necessary."

She was listening with sunbright alertness. Her cheeks felt hot.

"At that point, what's the next step?" she said.

"Listen, listen, listen." Cobb's gaze was penetrating. "Our volunteers aren't psychiatric social workers—they're capable, concerned people who won't panic in emergencies. Crisis hotline volunteering is about soft skills. Compassion. Patience. Empathy."

Caitlin stood unusually still.

"Always keep the focus on the caller—never yourself. Ask them their story. Find out if they have a support system—family, friends, therapists," he said. "Don't offer solutions. Your job is not to fix their problems. It's to work with the caller while *they* come up with a plan. And keep control of your own emotions. Don't let yourself get overwhelmed. People are calling from a dark place. You stay on the line while they figure out how to turn on a light."

She found she was having a hard time swallowing. When she breathed, her chest wanted to shudder.

"That's a big job," she said.

"We're here to provide comfort and encouragement. We're a gentle place for people to talk through their problems."

She took a second, letting the unexpected swell of emotion dissipate. She scanned the room. On the wall a schedule was posted, with volunteers' names.

"Do volunteers have regular shifts?"

"Most work a particular day of the week."

Wednesday. Jan. 2, 9, 16, 23, 30. Feb. 6, 13, 20, 27.

6 P.M.–Midnight

Vanessa Guzman, Kyle Detrick

She perused the schedule long enough that Cobb said, "Do you have a particular question about our volunteers?"

There was a slight chill in his question. Not worry, but a quaver, a fuzz in the deepest reaches of its frequency. Static disturbing his thought processes.

"What's got your attention?" Cobb regarded her closely. "The schedule? Was there a particular day of the week you need information about?"

"No."

"You think one of our volunteers might have taken a call from . . ."

She shook her head. "Can you give me examples of how volunteers have dealt with tough calls?"

Cobb either believed her or was playing along. He spoke about some of their longtime volunteers, offering examples. He nodded at the schedule on the wall. "Ms. Guzman has worked here for five years. She's a schoolteacher in her day job. We pair veteran counselors with newer volunteers."

That provided a fortuitous opening. "So, she's paired with a rookie?"

"He's not a rookie anymore. Mr. Detrick came to us a year ago, via an outreach program from his church."

"How do volunteers from church programs tend to work out?"

"On the whole, very well. Occasionally we get volunteers who . . ." He sought for a diplomatic way to phrase it. ". . . struggle when talking to callers whose life choices conflict with their religious teachings."

"Suicide, drug addiction, sexual abuse—some volunteers feel an obligation to evangelize?"

He shrugged, confirming it.

"But not this volunteer," Caitlin said.

"To the contrary. Mr. Detrick is an excellent counselor—patient, encouraging, steady."

"Can you give me an example of how that works out in practice?"

He nodded at the schedule. "I heard Kyle keep a suicidal caller on the line while he got paramedics dispatched."

"Really."

"He calmly got the caller's address and kept them talking. He was compassionate, he drew the caller out, he kept them from losing control."

"I'm impressed."

She was. Caitlin knew that Detrick had won a powerful, fragile victory.

She knew how much fortitude it took the hotline volunteers to talk people back from the brink. Because she knew how it felt to be the person on the other end of the call.

Her cheeks felt flushed. She hoped Cobb wouldn't notice, or wonder why. She took a second to anchor herself and let the backwash of her teen desperation dissipate.

"How do those calls affect him?" she asked.

"He maintains his equilibrium."

"Meaning?"

"Nerves are a problem for many volunteers. Not Kyle," Cobb said. "Our counselors go through forty hours of training. But when reality hits—an actual crisis call—the training may not stick. The first time a counselor hears a caller say they're having suicidal thoughts . . . that's extremely anxiety provoking. Volunteers can lose the thread."

"Mr. Detrick doesn't let the calls get to him personally?" Caitlin said.

"He's in his thirties, more mature than some of our student volunteers, and that helps. He's a calming influence on the rest of the team."

Maybe Detrick was a genuine Good Samaritan. Or maybe he was an expert manipulator.

And maybe, Caitlin thought, he exhibited no anxiety when talking to desperate people because psychopaths feel no concern for others.

"How about afterward? Excitement? The shakes? A letdown? Prayers?" she said.

"Satisfaction and gratitude," Cobb said. He tilted his head back and forth. "The occasional fist pump."

"Does he like to talk about calls afterward?"

"Why are you so interested?"

"I need to know the dynamic. How callers and volunteers influence each other. It can give me psychological insight into the UNSUB we're seeking. It might guide how we eventually talk to a suspect."

Again, Cobb looked skeptical. "All our volunteers talk about calls afterward. Some more enthusiastically than others." He pinned her with his gaze. "Should I be worried about the safety of the center, or my volunteers?"

She shook her head, and meant it. "We have no indication that the man behind these killings would target you, your volunteers, or the center. If that changes, we'll inform you."

He nodded but didn't look reassured. She couldn't blame him.

24

Caitlin left the crisis center with brochures, including a primer on crisis telephone techniques, and a flashback hangover. She felt a physical memory—of despair constricting her chest like a strangling vine. As she sank into Austin's rush hour traffic, she turned on the radio and spun until she found Beyoncé, "Freedom."

The song was driving, soaring. Even—especially—the quiet line about telling your last tear to *burn into flames* . . .

She turned it up. The song thundered through her, flushing the black-blood sensation that had tried to creep into her veins.

When she pulled into the Solace sheriff's station at six, she was tired, but buzzing. Under another violet sunset, headlights cruised up Main Street. Inside, she found Emmerich conferring with Chief Morales, coffee cups in their hands. Morales had sooty circles beneath his eyes. Emmerich cocked an eyebrow at her.

"Kyle Detrick has volunteered at the crisis hotline for a year," she said.

Both Emmerich and Morales understood: Detrick had been a volunteer for several months before the Solace abductions began. Whether that mattered, she didn't know.

"The director of the center describes him as outstandingly even-keeled on acute crisis calls."

Morales seemed to parse her body language. "You think that's a bad thing?"

"He pumps his fist and retells his victory stories," she said. "That could be overenthusiasm. Or a salesman bragging that he sold life to the desperate. Or it could signify a love of glory."

"That's not criminal. Not when you've talked someone off the ledge."

Emmerich set down his coffee. "You think Detrick has a hero complex?"

From his tone, and posture, he was inviting her to explore the implications.

"Maybe," she said. "And maybe his elation arises from playing God."

She thought of the FBI *Crime Classification Manual:* Mercy/Hero Homicide.

Mercy killers murdered in the genuine belief that they were relieving their victims' suffering. Hero killers recklessly committed homicide by inducing a crisis so they could save the day. They were firefighters who set a blaze, then arrived to fight it. They were nurses who caused patients to code, so they could revive them. They reveled in the rush and the praise that came from bringing people back from the brink. When they botched it, their victims died.

"We don't profile the UNSUB as committing hero homicide," she said. "There are no signs that the killer attempts to resuscitate his victims or mitigate their injuries. The suicidal ideation at the crime scenes indicates destructive rage. From the moment the UNSUB chooses a target, he intends to kill."

Emmerich's expression said, *But?*

"But the way Detrick revels in his hotline wins does echo the behavior of hero-killers."

They schemed their way into positions where they could control and target the vulnerable—critically ill patients, sometimes infants. In emergencies, the killer was conveniently present and became unusually excited while taking part in rescue or resuscitation efforts. Afterward, the killer frequently talked about the emergency.

"I know it doesn't fit—but it does," she said. "Detrick's excitement, his sense of victory, the way he seems to regard saving people from suicide as *his* success—by volunteering at the crisis hotline, he makes sure he's right there when desperate people reach out for help."

Morales took a final swallow of his coffee. "Isn't that the point of the hotline? To be there?"

He's amazing. She once again heard Brandi the receptionist, telling her to leave Captain America alone.

But Caitlin couldn't quell the itch. "I can't kick this feeling that Detrick is involved in volunteer work for the wrong reasons."

"He loves the stimulation?" Emmerich said.

"Maybe he *needs* it."

Psychopaths had more basic aggression than other

people—sometimes from birth. She ran through it for Morales and Emmerich. Medical research suggested that genetic, neurochemical, and hormonal factors could lay the groundwork for a personality to develop in a psychopathic direction. In diagnosed psychopaths, the autonomic nervous system tested at lower-than-average sensitivity. That helped explain why psychopathic people were sensation seekers. They had a high threshold for achieving pleasure and excitement. They literally couldn't feel happiness from watching the violet sunset, or singing along to Beyoncé, or laughing at a colleague's joke. To experience emotional satisfaction, they needed a jolt, a shock, a sharper experience.

"When psychopaths finally *feel,* what they tend to experience is either manic exhilaration or blind rage," she said.

Emmerich nodded.

"Detrick apparently reveled in stopping a caller from committing suicide. The UNSUB stages his victims' bodies as if they killed themselves."

Emmerich waited for her to draw the conclusion.

"Exhilaration and rage," she said.

She thought about the hotline. She had told Darian Cobb, honestly, that the center's counselors were not in danger. But what about the people they counseled? Were they phoning an emotional arsonist?

Did Detrick choose victims from among vulnerable women who called in crisis?

To Morales, she said, "Have you obtained all the victims' phone records?"

"Including the Dallas victim. Detective Berg printed copies."

"Excuse me," she said.

"Find something," Morales called after her. "Something solid."

In the detectives' room, she found the records. Laying them out on the table, she got a ruler and, line by line, began to cross-check them against the number for the Westside Crisis Hotline. *Show me a connection.*

Victim by victim, number by number, month by month, she went back a year, checking whether any of the six abducted women had phoned or answered calls from the hotline.

Nothing.

"Jesus." She ran her fingers through her hair. None of the missing women had called the hotline. Not one.

She needed more information.

What had triggered the UNSUB to start killing in Gideon County? Why was his pace accelerating? If Detrick was the UNSUB, did his hotline work connect to the murders?

Detrick had been on duty a number of times preceding an abduction. Did phone calls to the hotline trigger him? Calls from women? Calls about a particular subject?

Motion beyond her computer screen led her to raise her head. "Yes?"

Rainey stood near the door, putting on her coat. "I said, chow time. You usually pop up like a prairie dog when anyone mentions food."

The room had half emptied. Around her, tired faces

leaned over files and screens or hung on phone lines, pens in hand. Roll call for night shift was going on down the hall.

On a whiteboard, a detective had written *Tips called in: 452. Tips cleared: GET TO WORK.*

Four hundred fifty-two suspects they were investigating. And, she was convinced, all but one of them off base.

The itch under her skin grew stronger. She checked her watch. Six forty-nine P.M. February 13.

Wednesday.

She stood, grabbed her coat, and followed Rainey to the door. "I'm starving."

25

When they arrived at the Holiday Inn Express, the taco stand across the street was hopping. The cherry-red dregs of sunset striped the horizon. Caitlin's stomach felt empty, but rife with beating wings. She hadn't eaten since breakfast.

They got out, pulling backpacks and briefcases, file folders and books, with them. The others turned toward the lighted hotel entrance, but Caitlin pointed across the street.

"Local culture. It's important to understand our environment. Come on."

Emmerich demurred. "I have reports to write."

"Gotta fuel your engine."

He smiled, a rarity. "Fine. We need Jet A to keep running."

They crossed the street, perking up as they heard the sizzle of the grill.

Twenty minutes later, they gathered wrappers and stood up from a picnic table. Rainey sucked habanero sauce from her thumb. Emmerich downed the last of his iced tea. Caitlin felt replenished. The conversation was relaxed as they crossed the street to the hotel.

But Caitlin felt unsated. Her obsessive need to know had stirred. She wanted a glimpse into Kyle Detrick's mind.

The lights in the hotel lobby were bright, the lanky clerk half attentive behind the front counter. He mumbled a welcome.

Rainey's phone rang. She answered a video call. "Hey, Dre."

She broke into a smile—the deep, enamored smile of a mother. Caitlin caught a glimpse of the screen: a boy, ten years old, sitting at a kitchen table. Behind him, his brother ran across the view.

"Dad said you could help me with my math homework."

"Word problems?" Rainey said.

"What else?"

Rainey's smile tightened at the edges. Caitlin guessed that word problems were Dre's nemesis.

"You'll get through it," Rainey said. "Learn how to handle these problems and the rewards of straight-up math await you in seventh grade."

"Ma. That's *two years* from now."

Caitlin smiled.

Rainey dropped onto a couch in the lounge area and put earbuds in. "We get this homework done, you and T.J. can play *Mario Kart* for half an hour."

Caitlin headed for the elevators and pressed the button. Emmerich sauntered up. He had a Churchill biography tucked under his arm, but his head was bent toward his phone; answering e-mail. When the elevator came, he barely glanced at Caitlin as she entered before him.

She guessed that meant he trusted her to take point and keep the demons from leaping on him as he thumbed a reply.

The doors opened on her floor. "Good night, sir."

Belatedly, Emmerich looked up. He caught the door with his hand just before it closed.

"Checking out the hotline was a good call," he said. "I think your instinct's right. But Morales is right too. We have to develop solid evidence."

"Working on it."

He released the elevator door. "Good night, Hendrix."

When the door of her room clicked shut, Caitlin paused. She asked herself: *Is this really what you want to do?*

The answer came: *Abso-fucking-lutely.*

She threw the dead bolt and the security latch on the door. She dropped her bag on the credenza. She removed her handcuffs from the back of her belt and her holster and Glock from her right hip. She pulled off her boots and changed into jeans and a hoodie. She got her phone and sat cross-legged on the bed.

She knew she was about to go out-of-bounds. She told herself, *Emmerich wants me to develop solid evidence.*

She sat for a minute, slowing her heart rate. She hopped up and turned off the overhead light. The dimness of the desk lamp lowered the mood. This would take extreme calm, and deep conviction, and a clear head. But she had to replicate the atmosphere.

Of that night, long ago.

She opened an app on her cell phone and put in earbuds. She told herself: *Go back. Back then. Feel it.* She knew she couldn't fake it. She felt a stinging pressure behind her eyes and a thumping in her chest.

She got out the brochure that Darian Cobb had given her at the Westside Crisis Center.

She thumbed the number into her phone keypad. Before she pressed CALL, she blocked her caller ID. She hit ACTIVATE on the app. It was a voice modulator.

She pressed CALL.

One ring, and the phone was picked up. "Westside Crisis Hotline."

It was a female voice. The second volunteer who took regular Wednesday-night shifts.

"This is Vanessa. Who's this?"

Caitlin hung up.

She sat still, her heart drumming against her ribs. This was stupid. Juvenile. Underhanded. She counted five minutes on the clock, quieting herself. Blew a breath through pursed lips. She raised the phone again and called back.

The number rang. Once, twice.

"Westside Crisis Hotline."

Her pulse pounded in her temples. She tapped her screen to activate the voice modulator. From her chest to her fingertips, her nerves rang. It was the electric thrill of the hunt.

"Hello?"

"I'm here," she said.

"I'm Kyle. What's on your mind?"

26

Detrick's voice sounded friendly and comforting. Even through the phone, his baritone was warm and came through crisply.

"I'm here to listen," he said.

She closed her eyes. He seemed *present*.

"Is it just you?" Her mouth felt dry. She wasn't going to have to fake anxiety. "Is anybody else listening?"

"Another volunteer is here tonight. But this conversation is just between us."

She took a minute. "I've felt . . . really alone for a long time. But talking is hard."

She heard her voice altered by the modulator: skewed toward soprano. She sounded younger, late teens or early twenties.

She felt a ghostly presence: the fifteen-year-old she'd been, isolated and badly depressed, too ashamed to tell her parents she was sinking.

Go, she told herself. *Dive*. There was no other way to do this effectively.

"I thought—if I called this number, maybe I could talk, if it's to one person."

"I'm the guy. I'm glad you called." He maintained the calm, attentive tone. "You sound upset. I'm concerned—what's bothering you?"

She sighed. "I don't know how to start."

"Maybe by telling me your name. It's easier to talk when I can picture the person I'm talking to."

"Rose." It was her middle name. First rule of lying: Seed it with truth.

"Rose," Detrick said. "That's lovely."

Spoken soothingly, in his rich baritone, it sounded lovely indeed.

This guy was good.

"I can tell it was difficult for you to pick up the phone," he said. "Take your time."

She closed her eyes. "I feel like I can't move. Like I can't breathe. Like a wall of thorns is wrapping around me." She tried to inhale. "It's crushing me. I . . ."

She stopped. She was no actor. The only undercover work she'd done was back in Alameda Narcotics. But making a street buy as part of an op to locate a meth lab was different from convincing this man she desperately needed his emotional support.

She slid off the bed and sat on the floor, facing the window and the night beyond. She pulled her knees up to her chest.

"I'm suffocating," she said. "And I can't see any way out."

"I'm here, Rose," Detrick said. "Have you talked to anyone about how you feel?"

"I can't."

Remembering: Mom in the next room, two A.M., sophomore year in high school, the night thick around her, the banshees crawling through her head, practically stopping her breath.

"My mom, I can't—they don't—I can't talk to her."

"You sound like you're having a really hard time," he said. "Okay. Rose, I'm here."

His reiteration seemed like a real lifeline.

She reached deeper. "I'm scared."

His voice took on a stronger tone of authority. "Are you safe right now? This minute?"

This was the script for crisis hotline volunteers. Step one: Assess whether the caller is in acute crisis, a danger to herself or others.

"Nobody's trying to break down the door, if that's what you mean," she said. "Yeah, I guess I'm safe."

"Okay, that's good. But it sounds like you're really down," Detrick said. "Do you want to tell me about it?"

She sat there and let her old terrors well up, and all the pain that she had tried to shed.

"People say the blues pass, but that's not true," she said. "Not even close. I know because people said that to my dad. Said the sun would come out, everything was going to be fine, he just needed to focus on the positive and cheer up."

The scars on her forearms, beneath her tattoos, gleamed white under the desk lamp.

"Then he tried to take his own life," she said.

"That must have knocked your world out of balance."

"He was what I was hanging on to. Then he was gone from the house and our family. Mom tried to keep the truth from me, and to be everything for me. But I needed him. I felt so empty—so . . ."

She fought to say the word she meant.

"Forsaken," she said. "And the night terrors still came, and he wasn't around to protect me from them."

"It sounds tough. And that you've been battling depression for a long time."

She pulled her sleeves down over her forearms. "Years."

"You don't sound that old, Rose."

"I'm twenty."

That was an intuitive calculation on her part. She wanted him to think she was within the age range of the UNSUB's targets.

He said, "Am I correct in understanding that you feel really sad, afraid, and depressed?"

"You win the carnival prize."

"Have you ever felt this bad before?"

"In high school. After my dad attempted suicide. People looked at me differently. We lived in a small town and everybody knew about it."

"That must have been an additional source of pain for you," he said.

"I felt like a pariah. I could sense people's stares, even behind my back. Talking under their breath as I walked past in the cafeteria. 'That's her. Poor girl.' A few asked me if he was going to do it again. If we had to remove his guns from the house. The worst were the people who told me he was going to hell."

She nearly spat the word *hell*. "He was in agony. Now I know he was suffering. I know how bad it was getting, until something finally broke his back emotionally. But hearing that—and it wasn't just my school classmates, it was their parents, it was people I'd see in the supermarket or the library—'Suicide is a sin. Your father needs to repent and accept Jesus in his heart . . .'"

Detrick held off a beat. "Texas."

She clamped her lips shut. *Remember that you're supposed to be a local.*

"They were well-intentioned. Mostly," she said.

Detrick's voice lightened. "God save us from people who think they know what's best for us."

"Amen."

After letting the moment crystallize, he said, "You're talking a lot about your dad. Is he still in your life?"

"No."

He was dead. She didn't share that. Mack's memory, as fraught as his life and their relationship had been, needed to be protected.

"My parents divorced," she said. "I don't have any contact with him."

"But you're holding on to what happened to him. Is there a reason for that?" Detrick asked. "You sound angry at him, but like you also miss him."

Clever bastard. "That about sums it up."

"Really?"

"What else do you want me to say?"

"It sounds like something kicked off this latest round of depression, but you haven't told me about it. You seem angry and in pain. What's going on?"

"It's a wave. It comes in regularly, like the tide," she said.

He let a silence extend. "Do you feel like your father visited his sins on you?"

Okay, that was off.

"I don't mean literal sins," Detrick said. "I mean, do you feel especially like your father's daughter somehow? Compared to being your mama's little girl?"

A weird feeling sank through her—like a needle had been driven into the base of her neck, at the spine, and was being threaded around her lungs and heart.

"I'm afraid I am him," she said.

"How so?" His tone remained concerned, but definitely curious.

"After his breakdown . . ."

Keep it vague. But she remembered coming home from school and finding police cars out front. Running inside, feeling terror pierce her when she saw the uniformed officers in the kitchen with her mother. Begging, *Dad—where's Dad? Is he okay?*

She'd thought he was dead, cut to ribbons in an alley. But it was his partner who had died at the hands of a serial killer. Mack had reached the scene too late to prevent it.

Hours later, he drove off a bridge.

When firefighters pulled her father from the river, he raved, punching, screaming at them. He spent the next six months in a locked psychiatric ward.

"He was never the same," she said.

"And you think his poison runs in your veins."

The words struck like lightning. Though the room was dark, her entire field of vision seemed to blanch white.

"Yes." A crack caught the end of the word.

"You sound so afraid, Rose."

Lock it down. She tried, and couldn't.

"I'm terrified," she said. "I know the tendency to depression can be inherited. And that how you grow up influences how you handle the world. Nature and nurture. And you're right, I'm like him. So goddamn much." She tried to breathe. "What if the urge to commit suicide is embedded in me too? What if trying to kill yourself is a flaw in your life—like an aneurysm, that can fail at any time and take you down?"

Over the line came the sound of Detrick drawing a long breath. He took a beat. When he spoke, his voice was intense—not rough, but intimate.

"Have you ever contemplated suicide?" he said.

"Yes."

"Have you thought about how you would do it?"

"Many times."

"Have you considered a particular method?"

On the surface, it sounded ghoulish. But she knew from experience that this was one of the most important parts of a volunteer's script. Detrick remained level and empathetic. His steady compassion was almost irresistibly alluring.

"Yes," she said, "I've thought about how I'd do it."

"How, Rose?"

She felt the subtle pull of his voice, a tone that begged to be trusted. *Resist.*

"Why are you doing this?" she said.

"Doing what?" He sounded genuinely surprised.

"Why do you volunteer at a crisis hotline? What do you get out of it?"

"We should talk about you," he said.

"No, I want to know."

He took what seemed a thoughtful pause. "Everybody deserves a friend, and to talk to somebody who can help. And right now, that means hearing about what's upsetting you."

She played his game: She let the silence hang. It was an interrogator's technique. A journalist's technique. The shrink's technique, to give a patient breathing room. Create silence, and people want to fill it. And, she thought: It was the trick behind knowing that if you ask a narcissist about himself, he'll be helpless to keep quiet.

She could hear him breathing over the line.

Then, in the background, she heard the other volunteer on a call. "*That's good. I'm glad to hear it. You take care. Bye.*" And the other phone clacked back into its cradle. A chair squeaked. A door opened, and closed.

A few more seconds passed. She realized: Detrick was now alone in the office.

She spoke quietly. "Why do you spend your time talking to suicidal people?" A rage she'd thought was extinguished heated, red and sharp. "Why do you care? What do you get out of it?"

"That's a hard attitude. Who are you so angry with?"

"You get off on hearing people suffer? Does that make you feel superior?"

"You've got some fight in you. I can hear it. That's good."

He was a fencer—skilled at deflection. But she wanted him to attack. She remembered how, when she'd called the crisis hotline in the East Bay, she had been full to the brim with *fuck you*. She had torn into the woman who took her call, until she'd spent all her emotional ammo and was left disarmed, forced to face herself without defenses.

It had been terrifying. She'd felt out of control. Hated that. In the end, she hung up on the volunteer. That had been a mistake. A week later, she cut herself too angrily and ended up in the ER.

"You want to get mad?" Detrick said. "Get mad. Go on. But please, Rose. This is important. How would you do it?"

Her head was thumping. Her mouth felt parched. She was clutching her knees, her feet cold on the hotel room floor. She felt very small.

"I'd cut my wrists."

He kept quiet.

She looked at the scars on her arms. "I'd cut at an angle, along the length of the artery. A bunch of times." Her pulse pounded in her forehead. "And I'd slip under the surface of a warm bath. Into floating darkness. It would be like . . ." Her voice grew soft. "Like falling through a field of stars, into the black nowhere."

The silence on the phone line stretched. She felt a sob welling up.

She'd never told anybody that before. But it was true. It had been true since she was fourteen. In the deepest empty nights, the lure sometimes called to her.

Detrick inhaled. "That's beautiful. But I want you alive."

For a second, it seemed that a jagged bolt of lightning had shot through the room. She was staring out the window. The stars came into focus.

"I want you to keep talking, Rose. Pour it out. What kind of blade would you use? Tell me how you'd feel, every second of the way down. I want you to keep talking." Another pause. "Did you hear me? I want you alive."

That word, *I*.

That word shoved her back from the brink. That, and a tone in Detrick's voice that seemed like more than curiosity.

The pull she'd felt ebbed. She stood up.

She thought: *Is it all about him?*

She put a fist over her mouth.

Under the low light of the desk lamp, her reflection wavered darkly in the wall mirror. Inside her head came a sound like a lightbulb exploding.

Control.

Well, wasn't this just goddamn great. Control was what they'd been talking about all along. Control and possession were the killer's driving goals. Control was what she'd been clawing for since she was a child. Control over herself and her life. The quest for control was what had led her to become a cutter.

Perfect control was impossible. But she could damn

well control one thing—she knew she couldn't *lose* control ever again, not even to catch a killer.

"Rose?" Detrick said.

His voice was pleading. Jesus God, his sway had felt so strong and immediate. Fear washed over her like icy water. She hung up.

She stood in the dark, chest heaving. She whispered, "Oh my God."

She couldn't see straight. She turned in circles, paced, and ran her fingers through her hair. What had she done?

Her nerves were crawling. She had to get out of the room.

She yanked off her hoodie. She changed into running gear and took the stairs to the ground floor. Outside, she pounded the frontage road along I-35 for five hard miles. The scars on her arms throbbed. When she came back through the doors of the hotel, there were lines where the tears had run down her cheeks.

27

The breakfast lounge at the hotel was busy at seven thirty A.M., full of business travelers fueling up before hitting the interstate. The white sun slanted across the floor. The room smelled of shampoo and aftershave and sugar. Caitlin strode in, poured a large cup of coffee, and joined Rainey at a table by the window, apart from the other diners.

Rainey looked up from her phone. "Those four hundred fifty-two tips called in to the sheriff's office? I've been searching them for descriptions that could match Detrick. A dozen possibles." She scrolled down the screen. "This one—girl named Madison. 'Man watching me outside my apartment building.' Caucasian, tall, dark hair, dressed like a banker. 'Thought he was a cop but he split when my mom appeared.' She lives a quarter mile off I-35."

"Definitely."

Rainey shifted her attention. She evaluated Caitlin's crisp white button-down blouse and the black suit she'd bought on sale at T.J.Maxx. "You look particularly fed-like today."

Caitlin smoothed her hair. She'd pulled it back into a tight French twist. She blew on her coffee.

Emmerich set a plate and cutlery on the table. "I got Detrick's cell records."

On his plate was a waffle cooked in the shape of Texas.

"And you think street food is bad for you?" Caitlin said.

"When in Rome."

As usual, Emmerich's suit was impeccable, but creases were showing at the elbows. His glance assessed her appearance in a heartbeat. He didn't comment but seemed to file it away.

He took out his phone and thumbed to a download. "The records show that on the nights when women disappeared, Detrick's phone never left his neighborhood."

Caitlin set down her coffee cup. "Seriously?"

She and Rainey exchanged a glance.

Emmerich said, "I have a year's worth of call records, data usage, and cell tower registration logs. We'll correlate those to his work schedule, but from a cursory review, he's wedded to that phone. It's always with him, always on the move. *Except.*"

He eyed the bottle of syrup on the table but couldn't make himself cross that line. He cut a bite of the waffle and ate it dry.

He looked up, eyes canny. "Except, on the six nights

when victims disappeared, his phone pinged the tower two hundred meters from his house."

Excitement began to heat in Caitlin's chest. It nudged aside the vague shame and sense of unbalance she'd felt since the unsanctioned call to the crisis hotline.

That's beautiful.

Bleeding to death. Her description had brought out Detrick's poetic side. *But I want you alive.*

She blinked away his hovering presence. "Detrick's phone was at home all six nights. But . . ."

"He gave us alibis for those nights," Rainey said.

"He said he attended a Longhorns basketball game. Real estate seminar. A concert."

Emmerich shook his head. "The phone didn't."

Rainey said, "So either Detrick left it home, or his alibis are lies."

Emmerich nodded. "Detrick wanted to make sure no evidence could place him near the abduction sites."

It wasn't proof. Not even close. But it went to Detrick's credibility.

"Where I come from, we call that consciousness of guilt," Caitlin said.

As the word left her mouth, her throat went dry. She drank her coffee. Guilt. Yeah. The kind you feel after making stupid mistakes. Like calling the suspect under false pretenses.

She felt reckless for opening herself up to Detrick on the hotline. Yet she couldn't shake the truth that he *understood* her. He *saw* her. If she'd been in true crisis, he could have pulled her from the void.

Whatever he was doing, he was a master at it.

She stood. "Ready to go?"

Rainey was finishing her coffee. "What put the bee in your bonnet this morning?"

"The phone records should help move the needle with the detectives here."

"Should." Emmerich's eyes were narrow in the sharp sun coming through the windows. "You have something else to help move that needle into the red zone?"

Go for it. She nodded.

"We're gathering evidence on Detrick, but it's highly circumstantial. We don't have enough for a search warrant, or to obtain DNA."

"Not yet."

"And Saturday night is approaching." She leaned on the table. "I have a plan. I want to surveil Detrick."

"That's not a plan."

"Openly."

Emmerich set down his fork. Raised an eyebrow.

"Give me the chance to follow him in plain sight. I want to dog him," she said.

"Tip our hand."

"If he's innocent, great. If not, I'll force him to be on his best behavior."

Emmerich thought about it. "If he's the UNSUB, you'd be applying pressure as his urge to kill is building. He'd only be on his best behavior for so long before he acts out in response."

"We profiled him as believing he'll outsmart us. I can turn that against him."

"It's a risk."

"I know."

He didn't move, but his gaze retreated as he thought about it. "I'll give you seventy-two hours."

She clenched her fists. "Thank you, sir."

Her stomach was already tying in knots. But the feeling that overcame her was excitement.

Her phone buzzed in her pocket. She nodded at Emmerich and headed for the door. She was pumped.

When she looked at her phone, her mood grew even better. Sean had texted her. It was his flight itinerary, with the message Virginia is for . . .

She texted back: Fed love.

For the first time in a week, she genuinely smiled. Grabbing the keys to the SUV, she headed outside.

At the wooded house outside the city, he lay in bed and listened to the car back out of the drive. Emma was taking Ashley to school, then going to work. It was unusual for them to stay over on a weeknight, but a power outage at her apartment complex had emboldened her to ask if he'd mind. The night had turned into an adventure for Ashley. They built a fort in the living room from sheets and sofa cushions, and the little girl slept inside with her books and Disney princess doll and a flashlight. It reminded him of his own childhood, his grandparents' house, crawling beneath the dining room table when the angry voices became too loud.

The engine faded. Quiet descended. He waited, listening, ensuring Emma was gone. The only sound he heard was birds shrieking in the trees.

He stretched and got up. He had appointments later in the morning, but right now had a good half hour before he needed to shave and shower. He opened the closet and pressed on the false wall in the back. It opened with a muffled click.

The corkboard with his collection swung into view. The sun reflected off the photos. A warmth filled his chest.

Shana Kerber was there now. She'd been a wildcat, that one—with that little cheerleader body, those frosty eyes, ready to lunge at him when he wouldn't hand over her squalling baby.

But she had been mentally disarmed by his appearance.

It always worked. Long enough for them to hesitate. And hesitation—like an initial faltering, superficial cut across a vein—did no good.

So Baby Mama now sang with the unearthly choir on his wall. In the first photo, her eyes were riven with terror. With knowledge. She stood bolt upright, against a wall, her hand raised to keep him back. That was always a brilliant moment, and it was rare to capture it—when disbelief crumbled, and reality set in. Her situation. Him. He ran his fingers across the surface of the photo, savoring it. His breathing quickened.

The second photo was Baby Mama, after. Baby Mama, taken. He'd snapped it mere moments after the change. Her eyes still gleamed, but saw nothing. Her lips—her red, full lips—were softly parted. Her flesh was still at 98.6 degrees. The white nightgown draped her figure like cling wrap.

The heat in his chest spread, and descended. His bare feet were cold on the floor. His jeans were unbuttoned.

Beside Baby Mama was Debbie Does Dallas. The look on that one's face was the one he loved most. *Truth*. She had understood where she was, and that she had no say, no choice, no way out.

That was the look he'd always sought. Since *her*. He stared at the photo of Dallas, but saw *her* face. Heard *her* voice. Felt *her* yield beneath him. He cried out and sagged against the closet door.

Dallas had been a brilliant moment. But it had been five days. Sometimes they lasted two weeks or longer before they gave it up. Before he got to see their epiphany, and submission.

But now he felt the hunger again, the need, the want.

He hoisted his jeans. He had a busy schedule planned, full workdays the rest of the week. Saturday . . .

Shithead cops. It was better when he could simply fade into the background—when the women merely went away. Why would anyone miss them? This nation was full of women. They fell out of sight all the time. Runaways, prostitutes, mothers bolting on their kids. There shouldn't have been such a fuss, not in this crowded, teeming stretch of Texas. Nobody should have wondered where they went.

That was the lesson he'd learned, last summer, on the phone call.

Why do you care? she'd said. *Why help women like that? Losers, beggars, hanging on to you. Crying, sucking their thumbs, wanting you to make it all better. Why? Who'd miss them? Most women who disappear are never even reported missing.*

It had been a bolt of electricity. Her nasty, excoriating voice, lashing him. But with illumination.

You listen to women, she said. *Why not give them what they want?*

What they deserved.

Tell me you don't picture them dead. That you don't secretly hope for it.

He had been breathing so hard by then, he thought he might use up all the oxygen in the room. *I do,* he thought. *I do, I do, I do.* And for every one he listened to, why not take another?

What are they doing, except using up your life? the caller had said.

Too damned right.

And they *did* want it. He knew; he'd known since the day he was five and opened the bathroom door and saw his mom in the bathtub, floating, head back, submerged, her naked flesh poking above the surface of the water, gleaming, wet . . .

He stepped back from the closet wall. The photos were beautiful. Always Polaroids. Never on your phone, never on your computer. Never, ever, in any form where it could be uploaded to the eternal cloud. Simple was best. Old-school.

Maybe he should wait. The cops had ginned up a show.

No. Screw 'em. He had once tried to suppress his need, but no more.

He thought of the young barista he'd scouted, Madison Mays. Her ass was tight. Her face was unblemished by awareness. If her mother hadn't opened the door, Barista might now be singing with the choir. He'd been pissed off. Still was. Even though he had Dallas instead. Instead was never good. Both was better.

The world was full of women, but Barista was the one he wanted right now. Maybe he could still have her. He simply needed to be careful. Blend in. Like always. Nobody would see him, even in plain sight.

He smiled. Saturday night was only two days away.

28

Caitlin was parked directly across the street from Castle Bay Realty, downing an Americano, when Kyle Detrick pulled into the parking lot in his twinkling-clean Buick Envision.

He parked in his usual spot, got out, and headed for the office doors. He was strutting, looking as alive as if he were a vampire who had just drunk arterial blood. His color was high. His black jeans were tight, his cashmere sweater adhering to well-toned abs. His houndstooth blazer matched his cowboy boots. He swiped a look at his reflection in the tailgate of another SUV as he passed. He was whistling.

He grabbed the building door's handle, and saw her.

She had on shades and was draping one hand over the top of the steering wheel. She took another swallow of the coffee.

Traffic passed in front of her. Detrick held on for a second, as if double-checking that she was really there, and went inside. The door shut hard behind him.

From her spot in the shade along the curb, Caitlin had

a clear view of the building's front and side doors, and an unobstructed line of sight to the lobby. At the desk, Brandi greeted Detrick effusively, swiveling back and forth on her chair and laughing at a remark of his. He paused a second to enjoy the attention. He headed deeper into the building without looking back at Caitlin.

Cool customer.

So far.

She set the Americano in the cup holder. She knew better than to fill up on liquids while on surveillance. The coffee was a prop, meant to give Detrick the sense that she was primed, and supplied, and comfortable, and settling in to binge-watch.

She normally disliked stakeouts. Hours of tedium, with the potential to miss a critical piece of action if you looked away for ten seconds. She dealt poorly with anticipation. Hated uncertainty. She always preferred to act—not to sit in a car hoping for action. But this was different. Sitting here *was* action, an attempt to spur a reaction.

Keeping an eye on the building, she phoned the Westside Crisis Hotline. It was time to be up front with the director, Darian Cobb. He wasn't in. She left a message asking him to call.

At ten forty-five A.M., in the Castle Bay lobby, Brandi answered the phone, looked up stealthily, and covered the receiver to talk. She glared out the plate-glass windows at Caitlin. A minute later Detrick sauntered into the lobby, shot Brandi a thumbs-up, and came outside. Ignoring Caitlin, he climbed into the Envision and drove off. Caitlin pulled into traffic a hundred meters behind him.

She followed him for twenty minutes as he headed north from downtown, to an apartment complex where he met a couple in their early thirties. She parked on the street and took photos with a Canon camera, which had a big, obvious lens. Detrick ushered the couple into his SUV and spent the next two hours driving them around neighborhoods on the fringes of the city, showing them homes. Caitlin took photos of every stop, and wrote down every address, and made a note to check how many homes listed for sale in the Austin metro area were empty. A Realtor who had a key to a lockbox and knew of unoccupied buildings could make good use of them late on Saturday nights, if he wanted to stash a kidnapping victim somewhere. He wouldn't leave victims in a vacant house for long, however, because a thousand other Realtors also had lockbox keys and could enter at any time.

She followed Detrick when he took his clients to Tacodeli for lunch. The restaurant was bustling, the line to order thirty-five deep. Caitlin parked, strolled in, and used the restroom. She was filling her empty coffee cup with water when Detrick spotted her. She held his gaze, went back outside, and climbed into the Suburban. In its side mirrors, she could see Detrick staring at her.

About four thirty, he returned to the office. In the lobby, he spoke to Brandi. When he went into the interior of the building, Brandi got up from the front desk, bustled around at a side table, and came outside holding a napkin piled with chocolate chip cookies. She marched across the street to Caitlin's Suburban.

Caitlin let her stand outside the driver's door for a minute before putting down the window. She felt stiff from driving around all day sitting on her ass, but gave Brandi her most tranquil look.

"May I help you?"

Brandi's back was straight. She was wearing a ruffled white blouse that looked like clouds clinging to a mountain valley. Today's necklace was a gold-dipped charm shaped like Texas. The southern tip of the state had lodged in the shadows between her breasts.

"Mr. Detrick thought you might need refreshments," Brandi said. "You're looking kind of wilted."

Caitlin took the cookies and set them aside. "Kind of you."

Brandi crossed her arms. "You have no cause to do this."

"How long has Mr. Detrick driven that Buick Envision?" Caitlin said.

"None of your business."

"Did you know he erased its GPS history?"

Brandi's chin rose. It looked like righteous dudgeon, or an urge to gut Caitlin like the deer she hunted.

"He told me. The government has no legitimate reason to know where he drives. He takes clients to view prospective homes. He deals in people's most personal life decisions—where to start a family, where to put down roots. The FBI has no business prying into where people decide to live out their dreams. If it weren't for your scare tactics, he wouldn't have had to take this stand. But he did." She looked Caitlin up and down. "And fixation is unattractive. Leave him alone."

"Did he tell you we can't confirm his alibis for the nights women went missing?" Caitlin said.

Brandi's lips slowly parted. Color rose on her neck.

Caitlin started the engine and jammed it in gear. "Appreciate the cookies."

She pulled out and swung a U-turn, leaving Brandi standing in the middle of the street. While the two of them were talking, Detrick had come out the side door of the office building and climbed into the Envision.

Nice try, sleazehead.

He sped away, but she followed. He drove south through downtown and crossed a bridge over Lady Bird Lake, shifting lanes through sluggish traffic. He was apparently trying to lose her. Five miles down Lamar Boulevard, in a gentrifying neighborhood where sleek new apartment buildings and luxury movie theaters competed with ramshackle honky-tonk bars, he turned into a strip mall. Caitlin pulled in behind him.

By the time she got out, he'd headed into a liquor store. She walked in, pulled off her shades, and strolled along an aisle perusing New World reds.

He bought a six-pack of Lone Star and turned from the register to find her waiting inside the doors. He sauntered toward her.

"Where are you headed?" she said.

"I have to say, I'm flattered. I've never felt like such a wanted man." A smile graced his lips. "It's sort of . . . hot."

His sunglasses were propped on top of his head. His cologne had faded into a heated, physical scent. His gray eyes were a cool counterpoint.

"I hear your GPS got wiped," she said. "I'm here to make sure you don't get lost."

"Leave a trail of bread crumbs, so you can find your way home."

His tone was light. She caught not a hint of resentment or even annoyance.

"I'm not the one who loses things in the forest," she said.

Once again, for a microsecond, his eyes tightened, like he'd recognized a glitch. Then his smile turned up to full wattage.

"What a life you lead, Agent Hendrix. Have fun."

He brushed against her as he walked past and out the door. She fought off a shiver.

He drove away. She stuck to him. After wandering and burning time, he finally headed home at eight forty-five P.M. He seemed to think he could outlast her.

Jackass had no idea.

His house was off the main roads in a south Austin neighborhood near I-35. It was—according to the Castle Bay Realty website—what Realtors called a "dark skies" neighborhood. That meant it was marketed to stargazers.

To a cop, it meant that there were no streetlights. No sidewalks, few signposts. Under the winter night, the street was coal dark. Beyond her headlights, Caitlin glimpsed lantana and manzanita and cedars lining the street. She idled while Detrick parked on the driveway, flicked his remote to lock the Envision, and went into the house. He flipped on a light in the living room and looked out the window. She knew he couldn't see her inside the darkened Suburban. But somehow, his eyes seemed to pierce her. He shut the curtains.

She pulled slowly away.

Friday morning, she was back, six thirty A.M., outside his place with her laptop open, answering e-mails and making calls. She wore a black peacoat over her black V-neck sweater, black jeans, and Doc Martens. She'd pulled her hair back into a braid. She was parked so that when he came out and saw her in the car, the rising sun would reflect off her sunglasses.

Detrick emerged at seven thirty, looking fresh and dapper. He walked jauntily to his Envision, shooting her a salute as he climbed in.

He spent the morning again taking clients house hunting. He maintained his cool, acting as though she wasn't right behind him. Around noon, he dropped a client at home and drove to a gas station. When he got out to fill the Envision's tank, Caitlin pulled up at a pump on the other side of the fuel island.

Detrick looked over and actually laughed.

Caitlin got out and unscrewed the Suburban's gas cap. Detrick set his pump to fill automatically and leaned back against the side of the Envision, ankles crossed, looking supremely relaxed.

"I've always wanted a fan," he said.

"I'm amused that's how you see this." She stuck the nozzle in the Suburban's tank.

He shrugged. His smile, she had to admit, was dazzling.

"You could be a recruiting poster for the FBI," he said. "You're dogged. Spunky. Much more appealing than the agents you see in the movies. I mean, *Die Hard*?"

She had to laugh. "Agent Johnson and Special Agent Johnson, going up in a ball of ignominious flame. 'We're gonna need some more FBI guys, I guess.'"

"Or *Fargo*."

"Two feds having lunch in their car, Billy Bob Thornton strolls past, pulls a machine gun from under his winter coat, then crosses the street and carries out a mob massacre under their noses. It's perfect." She tilted her head. "What's the weirdest call you've ever taken on the crisis hotline?"

He looked her up and down. She felt a static charge.

"Seriously?" he said.

She nodded.

"Chronic masturbator."

She raised an eyebrow, as if blandly curious, encouraging him to divulge more. Inwardly, thinking: *You gotta be kidding*.

"Told this incredibly personal story about her tormented life. Started talking faster, then panting. Then moaning."

"Her."

"As afterglow, she asked me intrusive questions about *my* life."

His eyes were alight. He was delighting in trying to knock her off-balance.

"That's a hell of a hobby," she said.

He finished filling the tank. "I'm done with work at five. After that we can go for a drink. Sixth Street, music, dancing. I can tell you the dirty details about that call. You look like you came dressed for a cocktail in a packed bar."

"No, thank you."

"You shouldn't miss Austin after dark."

"I'm not missing a single thing."

He replaced the hose and got in his SUV. He gave her a sultry look as he started the engine.

As he drove away, he mouthed, "Your loss."

29

In Phoenix, a warm Friday afternoon was turning cool as the golden sun sank over the desert. Lia Fox parked outside her apartment complex. Sprinklers misted the lawn. The air was still, but it felt like sand was blowing past her, grating on her skin.

Inside, she bolted the door, dropped her keys on the kitchen island, petted the cat when it pranced in, and poured a glass of Sauvignon Blanc. She drank half of it in one go.

There was no news about Aaron Gage. No updates on the cases in Texas. No arrests, no wanted posters, no drawings of the suspect. The FBI hadn't called her back.

She kicked off her heels. "What did you expect, idiot?"

She'd called in a tip. That was all. The agent, that redheaded woman who looked like she played volleyball, had expressed concern and scanned her with eyes that seemed to fire X-rays. Maybe the woman had followed up. Or maybe the woman thought she was a wacko. *"I have to ask—at that point, why didn't you call the cops?"* Lia guessed it sounded bad. But times had been bad. The

FBI didn't have to know about her private life. Just about her shattered love life.

Aaron. She thought of his hard body, his handsome face, his hands on her, his out-of-focus smile when he was drunk. She thought of a group picnic and her longing for him to pay attention, to really look at her. She thought of the moment when she was actually *seen.* It wasn't by Aaron Gage. The sensation overcame her again, after all these years—a bone-deep shiver of fear and pleasure and shame and a topsy-turvy longing to *let go.*

She poured another glass of wine.

She thought of the insults, the shouting, the way Aaron ignored her and passed out and *that night, that night, that night.*

Her breath jammed halfway to her lungs. She swallowed and drove away all the images from afterward. The notes and the dolls and freaky fucking Slinky, limp and dead-eyed in the backyard.

The evening sun bounced off the frames of photos on her living room wall.

She picked up her phone and dialed. "Mom. Hi."

Her mother was surprised to hear from her. It wasn't Sunday, or a birthday. Lia's gaze lingered on a photo on the side table. Happy times, mother-daughter intimacy. Smiles and big hugs. Mother's Day.

"No, I'm fine—I just wanted to catch up. You heard from . . ."

Her mom went on, about her beloved dog Tizzy, about her brother John and his perfect family, about her little sister Emily and Emily's perfect semester in college.

Mom had never forgiven Lia for quitting that tight-ass Christian college in Houston. Emily didn't go to a Christian college, but did li'l sis get grief about that? *Noooo.*

Mom never asked about Lia's life. Mom had learned years back that Lia's answers gave her nothing but anguish.

"No special reason. I just wanted to hear your voice," Lia said.

Mom didn't know about Slinky, or the dolls, or how Lia had threatened to kill herself the night of the fire, and how screaming the threat at Aaron hadn't stopped him from drinking himself into a conflagration.

And more. More more more.

"Never mind," she said. "I'll talk to you next weekend."

She hung up. The grating sensation, sand under her skin, grew worse. She finished the second glass of wine and checked the locks on the doors. She wished the FBI would call.

She stared at the walls, and wondered where he was.

In his darkened kitchen, Kyle Detrick stood at the sink and stared out the window. Across the street, barely visible in the winter darkness, the FBI Suburban sat black and sinister at the curb.

He could sense her depthless eyes, staring, pinning him, like a viper. He could practically hear her breathing.

He could hardly believe she'd asked about the call to the crisis hotline.

Weirdest call? No. Most memorable. Most affecting. Most . . . transformative.

He hadn't even lied.

August, last summer. Late on a Wednesday night. The girl's voice on the line, hard and ragged.

Met a guy and I loved him so bad. My parents tried to stop me from seeing him. Said he was wrong, I was too young. I ran away. We robbed 7-Elevens and a Waffle House. He died.

She was panting by that time. *I lived on the street. Fucked men for money.*

By that point, he wasn't about to hang up. After she climaxed, she sighed and said, *Wow.* She asked him how he liked it. For once, he found himself speechless.

She laughed. *Bang-bang, huh?*

His blood had risen and hammered in his temples.

Your turn, she said, lighthearted and vicious. *What's your story?*

He couldn't figure her. He'd asked: What are you doing?

There must be somebody who makes you so crazy you want to kill, she said. *Kill them, kill for them, kill yourself. I want to know. If you don't tell me, I'll shoot myself.*

She had called to see what she could get out of *him*. It was . . . eye-opening.

Isn't there somebody you hate that much? You want that much? she said. *Tell me.*

His past, the lockbox where he kept his heart, his pain, the need and awful sense of the world being dead and empty . . . she had laughed over the phone and said, *What are you waiting for?*

On the phone, he'd felt the lock slip. He wanted to tell her.

But she hung up. Left him cold under the burning lights in the crisis center phone room. He had tried to shut back down, but she had turned a key.

A week later, he saw her outside the center. At first, he didn't know it was her. Sitting on a bus stop bench across the street. Summer twilight shading her features. Blond, smoking. Watching. He went to the window.

She raised her hand, made a finger-gun, and mouthed, *Bang-bang.*

Of course she knew he was working that night. He stood at the window.

She didn't come in. She waited.

At midnight, when he finished his shift and crossed the street, she rose from the bench. She ground out her cigarette under the toe of her boot. She had a black cat tattoo over her left breast. She was breathing hard, and under the streetlight, the cat seemed to flex and stretch its claws. For a minute, she looked like she wanted to throw her arms around his neck and let him pick her up and sweep her away. Like she wanted to open herself to him, and eat him up.

He stepped under the streetlight. He raised a hand to speak to her. He meant to talk gently. But she saw his face.

She turned and ran like a deer. And he ran after her.

Now, in his kitchen, he stared out the window at the dim black form of the SUV across the street. If Caitlin Hendrix thought a badge and a gun and those ripe lips could shake him up, she didn't know whom she was dealing with.

30

Detrick stepped outside his door at nine forty-five Saturday morning. He wore his houndstooth blazer with jeans and boots. He was carrying an armload of OPEN HOUSE signs. He dumped them in the back of his Envision, slammed the tailgate, and stared across the street at Caitlin. No smiles this morning. He paused, seemingly thinking, and crossed the street.

She put down the Suburban's window.

He stuck his hands in his front pockets, Mr. Casual. "You must be getting tired of this."

She took that to mean *he* was getting tired of it. "Did you stay home last night?"

He looked away. It was a casual gesture, but she sensed calculation beneath it. Maybe he was wondering if she'd maintained surveillance on his property after he heard her drive off last night. She hoped so.

"All night. All alone." His gray eyes turned back to her. "Just like you, I bet."

"Don't forget your phone."

Face flat, he crossed the street and climbed into the

SUV. The engine gunned as he pulled away. Caitlin turned over the ignition and followed.

Detrick drove two miles to the Sunset Valley Bank. Caitlin knew, thanks to research Rainey had done, that Detrick maintained his personal account here. He went inside, returned five minutes later, and drove away with a roar. Up the street he went into a bakery, came out with a pink box, and took off again.

His open house was in a neighborhood of old trees and cracked sidewalks. Caitlin parked up the street from a single-story ranch home, undistinguished and dispirited, though freshly painted, with potted hydrangeas lining the front walk. It was a Potemkin house. A false front.

Like Kyle Detrick.

She sat with the engine off. Inside the house, he paced near the front window.

Her phone rang. *Nicholas Keyes.*

"That multiplex theater video," Keyes said without preamble. "Where the woman disappeared after she went to the concession stand?"

Caitlin sat up straighter. "You said you were looking at slant routes and interceptions."

"I overlaid some *Madden NFL*–style software on the video. It allowed me to track the victim, then determine whether any other person in the lobby reacted to, or anticipated, her movements, even tangentially."

"And?"

"Sending it to you."

Caitlin opened her laptop on the passenger seat. She pulled up the video.

Keyes said, "See Veronica Lees, with a concentric circle underneath her feet?"

The video on Caitlin's screen now looked like an NFL TV replay. A blue circle spun beneath Lees's shoes, as if she were a wide receiver running a post pattern.

"This is excellent," Caitlin said.

"Keep watching."

Veronica worked her way across the foyer. As she joined the long line at the concession counter, a second circle appeared, yellow, around the feet of a figure far across the lobby.

"Whoa," Caitlin said.

The yellow circle spun below a figure in black jeans, a black shirt, and a black hoodie, wearing a black baseball cap. The figure's back was to the camera, but from the breadth of the shoulders beneath the hoodie, Caitlin judged it to be a man.

Veronica Lees worked her way closer to the front of the concession line.

For a few seconds, the figure in black remained stationary. The yellow circle spun beneath his feet. From within it, a yellow arrow appeared. It stretched into a line heading across the lobby toward the far side of the multiplex—to the hallway from which Veronica had first appeared. While Veronica paid for her box of candy, the figure in the hoodie zigzagged through the crowd along the path of the arrow. He never got within thirty feet of her. He headed to the hallway and out of sight.

It was subtle, and had been hitherto impossible to discern because the figure reached the hallway to the theaters before Veronica did and disappeared around the corner.

"Holy crap," Caitlin said. "He got ahead of her and was waiting when she turned the corner."

"Like a cornerback getting ahead of a wide receiver. The quarterback throws deep, and the defender is in position to intercept," Keyes said. "You can't see the man's face, not in any of the shots. He knew where the cameras were. But he keeps watch on her from the time she enters the lobby until she reaches the concession stand. Then sets himself up to intercept her."

"You're—"

"Sending it to the sheriff's department as we speak. Judging from the height of the counters in the lobby, which I've confirmed, the guy in the hoodie is 1.85 meters tall."

A chill ran up Caitlin's neck. "Same as the Dallas garage. Same as the guy I'm watching through the window of this suburban house."

Uncertainty entered Keyes's voice. "The software is picking up some strange artifacts in the video—I'm going to dig a little deeper. But this, I have high confidence, is legit. That's the UNSUB."

"Thank you."

"It's what I do." Keyes clicked off.

Caitlin sat, her pulse racing.

A car pulled up, a hatchback with a BABY ON BOARD sticker. A young couple emerged, removed a car seat like they were handling nitroglycerin, and headed inside. They looked South Asian, hopeful, intrigued.

Shana Kerber had been young, hopeful, a mother with a baby about the same age.

Caitlin's phone rang. *Sean.*

"Hey, babe," she said.

"Thinking about the itinerary for my visit," he said. "Maybe rent a boat and head out across Chesapeake Bay. Knock the walls down at some little B and B. Then tour the Air and Space Museum. Photograph the wreckage of our democracy. Eat candied apples."

It was early in California. It sounded like he was outside.

"You warming up on the sidelines?" she said.

"Sadie is. Peewee soccer."

"She's four. She can't even write her name."

"She burns calories. She learns to socialize. Field position doesn't exist. Both teams cluster around the ball at all times, like a swarm of bees in the middle of the field."

"You love it," she said.

"Damn straight."

She leaned back, soothed by a sense of connection with Sean. "Don't shout instructions at her. Coaches hate it when parents do that. It confuses the kids."

"But I am the coach."

She laughed. "I can't wait to see you."

"Me either." The phone went muffled, and he talked to another parent on the sideline. She heard, "Band-Aid," and "juice box." When he returned to their conversation, he sounded distracted.

"Something going on?" she said.

"Just work."

ATF explosives cases were never just work. "What's up?"

"Bombing in Monterey," he said. "Last night. Pipe bomb rigged with a tripwire outside the Defense Language Institute."

"Casualties?"

"Motorcyclist hit it at speed. Wrecked and took shrapnel, but he survived. Lucky as hell."

She turned to her laptop and pulled up a news article on the bombing. "DOD installation. You think the military was the target?"

"That's the working theory. We're meeting with the police in Monterey this afternoon."

He sounded intense and focused. Bombs brought all hands on deck.

Sean lived for this.

"I'll call you tonight," he said. "Your Saturday off to a good start?"

Inside the open house, Detrick shook hands with the young parents.

"Peachy," she said. "Drive safe, babe. Get the bad guys."

"You too."

The electricity in his voice was contagious. She hung up, buzzing.

Outside the open house, another car pulled up and a couple got out. Two men, early thirties, fit and dressed in spiffy casual for a Saturday of house hunting. They paused on the front walk to point out features of the home, heads together, before heading inside.

Caitlin climbed out and followed. Her pulse was up.

Inside the front door, a stack of glossy brochures sat

on a table. She picked one up. In the living room, the two men were assessing the fireplace and the home's feng shui. In the back of the house she could hear Detrick's voice, bright and smooth, as he answered the South Asian couple's questions. The baby fussed.

Detrick returned to the living room with the parents, sounding jolly and informative. He saw Caitlin, and his voice faltered.

He greeted the new couple, suggested they check out the kitchen, urged the young parents to explore the backyard. When they left the room, he approached her.

"This is getting old," he said.

"You've only worked as a Realtor for nine months," she said. "Before that, you were a salesman for a home alarm system company."

Rainey, in addition to digging up Detrick's financials, had obtained his tax and employment records. He shouldn't have been surprised. Yet he looked alarmed.

"Keep your voice down."

"When did you move to Austin? How long after you dropped out of Rampart College?"

The gay men in the kitchen turned and surreptitiously listened.

Detrick stepped closer to her. The previous day's suggestive banter had disappeared.

"I've played nice. But this is no longer funny. You're obsessed with me."

"What do you know about obsession?" she said.

His expression curdled. "Stay away from me."

"Where were you Saturday night?"

His expression went flat, and hot, like a griddle. He leaned in and lowered his voice. "You're harassing me. I won't have it. I'll call the sheriff's office in Gideon County and have you taken off this investigation."

"They would love to talk to you. Call and make an appointment. Ask for Detective Art Berg."

"Don't be clever." He said it cuttingly, but realized she had outmaneuvered him. "I'll take it up with your superiors."

She held out her card. "The main switchboard will connect you to my unit chief. Special Agent in Charge C.J. Emmerich."

Behind him, both couples were staring. The two young men exchanged a perturbed glance and sauntered out the front door. Detrick's posture tightened. He nearly called to them, but they hurried down the front walk, casting *what the hell was that* looks over their shoulders.

Detrick glared at Caitlin's proffered card. "There are other avenues I can take."

"The press, you mean." She lowered her hand. "They're drooling for fresh information on these murders—they'd interview you in a heartbeat. Splash it on page one, broadcast it at the top of the hour. Your face will be recognizable from Waco to Laredo." She smiled. "Fine with me. Reporters, photographers, a couple of news vans—that multiplies the work force. I won't have to cool my heels driving around behind you all day. They can keep eyes on, and I can finally take a break and try Tomo Sushi."

His eyes remained remote. Something was working, feverishly, deep behind his gaze, but he screened it. His shoulders were tight.

"You're pathetic. This isn't a federal-caliber investigation. It's compulsive desperation." He nodded at the door. "Leave."

She dropped her card on the table in the entry hall. Back in the Suburban, she gripped the wheel, pulse thudding.

The bastard was rattled.

31

Detrick pulled into his driveway at eight forty-five P.M., after a second open house at a condo near Zilker Park and a long shopping trip to Whole Foods in downtown Austin. The hot sauce section in the store took up a hundred yards of shelf space. Caitlin had felt conspicuous by her paucity of visible tattoos.

Detrick killed the headlights and tromped into the house. Caitlin parked fifty yards up the street, climbed out, and stretched. Her nerves were tight.

Saturday night.

Satellite views of the property showed that the next street over was a cul-de-sac. There were no bus stops within a mile and a half of Detrick's house. The Dodge Charger registered to him was parked in the garage, not stashed a mile away. But if he tried to slip out of the house, she had an infrared app on her phone and a night-vision rifle scope.

Rainey pulled up behind her and climbed out.

Rainey's braids fell across the shoulders of her ruby-red fisherman's sweater. She handed Caitlin a sack from

Torchy's Tacos. They'd decided that trying every Austin taco joint should be a team goal.

Caitlin's stomach audibly rumbled. She pulled a taco from the bag and bit into it. "Good God. I would knock over convenience stores to keep myself supplied with this."

"I already ate the chips and guac," Rainey said. "Status?"

"He's so over me, he won't even look at my vehicle. I could be wearing a wolf mask and antlers and he'd pretend not to see me."

"Tick on a hound, baby. You're driving him nuts. Good," Rainey said. "The next eighteen hours will be critical. You ready?"

"I have a full tank, a camera, handcuffs, and an extra clip." And enough adrenaline to overpower her fatigue. And, if that failed, NoDoz.

They turned toward the house. The kitchen overlooked the street. The lights were off.

"He's standing there in the dark, staring back at us," she said.

"If he's a psychopath, his defensive response will be to act out to restore control. He'll try to put something over on you."

"If he tries to climb over the back fence . . ."

"I'll be parked there, waiting."

Rainey got in her vehicle and pulled away.

But it was seven fifteen A.M., with the morning sun spearing her eyes, when Detrick strolled out his front door, picked up the Sunday paper, and walked to his SUV, twirling the keys around his index finger.

Caitlin straightened, suddenly wide-awake. "Ostentatious display, bastard." She started the engine and phoned Rainey. "He's on the move. And making a point of showing me he slept nice and cozy in his own bed last night."

"We're done here, then."

"I'm not."

"You're going to run out of steam."

"Any reports of—"

"No."

No women had been reported missing overnight. That was good news. Possibly probative news.

Detrick fired up his Envision, backed out, and roared past Caitlin.

"Your seventy-two hours are almost up," Rainey said.

"I'm not done yet."

Caitlin ended the call, put the Suburban in gear, and followed Detrick. Part of her was thinking, *He's got to be ready to explode.* Part of her was thinking, *If I'm wrong, I've wasted three days when I should have been hunting the real UNSUB.*

Twenty minutes later he stopped outside a wooded apartment complex on the hilly west side of town. Caitlin's eyes were gritty, her clothes clinging to her, her mouth dry. She needed coffee. And a shower. And eight hours' sleep. The fatigue swelled and ebbed behind her eyes. But her reserves of adrenaline were amping her up.

Slip up, you son of a bitch.

If he was the UNSUB, if he was the one who struck on Saturday nights, he had to be fuming. Had to be boiling with rage at being thwarted.

Come on. Show yourself to me.

He had barely exited his SUV when a woman in her thirties strolled from the apartment building, waving. A little girl was at her side, as skinny-legged as a fawn, skipping toward him. Caitlin recognized them from the photo in Detrick's office. *A friend.*

The woman was slight, wearing a modest azure dress. The little girl bounced up to Detrick, jumped up and down, and laughed when he said something to her. He chucked her under the chin. The woman smiled meekly and stood with her hands clasped. Detrick swept an arm around her shoulders, took the little girl's hand, and ushered them to his Envision. Lord of all he surveyed, beloved of children and small animals and all the birds in the air.

He drove them to the oak-dotted campus of a megachurch.

After two hours of songs and sermons, Detrick drove south with the woman and girl on I-35. In San Marcos, forty-five miles down the road, he pulled off at a gargantuan outlet mall. He parked, helped the little girl out, and took his girlfriend's hand. They strolled toward a food court.

Caitlin followed, and phoned Emmerich. "He's trying to wear me down."

Or else he's being exactly the clean-shaven daddy stand-in we refuse to believe he is.

"You got through Saturday night. That was big—and vital. But you sound exhausted," Emmerich said. "Nothing's going to happen on a Sunday morning. Come back to the sheriff's station."

The fatigue muttered, *I surrender.* Her hunter's instinct hissed, *I can't let up.*

"Soon." She ended the call and followed Detrick deeper into the shopping center.

They walked along the promenade, past a juice bar and a candy store, toward the food court. They seemed to be headed to an Olive Garden. Detrick let go of the little girl's hand and told her she could run ahead. The meek woman at his side chattered away but kept her hands folded in front of her. Caitlin was fifty yards behind.

They strolled past a coffeehouse on a corner. Detrick glanced at it. A flare of light caught its plate-glass windows, reflecting from a passing pickup. Abruptly, the truck's brakes squealed and it jerked to a stop, avoiding another car. Detrick and his girlfriend turned at the sound, then kept walking. Inside the coffeehouse, a barista straightened, caught by the commotion.

As she turned back to a rubber tub full of dirty dishes, the back of her black uniform shirt rode up. Stuck in the waistband of her jeans was a .40 caliber pistol.

Texas. Open carry was legal. Leave a tip.

She was in her teens, petite and athletic. And blond. She struck Caitlin as having a figure and features remarkably similar to Shana Kerber's.

Caitlin stopped. She had seen the girl before.

The teenager had come to the Solace sheriff's station with a tip. Caitlin had seen her at the front desk, speaking rapid-fire, indicating the height of a man who had stood in the shadows and spooked her.

Detrick and his girlfriend went into the restaurant and took a table by the window.

Caitlin backed up and went into the coffeehouse. Creds out.

Contemporary Christian music played over the speakers. Kids were eating muffins and throwing crayons. The girl's eyes went as round as pie plates.

"Madison Mays," she said, when Caitlin asked. Rainey had mentioned a tip from a girl named Madison.

"Yeah, I told the sheriff's office. The man I saw was dressed like a banker—coat and dress shirt, no tie. But I didn't get a good look at his face."

Caitlin's heart was pounding. Her exhaustion and doubts evaporated.

Detrick had just walked past a coffeehouse where a potential witness worked. Maybe it was coincidence. The mall was heaving with people. Or maybe he was scouting this girl.

From the coffeehouse, there was no direct line of sight to the food court and the Olive Garden. Caitlin couldn't drag Madison into the open for Detrick to see. She couldn't contaminate a vital potential ID, either, by showing the girl his photo.

Caitlin scribbled on the back of her business card and handed it to Madison.

"Here's the number for the sheriff's office investigative unit. I'm going to have them call you. Detective Berg will arrange for you to look at photos, to see if you can identify the man."

Madison clutched the card. "Okay."

"What's your phone number?"

Madison gave it to her. Caitlin texted it to Berg, Emmerich, and Chief Morales. Arrange photo lineup for witness. May be something solid.

Madison pressed a hand to her stomach, nervous.

"You did the right thing, and you're going to do an even better thing." Caitlin extended her hand. Madison took it with trembling fingers. "Be very cautious about your safety. And I'm glad you're thinking about how to defend yourself. But a handgun should be in a holster, and for a license to carry it, you need to be twenty-one."

Madison's eyes widened.

"Do you know how to use that revolver?"

The girl blushed scarlet. "I . . ."

"Get training. This week. There's a guy in Solace who offers self-defense and firearms courses. I saw him on the local news. He looks like Wyatt Earp. Call him."

Caitlin walked out. Her skin was tingling.

Detrick had tried to put one over on her. He'd tried to regain control by indulging a predatory craving in plain sight. But he didn't appreciate the scope of the information Caitlin had, or the resources she could access. He had a blind spot.

She strode around the corner to the food court. Inside the restaurant, he sat with his good friend and her little daughter. Caitlin paused, standing in the sun, until he saw her. His face was waxen—a GI Joe doll that could have been ablaze inside, without ever losing its bland smile.

32

Caitlin turned into Detrick's street at nine P.M. Sunday night. She gunned the engine so he'd know she was there. She pulled a U-turn and parked behind Rainey. Through the back window of the Suburban Rainey was driving, the light from her laptop screen lit the interior of the SUV electric blue.

Caitlin got out and strolled over. Rainey put down the window.

"He's locked up all tight and tidy. He and the girlfriend and the little girl."

"Thanks," Caitlin said.

"Emmerich gave you seventy-two hours."

"I'm on my own time."

"Terrible way to spend it. Ordinarily, that is."

"Small risk for a potentially astronomical reward."

"*Black Mirror* marathon on my tablet tonight, if you need a break and want to watch with me."

"You know how to throw a party."

"You don't find dystopian satire relaxing?"

"Have fun."

Rainey started the engine and pulled out. Caitlin stood in the street for a minute, hands in the back pockets of her jeans, facing Detrick's house.

I'm not wrong.

She stated it emphatically, deliberately, if silently. But deep below the surface, where the old whispers, the doubts and fears and uncertainties swam, a small voice said, *Maybe you are. Maybe the real UNSUB is out there, right now, hunting.*

She climbed back in the Suburban and waited.

The dawn was blinding along the edges of the horizon, blazing gold, when Detrick's girlfriend came out the door and began piling items into his Envision. Caitlin had her name now: Emma Lane. Her little girl, Ashley, soon followed.

Caitlin rubbed her eyes and rolled her neck.

Detrick came out wearing jeans and a ski jacket. A computer case was slung over his shoulder. He was pulling a black roller suitcase.

Caitlin sat up straight. "Well, well."

Detrick pointedly ignored her as he helped the little girl into the SUV. He swung the suitcase into the back of the Envision with an ostentatious flare. When he drove away, Caitlin was right behind. It didn't take long to confirm his destination.

She punched in Emmerich's number.

He picked up on the first ring. "Time to fish or cut bait. What do you have?"

"Detrick's heading to the airport."

"How interesting."

"I'll keep you posted."

Austin's airport was ten miles east of downtown on the wide green prairie near the Circuit of the Americas racetrack, where Formula 1 held the US Grand Prix. The airport's main terminal was buzzing, packed with traffic and travelers lined up at curbside check-in.

Detrick turned into long-term parking. Caitlin watched to make sure he didn't pull a fast one and drive straight out the exit. She was standing on the sidewalk outside American Airlines Departures when the parking shuttle drove up and disgorged Detrick, Emma, and Ashley. He offered a glare of studied disgust, then ignored her.

"This seems unusually spontaneous," Caitlin said.

He walked past her. Emma trailed him, shoulders hunched, head dipped, eyeing Caitlin from under her bangs.

"Where you off to?" Caitlin said.

Detrick kept going. The automatic sliding doors opened.

"What's the occasion?"

The little girl, Ashley, was pulling a kid-size roller suitcase, hot pink, covered with rainbows and fairies. Sadie Rawlins would have loved it. The little girl stared up at Caitlin, her head swiveling as she passed.

"Who's that lady?" she said.

Emma grabbed her daughter's hand. "Nobody."

She pulled Ashley close, but that only made the girl eye Caitlin with greater curiosity.

"She was outside Kyle's house too," Ashley said.

Detrick said, "She's not a nice person. Ignore her."

That was interesting. Caitlin followed them into the terminal, feeling like a hornet that had just been swatted at. Noise echoed off the cavernous ceiling. Detrick strode directly to security, where the line snaked like the Matterhorn's at Disneyland.

Caitlin let him get in the queue, and stepped close to the crowd-control barrier.

"Leaving me, Kyle?"

He exhaled with deliberate exasperation and stopped. His expression mixed disdain and weary righteousness.

"I'm taking the people most important to me on vacation." His eyes were flat. "To escape FBI harassment."

The line moved. His boarding pass was in his hand. Caitlin stepped back and he put an arm around Emma's shoulders, nudging her forward.

"Enjoy it," Caitlin said.

She backed away to the front windows of the terminal. A few minutes later, Detrick cleared security. Just before he disappeared with Emma and Ashley into the airside crush of the terminal, he turned and looked directly at her. He took his time. He raised his hand, and smiled, and waved good-bye.

Caitlin's pulse felt thready. "See you, Kyle."

33

Outside the motel room window, the view was hushed. Flagstaff, Arizona, had pathetically anemic nightlife. It sat at the intersection of I-40 and I-17 in the mountainous north of this mostly empty state. It had pine forests and a college and highways that led to the Grand Canyon eighty miles farther north. Which meant it had scattered winter tourists and half-empty tourist bars and cheap motels. Like the one where he was ensconced after a week of sightseeing with Emma and Ashley. Five days of driving around picking up colorful rocks and staring at massive holes in the ground.

It was Saturday night.

Detrick stood at the window. One table lamp was on in the room, low, casting shadows. The street outside was quiet. Snow swirled beneath the streetlights.

Behind him, Emma checked on her sleeping daughter. Ashley looked like a comatose monkey. Kids, it seemed, could be paying attention to you one second, then be limp and gone the next. Lights out. She wouldn't stir for the rest of the night.

Emma approached his side. She whispered, "Shall we watch TV?"

He scanned the street. Saw no prowling cop cars. No suspicious pedestrians, no FBI vans disguised as utility trucks. They were registered at the motel under Emma's name.

Emma stepped closer. "It was a lovely day, Kyle."

She folded her hands. She knew not to touch him unless he invited her to. But she was close. Pressing.

"This trouble's going to go away," she said. "Everything's going to be okay."

At the far end of the street was a bar. Its neon sign blinked red through the falling snow. Women went in and out.

He sensed Emma, breathing on him. Everything was pressing. His need felt overpowering.

He licked his lips. "I'm gonna get a drink."

"But . . ."

He turned his head to stare at her. She took a step back.

He centered himself. She was so amenable, Emma. So caring and grateful and unquestioning. She trusted him. She was normal. That was what normal women did: trusted. It always made him glad to have her at his side. She wasn't a showstopper, but her thorough devotion was what the women at church called a blessing. That's what he was: blessed.

He closed the curtains and softened his voice. "One drink."

For a second, she held on to something—resentment, maybe. That was unacceptable.

"I've had a horrendous time since this crap with the FBI began. It's ridiculous. Somebody started a rumor about me. Somebody's trying to wreck my life. And I'm going to get to the bottom of it. But right now, I need a few minutes to blow off some steam."

She sagged, but softened. "I know."

"I'll bring you back something. Pie."

Her smile was less reluctant now. "Cherry."

"Atta girl." He pulled on his ski parka. "Don't wait up."

He went out the front door of the motel. The Roundup, the place was called. A giant cowboy on the sign out front, twirling a lariat over his head. It beckoned, *Welcome, rubes.*

He sauntered down the street. Spotty late-night traffic eked its way through the falling snow. He strolled to the end of the street, toward the red neon sign outside the bar, and pushed through a rough wooden door.

Inside, it was humid and hot with bodies and the smell of beer and overamplified classic rock from a band crammed in the corner. Detrick worked his way through the packed room, checking out women. At the bar he ordered a Coors and drank it, eyeing the crowd in the mirror. When the beer was gone, he strolled down a back hall, toward the men's room. The mindless chatter and off-key guitar solo faded.

The hall was empty. He passed the men's room and ducked out the rear door into an alley.

The cold bit him, bright and invigorating. Sticking to dark side streets, he doubled back to the parking lot at the Roundup.

A minute later he was rolling up the highway into the mountains.

The rustic town of Crying Call was twenty miles north. This was where low-budget travelers, backpackers, mountain bikers, and college students on weekend getaways stayed. It was at seventy-two-hundred-feet elevation—high enough to cause even the fittest athletes to grab for breath when they first arrived. But he'd been at elevation all week long. His bloodstream was packed with oxygen now. It was coursing with strength.

Detrick parked in an unlit lot with a good view of a busy tavern. Muffled music throbbed from inside it.

The snow was coming down thicker here, fat and slow, softening the street. The view was white. Virgin. He turned off the engine and killed the headlights and sat in the dark, breathing.

He sat for half an hour, scanning all four directions. He saw no sign that he had been followed. He sat for another twenty minutes.

A young woman stepped out the tavern door into the frosty air.

She was slim, ethereal, with beautiful long blond hair. And she was alone.

She paused on the sidewalk to dig through her purse, swaying like she was tipsy. Detrick zipped his parka. On the passenger seat was a cowboy hat he'd bought that morning at a Flagstaff tourist shop. He put it on and got out.

Snow stung his face. The street was deserted. Nobody was tailing him here. Nobody was holding him back, blowing his chance, keeping him away from Madison Mays, *ruining* everything.

The hat was black, matching his parka, contrasting with the snow. He crossed the street toward the tavern. Ahead, the blond ducked her head and sauntered along the sidewalk in his direction.

Detrick pulled the hat low on his forehead and checked the shadows. Down a cross street he heard a dog and saw a parked pickup truck. Everything was dark.

There was no traffic, no spying eyes. *Now.*

He cried out and went down on his knees.

The woman tented a hand over her eyes. "Are you okay?"

He struggled to rise. "Fine . . ." He slid to the sidewalk.

The woman rushed up. She wasn't as young as he'd first thought, but still late twenties. Her cheeks were red with the cold. Her jeans were tight. She had that cheerleader body. The snow was clinging to her blond hair, creating a halo.

He looked up at her with wide eyes. "Apologies. Prosthetic leg. Doesn't work great on icy sidewalks."

"Omigosh. Let me help you up." She crouched at his side. Her hand went to his elbow. Steadying him, she tried to help him get his weight underneath him.

He offered a rueful smile, slowly getting to one knee, using his free hand to brace the leg that had seemingly given out. "Almost there."

Her eyes were wide with concern and curiosity. "Was it an accident?"

He'd had no excuse to bring his crutches on this

vacation. Not like in Dallas, or on the college quad where the girl had stepped out of her dorm. So tonight, he had to boost the pity angle.

Levering himself awkwardly upright, he gripped her shoulder and held on like he might topple again. "Afghanistan."

"Oh." Her face went sad. "Thank you for your service."

She put a hand to his chest to help him balance, then let him wrap an arm over her shoulders. Leaning heavily on her, limping, he nodded at the dark parking lot.

"I'm over there."

The altitude, and the effort it had taken for a disabled war vet to stand up, could easily explain his hard breathing. The snow, the street, the night, all pulsed in his vision. His rich, hungry blood was pounding in his heart, his temples, his hands, ready inside his gloves. Even through their thick coats, the girl felt supple underneath his arm. She steadied him as they crossed the street.

Now, he thought. *Now now now, finally oh yes, always, now.*

They approached the car. He unzipped his ski jacket and reached inside.

On the cross street, a truck door creaked open. "*Freeze.*"

Detrick spun, shocked. From the snowy dark a figure jumped out of the parked pickup and charged at him, watch cap pulled low, parka half zipped.

Gun in her hand.

"FBI. Don't move."

Caitlin materialized, face fierce under the neon tavern light, weapon raised.

Detrick didn't move. He couldn't. Couldn't think, couldn't breathe. He glared.

The sneaky bitch.

His tongue loosened. "You are fucking kidding me."

Caitlin walked toward him, side on, that gun in her hand steady and level. It was an infuriatingly arousing sight.

Unforgivable bitch.

"You can't be serious," he said, louder. "I step out for a drink and this is your response?"

"Both hands behind your head," Caitlin said.

He shook his head. Then. Then . . .

The blond swiveled out from under his arm and twisted his hand behind his back.

34

Caitlin walked toward Detrick across the parking lot, Glock leveled, blading her body to reduce her target profile. Under the tavern sign, the falling snow flared into shards of light. Detrick had frozen, half twisted, shoulders canted, gargoyle-like. His eyes were in shadow beneath the brim of a black cowboy hat, but his mouth, fighting to form a smile, instead looked like a rictus.

At his side, Special Agent Arinda Sayers spun neatly from beneath his grip. Hand on his right wrist, she twisted his arm behind his back and pushed him against the snow-dappled side of his rental car.

He hit the chassis with a metallic *thunk*. Under his breath he muttered, "*Shit*."

Sayers, an FBI agent from the Flagstaff Resident Agency, kicked Detrick's feet into a shoulder-wide stance.

"You double-teamed me?" he said.

A curse escaped his mouth. He was figuring it out.

"What'd you do, put a GPS tracker on my rental car before I even picked it up at the airport?" he said.

The shock was bright in his gray eyes. That was precisely what she'd done—twice. Because he had figured that the FBI might do exactly that, and tried to outsmart them by requesting a last-second upgrade at the airport car rental counter. But she had warned the rental company to expect that ploy, and managed to get the tracker on the replacement car.

He craned his neck to get a look at Agent Sayers. Her blond wig was askew, falling over one eye. She pulled it off. Detrick spat, *fuck*.

Caitlin's pulse was thundering. Despite the snow and the blistering cold, she felt hot, all the way to her fingertips. She pulled her handcuffs from beneath her parka and snapped them around his wrists.

Sayers raised her wrist to her face and spoke into a radio. "Suspect is in custody."

"What the hell?" Detrick said.

He was breathing hard. Then, like he was shutting off a floodgate, he exhaled and seemed to spin down. The rage left his voice.

"This is a misunderstanding," he said. "I'm hurt. You"—he nodded at Sayers—"you lied to me."

"How's that?" Sayers pressed her forearm against the back of his neck, holding him against the car.

"You pretended to be drunk. You pretended . . ."

When his voice trailed off, Sayers didn't fill in the rest. *You pretended to believe me.*

Down the street came two police cruisers, lights flashing.

"Which leg is prosthetic?" Sayers said.

"Come on, can't you take a little hyperbole in the name of romance?" he said.

"Which branch of the military did you serve in? What was your unit in Afghanistan?"

"Nobody could have taken that seriously."

Caitlin holstered her gun. Her adrenaline was jacking. Everything seemed sharp-edged and bright.

Detrick had not only been caught in the act—he was confessing to the ruse. She couldn't help thinking of Aaron Gage, an actual combat veteran, carrying on strong after suffering catastrophic injuries. She swallowed the acidic taste in her mouth and dug through Detrick's jeans pockets. She unzipped his ski jacket and pulled it open.

"Huh," she said.

In an interior slash pocket was the item that had caused the metallic *thunk* when Sayers shoved him against the car. It was a tire iron.

The handcuffs Detrick was carrying were in an outside pocket. Caitlin held them up. They reflected in the police cruisers' spinning lights. Two officers got out and approached.

Detrick spat, "You have no idea what you're doing."

She hauled him upright. "I'm arresting you for attempted kidnapping."

She had him.

35

With flashing lights strobing red and blue across the road, Crying Call looked arc-lit and shadowed. From the tavern parking lot, the road led to the town square. A red stone courthouse stood on one side and, next to it, the police station and city jail. Caitlin followed the Crying Call police cars. In the headlights of her rented pickup truck, the rear of Detrick's head was brightly illuminated in the back-seat cage of the cruiser, behind the Lexan partition.

She felt triumphant and relieved—and chilled. Detrick's rental car was being loaded on a flatbed tow truck for transport to Impound. Inside it, she had found a DISABLED placard hanging from the rearview mirror. It would have been the final prop that convinced a real victim he was a wounded vet—a sign that led women to lower their guard and approach the vehicle that would spirit them to their deaths. The rental car's child safety locks were engaged. Once inside, a victim couldn't open the doors.

Quite a coup de grace.

But the DISABLED placard and child locks weren't all of it. She'd also found a handheld spotlight and a badge wallet with a toy detective's shield. Detrick had a backup ruse ready to go at the right moment.

She saw now how he must have taken Phoebe Canova from her car at the railroad crossing in Solace. Wait for the crossing barrier to swing down. Pull up behind Phoebe's car as a freight train passes, blocking any escape path. Aim the spotlight at her and walk toward the driver's side with his fake badge prominently displayed. When Phoebe lowered the window, ask her to step out of the car. And he had her.

Special Agent Sayers had stayed behind at the tavern parking lot, supervising the impounding of the car. The Flagstaff Resident Agency was contacting a judge who would issue a search warrant for Detrick's room at the Roundup Motel.

Caitlin's fingers tingled, chilled. Ahead, in the police cruiser, Detrick turned and squinted at her over his shoulder. The headlights turned his features cold.

At the jail, the Crying Call officer got out and opened the back door of the patrol car. Caitlin jogged over, her breath ghosting the freezing air.

"May I?" she said.

The officer stepped back and extended a hand. His expression was droll. "All yours, ma'am."

She beckoned Detrick with a small, dismissive wave. He wriggled out. She led him by the elbow into the police station, with the local officers following like her knights at arms. Detrick hunched into his parka, absorbing the atmosphere: the cold lighting, the scarred counter of the front desk, the cheap linoleum, the brick walls. The station had been built when this was a frontier town.

Still not much more than a frontier town now.

The desk clerk pointed down a hall. Caitlin led Detrick into the jail wing, through a door with a buzzing electronic lock. A desk sergeant waited on the other side.

"Process him," she said.

The FBI team arrived in Crying Call four hours later, after flying into Flagstaff on a Bureau jet. It was two A.M. when Emmerich walked through the door of the police station with Rainey. The Crying Call chief of police met them in the lobby, looking alert and grave. The attempted kidnapping was a state crime, not federal, so his department was in charge. But he had already formally invited the BAU to assist in the case against Detrick. He shook Emmerich's hand and gestured to the back of the station, which was twenty feet from the front.

Caitlin was waiting for them. Emmerich walked over to her. Behind his somber demeanor, his eyes were animated.

"Well done."

"Agent Sayers was a star," she said. "She deserves a lot of praise."

His suit was creased, his white shirt tired, but his gaze was sharp. "Noted."

She nodded. He stood there another second, and his expression seemed to fill with satisfaction. Maybe pride. He nodded back.

Energy flooded Caitlin's system. And relief.

The police chief, Hank Silver, led them to the station's Investigations section. It was the size of a single-wide trailer. Detrick had been taken to an interrogation room. The chief showed them a CCTV video feed.

Cuffed, isolated, Detrick looked antsy. He sat, his feet shackled to a ring in the floor, squirming in his seat.

"How'd he handle being booked?" Emmerich said.

"He acted like it was an insult," Silver said.

"Good."

"At first he was self-important about it. Couldn't believe he was being treated 'this way,'" the chief said. "Then he got angry. Didn't say anything, but looked like he was ready to blow. He's been cooling his heels in there since ten P.M."

"Has he said anything? Asked for a lawyer?"

"Nope."

Emmerich watched the video feed. "He will. Sooner rather than later. We need to talk to him before he gets himself together and decides that's the avenue he wants to take." His tone turned diplomatic. "We'd like to take the lead on interrogating him."

"All right with me," Silver said. "You've been after this guy and it's your show."

"Thank you."

Emmerich turned to the team. "He's stewed long enough. We should conduct the interrogation now."

Rainey was peering intently at the screen. "Teri Drinkall."

Chief Silver said, "Excuse me?"

"She's the woman missing from the Dallas parking garage. It's been two weeks since she disappeared but we know he kept at least one victim alive that long. We have to find out if Teri is still alive."

"You think he'll tell you?"

"We can work on it. The police searched his house in Austin tonight, but it's been sterilized."

Emmerich looked grave. "The odds are slim, but not zero. For any chance to save Ms. Drinkall, we need Detrick to talk."

The Investigations office was chilly, the furniture nicked and cheap. Emmerich crossed his arms.

"Strategy?" he said. "Suggestions for how we approach it?"

Rainey had dark rings beneath her eyes but was straight-backed and thrumming with energy. "You should lead the interrogation."

"Because?"

"Detrick's a narcissist who'll want to impress the guy running the show. His personality is organized around gaining and maintaining power," she said. "Omnipotent control is the source of all his pleasure and pain. He'll want Special Agent in *Charge* Emmerich to admire his audacity."

"Agreed." Emmerich considered it. "He sees himself as a master of all games. He's going to want to talk to authority figures as if we're on the same plane. If I can convince him we're working this investigation with him, collegially—all in it together, if not exactly from the same perspective—he may talk to me like I'm a colleague."

The chief shook his head. "You gotta be kidding."

"I've seen it happen more than once. We give him some time, convince him we're as fascinated by these murders as he is, and he may break down and discuss the case in detail."

"Like Rader," Rainey said. To Silver, she added, "Dennis Rader, the BTK killer—when he was finally captured, he confessed to the arresting officers at length. He said he'd always envisioned that if he were apprehended, he would sit down with the lead detective over a cup of coffee and discuss the case."

"I take it he was mistaken," Silver said.

"As he discovered after confessing to ten murders."

Caitlin had her hands jammed in her pockets. Detrick wasn't Rader. Detrick knew he'd been a suspect and thought he'd outwitted them. Emmerich's idea was good, but Detrick would be tough to wear down.

Emmerich turned back to the video feed. "Detrick believes implicitly in his ability to manipulate women. I want to turn that against him." He looked up. "Hendrix. You come with me."

Caitlin couldn't hide her surprise. This was an opportunity. Something she wanted. And she wanted to hear Emmerich's reasoning.

"Sir?"

"Rainey's older than Detrick," he said.

Rainey raised an eyebrow, wanting to see where he was going.

He turned to her and spread his hands, softening his words. "And we don't know enough about his relationship with his mother to tell whether he'd regard you as a Madonna or Mommy Dearest."

"Fair point," Rainey said.

"But he's attracted to Caitlin." Emmerich paused, staring at her frankly.

They all stared at her. Strangely, she didn't feel awkward.

"You can use that to turn the tables on him," Emmerich said.

Caitlin thought about it. "So, to him, am I a virgin or a whore?"

"Maybe Sleeping Beauty. See which way he jumps and trip him up."

They headed down the hall. The interrogation room door had a laminated sign that read NO WEAPONS. Chief Silver peered through a peephole and unlocked the door with his jangling key ring. Giving Emmerich a sober nod, he opened it.

Caitlin and Emmerich entered. The chief followed.

At a particleboard table, Kyle Detrick sat on a tired plastic chair. His eyes were rimed with fatigue. His stylish ski fleece smelled of sweat. Under the buzzing fluorescent lights, his looks were darker, deeper edged.

Emmerich dropped a brown FBI file folder on the table. The walls in the small room deadened the sound.

He turned to Silver. "I don't think we need the handcuffs."

The chief ran his tongue around the inside of his cheek.

Across the chipped table, Detrick raised his chin. He seemed assured and self-satisfied.

Silver looked like he really, truly wanted to punch him in the nuts. "Not when he's so outnumbered. Hold out your hands."

Detrick raised his wrists and the chief uncuffed him.

"Knock when you're done." Silver left, closing the door. It locked with a rough click.

Detrick stretched his fingers and rubbed his wrists. Emmerich took off his suit jacket, draped it over the back of a chair, and rolled up his shirtsleeves.

"Getting an FBI team to a mountain town in the middle of the night—you managed quite a feat, Mr. Detrick."

Emmerich sat. Caitlin took the chair next to him. Detrick refused to look at her.

Emmerich rested his hands on top of the file folder. The FBI seal was prominent. "You know why you're here?"

Detrick leaned back in the chair. He couldn't move far—though his hands were free, his feet were still shackled to the ring in the floor. "Somebody's got a hard-on for me."

He smiled and tilted his head at Caitlin, coyly.

"Why do you think that is?" Emmerich said.

"I'm insulted—and not a little shocked—at the way I've been treated. They actually call it being 'processed.' Like I'm a bull being led to the slaughter. Photographed, fingerprinted—and that cotton swab they ran around the inside of my cheek."

Emmerich remained impassive. "That's to gather saliva and epithelial cells for a DNA sample."

"We all watch *CSI*," Detrick said.

But hearing that his DNA was going to be analyzed seemed to set him on edge. His eyes took on a wary cast. Caitlin thought: *He doesn't know for certain whether he left DNA at any of the crime scenes.*

Emmerich pulled a sheet of paper from the file folder. The arrest report.

"Tire iron, handcuffs . . ."

Detrick shifted. His glib smile returned. "It was late. I flew in and couldn't legally bring a firearm on the plane."

"You normally carry a firearm?" Emmerich said.

"No. My point is, I don't know whether to be more amused or outraged that she actually arrested me for pulling a joke."

"Wounded vet?"

"Is that what the bait agent told you?"

"'Bait'?"

"The fake blond. The lure. You know—what predators use to entrap you."

"You had a weapon on your person, and restraints. You were carrying a kidnap kit."

Detrick shook his head, looking disgusted. "It's a game."

"The DISABLED placard?"

Detrick shrugged. "Chicks dig guys with a limp. No law against plumage."

"You a peacock?" Emmerich said.

"What can I tell you?"

"The child locks in the car were enabled."

"I came on vacation with a six-year-old." He spread his hands like, *Duh*.

"We'll be talking to Emma," Emmerich said. "What did you plan to do with the young woman you were leading to your car?"

"I wasn't leading her anywhere. We were going to party."

Emmerich nodded, as though digesting that. "Why do you think we came to be interested in you to begin with?"

"No idea."

Emmerich's expression was one of concern and curiosity. "Really?"

Detrick paused, gauging Emmerich's sincerity. "Somebody doesn't like me. That's all I can think. Professional envy, maybe someone I outmaneuvered on a deal."

"Who might that be?"

"Could be anybody."

He glared at Caitlin. She returned the look.

Detrick turned back to Emmerich. "You guys are really over the top, you know."

"We're the FBI," Emmerich said.

"I've done nothing illegal," Detrick said. "You have to see that. I come up here to get away for a while, bring the girlfriend and her kid, but you know, after a week, all she wants to do is watch Disney and sip lemonade. I've been cooped up. I just wanted to blow off some steam." His smile returned. "You understand that, right?"

Buddying up to Emmerich: Caitlin had to admit surprise that the profile fit Detrick so well.

"You wanted to paint the town red," Emmerich said.

Detrick shrugged and gave a little-boy smile. "Saturday night. You can't blame a guy for trying."

Caitlin leaned back, thinking, *Is that what you said to Teri Drinkall right before you clubbed her in the head?*

Detrick sighed and finally looked at her. "I don't mean to sound facetious. But come on."

She tilted her head, as though perplexed and even regretful. "You think I've been too tough with you?"

"You're a wildcat."

She didn't react.

He took it as encouragement. "You're a player, I get that now. Whoever put you on to me, they have some ulterior motive. And I can even see how you'd be ethically obligated to follow up. But my God, under that gun belt, you're a demon."

Heat filled her chest. It was half shock, half excitement. He thought he could get to her with insults that had an undertone of sexual come-on.

"These charges are bogus," he said. "You know that. I see that you want me to sit here and sweat it, but we both know we're doing a dance. Right?"

"What kind of dance do you think you're doing?"

She let soft curiosity color her expression. He was

trying to beguile her into dropping the charges. He truly thought he could wing this and woo her.

She'd seen men attempt this strategy before: frat boys she pulled over for speeding; drunks on a park bench who thought that slurring, "Hey, baby," would convince her and other runners to give them a kiss. But she'd never seen it from a man facing felony charges.

Detrick gave her a Don Juan smile.

His sexual attraction to her was so overt, and his smile so confident and hungry, that a cold feeling of doom descended on her. She saw his instinct to manipulate and toy with people. She saw how he'd used it in the hotline call she'd made. Her stomach hollowed.

Emmerich flipped through the case file. "You know this is about more than attempted kidnapping."

Detrick leaned back and ran a hand through his dark hair. "I know that's what you think."

Emmerich read a note in the file. "Teri Drinkall. Where is she?"

"No idea who that is."

Emmerich looked up. "Please."

Kyle raised his hands, like *You got me*. "I'm not going to admit to anything. You know that."

"Six women, six disappearances. So slick, so smooth. It took exquisite planning." Emmerich pondered it. "I do admit, these crimes took daring."

Detrick's eyes flashed. "Whoever's doing it is a prodigy."

Emmerich nodded pensively. His long pause signaled Caitlin to take the lead.

She waited a moment. She needed Detrick to think he

had the upper hand on her. He wanted to see himself as Emmerich's equal but would want to squash her—in front of her boss.

Quietly, thoughtfully, she asked him, "So who do you think did it?"

Detrick scoffed. "You want my opinion?"

"I do."

"You've played dirty with me from the beginning. And now you want my help?"

"You studied psychology. You're trained to talk people through their most extreme, darkest moments—including people who threaten violence. Yeah, I think you can supply insights into the killer's mind."

He eyed her skeptically.

Caitlin said, "The white nightgowns. What do they symbolize?"

Detrick didn't move, but his attention zeroed in on her. His voice quieted, as hers had.

"You want me to say the white symbolizes purity?"

She held his stare. He breathed in, and out.

"That's not what this guy is about," he said.

Her pulse ticked up.

"Study the psychology of fairy tales," Detrick said. "The Maiden represents innocence, yes—but also naïveté. Which gets her into trouble."

"Snow White eating the poisoned apple."

"They fall for it every time."

Caitlin heard, *They brought it on themselves.* "But the Maiden also represents desire. That's why the hero is out to rescue her." She leaned in. "Tell me about the suicide hotline."

He eyed her up and down. The warmth returned to his voice. It went beyond seductive to heart grabbing.

"You came close, didn't you?" he said.

For a terrible second, she thought he knew she had phoned him on the crisis hotline. She fought to keep her face blank. But she knew that microexpressions couldn't be hidden.

Then she realized something worse: Detrick didn't know she had called the hotline. He had no idea. He didn't recognize her voice from the call; he wasn't fishing to get her to confess.

He had intuitively found her vulnerability.

She couldn't expose her soft underbelly to Detrick. He'd already glimpsed it—she had to stay opaque. She tried to close herself off. She feared that if she spoke, the slightest quaver in her voice would give him another opening. But she couldn't sit there like a ball of putty. And she couldn't let Emmerich think she had something to hide, which she damn well did.

"You mean I came close to playing the Maiden?" she said.

"No. You've been fixated on my volunteer work since I first mentioned it. As if offering a hand to people who are drowning is something to be suspicious of," Detrick said. "That fascinates me."

"Really?"

She wanted to reel out the line, to let him grab the

hook. But she was seeing exactly how deft he was at creeping past emotional defenses. He was probing, trying to get her story out of her, seeking soft spots, trying to sink the hook into her instead.

"My pastor is the one who urges his congregation to volunteer with the needy," he said. "It's fortunate that my background in psychology made me the right person for the hotline job."

"The suicidal ideation in the Solace murders has disturbing echoes for me," she said.

"What's your story?"

"The Polaroids of the killer's other victims indicate he's possessed by fantasies of suicide. What do you make of that?"

"Your cheeks are flushed," he said.

"Do you think the people who call the hotline are naive?" she said.

"You wouldn't have used a firearm. You're a tough chick, but that's too messy even for you," he said.

"What do you say to women who are in pain?"

"Pills, maybe."

Power. That was it. That was what he loved. She could see it—the brightness in his gray eyes, the way he licked his lips, the color in his handsome face—power was what made him *feel*. He could pull people to safety or kick them into the abyss with a sharply worded response. He held them in his hands. Exhilaration and rage. Hero and destroyer. He was both. He was God.

He leaned forward on his elbows. "It was bad, wasn't it?"

"Is this how you treat hotline callers—you pepper them with accusations? Do you actually know anything about young women's emotional lives?" She tried to look thoughtful. "As a crisis hotline volunteer, you're supposed to be good at listening. But do you have any clue how to discern real despair from a passing bout of the blues?" she said. "You think you can dig out my darkest secrets? You want me to say I thought about ending my own life? Way back when, after a breakup, crying in my dorm room, listening to Death Cab for Cutie?" She managed to smile. "Once upon a time, I was sad. I cheered up."

He steepled his fingers. "The pull never goes away. Ever."

She kept a poker face. The heat in her chest had turned caustic.

Detrick didn't want to help the anguished people who called the hotline. He wanted to control them.

Quietly, he said, "I know nothing about the killer's victims. But the way you're talking, they never saw it coming."

Liar. She wanted to shout it at him.

He knew. They all saw it coming, if only for a fraction of a second. That was what he wanted, above all else.

"No," she said. "They saw themselves betrayed. You stole their lives from them."

"That's your fairy tale." Detrick leaned back, smiling with satisfaction. "I want a lawyer."

That was the falling blade. After a moment, Emmerich and Caitlin stood.

Detrick leaned toward her again, smiling darkly. "I'm going to leave this place a free man. I'm going to waltz out of here with a smile and a wave, and you're going to have to swallow it."

36

Crying Call was the county seat, and Monday morning the county courthouse on the town square dominated a piercing blue sky, red brick against the blinding white snow on the surrounding mountains. Caitlin and her colleagues walked in at ten forty-five for Detrick's arraignment.

Caitlin was buzzing with an adrenaline hangover from his arrest and interrogation. She jogged up the courthouse steps ahead of Emmerich and Rainey and pulled the door open as if she wanted to Hulk-rip it from its hinges.

"Know you're still angry about how Detrick ended the interview," Rainey said, "but cool your jets."

They headed inside. Caitlin shot her a look. "He toyed with us."

"He's in jail, and we're about to watch him enter a plea, then be hauled straight back to a cell. This is a win."

"True," Caitlin said, less sharply.

They walked briskly along the hall toward the courtroom. Their heels clacked on the polished tile floor.

"It would be great to see him hauled back to his cell

with a cattle prod up his ass." Caitlin instantly raised a hand. "I'm joking."

"No, you're not." But Rainey's glance was amused. "You did okay, interrogating him."

"He admitted nothing."

"Didn't he?" Emmerich said.

When Detrick had asked for a lawyer, they'd left the interview room. Emmerich had maintained a Zen calm. *First move in a long game,* he'd said. *Good job.* But Caitlin had been fuming. More than a day later, she still was. Impatience was a flaw of hers.

Chill. Out, she thought.

She knew intellectually that the interrogation had been productive. That wasn't what was eating at her.

Detrick's smile seemed to follow her everywhere, even when she shut her eyes. And he *knew.* He sensed that she'd nearly committed suicide all those years ago. Sensed that it was her greatest fear. He was waiting for her to come back to him, to discuss it, to let him lure her into the longing, the desire, the heavy cloak of depression, and the desire to *end it.*

She spoke through gritted teeth. "He forces young women to die watching their blood run from their own veins. He uses them as surrogates for whoever twisted him to begin with. It revolts me."

Rainey said, "Focus on the how. Don't try to figure out the *why.* You won't cure him or stop others from becoming him."

"I know."

Emmerich smoothed his tie. "We're here to see that he stays behind bars. We want our presence to add weight to the prosecutor's request for maximum bail."

They rounded a corner. Morning light fell through a tall window at the end of the hallway, stinging their eyes. The courtroom doors were ahead.

Emmerich slowed. "Caitlin? A minute, please." He told Rainey, "We'll be right in."

Rainey nodded curtly and headed down the hall. Emmerich stepped to the window. Caitlin thought, *Uh-oh*.

He kept his expression neutral. "You'd better tell me everything."

The poker face didn't work with Emmerich. She knew her cheeks had flushed a deep red.

"It's old news. Not an issue. I . . ."

"Not right this minute. But Detrick managed to get under your skin. When we have more time, I need to know what pushed your buttons. So you can strategize a way to deflect him."

"Yes, sir."

He held her gaze a second. She nodded tightly. After a freighted pause, he headed toward the courtroom.

He held the heavy wooden door for her. Inside, the room was full. They took seats on pew-style benches beside Rainey and Special Agent Arinda Sayers, who had driven in from Flagstaff.

Reporters filled the back half of the public gallery. A public defender sat at the defense table with a stack of files a foot tall. The county criminal attorney—the prosecutor—entered, hauling a heavy briefcase. He was tan and looked like he spent his off hours tossing hay bales from the back of a pickup truck. He shook hands with the police officers in the room, then with the FBI group. The court reporter entered.

The clerk came in from the judge's chambers and said, "All rise."

They stood and the judge entered, his robe flaring, his face a flatiron as he surveyed the packed room. They sat.

The doors opened and the morning's prisoners were brought in. The crowd stirred. The prisoners were shackled together, dressed in baggy orange. They shuffled up the aisle, escorted by uniformed sheriff's deputies.

People rose in their seats. Reporters scribbled. An artist began frantically sketching.

Kyle Detrick walked in the center of the hobbling line like a playboy prince stuck boarding economy on a long-haul flight. His shoulders were thrown back, his cuffed hands loosely clasped in front of him. He looked world-weary and above it all.

Women in the gallery, and a few men, put their heads together, murmuring excitedly. Caitlin heard someone whisper, "Omigod, he's gorgeous."

The judge cracked his gavel. "Quiet in the court. We will have no eruptions, no commentary, no talk from the gallery. Or you'll be ejected."

The women behind Caitlin quieted down, but she still heard them squirming on the bench, straining to get a good look at Detrick.

This was going to be a circus.

◆ ◆ ◆

Detrick's moment in the spotlight took two minutes. His name was called. The bailiff unshackled him from the chained prisoners. He sauntered through the gate, took a contemptuous look at his young public defender, and stood at the defense table like a prophet beleaguered by petty fools.

The clerk read his case number. The judge asked if he was ready to enter a plea. Detrick raised his chin and said, slowly and firmly: "Completely. Thoroughly. Not. Guilty."

Titters and hubbub. Rainey muttered, "Lord have mercy, he thinks he's O.J." The judge smacked his gavel again.

The prosecutor asked for maximum bail. The court-appointed defense attorney got nowhere arguing against it. Detrick lowered his head, shaking it sadly. Caitlin wondered why he hadn't hired his own attorney. Insufficient funds? Or did he think this was a game and that his lawyer didn't matter?

She glanced around. She didn't see Emma Lane in the gallery. But she saw more clearly the other wide-eyed women in attendance. She saw their fascination and excitement and adjusted her opinion. Detrick's arrest wasn't going to be a circus. It was going to be a spectacle.

The judge bound him over for a preliminary hearing.

The bailiff approached, took his elbow, and led him from the defense table back to the chain gang. At that point, Detrick got a panoramic view of the crowd. The women, the reporters, the heat, the barely contained frenzy.

He managed to keep his face flat, but his posture seemed to shift. From Caitlin's seat, he looked like he actually grew taller.

His gaze landed on her. She couldn't read it. But she felt the chill emanating from him, like she'd been dumped in a snowbank.

The bailiff sat him down and shackled him. Emmerich stood. He led the other agents from the courtroom.

A TV crew was waiting in the hallway. Caitlin stutter-stepped, caught off guard, but Emmerich forged ahead. When a national correspondent put a mic in his face, Emmerich said, "The Crying Call Police Department will have a statement for you soon."

Caitlin followed him out of the courthouse to a Bureau SUV. When they got in, she let out an audible breath.

Emmerich said, "Buckle up. It's only starting."

37

Emmerich and Rainey flew back to Virginia Monday afternoon, while Caitlin stayed an extra day to confer with the Crying Call police and the prosecutor's office. In Flagstaff, Special Agent Sayers executed a search warrant on Detrick's motel room and tried to interview Emma Lane. She found nothing probative in the room. Emma refused to talk.

Tuesday morning Caitlin drove to Phoenix to catch her flight to Washington. She planned to return to Arizona in just under two weeks' time for Detrick's preliminary hearing.

The day was crystalline. On the way to the Phoenix airport, she detoured to the offices of Crandall McGill.

She found Lia Fox behind the front desk, her inch-short hair the black of a broken television screen.

Lia nearly jumped from her chair. "I left you messages. You've been in Crying Call. Jesus. What the hell."

"I wanted to speak to you in person," Caitlin said.

Lia glanced past Caitlin's shoulder at the parking lot outside. "Did you come alone? Were you followed?"

"By whom?"

"Anybody. His friends. The media."

Caitlin couldn't believe that Lia was always this stunned and jumpy. Even on Wall Street trading floors where brokers ran on cocaine, nobody was this stunned and jumpy.

"Nobody followed me. I came to thank you."

"Thank me?" Lia spoke in a stage whisper. "I asked you to keep my identity confidential."

"I have."

Lia's eye twitched.

Caitlin had been certain, the first time she spoke to her, that Lia was withholding something. This wasn't dissuading her.

She softened her expression. Gently, she said, "I'm here to express my appreciation. Your information was vital in allowing us to arrest Kyle Detrick. But I'm concerned— something's upsetting you. Detrick is behind bars. That should reassure you, but it's not. Please, tell me."

Lia pressed her lips tight. Her eyes were as dark as her hair, pupils wide. Looking at them was like staring into nothing. She scanned the parking lot again and nodded Caitlin into a break room.

She shut the door and crossed her arms. "What the hell happened after I phoned you in Texas? I gave you Aaron's name but Kyle's the one locked up in Crying Call?"

Caitlin sat at a table and pulled out a chair for Lia. "Have a seat."

Lia dropped onto the chair. "You're positive it's Kyle Detrick. It's not Aaron."

"One hundred percent. It couldn't be Aaron."

She told her what had happened to Gage in Afghanistan. Lia put a hand over her mouth.

"But Kyle . . ."

"I arrested him," Caitlin said, "in the act of attempting to kidnap a woman."

"Oh my God."

Caitlin filled in the details. Lia listened, lips parted, shaking her head.

"You didn't tell Aaron the name I use now. Tell me you didn't. Or Kyle."

"No. Detrick doesn't know you've been in contact with the FBI," Caitlin said. "Can I ask why you never called the police about the stalking? The real reason, I mean. I don't care what you did. I just want to fill in the blanks."

Lia hung on for a few seconds, shoulders hunched. Then seemed to decide: *Screw it.*

"I lived with some older students. We ran a dispensary from our apartment."

Caitlin nodded slowly. "Weed? Adderall?"

"And Xanax."

Recreational pharmacy—yep, that would keep somebody from asking the cops to come around. "Why did you change your name?"

"After the fire, and the breakup, I quit Rampart and left Houston. My whole college experience was a mess. I wanted a fresh start. And I wanted to get the hell away from Aaron."

Caitlin nodded encouragingly.

"I stopped going by Dahlia. Or Dahli. That kind of became a sick nickname. I didn't want to hear it ever again," she said. "Fox—that's a name I took years later, when I got married."

Caitlin glanced at her ring finger.

"We lasted eighteen months. But I hung on to the name." She shrugged.

Caitlin nudged her further. "Something else is upsetting you."

Lia's foot began to jitter. She shut her eyes and shook her head tightly. From the hallway, voices approached. Lia jumped up and locked the door. The knob rattled.

She said: "Cleaning crew. Come back later."

Caitlin stood and walked over to her. "What is it?"

Lia shook her head.

"If you're frightened, let me help you," Caitlin said.

Lia returned to the table and flopped back in the chair. Caitlin sat down beside her, took her hand, and squeezed.

Lia nodded. "It's just—everything's getting turned inside out."

Caitlin held tight to her hand. "Please, just tell me."

"Off the record. None of this can go in your report," she said. "Fine. I cheated on Aaron with Kyle."

Caitlin kept her expression compassionate. Thinking: *Well, that's a big nasty surprise for Lia at this point.*

"I'm rethinking everything. That night." Lia's black eyes stared at Caitlin. "I don't think Aaron caused the fire. I think he passed out. I think Kyle set it."

"Why?"

It was a puzzle piece that slotted squarely into the profile of a psychopathic sexual sadist, and it felt intuitively right to Caitlin, but she needed to hear Lia's explanation.

"Kyle's the one who woke me up and got me out of the apartment." Her expression was one of curdled horror. "I think he was trying to kill Aaron and 'rescue' me."

Hero and destroyer.

Caitlin held on to Lia's hand. Lia cast her gaze at the floor.

"He did it to win me back," she said.

"The fire happened *after* you slept with Detrick?"

Lia tipped her head back. "Stupid. Sleeping with him was stupid."

"After the apartment burned, you broke up with Aaron but didn't accept Kyle's advances again."

Lia looked at her. "Exactly."

A clearer image of the college disaster took form in Caitlin's mind. Lia had cheated on Aaron Gage with his handsome, clean-cut roommate, Kyle Detrick. But she'd broken that off.

So Detrick set a blaze and led Lia to safety. Aaron Gage had been lucky to rouse himself and get out, instead of dying in the fire. Aaron would have been collateral damage, not the target, but he would have been just as dead. But being rescued by Sir Kyle hadn't rekindled Lia's desire for Detrick. Instead, he suffered her fresh rejection.

Lia scratched at her arms. "I think Kyle might be the one who harassed me afterward."

"I think that's a legitimate deduction."

"He killed my cat." She stood up. "Then he went off and started killing women."

"Yes."

"Jesus hell."

Somebody knocked on the door. "You all right in there?"

"One minute. One more minute." Lia almost shouted it.

Caitlin stood. "This could be important. Did Kyle ever talk about suicide?"

Lia's chest rose and fell. "You mean the game?"

"What game?"

"He liked me to lie still and pretend I'd tried to kill myself. Play like I'd OD'd, or shot myself, or slit my wrists." Lia's face was pale. "Then he'd come in and find me. He'd bang me back to life."

"That was what he enjoyed?" Caitlin said.

"He didn't seem to enjoy the sex at all. It always seemed to frustrate him."

The knocking came on the door again. Lia looked at it anxiously. "That's all. I can't talk anymore."

Caitlin handed Lia her card. "If you change your mind—about even the smallest thing, or just want to talk—please call me."

Lia nodded, lips pursed, avoiding her eyes. She unlocked the break room door and escorted Caitlin out.

On the sidewalk outside, Caitlin put on her Ray-Bans.

Patience. Emmerich's voice—her father's voice—echoed that interrogation wasn't a one-step process. You had to give it time.

And Detrick was locked up.

For now.

38

Arrivals at Dulles was jammed, hot, and noisy. The low ceiling and constant flow of people created a writhing scene. Caitlin stood beside a pillar, peacoat buttoned to the neck, lips dry, nerves singing. At her side, Shadow sat, big ears pricked, head swiveling at the marvel of so many unfamiliar bodies, so much commotion, such crazy new smells. The dog rose to her feet, skinny black legs and white paws itching to break into a run. Caitlin tightened the leash.

"Sit, girl."

Shadow lowered her tail back to the tile floor but looked like a sprinter ready to bolt from the blocks. Caitlin felt the same. On the overhead screens, the flight from San Francisco showed AT GATE.

She'd been back four days, barely caught up at work, and had already booked her return flight to Arizona for Detrick's preliminary hearing. But this weekend, the next two days, were her own.

And Sean's.

She nearly leaped as she saw him come through the

doors toward her. Her smile was so wide it ached. Shadow caught her excitement and abandoned any pretense of obedience. She stood, head tilted to Caitlin, then saw him too. Her tail wagged like a flailing whip.

He had that slow stride, and a duffel tossed over his shoulder. Hair freshly cut, brown eyes scanning the crowd as if for threats, until he saw her, and all his defenses, his reticence, gave way to the smile that could wreck her in nothing flat. She meant to play it coy, to deliberately act like she always hung out by baggage carousels on blustery winter days, but instead she was laughing, and her arms were so tight around his neck that she hardly realized he'd lifted her off the floor and was still kissing her. Even as families and baggage handlers and aircrews flowed around them, and Shadow yipped and jumped and whimpered at their knees.

She broke from the kiss and leaned back to look at him. "About goddamned time."

"How many other guys did you jump before I got here?"

"None. Well, maybe that Air France captain. And the Redskins defensive line, when they came through." She kissed him again. "I missed you."

"You too. Like nothing else."

He wrapped an arm around her shoulders and they walked out into the frigid, windy day. His straight-out expression of emotion, without jokery, was something new. Sean had always been extroverted and expressed himself more easily—verbally and physically—than she did. But since nearly dying, he'd given up most efforts to artificially clothe himself in cool. At least around her. On the job, from what she gathered, he was still the chill and steady federal agent he'd been before.

But this—almost instant relaxation, readiness, openness—was something she loved.

"Good flight?"

"Better now." He squeezed her shoulder. Shadow barked.

Sean took the leash from Caitlin and they headed to the parking garage, talking animatedly. Caitlin ran him through the details of the Detrick case. He'd watched the news and heard the short-form version, but by the time they reached her Highlander, she was speed-talking about the arrest.

"He was convinced he'd outmaneuvered us. He was careful—but had an untrained civilian's level of counter-surveillance. He had no idea we were tracking his rental's GPS the entire way. That allowed the Flagstaff agent to circumvent him and get to that local tavern before he got out of the car," she said. "Agent Sayers. Young, sharp, willing. She's going places."

"Emmerich trusted you."

"He did. It paid off."

The look she gave him said: *Thank God*. She could express her relief with him. She knew following Detrick to Arizona had been a risk. If she'd been wrong, her time and their whole case could have been taken for a fatal detour.

Sean eyed her over the top of the Highlander as they climbed in. "You got him."

She paused and put her hands on the roof. "I fucking did."

He smiled. Shadow jumped in the back and they pulled out.

The drive to her apartment outside Quantico took them down I-95. They turned on the heat and the music and Sean whistled to Shadow, who scrambled over the seats and squirreled onto his lap. The dog licked his face and curled into a ball, happy.

"Drop your stuff off, dinner in Georgetown, tour of the wreckage of democracy, and a night of debauchery," Caitlin said. "Sound good?"

"Shadow stays home, though."

She laughed. Shadow yipped and batted her tail against Sean's leg. He held his hand out. Caitlin took it. He watched the brown winter grass and grasping bare branches of the trees go by along the interstate.

"Thank you for coming," she said. "I need this."

He squeezed her hand. "You're not the only one."

Heat filled her chest. It was relief and gratitude and sheer longing. And, despite Sean's presence—his own heat and laughter and the promise of what was to come—a pang, the underlying melancholy, rose to prick her. He was here but would soon be gone again.

"Work heavy right now?" she said.

"Challenging. This bombing in Monterey. It wasn't foreign-based terrorism, from what ATF can determine. Nobody's claimed responsibility. No demands have been issued, no manifesto published, no attempts made at extortion."

She judged the tone of his voice. "You think he'll hit again?"

"The bomb was packed with screws and razor blades. He wanted to maximize the carnage," Sean said. "And he . . . or she, or they . . . took care not to leave fingerprints on any of the components."

"The bomber knew that fingerprints can survive an explosion?" That implied the offender was both sophisticated and meticulous.

"Device had a simple trigger, used externally threaded steel pipe, common supplies. But the guy wanted to put a personal stamp on the blast," he said. "The bomb was wrapped with barbed wire."

She eyed him. "Barbed wire."

"A signature."

Cold intensity filled Sean's voice. Caitlin tried to judge where his deepest worries lay.

She said, "Do you think . . ."

Sean's phone rang. He dug it from his jeans pocket. A stony look overtook his face.

"Boss," he answered.

She drove, tires droning, listening, half excited and half anxious.

"When?" Sean went still. "SFPD—okay. Yeah. Soon as I can."

He ended the call. Stared out the windshield, then turned to her, troubled. Caitlin's stomach sank.

"Another bombing?" she said.

"Financial District. Two hours ago."

Downtown San Francisco. Lunchtime.

"Casualties?" she said.

"One confirmed dead. Seven injured."

"Shit."

On Sean's lap, Shadow raised her head, eyes full of the concern only a dog can express.

"Bomb was placed in the lobby at a biotech firm. Blew out the plate-glass windows, shredded people on the street. Killed a security guard." He looked at his phone. "Peretta is sending me everything they have. Videoconference in forty-five minutes."

Caitlin's jaw tightened, but she kept her hands steady on the wheel. "What do you need?"

"Access to a SCIF."

SCIF: Sensitive Compartmented Information Facility. In the terminology of security, defense, and intelligence, it was a secure room that guarded against electronic surveillance and data leakage. She was startled. Requiring a SCIF indicated that this had been bumped up to a case with national security implications.

"There's one at Quantico," she said.

"Do we have time to drop Shadow off?"

"She can come with."

Sean peered out the windshield, a thousand-yard stare. The afternoon sun was a streak behind his head, putting him in stark silhouette. He was already half gone.

Two hours later, as Caitlin sat at her desk, with Shadow curled up asleep beneath it—breaking a slew of regulations, but she didn't care, because it was Saturday—Sean emerged from the SCIF and found her in BAU-4's section of the floor. She was tired and had caught up on only half her e-mails and file reports and reading. The sun had dropped to the edge of the western horizon, raging orange between the scarecrow branches of the trees.

Sean strode up, purposeful. When he approached, she knew it was bad news.

"Tonight?" she said.

He nodded. "I'm sorry. They need me to work the crime scene and the evidence."

Two feds? We'll work it out.

Her smile wouldn't come.

Then the look in his eyes overwhelmed the disappointment she felt at losing their weekend. Whatever was going on with this bomber, it was bad.

She whistled to Shadow. "I'll drive you back to Dulles."

They headed out the door. A few minutes later she was pulling onto the interstate.

"Do we have time to stop by your apartment?" Sean said.

Her gaze was longing and hurting and crazy. He gave the look back.

At an exit for a state park, she swerved off the highway. She pulled deep into the woods, a thin scrim of dust blowing behind the Highlander. She drove onto the grass and into a stand of trees. Jerked to a stop.

She killed the engine. Her hand lingered on the ignition. "It's cold out there."

"It's what we've got."

They jumped out. Shut the doors.

Around the far side of a thick chestnut, they grabbed each other. Unbuttoned each other's coats, fumbled with zippers. Sean's bare skin, when she found it, was smooth and hot and sent a shiver from her fingers up her arms and down her spine. His hands slid beneath her sweater and down the back of her jeans. She pressed her mouth to his. Her breath came rapidly. Sean gazed at her, eyes wide-open—he never made love with his eyes closed— and leaned back against the trunk of the tree and hoisted her up. She wrapped her arms around his neck and her breath blew frosty in the tingling air and she gasped, madly, clawing him, needing it, needing it all.

39

Caitlin pulled into Crying Call a day ahead of Kyle Detrick's preliminary hearing and saw four TV crews parked in front of the Gothic brick courthouse. One from Phoenix, one from Flagstaff, and two from national cable networks. She cruised around the town square, getting a feel for the scene. A reporter stood on the courthouse steps, talking to the camera, gesturing with her notes for emphasis. Heavily bundled people walked along the square. The diner across from the courthouse was packed. Piles of dirty snow lined the gutters.

She parked behind the police station. The air was clear and brisk, the sun canted between peaks of the pine-covered mountain range to the east. A series of storms was forecast to roll across the western US in the next week, but this was a bluebird day. She buttoned her pea-coat for the short walk to the station door.

Inside, the bright winter sun reflected off the scuffed linoleum. Phones rang and computer keys clicked, but the place was quiet. A uniformed female officer at the front desk looked up.

"What's happening?" Caitlin said.

"Same old. Boredom, anxiety, crime. Our celebrity has been behaving himself."

The officer's nametag read VILLAREAL. She nodded toward the back of the brick building, where Crying Call's six jail cells occupied an isolated block of the building. No windows, no way to get a message out unless the jailers arranged it.

"It's been a show," Villareal said.

"Tell me about it."

"You'd think he was a movie star. You remember that good-looking criminal a few years ago, his mug shot with luscious lips and piercing pale eyes—it went viral, people called him the 'handsome felon.'"

"Bad boy with a soulful stare."

"Our guest back there is the new version." Villareal tossed her head in the direction of the cells. "Complete charmer. Though he's not fooling me. But at least he doesn't throw his piss at the bars, or call me the c-word. He's happy to eat the fast food we bring in."

"Not your usual prisoner."

"He's the opposite of a problem."

Caitlin nodded, wondering how deeply Detrick had greased his way into his jailers' good graces.

Villareal sighed. "Making friendly small talk with the guards isn't an issue. They are." She nodded pointedly out the front window.

"The news media?" Caitlin said.

"Them, and the others. The admirers."

Caitlin grimaced. "SKGs. Serial killer groupies. It's a real thing."

"Before we put a lid on it, a couple of national reporters visited the jail and interviewed him. That *really* brought the fans panting."

Outside, women stood on the sidewalk in front of the courthouse, snapping photos, selfies, photobombing the television reporters.

"They're waiting to see if he's taken next door for any court appearances. Nothing's scheduled today, but that doesn't stop them. I do."

"They come in here?"

"Wanting to visit him. And more."

Caitlin wasn't surprised that carrion crows of all varieties had descended on Crying Call. She'd seen the Facebook groups that had sprung up, protesting Detrick's innocence.

"I bet. Hybristophilia—it's a sexual attraction to criminals. Arousal by outrage," Caitlin said. "I presume they try to wrangle conjugal visits."

"At least Detrick doesn't scream at us when we drag them away."

Yeah, Caitlin thought: Detrick was perfection incarnate. Mr. Wonder Bread, congenial and compliant.

The police chief came out to the desk. He extended his hand to Caitlin. "Heard the latest?"

"Fill me in. But I'm guessing—Detrick loves this circus."

"That ain't the half of it. Come on back to my office."

◆   ◆   ◆

He could hear them.

From his bunk in the cell, between the cold steel bars, their voices echoed. Muffled, indistinct, but their pitch and tone came through.

Caitlin Hendrix was back. All the way from Virginia, two thousand miles to this pissant town. Just for him.

They couldn't keep away, the women—they just couldn't.

The bitches.

His girlfriend, Emma, was gone. She'd left him after a single visit to the jail. Came in looking like she was sitting on a cheese grater, face contorted, wouldn't hold on to his gaze no matter how many times he called her by name. She'd embraced him, but dutifully, pushing dark glasses up her nose and talking about how *awful* it was that the police and FBI had searched the motel room, how *intrusive* and *disturbing* for Ashley.

They didn't find anything, though, he said. *Right?*

She looked at him then. Looked at him and said, "I'm going home."

Never mind. Nobody in the media had gotten Emma's name. Nobody was going to chase her down and try to worm information out of her. Not that she'd have anything bad to say about him. Her own fears were what had driven her off.

Didn't matter. Emma was gone, but panty throwers had lined up to replace her.

Strangely, that made jail tolerable.

At first, he'd felt out of control. Wild. Caged. He'd

never been arrested before. He had wanted to lash out. Only his incredible intellect and discipline allowed him to keep from cutting these rubes down verbally—and that bitch who'd just walked in, Hendrix, physically.

But after he talked to the FBI and saw the looks on their faces when he lawyered up—and he guessed he was now the type of guy who used the term *lawyered up*—he found strange depths in the experience of being in custody.

He was the lion in the zoo. And like the lion, he could roar.

So, when the panty throwers couldn't get in to see him—after the first one . . . the jailers wised up after she lifted her top to show him her tits—he sent a message out, through his public defender, requesting visits from people attached to legal organizations and charities and public service news media and social justice groups. And they came.

So many of them came that the jail had to create a liaison for him, in addition to his lawyer. A paralegal from an Arizona legal aid charity. He had a link to the outside world. A mouthpiece if he wanted it—a conduit if he needed to forward requests or speak to people on the outside.

Meanwhile, he used the women who contacted him: to raise money, to give interviews, and to gather information. Some of his fans had access to confidential databases. They provided him with names, addresses, and background on people he was interested in. He didn't have a computer, but he had a legal pad his jailers let him write on. And he had his perfect memory.

He was the center of attention—he gave himself that. It was not what he wanted, but it was his, and he needed to use it to his best advantage, to make this a win.

Her voice, Hendrix's voice, was too bright, and impossible to decipher. She was talking to the desk clerk, and now to the police chief.

Hendrix being here meant that his court date was only a day away. Detrick steepled his hands on his chest and stared at the ceiling. He knew that outwardly he appeared serene. It baffled the town cops who brought him his meals and chatted with him as they hauled drunks to and from the neighboring cells.

One day to the preliminary hearing. He sat up and opened the lawbooks at the foot of the bed. He had work to do.

The chief closed his office door. "Yesterday Detrick rejected his court-appointed attorney and demanded to represent himself in court."

"The judge permitted it?" Caitlin said.

"He did. Recommended strongly against it, and Detrick's public defender had it read into the record that this was over his objections. Detrick insisted. He's going into the hearing tomorrow *in pro se*."

"Adding jailhouse lawyer to his résumé." She considered it. "Surprising, but not. His driving motive, his base need, is *control*. He can't relinquish it."

"That I can see," the chief said. "It could be a total fuster-cluck. What happens if he's convicted and argues for a new trial based on incompetence of counsel?"

"Cross that bridge when you come to it."

Silver sat heavily in his desk chair. "One thing you should be aware of. Because Detrick's now his own counsel, he gets to review all the evidence against him in discovery."

"He already had that right, as the defendant."

"But defendants never bother looking at the evidence. Trust me on that. This guy is something different." He looked up from under heavy eyebrows, his expression portentous. "He went through it all with a fine-tooth comb, including the affidavit you wrote out supporting his felony arrest."

"Yeah?"

"Which mentions a confidential informant."

Caitlin frowned. "That's not unusual."

"Any thoughts on whether he might know who that is?"

She shook her head carefully. "I don't know. But the confidential informant is, for now, confidential."

"Good."

The chief's phone rang. When he answered, his shoulders lowered, as though he'd been abruptly laden.

"Coming." He hung up. "We're getting calls from all over. People see the newscasts, hear about those women you found laid out in the woods down in Texas. They see the Polaroid photos." He sighed. "Families of young women who've gone missing. They're phoning us from across the country, hoping we can tell them if Detrick killed their daughters. The numbers . . . it's disturbing."

"Very much so. Was that . . ."

"Not a call. A warning. Another family just walked through the front door. You want to be the one to tell them we can't help?"

40

At a free desk in a corner of the cramped police station, Caitlin listened to the story. The stricken parents sat across from her, bunched in their coats, ruddy and strained. Turk and Mary Jane White had flown from San Antonio to Phoenix, then driven to Crying Call, hoping for some answers. Mary Jane held a wet tissue balled in her hand. She pulled a photo from her purse.

"That's her. The most recent picture I have. That's Sonnet."

Caitlin took the snapshot. Sonnet White looked disturbingly familiar. She had the willowy blond looks of so many of Detrick's victims. But Caitlin didn't recognize her.

"When was this taken?" Caitlin said.

"Last year." Mary Jane dabbed at her eyes.

"Ten months ago," Turk clarified. "She won't have changed much."

Caitlin did them the respect of looking a long time at the snapshot, but she was sure she had never seen Sonnet's face. The young woman was not among Detrick's eerie photo gallery.

Caitlin held the photo up. Gently, clearly, to ensure that Mr. and Mrs. White would hear and process the information, she said, "Your daughter is not in any of the photos we've recovered from the crime scenes."

Mary Jane sagged and pressed the tissue to her eyes, collapsing with relief, but Turk's eyes stayed steely.

"You still don't know for sure if he's got her, though," he said.

Caitlin hung on to the photo, examining Sonnet's features. She was beautiful, in a hard way, and her gaze was distant. Her tattoos were extravagant. She looked to be in her early twenties.

"I have no evidence that the offender has ever crossed paths with her," Caitlin said. "Do you have reason to believe she knows Kyle Detrick? Did she spend time in Gideon County, Austin, or San Marcos?"

"We . . ." He trailed off, hesitant.

Mary Jane looked up, her eyes brimming. "We don't know where she's been. We originally reported Sonnet as a runaway."

Turk said, "Mary Jane."

She cut a harsh look at him. "No point in hiding it now. We came all this way. We should explain." She straightened. "I admit she has problems. Sonnet. Trouble . . . with . . . drugs, and unsuitable men, and the law . . ."

Turk averted his gaze.

"But after seeing those photos the FBI found. All those girls who look so much like her. We got to fearing that maybe she didn't run away after all . . ."

Mary Jane broke down and leaned into Turk's arms. Stiffly at first, then with rough agony, he clasped her to him. The look he gave Caitlin was tormented.

His voice was a rasp. "Keep the photo. I wrote her cell phone number on the back. She won't answer a call from us, but maybe if you try. Please, keep it. In . . ." His voice broke. "In case."

They left, Turk with an arm over Mary Jane's shoulders. Caitlin rubbed her eyes. She couldn't relieve their anguish. Or that of the other families who had phoned the Crying Call PD, begging for help.

So many missing.

Through the front window, she watched Turk hold the door of their car while Mary Jane got in, crestfallen.

Sticking the photo in her back pocket, Caitlin walked to the front desk. "I want to see the prisoner."

Villareal scrunched her mouth to one side. "You can't interrogate him. He lawyered up."

"I was there. But now he's his own lawyer. Who can give permission to speak."

With a shrug, the desk officer picked up the phone, talked briefly, and pointed over her shoulder. "They'll admit you."

At the back of the station, Caitlin waited for the door to the jail unit to buzz open. A young officer waited on the other side.

His thumbs were notched beneath his belt buckle. "Miss."

"How's the prisoner behaving?"

"He's a cream puff."

There was no sally port. The officer pulled out a key ring, opened a locker, and let her place her Glock and her drop-point knife inside. He locked it, then led her around the corner. The jail had six cells, three on each side of a central hallway.

Detrick was watching.

He sat on the thin cot in the cell, legs outstretched, leaning back against the cinder-block wall. He'd heard her voice approaching and had assumed a pose.

The young officer said, "See you in a few."

He left her alone. Only one other cell was occupied, next to Detrick's, by a gray-faced man passed out and reeking of whiskey. Caitlin stopped, leaned back against the bars of the empty cell opposite Detrick's, and took a studied look at him.

Two weeks in jail had cost him his winter tan. His face was paler and thinner. It brought out the lines of his jaw. His hair had grown out just enough to fall over his forehead in a Superman curl. The stubble on his cheeks kept him from looking too young. The orange shirt and loose pants hung on him like he was a model.

An empty KFC box sat on the floor, smelling of grease and salt. Detrick had a lawbook open on the cot beside him. He ran a finger down the page, as if he were stroking a woman's back.

"Here for your session?" he said.

"I missed your feeding, but I thought I could still get a look at you in your new habitat." She spoke offhandedly, but her heart had begun to pound.

"I knew you couldn't stay away," he said.

"Since you're now representing yourself, I presume you've seen the list of witnesses the prosecutor is going to call at your hearing tomorrow. I'm eager to testify."

He closed the lawbook. The gray of his eyes seemed peculiarly piercing. Maybe it was the lights.

"Don't pretend you came to rub it in," he said. "That's not why you're here, ogling me."

"I'm here, *Counselor*, to emphasize what a disaster you're facing. The evidence against you is overwhelming."

"You want me to hear you out. You want me to tell you how to stop yourself from going down that dark path. The one that ends with you blowing your brains out. You want me to save you."

She smiled. She tried to laugh. Her heart was hammering.

He leaned forward. He had a coiled, sleek energy. "You should see yourself right now."

He uncurled from the bed like a sidewinder rising to strike. Sauntered to the bars of the cell and hung his hands on a crossbar. Shadows from the overhead bulbs striped his face.

"But it's not a gun, is it?" he said. "Because a gun's your lover. You feel naked without it on your hip right now, I bet. You'd never want it in your brain." He looked thoughtful. "Would you?"

She stared at him. "Tell me where Teri Drinkall is."

His gaze slid over her. A shiver cascaded down her shoulders.

"That's the woman from Dallas?" he said.

Cocksucker. "If she's still alive, telling me will open a whole world of possibility to you. If she's not . . . telling me will still make a difference to your sentencing."

"Sentencing? The only sentences involved here are going to be the ones in the blockbuster memoir I write about my false imprisonment and exoneration."

"Tell me today, and I can do something for you. Get to court, and you'll bear the full weight of Arizona law. Which, you should know, is even harsher than Texas law."

"You want me to talk about the dead women, right? How they all had their wrists slashed."

Something about the way he said *slashed* caused the breath to catch halfway to her lungs.

She saw again the cuts in Phoebe Canova's wrists. Angled, deep, four inches long. Not a cut. A *gash*. *Slit*. *Slash*. And the knife that made them, razor sharp.

It was Detrick's freakish sexual metaphor. Slitting their wrists was a substitute for sexual penetration. It was how he got off. The cuts on Phoebe's wrists had looked wide, like the edges of a crevasse. Like a petal opening. They'd been probed, with the knife at the very least.

Good God. How did he get so twisted? Why?

Don't ask why. You'll go crazy. She stared at him, trying not to let her racing heart give her away.

"You're never going to control it," he said. "You can't."

"Control is for you, isn't it?"

Her hands were clasped behind her back. She dug her

nails into her palms, to force herself to focus. And to boil off her raging anxiety.

His expression, despite it all, looked every bit as seductive and concerned as it had the day she'd met him in his Austin real estate office. He was wearing the mask. The face of sanity, of allure, of reason and hope. It was amazing.

She thought of the parents jamming the police department's switchboard. Of Turk and Mary Jane White, crushed by the not knowing, raked by the fear that this man had taken their daughter, Sonnet. She thought of the faces in the Polaroids. Of terror. They were the reflection of his true being. They were his real self, projected and captured in the moments before he killed them.

She pulled the snapshot of Sonnet White from her back pocket. "Where's this girl?"

He eyed it, almost lackadaisically. "Who's that?"

Holding the photo up, she took a step toward him. He sighed, bored. But he took a minute to judge the photo. Something skittered behind his gaze, then was gone. A reaction, fleeting. Familiarity, or want. Or just pattern recognition. Caitlin took another step toward him. She would have shoved the photo down his throat if she could.

"Nice," he said. "I like. What's her name? Got her number?"

"Tell me what you did to her."

Detrick's gaze shifted from the photo. It painted Caitlin up and down. "Have you ever considered going blond?"

The sick shiver wormed down her spine. "I'll see you in court."

He smiled. "It'll be good to talk without these bars between us."

He grabbed the bars with both hands and leaned back, stretching. His gray eyes seemed to devour her.

She walked out.

41

She was still stressed out when she checked into her motel. Blood resounded in her ears.

Detrick's gaze, his insidious composure, his male-model pose, his . . . *Ready for your next session?*

She pulled off her suit jacket. It caught on the cuff of her blouse. A button sprang free and hit the wall with a click.

She checked her e-mail. Special Agent Sayers was driving up late in the afternoon. They'd meet with the Crying Call prosecutor to prepare to testify at Detrick's hearing. Rainey was coming in the morning to work with the county criminal attorney's office to develop the case for what they presumed would be a long trial.

Caitlin snapped copies of Sonnet White's photo, front and back, and sent them to Nicholas Keyes at Quantico. *Last seen early August, San Antonio. If there's any information we can give her parents, it'll help.*

She yanked off her boots, unzipped her roller carry-on, and hauled out her running shoes. She tried to loosen her jaw.

She grabbed her phone and called Sean.

"Babe," he said. "I've got three minutes."

His voice made him sound under even greater strain than she felt. She'd called on the spur of the moment, without considering his workday. She was not thinking clearly. She walked to the window. Outside, craggy red mountains were dappled with pines.

"What is it?" she said. "The bombing case?"

"It's deeper and weirder than it first looked." Sean exhaled, hard. "Everything okay with you?"

"Tell me what's going on."

"The second device, the one that exploded in the Financial District—it was more sophisticated than the first. Screws and razor blades again, but detonated remotely with a cell phone. And it used PETN and boosted TNT," he said. "The guy has access to high explosives and he's improving his technique."

That was all bad. She paced by the window. "Any indications yet of motive?"

"Monterey device targeted a DOD facility. San Francisco, the biotech firm that was hit has links to the defense industry."

"You think this is political?"

"Maybe." A pause. "Last year, a primitive device was found in a trash can at Columbia University Medical Center. NYPD defused it. It may have been the bomber's first attempt."

"A hospital? Jesus."

"Right now, it's all air and suspicion. Nothing solid."

The stress in his voice told her that the case was more

than serious. It was alarming. And it was on his shoulders.

"You think it's a single offender?" she said.

"Security footage from both the Defense Language Institute and the biotech firm shows a single suspect placing the device. Five-nine, hoodie with a full-length duster over it, sunglasses, gloves. Maybe Caucasian. We can't determine sex."

But most bombers were male. She continued to pace. "You're worried he's going to strike again soon."

"Two bombings in two weeks? Yes." He paused once more and lowered his voice. "The video footage—there's something. It's hard to explain. But when I watch it, I get déjà vu."

She slowed. "How so?"

"It's like I'm getting a visual echo. Seeing a shadow that's not there. The hair on the back of my neck stands up."

She stopped. "Sean?"

"I don't know." He breathed. "Never mind. I'm seeing things."

"You don't see things, Rawlins. Unless they exist."

"Never used to. Forget it—I gotta go." Apologetically, he added, "Everything okay with you?"

"Fine. Love you."

"You too." A *beep* said he'd ended the call.

She crossed her arms, holding tight to the phone. She was even more amped up than before she'd called him. She changed and headed out for a long run.

The afternoon was sunny, the temperature hovering in the low forties. Above the mountains, a sheen of white cloud was bearing down from the northwest. It added a portentous grandeur to the day. She warmed up for a mile, sticking to the shoulder of a two-lane highway that led into a national forest. The air stung her lungs. Her legs felt sluggish from the cold and the altitude.

Sean had sounded so uneasy. Déjà vu. An echo. A shadow. *Never used to . . .* He was talking about the attack that almost killed him. He was talking about the Ghost.

She hated hearing the doubt in Sean's voice. Hated that the Ghost had crawled into his head. Hated, above all, the idea that the Ghost could have any connection to these bombings. She fought a shiver.

She wished she could provide insight into the bomber's motives. She needed to help someone.

The air smelled like snow. The road gradually ascended, and as she warmed up, the strain of the altitude became a welcome challenge. She managed to pick up her pace.

It'll be good to talk without these bars between us.

Detrick's words crackled in her mind. Cold eyes, cobra smoothness. Heartless and predatory. She accelerated. After two miles, blowing hard, she reached a scenic overlook.

Crying Call nestled in a river gorge, with raw peaks on either side. The red stone, the dark green of the pines, the white glaze of snow, and the arching, varnished sky spread around her. She stopped at the overlook and inhaled it all. Her heart was pounding, but with life. A hawk swooped past, screeching. She smiled and pulled out her phone.

The selfie was poor, but it caught the splendor of the view. She wiped her sweaty hand on her fleece and sent the photo to Michele, with a message: Not a bad day at the office.

She took another minute to savor the scene and started back down the mountain. Her second wind lifted her to a solid, fast clip. When her phone buzzed in her pocket, she kept going—the motel was in sight. A big rig rumbled past, blowing strands of hair around her face. She sped up and raced to the lawn of the motel like a sprinter crossing a finish line.

She bent and put her hands on her knees. After a minute, she straightened and pulled out her phone.

It was a reply to the message she'd sent at the top of the hill. Not as good as mine. The photo showed Michele coming through the doors of the ER, shooting an exaggerated thumbs-up. Outside, it was pouring rain. Her hair and scrubs were soaked.

Caitlin laughed.

The breeze gusted. The hawk circled high overhead, a silhouette, soaring.

42

The wind woke Caitlin at six A.M. Tiptoeing across the cold motel room, she pulled back a corner of the curtains. The morning twilight was thick with driving snow. Fat flakes battered the window.

"Oh boy."

She wasn't a winter driver. She handled rain like a pro, thanks to growing up in the Bay Area, but snow was still foreign to her. The two blocks to the Crying Call Courthouse proved a grinding, slippery drive. She felt like she was steering a bumper car.

The town square was packed with an extra helping of news vans, but they were vague shapes through the heavy snowfall. She could barely see across the street to the park in the center of the square. The businesses on the opposite side were invisible. She parked the Suburban, tucked her head into the collar of her peacoat, and ran up the courthouse steps, boots sliding on the granite.

Inside the courthouse entrance, there was a mad buzz to the air. The heater was blasting. The tile floor was wet. The lobby was crammed with locals, gawkers, reporters, and camera crews. Spotlights glared from shoulder-mounted television cameras. A new security checkpoint had been set up, manned by county sheriff's deputies.

A throng waited to pass through the metal detector. Caitlin approached, flashed her creds, and surrendered her gun to a deputy. She put her shoulder bag in a plastic tub on the X-ray conveyer belt.

She checked her watch. She had twenty minutes. Behind her the door opened and, in a blast of icy air, the prosecutor came in carrying a fat legal briefcase, wearing a hooded ski parka. She raised a hand in greeting. In the security line, people were excited, murmuring, gossiping, hoping to get a view of *him*.

"He's *so* hot," a young woman said.

"If he put his hands on me, I wouldn't fight," another said.

Yes, you would. And you'd scream.

Caitlin breathed and told herself to stay calm. But she couldn't help counting the blonds in the line. They seemed to fill the hall on either side of the metal detector, like an eruption of the Children of the Damned.

In her bag, her phone rang. She grabbed the purse from the X-ray belt and dug the cell out. *Nicholas Keyes.*

"Caitlin." Keyes's voice was rushed. "The young woman in the photo you sent. The San Antonio runaway, Sonnet White. You're not going to believe this."

Caitlin inched forward in the line. "What?"

"She called the Westside Crisis Hotline."

Caitlin stopped. "When?"

"Last August. Three weeks before the Texas killings began."

"Keyes," Caitlin managed to say, instead of *Jesus Christ*.

"Got no hits on her from ViCAP. Could find no reported arrests in Texas or neighboring states, no deaths under the name Sonnet White or Jane Does matching the woman's physical description. I thought I might get a hit when I scanned her photo—that one tattoo is distinctive."

Caitlin nodded. "The cat over her left breast."

"But nada. Then I got her cell records. She called the hotline on Wednesday, August first, at eleven twenty-two P.M."

Caitlin felt electrified. "How long did the call last?"

"Twenty-two minutes."

"Is she still using that cell phone?"

"No. After she called the hotline, there's activity for another week. The last recorded entry is data usage just before midnight on August eighth."

The subsequent Wednesday. "Detrick worked the phones Wednesdays six to midnight."

Caitlin's stomach clenched. Her astonishment blended with the sinking knowledge that Turk and Mary Jane White's daughter had probably crossed paths with Detrick.

Ahead of her, the queue stirred, as if a shiver was slinking down the line.

"Send me everything. Copy Emmerich and the team, and Detective Berg in Solace," she said. "Flat-out amazing, Keyes. Flat-out thank you."

"Code received. You're fuckin' welcome." Keyes ended the call.

In the courthouse lobby, heads turned. The hubbub rose to a racket. Caitlin's head was pounding.

Beyond the metal detector, where the entry hall ended in a T-junction, the elevator doors had opened. Detrick stood inside, flanked by Crying Call police officers from the jail.

They held the door and he stepped out. His eyes drank in the crowd in front of him. For a second, he seemed to grow, like an oxygen-fed flame.

He'd shaved and washed his hair and was dressed in his own clothing—the tweed jacket and dress shirt she'd seen him wear while showing houses in Austin. He didn't quite smile, but his step had a swagger to it.

The woman in front of Caitlin blurted, "Oh my God."

Reporters shouted questions. Detrick raised a hand and waved to them.

Caitlin stopped dead again. Detrick was unshackled.

He strolled along the hallway between the two officers, one of whom was the young patrolman who'd admitted Caitlin to the jail yesterday. She felt light-headed. Mr. Congeniality had convinced his jailers to spare him the indignity of arriving in handcuffs.

He saw her. He smiled and winked at her.

The officers led him out of sight. Uneasy, she beckoned one of the deputies manning the security checkpoint.

"Ma'am?" he said.

"The defendant who just went in—Kyle Detrick. He wasn't cuffed."

Women on either side of her turned at the name *Kyle*.

The deputy said, "It's optional when prisoners are under guard."

She held up her credentials again. "I need to get through."

The woman in front of her said, "I was here first."

Caitlin looked over her shoulder for the prosecutor. He was on the phone and simultaneously talking to another lawyer. She whistled to get his attention.

When he looked up, startled, she called, "Get in there. No shackles on Detrick."

He frowned. The bailiff said, "All right, ma'am."

She circled the complaining groupies, dropped her shoulder bag on the X-ray belt, and cleared the metal detector. The hall beyond was crowded and noisy. She headed for the courtroom. She got fifteen feet and chaos erupted.

A fire alarm rang. People shouted. Caitlin ran.

She shouldered through the crowd. "FBI."

She turned the corner. The hallway outside the courtroom looked like mayhem.

The fire alarm shrieked. Bailiffs and blue-shirted police officers dashed into the courtroom and immediately back out. Spectators ran to the tall window at the end of the hall, which overlooked the square outside.

She grabbed the sleeve of a rushing bailiff. "What happened?"

The bailiff's shoulder radio blared with unintelligible voices. His face was fraught.

"When Detrick approached the courtroom, the crowd started jostling for a closer look at him. The cops escorting him moved to break them up, and the fire alarm went."

"Detrick pulled it?"

"SOB's quick."

The alarm bell was on the wall five feet above their heads, screaming.

"Where'd he go?" Caitlin yelled.

The bailiff looked around, uncertain. At the end of the hall was the door to the fire stairs.

He pointed. "Stairwell?"

"Go," she shouted.

Caitlin sprinted back through the crowd to the security checkpoint. She retrieved her Glock. She rushed out the front doors of the courthouse, into a whiteout.

43

Caitlin ran down the steps of the courthouse into the blizzard. Coat open. Stack-heel boots slipping on the steps. Weapon in her hand. The snow skewered her, blowing almost horizontally, stinging her face, hitting her in the eyes.

She raced around the side of the building toward the fire exit. Behind her came muffled voices, people rushing from the courthouse. She skidded on the slippery sidewalk. Outside the fire door, two sheriff's deputies were examining the pavement. The snow was four inches deep. Footprints led in multiple directions.

One deputy pointed toward the town square. "That way."

They ran past Caitlin toward the square, weapons drawn. The storm erased them to gray outlines within seconds.

Caitlin almost followed, her nerves singing, but stopped herself. She scanned the crazy trails of footsteps outside the fire door. Multiple shoe prints in the snow.

Look. Think.

The deputies' footsteps were the clearest. Heavy rubber-soled boots, heading in tandem toward the square. Beneath them were a smaller, less defined set of prints. Running shoes.

Detrick had come to court wearing the clothes he'd brought to Arizona. His tweed jacket. Dress shirt. Jeans.

Cowboy boots.

The bastard wore cowboy boots. That's what he'd had on the night she arrested him.

She tented her cold fingers over her face to keep the snow from blowing in her eyes. And she saw the prints. The sole and clear heel of cowboy boots.

Heading away from the town square, west, between buildings.

She yelled for the deputies, but the wind swallowed her words. She ran, slowly, holding her Glock low by her side, trying to follow the footsteps even as the gale erased them.

She turned down an alley. Needles of snow funneled between the brick walls of the buildings that lined the passageway. She couldn't see more than six feet in front of her.

The wind rose to a shriek. Beneath it, she heard a voice.

"Should have done yourself."

She raised her gun, backed against a wall, and swept her gaze in a steady arc, looking for him. The voice was indistinct, shredded by the storm. She couldn't pinpoint it. She was breathing like a run-out horse.

"Gonna wish you had." The voice slithered over her again, more distant. "You'll see."

West.

She raced from the alley, her feet sinking into six-inch-deep snow. The whiteout swallowed her. The air howled. She was in the open, on the far side of the square. The ground beneath the snow turned gritty as she ran across a gravel verge.

She came to the highway. She stopped on the shoulder, looking north and south—and saw nothing. Just white. She could barely hear the rumble of engines and swish of tires.

Then she heard screeching brakes.

Her shivering skin contracted. Teeth chattering, she swiveled toward the sound and instinctively backed up a step.

The crash came as a loud *bang*. Metal shrieked. An engine roared, downshifting.

A jackknifed semi materialized from the whiteout.

It appeared on the highway like a metal mountain, canted, headlights scattering snow, trailer coming around and around, skidding at her out of the blizzard.

"Jesus." She dived for safety.

She hit the gravel flat on her belly, Pete Rose sliding for home, and rolled. The big rig raked past her, ghostly and huge. Sparks flew from beneath it, rooster-tailing orange as it dragged an object along the asphalt. It muted back into the storm, a fallen beast going down at far too high a speed.

It caught on something and flipped.

Behind Caitlin, a telephone pole creaked and ripped from the gravel verge. So did the next pole down the line. Wires dropped to the ground around her with a wet slap. She scrambled to her feet and out of the way as a string of poles was yanked out of the ground like Lincoln Logs. They toppled with a thunderous clatter.

The eighteen-wheeler continued to squeal down the highway on its side, sweeping other vehicles in its path. There were no horns, only brakes and the continuous crunch of metal.

She climbed to her feet. Chest heaving, she ran toward it.

A hundred yards down the road, the tractor trailer finally stopped. A massive pileup completely blocked the highway.

The only road out of town.

Two trash cans were twisted and crushed between the fenders and front wheels of the tractor's cab. That's what had caught beneath the big rig, sending the orange flare of sparks along the road as the truck skidded past her.

Trash cans, in the middle of a highway. Detrick had engineered the accident.

Her Glock remained in her hand, her index finger freezing as she held it outside the trigger guard. She turned in a circle, looking for him, but saw nothing.

On the bitter wind came the stench of gasoline and burned rubber, and the sounds of shouts and moaning. A strange, animal screaming. Stomach knotted, she ran toward the pileup.

Detrick was gone.

44

The coffee was lukewarm. Caitlin's hair was plastered to her head and stippled with ice crystals, her peacoat was soaked through the shoulders and sleeves. Her leather gloves did little to cut the numbness in her fingers. Through the blowing snow, the blue and red flashing lights of the fire trucks and ambulances were dimmed to muffled pastel colors. Tow trucks were hooking winches to the crushed vehicles in the pileup.

An Arizona state trooper approached, heavy jacket zipped, snow crusting the broad brim of his tan campaign hat.

"They're transporting the last casualties now. Broken bones." He eyed the hundred-yard span of the wreckage. "No fatalities. We dodged a big one."

"No kidding." Caitlin eyed the smashed tractor cab of the eighteen-wheeler. "Get anything from the driver?"

"He saw the trash cans in the road when he was almost on top of them. With the snow, he couldn't tell what they were. He swerved and lost control." The trooper shook his head. "No question somebody pulled them onto the highway. What a bastard."

She nodded. Her face was chapped, her nose running.

The trooper said, "Thanks for your assistance. Go inside, get warmed up."

She shook his hand. This was his patch, and working in these conditions was hellish. And he did it every day.

A voice called to her. "Caitlin."

Through foot-deep snow, Brianne Rainey trudged toward her along the shoulder of the highway. Her black parka was zipped to her chin, combat pants stuffed into L.L.Bean boots. The flashing lights illuminated the bright yellow letters FBI on her watch cap. Her eyes were narrowed in a cold grimace, but Caitlin felt a warm reassurance at the sight of her.

Rainey put a hand on Caitlin's back. "No fatalities."

"Incredible luck."

The pileup was a stinking, twisted mess. The big rig had been carrying live chickens. The smashed trailer, its back doors open, echoed with the frantic cries of frightened and dying birds.

Caitlin inhaled through chattering teeth. "Detrick used the storm to his advantage. He caused the wreck to slow us down at least. To keep us from following his escape route out of town at worst."

The highway was the single major road in and out of Crying Call. To reach the town, the bulk of emergency vehicles had been forced to take a winding fire road through the mountains.

Sticking to the verge of the highway, they picked their

way around the wreckage. Beyond it spread a vast wilderness. The pine-covered peaks were invisible. Beyond fifty feet, everything was invisible.

"Who's responding?" Caitlin said.

"City, county, state troopers. Forest Service in the mountains. Air support if the weather lifts."

"When is that going to happen?"

Rainey shook her head. "Storm extends across four states."

Ahead of them, the highway was desolate, the snow blowing into deepening drifts. Finding Detrick was going to be a desperate endeavor. The gale had obliterated his tracks. It would prevent trailing dogs from picking up his scent.

Despite the sting of the snow, anger heated in Caitlin's chest. Every minute Detrick was gone made this disaster exponentially worse.

"You think he's on foot?" Rainey said.

"He's wearing a tweed jacket, jeans, and cowboy boots," Caitlin rasped. Her voice was half gone. "If he tries to hike out, he'll freeze."

Rainey looked at her funny. "Come on."

"What?"

She put a hand around Caitlin's back and led her toward the town square.

"You've stopped shivering. You're getting hypothermic. Inside, now."

In the police station, they found noise, bustle, urgency, and anxiety. Uniformed officers ran in and out. The two jail-wing officers who had escorted Detrick to the court-house without shackles sat in Chief Silver's office, slumped like dough. Silver paced behind his desk, phone to his ear, trying to coordinate the hunt for Detrick. At the front desk, Officer Villareal looked like she'd been stunned by an electric eel. But when she saw Caitlin and Rainey, she sprang to life.

"Hang up your coats. Radiator over there is hot. Get coffee."

Caitlin couldn't unbutton her coat. Rainey offered to help, but Caitlin muttered, "I got it."

She didn't. She walked to the radiator, used her teeth to pull off her gloves, and pressed her hands to the hot metal. It was agonizing, stinging relief.

Villareal brought a gym towel. "Your hair's going to melt in a minute."

"Thanks."

Caitlin draped it across her shoulders, over the frozen mass of her auburn hair. She pressed her legs to the radiator.

Rainey, watch cap crusted with ice, leaned against the radiator beside her. "I doubt the escape was spontaneous."

"No. Detrick . . ."

The heat paradoxically caused her teeth to chatter. She clenched her jaw.

After a minute, she started again. "He planned it. He knew the layout of the courthouse. He spent two weeks buttering up his jailers. Today he wheedled them into leaving his hands and feet free. He created the opportunity and seized it," she said. "He *winked* at me, Rainey. He was *grinning*."

Caitlin's hands warmed enough that she could fumble to unbutton her coat. She pulled it open and pressed as much of herself to the radiator as possible.

"His life as he knew it is over," she said. "There's no going back, no pretending he's innocent. And the escape makes him truly infamous. So what's he plan to do? Go underground? Cross the border, change his name, try to fade away?" She shook her head. "No way."

"No," Rainey said. "He has a blinding urge to kill."

Caitlin gave her an anguished look. "He's free. When that urge erupts, there'll be nothing to stop him."

Rainey pulled off her hat. "Something triggered Detrick last summer, and he started abducting and killing women in Solace," she said. "With every new victim he took, his inhibitions drained away."

"Psychopathology on display."

Rainey nodded. "He has a high threshold for physiological arousal. Killing became the act that satisfies it. And once a psychopath finds the prize button, he keeps hitting it. His reward system for sex, drugs, or crime goes into overdrive and doesn't turn off. He won't cut his losses. He has no shutoff valve."

"He indulged his rage and his drives. Hell—he tried to abduct a woman here in Crying Call, when he knew the FBI was on his tail. He convinced himself he could act with impunity."

"He's on an arousal jag. Pedal down, and the brake line's been cut."

In the chief's office, Silver banged down the phone. He turned to the jail officers who'd left Detrick unshackled. "You two." Caitlin caught a glimpse of their faces just before Silver slammed the door. They were braced for a verbal beatdown.

Rainey's gaze lengthened. "The *only* thing that will restrain his actions is fear of capture. And he's just gotten a huge boost to his sense of omnipotent power and control."

A full-body shiver overtook Caitlin, and the heat from the radiator flooded in. Her shoulders were screwed up tight. She concentrated and got them to drop an inch.

"Detrick's an expert at manipulating women. He's honed it to a high art. He feels infinitely superior to us," she said. "But he feels inadequate beside men who are accomplished and confident. That's one reason he impersonates cops and soldiers."

"He wants men with authority to appreciate his cunning," Rainey said.

"And he yearns to be recognized by them. If he can't have their admiration . . ."

"He'll take fear and disapprobation."

"He's going to want to rub law enforcement's nose in his success."

Rainey's brown eyes were grave. "What's his end game?"

"Stay free. Murder when he wants. Exact revenge on the world for daring to turn his life upside down," Caitlin said. "He's going to want to make a statement kill."

At the front desk, a phone rang. The desk officer answered and held the receiver up. "Agent Hendrix."

Caitlin frowned in surprise. With her half-numb fingers she worked her cell phone from her pocket as she walked to the desk. *No Signal.*

Villareal handed her the desk phone. "Cell towers are down between here and Flagstaff."

Caitlin thanked her. "This is Agent Hendrix."

"He escaped?" Lia Fox said. "He pulled a fire alarm and waltzed out of the courthouse like Fred Astaire? What the ever-fucking *hell*?"

Caitlin took a breath. "Every law enforcement agency in northern Arizona is searching for him."

"What kind of Barney Fife cops do they have in Crying Call?"

Lia's frantic voice carried beyond Caitlin's ear. Villareal turned away.

"What if he comes after me?"

"He doesn't know your name. He doesn't know where you live. Your number is unlisted. Your identity has been kept confidential."

Lia's voice cracked. "Like that's going to make a difference?"

Caitlin thought of Detrick in the storm. If he was on foot, maybe he would freeze to death. If he'd stolen a car or hitched a ride, he could be warm, safe, and rolling south.

"He's not a normal person," Lia said with blank panic. "If he tracks me down . . ."

"I'll contact the Phoenix Police Department and ask them to add a patrol to your neighborhood."

"Why not just send me a sympathy card?"

Caitlin let a silence hang. She understood Lia's fears, but something more was going on. "What else is frightening you?"

"That's not enough?"

"Please." She wished this was a video call. Wished she was in the room with Lia. She was missing major context, and the woman's voice only told so much. "Tell me."

Lia seemed to fight tears. "Nothing."

"If you're trying to protect someone, you don't have to do it alone." She eyed Rainey. "You have the FBI here to back you up."

"From here on, I got only myself," Lia said. "Don't you understand? He's loose. He'll figure it out."

She hung up.

Uneasy, Caitlin leaned across the counter and replaced the receiver. Rainey walked over.

"News is out and our source is scared," Caitlin said.

She thought about it. Outside, the snow continued to blow.

"You worried about her?" Rainey said.

Another shiver passed through her. Her fingers still felt icy. "Yes. But she's not the only one." She turned to Rainey. "I'm worried about Aaron Gage's family."

45

Rainey's face turned grave. "Aaron Gage's family. In Oklahoma."

Caitlin, finally warming up, took off her coat. "Detrick knows an informant supplied his name to the FBI. If he thinks it's Gage, he could go after them. They're easy to find."

She still had no cell signal on her phone. "Wi-Fi?"

The desk officer gave her a password. Logging on to the network, she put through a video call to Quantico.

Emmerich answered on the move, walking from the BAU office toward the exit. He wore a black ski parka. His computer case was slung over his shoulder. "I'm on the way. Wheels up in thirty. Flight plan filed for Flagstaff, but if this storm sticks, it'll be Phoenix."

"Great." She felt bolstered. "One thing's worrying me."

She explained her concerns for Aaron Gage's family.

Emmerich pushed through the building's doors into a gray day and headed toward his car. "I doubt Detrick would connect the informant with Gage. It's been eighteen years. He's probably stewing over the informant's identity, but it's more likely that he thinks somebody in Austin gave him up."

"I agree that he probably spent hours in his cell running through his contacts, trying to pin it on somebody. Except for one thing. During Detrick's interrogation, I focused on the white nightgowns."

"The victims were found wearing them."

"But Gage is the one who caught Detrick sniffing a nightie. Detrick might certainly conclude that Gage put us on his trail."

Emmerich stopped at the door of his Audi S5. "Point taken. Alerting him wouldn't be unduly cautious."

"On it," she said.

"See you soon."

She ended the call. Rainey looked concerned. She had her own phone on the Wi-Fi network.

"What?" Caitlin said.

"A series of storms is tracking in from the Pacific, and this one's a monster. I doubt he'll get into Flagstaff."

She showed Caitlin the radar map. The blizzard crossed a vast swath of the southwest, from New Mexico and northern Texas into Oklahoma.

"I don't know if that's good or bad," Caitlin said.

At a free desk, she called the Phoenix Police Department about Lia Fox. Then she phoned Gage's landline. She got a *Circuits Busy* tone. She tried his cell. *Call Failed.* Repeatedly. On the desktop's computer screen, she brought up the National Weather Service.

Storm sweeps east through Oklahoma, knocking out phones and power.

In the heated station, the ice on her hair was melting. The back of her blouse was wet. Rainey went to the station's break room and brought back cups of rank instant coffee. Caitlin took one gratefully, warming her hands around it.

Rainey drank hers in one long go. "If this storm extends across four states, our team's not the only ones who'll struggle to get anywhere. So will Detrick."

"I know."

That thought should have reassured her. But, as her father had once said, *Don't ever leave a warning until later. You never know when too late might show up.*

"It's not Aaron I'm worried about," she said. "It's Ann and Maggie."

She pictured Gage's young, no-nonsense wife and the little girl who had bounced into the house the day she and Rainey spoke to Gage. She called Quantico and asked Nicholas Keyes if he could find a cell phone number for Ann Gage.

Clicking noises. "Sending it to your cell," Keyes said. "You sound cold."

"I'm defrosting. Thanks for the info."

Caitlin placed the call from the landline. To her relief, Ann Gage picked up.

"Mrs. Gage. It's Special Agent Caitlin Hendrix."

There was a brief, surprised pause. "What's going on, Agent Hendrix?"

"Are you at home?"

"Oklahoma City. Why are you calling?"

She sounded under pressure. On the desktop screen,

the weather map showed Oklahoma City, one hundred twenty miles north of Rincon, socked in by the blizzard.

"Are Aaron and Maggie with you?" Caitlin asked.

"They're home. I'm at my grandmother's—she shouldn't be on her own during this storm. What's wrong?"

Caitlin was certain that Ann didn't know about Detrick's escape. "I have to pass along some news."

When Ann heard it, she went stone silent for a minute. "Is Maggie in danger?"

"We have no indication that Detrick plans to harm your family. But he's dangerous, and we want you to be aware of the situation."

"Have you told the Rincon cops?"

"My next call."

"Jesus. I'm stuck here. The city's solid ice," Ann said. "Get somebody to the house to warn Aaron. I don't care if you have to call Fort Sill to send someone out there in a tank."

"I'm working on it, Mrs. Gage."

Caitlin managed to get through to the Rincon Police Department, but they were nonplussed by her call, overwhelmed with blizzard search and rescue.

"It's a full-court press until the storm clears," a police lieutenant told her.

"I can't contact Sergeant Gage," she said. "He's disabled, and alone at home with his toddler—"

"I know Aaron. He's pretty self-sufficient."

"That's not my worry." She reiterated that an escaped

prisoner might have a grudge against him—a man considered armed and extremely dangerous.

The lieutenant, Bill Pacheco, said, "Yeah. I see the FBI bulletin coming in."

"It's urgent that Sergeant Gage be warned about the threat."

"I agree that Aaron should know this SOB is on the loose. But power's out and phones are down."

"I know how bad it is. I'm on the back side of it here in Arizona."

"All our officers are on the roads, pulling wrecked motorists out of ditches. I can't promise assistance for such a tenuous threat."

"I don't think the threat is tenuous." She found that her hands were shaking. She was still colder than she'd thought. She tried to keep her voice calm but insistent. "Please, Lieutenant. This man is beyond dangerous. I know the chance is slim, but I couldn't live with myself if I didn't warn Sergeant Gage. If one of your patrols is out his way—"

"All right." The man sounded pressed. "I'll see if an officer can go by his house."

"Thank you."

"And if you talk to him, let me know. Right away."

"That's a deal."

Relieved, she ended the call. She tried again to reach Gage but couldn't get through. Outside, snow whipped across the Crying Call town square.

46

In the end, the FBI agent's refusal to hang up was what got to Lieutenant Bill Pacheco. It was ten P.M. when the lashing snow finally eased. At Rincon police headquarters, Pacheco got a breather from directing the emergency storm response, but the dogged insistence of young Caitlin Hendrix played on his mind. He stuck his head around the door to the lobby and signaled the staffer at the front desk.

"Get me Aaron Gage's number."

He called the landline: *Circuits Busy*. The cell: *Call Failed*.

He walked to the operations room and asked an officer to pull up the GPS locations of all the department's patrol units. None was within twenty miles of the Gage home.

That was when the call came in from Oklahoma City. It was Ann Gage, a girl he'd known since high school.

"Bill. Bad shit's going down and I can't reach Aaron."

Pacheco was already zipping his jacket and heading for the door. "I know, Ann. I'm on my way to your house."

◆   ◆   ◆

"Again, Daddy."

Swaddled beneath a comforter, Maggie Gage cuddled against Aaron's side.

"Time for you to get to sleep, Tigger," he said.

"One more time. Please."

It was late, but Aaron couldn't resist his daughter's sweet-soft voice. The storm had amped her up. The snow, the power going out—it was all an adventure to Maggie. He and Ann had built a fire in the living room fireplace before the lights and heat cut out, so the small house was warm. And tonight, he planned to keep Maggie snug beside him. He'd tucked her into his and Ann's bed.

The wind whistled beneath the eaves. He only wished that the phones were up. No comms, and Ann in OKC taking care of her frail grandmother—it concerned him.

"One more time," he said.

Maggie nestled tighter into the crook of his arm.

"One morning at the puppy farm, Chevy was playing with her brothers and sisters," he said.

At his feet, hearing her name, Chevy stirred.

Maggie said, "Did they dig under the fence?"

"You bet. They were all mischief. Chevy kept a lookout."

He felt as much as heard the disturbance. It was an uptick in the volume of the storm. A brush of cold air swirling through the bedroom door.

Beside the bed, Chevy raised her head, tags clinking.

More quietly, Aaron said, "The puppies dug a tunnel all the way to the trees and hid there."

The front door had opened.

It wasn't Ann. Wasn't anybody he knew. Wasn't the wind. He'd shut that door tight—it wouldn't slip the latch.

In the living room, a floorboard creaked. A sound guttered in Chevy's throat. A growl. Aaron touched her back. Her hackles were up.

He lowered his voice to a murmur. "Maggie, I need you to be a good girl and do exactly what I say. No questions. Ask me questions after. But right now, do what I tell you. Got it?"

There was a tiny pause, and her voice sounded as quiet and serious as his. "Got it."

"We're going to play a game, like in the story with Chevy and her brothers and sisters. And just like the puppies, you have to be completely quiet. Not a peep."

She whispered. "Like this?"

"From now on, not a sound. Grab my hand and squeeze to say yes."

She did.

He stood and scooped her into his arms. On the hardwood floor, he took seven silent steps to the only room in the house without a window, the only room an intruder couldn't break into from outdoors. The master bathroom.

The wind drove against the walls of the house. He set Maggie in the bathtub.

He whispered, "Stay here until I come back. If anybody knocks, don't answer. Don't make a sound. Stay silent and invisible."

He turned and gave a low, sharp whistle. "Chevy, come."

The dog's tags clicked as she stood and padded into the bathroom.

"Sit."

Chevy settled herself beside the bathtub. Aaron gave the command the Labrador had not been taught as part of her guide dog training, but that she knew well.

"*Guard.*"

He reached out and touched Maggie's face. Her soft breath warmed his hand.

"I'll be back. Stay here with Chevy. No matter what."

She squeezed his hand to say yes. His heart clutched. This amazing goddamn kid.

He locked the bathroom door behind him. In the bedroom, he listened.

Apart from the low crackling of the fire, he heard no sounds inside the house—not the hum of the fridge, not the rumble of the furnace. The power was still out. Which meant the lights were off.

The intruder was silent. Not ransacking the place for cash or food or drugs. They were coming for him. Him and his little girl.

Ann had taken the pistol with her to Oklahoma City. He'd insisted. The Mossberg twelve-gauge was locked in the gun safe in the bedroom closet. But using it was out. The slightest miscalculation, and a shotgun blast could tear through the sheetrock walls and hit Maggie.

Nobody was getting to Maggie.

Heart rushing, Aaron imagined the house, felt its distances, knew the obstacles, its edges and choke points. It was six steps to the bedroom door. From there, the hall ran fifteen feet to the living room.

The hall was the place to mitigate his tactical disadvantages. The place to do this.

The hardwood floor was slick. He took off his wool socks for secure footing. Silently he unbuckled his leather belt and pulled it off.

Barefoot, he crept to the bedroom door. Grasping the ends of the belt in his hands, he held it vertically in front of him and pulled it taut. Step by silent step, he advanced along the hall, sweeping the belt back and forth in front of him as a defensive plane.

The living room would be dark. The hall darker. The light of the fire would keep the intruder's eyes from adjusting fully when he stepped into the hall. The narrowness of the corridor eliminated the possibility that the intruder could attack him from behind. And whoever it was, he didn't have a gun. 'Cause if he did, he would have come in shooting.

Aaron crept to the midpoint of the hall.

The guy had a knife and would come straight at him.

The intruder wouldn't think he had to dodge. He would lead with the blade. And ninety percent chance the guy was right-handed.

Aaron took a stance and moved the belt to his left, an inch from the wall. He held poised.

Then he heard it. Six feet ahead of him, to his right, a hand brushed the wall. The intruder couldn't see for shit and was trying to orient himself.

Aaron held motionless. He listened. *Hold, hold*. He felt the air shift.

He swept the belt to the right and looped it furiously around the spot where he felt the disturbance. Guessing. He snapped the belt tight.

It caught. He whipped it around flesh and steel. Yanked hard and pulled.

He wrapped the guy's wrist.

Hot pain sliced Aaron's forearm. The knife was big. Maybe a Ka-Bar, and the blade, trapped under the belt, had sliced his hand.

He heard a hiss. Surprise. Pain.

Move in. He yanked the intruder toward him, hauling him off-balance. He let go of the belt with his right hand. Wound up and smashed a palm toward the guy's face.

The blow connected with the side of the guy's head. A guttural sound came from his throat. Aaron swept the intruder's leg. The guy grabbed Aaron's shirt as he went down. They hit the floor. Aaron scrambled back to his feet, searching for the sound of the knife on the wood.

He listened, and lunged.

Lieutenant Bill Pacheco bumped along the gravel drive. Snow pebbled against the windshield of his cruiser. Ice-coated trees glinted in the headlights. The barn came into view, farm implements swinging. The house was dark. His headlights flashed against the front windows. The door gaped, a black hole.

He came out of the car with his holster unbuckled, hand on the butt of his gun.

On the porch, Pacheco stepped to the side of the door. "Aaron?"

Inside the house, Aaron Gage's landline phone rang. The phone company had restored service. But nobody was answering.

The wind sang through the glassy trees. Beneath it, Pacheco heard another sound. Ragged breathing.

He drew his weapon and swung inside the door, sweeping his flashlight in synch with his gun. Snow had blown several feet inside the house. Virgin, no footprints. The phone continued to ring. Pacheco's hair stood on end.

On the kitchen floor lay Aaron Gage.

He was rasping for breath. The beam of the flashlight illuminated a dark, sticky spread of blood around him. His shirt was punctured with stab marks.

"Aaron." Pacheco hit a light switch, but the power was out. He swept the kitchen. "Aaron, is the guy still here?"

Gage didn't answer. His hand clawed the floor, striping the blood like finger paint. "Maggie . . ."

On red alert, Pacheco knelt at Gage's side.

Gage swiped a hand and grabbed Pacheco's jacket. "Maggie. My daughter."

Pacheco put a hand on the side of Gage's face. The man was ice-cold. "Aaron. Is Maggie here?"

With a shaking hand, Gage pointed at the back of the house. Pacheco swung his flashlight up. And heard the dog bark.

"Hold on."

Standing on weirdly shaking legs, Pacheco crept down the hall. The barking grew louder. He heard the dog pawing a door. At the end of the hall, he swung into the master bedroom, then to the bathroom door. It was locked. The barking intensified.

"Maggie?" Pacheco said.

He heard only a tiny, smothered sob. Pacheco took the blade of his buck knife and pried open the latch.

When the door swung open, Maggie Gage's brown eyes were wide and full of tears.

She was crouched in the bathtub, unharmed, hands over her mouth to keep her sobs from echoing. The dog stood in front of her, ears back, teeth bared. It growled and snapped but didn't attack. Lather and sweat darkened its fur around the guide harness. Pacheco's heart was pumping.

From the kitchen came a distinct whistle. And Aaron's faint voice. "Release."

The dog backed off.

"Stay," Pacheco said.

The dog obeyed, panting.

"Wait here," Pacheco said to Maggie. "It's going to be okay. I'm help."

He cleared the house, leaned into his shoulder radio, and called for EMS. Returning to the bathroom, he holstered his weapon and pulled Maggie into his arms.

"I gotcha."

The little girl crabbed against him, shivering. In the living room Pacheco set her on the sofa, pulled off his jacket, and wrapped her in it.

"Daddy," she whimpered.

"He's here. I'm going to take care of him."

Pacheco rushed back to the kitchen, set his Maglite on the counter to provide a swatch of visibility, and knelt at Gage's side. The phone finally stopped ringing.

Gage was as pale as a sack of flour, his lips bluish. "Maggie. She's . . ."

"She's safe. She's fine."

Pacheco ripped open the buttons of Gage's shirt. His breath caught. Six stab wounds, each an inch and a half long, were spread across Gage's chest, seeping blood. Pacheco grabbed some dish towels from a drawer to put pressure on the wound—but there were so many wounds. He covered one and pressed, and put Aaron's own hands on two others.

"Hold tight, buddy." He heard the quaver in his own voice. "What happened?"

In the living room, Maggie's hiccupping cries softly resonated. "Daddy . . ."

Gage, hearing her, appeared to let something go inside. "Maggie." He inhaled and seemed to offer up a prayer. He looked as if his every wish had just come true. "Maggie . . . you did great."

"Who did this?" Pacheco said.

"Don't . . ." Gage wheezed. "Don't know."

"How many?"

Gage tried to swallow. "One."

Pacheco grabbed a glass from the counter and filled it from the tap. He lifted Gage's head and let him sip.

"Chevy . . . growled. Knew things were wrong," Gage said, more easily.

The dog, hearing her name, padded into the kitchen. Offering a low, desperate moan, she crept to his side and lay down. Her brown eyes were mournful under the beam of the flashlight.

"I . . . told Maggie to hide and stay quiet. Commanded Chevy to stay with her."

Pacheco pressed his hand to the dish towel. It had soaked through with blood. He checked the time. The EMTs would still be miles away.

"Chevy did exactly as you told her to," Pacheco said. "She damn well did. She guarded Maggie. She never moved from her side."

Gage nodded. Softly he said, "Good dog."

Guide dogs are working animals. Not pets. And Chevy had been on the most important duty of her life. But when Gage said, "Good dog," the Lab inched forward and licked his face.

Pacheco said, "Can you tell me anything about the attacker?"

"I cut the guy and managed to land a blow but . . ." He stopped, overcome by pain. "Neutralized the knife, but he had a second blade."

"Aaron, you saved Maggie's life."

Pacheco's hand was wet, and the dish towel was sopping. He couldn't stanch the bleeding.

He leaned again into his shoulder-mounted radio. "Where's EMS? I need them *now*."

Gage's breathing became ragged.

"Keep talking, Aaron. Talk to Maggie," Pacheco said. "She kept quiet. She was brave."

"Best . . . beautiful goddamn kid. Maggie . . ."

Pacheco's hands were hot in the frigid draft, wet with blood. "Stay with me, Sergeant."

On the kitchen counter, the phone rang again.

In the Crying Call police station, under cold fluorescent lighting and air full of the smell of scalded coffee, Caitlin leaned on her elbows, eyes closed, phone pressed to her ear. The number was ringing. *Come on, answer.* It had been ringing every time she called for the last half hour, but nobody had picked up.

Weary, she lowered the receiver. She was just about to hang up when a man's voice broke in.

"Who's this?" he said.

She straightened with a snap. "It's Caitlin Hendrix." She recognized the voice. It wasn't Aaron Gage. It was the Rincon, Oklahoma, police lieutenant, and he sounded all wrong. "Lieutenant Pacheco?"

There was noise in the background. A child's cry. The air went out of her lungs.

"Lieutenant."

It was only a single second before he spoke, but it stretched forever.

"I'm here." He paused. "Not soon enough. Aaron's gone."

47

Caitlin stared out the dark windows of the police station. Under the fluorescent lights, her drawn face reflected from the glass. It was midnight. A phone rang somewhere. The station was nearly empty, a male officer at the front desk.

The door opened. In a wash of freezing air, Emmerich walked in.

"I heard," he said.

Caitlin turned, hands hanging at her sides. "We were too slow."

"You did everything you could."

She pressed her fingers to the corners of her eyes. "It wasn't good enough."

Emmerich's black parka was dusted with snow. His response was blunt. "Sometimes it's not."

Buck up, she heard. She nodded.

His voice gentled. "It's a terrible blow. But what we do now is find Detrick."

"Yes, sir." Hesitantly, she added, "Something's off about the MO of the attack on Gage."

Rainey, working at a desk in the corner, looked up from her laptop. "Caitlin. C.J."

Rainey turned the laptop. "Got the Rincon Police Department on video."

Emmerich touched Caitlin's shoulder. "Hold that thought."

He stamped crusty ice from his hiking boots and unzipped his parka. They approached the desk where Rainey sat. On-screen, they saw the solemn, exhausted face of Lieutenant Bill Pacheco.

"Lieutenant," Emmerich said. "What can you tell us?"

"Not much yet. The storm's keeping the forensic unit from reaching the crime scene. It'll be morning at the earliest."

"With your permission, I'd like a member of our team to accompany them."

"You're invited. That's official."

Caitlin cleared her throat. "What do you know, Lieutenant?"

Pacheco's heavy gaze settled on her. "That Aaron Gage was a hero. He saved his little girl's life."

Caitlin wanted to nod, to respond, but her throat locked.

Emmerich said, "You think the child was the primary target?"

"Not sure. But Aaron fought like a son of a bitch. Went down swinging."

"You think he injured the UNSUB?"

Pacheco nodded. "He said he cut the guy. Got the

knife away from him. But the killer had a second blade Aaron couldn't see. Sliced his arm, got him down."

Rainey and Caitlin exchanged a look.

Pacheco caught it. "Your escaped prisoner. Slashing wrists is his specialty, isn't it?"

"With women he's subdued and restrained," Caitlin said.

"I'd say he put that technique to use tonight."

Caitlin's stomach tightened. "Possibly."

"You doubt it?" Pacheco frowned. "Detrick did this before, in Solace, didn't he? Shana Kerber. Late-night silent entry into a remote residence."

Her eyes felt scratchy. She hadn't eaten dinner. Or lunch. She was running on charred coffee and sick adrenaline.

"This attack is similar," she said, "but only on the surface. This killing doesn't follow Detrick's MO."

"I agree. But this was retaliation, not a sex slaying. Revenge doesn't play by the rules."

Emmerich drummed his thumb against the desk. "Detrick's arrest was a stressor that could have caused him to explode with rage." He turned to Caitlin. "You're the one who thought Detrick might attack Gage—why are you discounting that insight?"

"I was afraid Detrick would attack Gage's wife and daughter," she said. "Detrick kills women because he thinks they're lesser, weaker objects."

Pacheco said, "I agree that he may have come looking for Ann, and would have done something awful to Maggie if Aaron hadn't put a dent in him."

She turned square to the screen. "Detrick didn't kill Aaron. He doesn't have the balls to confront a man."

Pacheco leaned back and stared at the ceiling.

Caitlin pressed. "I know that right now, all likely motive and evidence points to Detrick. I'm telling you, it wasn't him. It had to have been someone else."

Emmerich said, "It's extraordinarily unlikely Gage's murder is coincidental. If not Detrick, who? Why?"

"I don't know."

Pacheco shook his head. "I'll talk to you after the forensic unit works the scene." A deeper fatigue settled on him. "Ann Gage can't get back from Oklahoma City until the ice storm clears. I have to check on Aaron's little girl."

It was the emptiest ending Caitlin could imagine.

Pacheco closed the link. Caitlin continued staring at the blank screen. She felt sick. She'd had Detrick checkmated. Now he'd flipped the board.

"Do you want me to go to Oklahoma?" she said.

After a pensive moment, Emmerich said, "I'm going. This murder is connected to Detrick's other killings, but in a way I don't understand. I need to get a handle on it."

She nodded.

He looked her and Rainey up and down. "You're toast, both of you. We'll pick this up in the morning."

They gathered their things and pushed out the back door to the cold night. The only vehicle in the parking lot was the Suburban Caitlin had arrived in.

"How'd you get here?" she asked Emmerich.

"Hitched a ride on a snow plow to the edge of that pileup. Walked from there."

At the motel, Caitlin closed the door to her room. She sat on the end of the bed, hands hanging between her knees. Her eyes stung with fatigue. She knew she should find something to eat but couldn't summon the will to move. She felt wrung out.

She had to pull it together. In the morning, she needed to be ready to fight.

Her colleagues were in adjacent rooms, but she felt isolated. An unspooling anger overcame her, and the sense of being unmoored and alone. The image of Aaron Gage fighting to save his daughter's life grabbed her like a claw.

She stood and paced, raking her fingers through her hair. After a minute, she pulled her phone from her pocket. She called Sean.

He didn't pick up. Outside, the wind wailed. She paced, pinching the bridge of her nose.

She called Michele.

She normally wouldn't put a load on a friend's shoulders, but she needed a loving voice.

Three rings, four. "Hey."

Relief flooded Caitlin. "Hi."

"Girl. You all right?"

"Long day in a lonesome town."

"Hang on."

In the background, Caitlin heard music. She wondered if she'd caught Michele out to dinner. She heard Michele walking down a hall. The music dimmed.

"Sugar, you sound fried," Michele said.

"Bad day. I just wanted to hear a friend's voice."

"You got it. Want to talk? Just want me to swear at you?"

Caitlin paced to the window. "Colorfully. Please."

"You first."

The music swelled as a door opened. Caitlin heard Sadie's voice, and Michele covering the phone to say, "You should get back to bed, sweetie."

The song sounded familiar. It was Gary Clark Jr., "Numb." Michele came back. "Sorry."

"Have I influenced your taste in tunes?" Caitlin said.

"What?"

"Only ever known you to be into hip-hop," Caitlin said. "Never blues."

Then she understood.

In the background, she heard Sean's voice. "Sadie, let Mommy talk."

A jolt went through her. She stopped in front of the window. On the phone, she heard the clink of a bottle against a glass, and something being poured. After a second, she heard the distinct *ting* of a wineglass being set on a granite countertop.

Michele was at Sean's, having a drink with him.

"You there?" her friend said.

"Yeah."

Am I ever.

"I'm interrupting you," Caitlin said. Her voice sounded disembodied.

"Not at all. I just had a long day too," Michele said. "Needed a Mommy break, and Daddy was handy. Wish you were here to join us."

"So do I."

Michele paused before resuming. Then Caitlin paused too—had she actually said that with a cutting edge?

"Girl, it's the end of a hard week and we're watching *Finding Dory*. Again."

"No, I understand."

Caitlin didn't feel jealous—not exactly—but this was throwing her. Shit, it had thrown her like a mechanical bull, practically straight through the wall. She realized she was staring at an indeterminate stain on the motel room's brown curtains. She turned away.

"Caitlin."

"I—it's just been one of those days."

"That's not what you're talking about. Woman? Come on."

The walls had stains too. For a disgusting second, she floated out of herself and imagined the room being processed by a crime scene unit in white Tyvek suits. Spraying luminol, hitting the UV light, and watching the bedspread and headboard and ceiling light up electric blue with bodily fluids.

"If you want to know what occupied my day, turn on the news," Caitlin said.

"What?" Michele said.

Caitlin squeezed her eyes shut. What was she doing? She trusted Sean. And Michele.

But she felt like she'd been kicked in the gut.

She didn't want to breathe, not in this rank room. The air seemed full of evil humors.

She gave it one more try. "I'm in Arizona," she said.

"I flew out to testify at Detrick's preliminary hearing, but . . ."

"I'm looking at the story now," Michele said. "Holy shit."

Distantly, Sean said, "What's wrong? 'Chele, you okay?"

Caitlin leaned against the desk. Sean and Michele's closeness—it should have been obvious. When she lived in California, things were different. She was with Sean every day and ran with Michele twice a week. Potentially difficult moments were limited to picking Sadie up or dropping her off.

She wasn't living in California now.

She had yanked up stakes and hauled ass to the East Coast. She was the one who bolted. To the job of a lifetime, yeah. But she was the one who pulled out of town and kept going, all the way to Virginia.

Where did she stand now? She didn't know. But it was painfully clear that she was on the outside of a family unit.

Michele said, "What a nightmare. Are you okay?"

"Exhausted." The bone-deep chill of the storm wouldn't leave her. "I just wanted to say hi. I'll talk to you when you aren't so busy."

"Cat—"

Caitlin ended the call.

48

The parking lot lights at the motel were on all night, a sickly yellow glow that crept through gaps in the curtains. At three A.M. Caitlin lay awake, her head pounding, all the anxieties of the world crawling over her like centipedes.

She turned on the light. Sat up. Hugged her knees.

She couldn't phone anybody at this hour. She didn't want to turn on the television. Outside, the wind blew.

Was Michele spending the night at Sean's?

"Stop it." She said it out loud.

She knew that wasn't happening. Knew Michele had lost any physical interest in Sean.

In Sean goddamned Rawlins, all six foot two inches of him, with his washboard abs and an appetite for lovemaking that was rowdy and unabashed.

She got up. The room was cold. Her Warriors T-shirt and pajama bottoms were thin against the mountain night. She pulled out her laptop. She knew that was a mistake, that it would suck her deeper into the nightforce of obsession and chronic fear, but she opened it up.

Forcing herself to concentrate on the case, she thought: *Lia Fox.*

If Kyle Detrick had made it to Oklahoma and murdered Aaron Gage, Lia was relatively safe, because it indicated that Detrick was fleeing east, traveling at high velocity away from Phoenix. But if it wasn't Detrick—if someone else had killed Gage . . .

She rubbed her eyes.

If Detrick wasn't the one who killed Aaron Gage, he could be anywhere.

The dawn came through the curtains too early. At the roadside motel, Kyle Detrick opened his eyes.

He stretched, luxuriously, enjoying the good mattress and soft pillow. The clean sheets and warm, cosseting comforter felt smooth on his naked skin. After a few minutes, he climbed from the bed. At the window, he peeked out. A heat shimmer rose from the parking lot, the desert sun already doing its work. Across the highway, saguaro cacti stood in the brown rocky soil like props in a tourist brochure. The desert stretched on endlessly, to red-stained hills and the horizon beyond. Welcome to Anthem, Arizona.

He smiled.

Dropping the curtain back in place, he stretched out on the bed and turned on the morning news.

Look at that.

He turned it up. ". . . still no sign of Kyle Detrick, who escaped from the Crying Call Courthouse Thursday morning."

It was a live report from the scene. The reporter was some Latino man in a puffy ski jacket and hat with the Phoenix station's logo. He sounded stern and aggressive. So self-serious, these local nobodies. The man stood with a mic in front of the big smash-up on the highway out of Crying Call. Wreckers were clearing the last vehicles from the road.

It had been like throwing a strike at the bowling alley, Detrick thought. They all went down like bowling pins.

The report switched to file footage shot at the courthouse during his arraignment. On the motel room bed, he propped himself up on his elbows and watched himself. Or rather, watched the version of Kyle Detrick that had existed before he buzzed off his hair and got himself some clothes that made him look like a trucker. On the TV screen, he looked self-possessed. Even as he stood in the courtroom with the stinking chain gang, he had risen above. His chin was up. He looked righteous. He had shown them all that the injustice he was bearing would not stand.

And he had not let it. His smile returned, wider this time.

He felt amazing. He was free.

The news report retraced his escape path, the reporter pointing at the side door where the fire stairs dumped out of the courthouse. The snow was trampled, footprints impossible to follow. The news team interviewed astonished and breathless townspeople in Crying Call, and courthouse fans exhilarated by his escape.

He tried to suppress a laugh. It was delightful.

The report cut to a Main Street bar. A local band had written "The Ballad of Kyle Detrick." The report briefly showed the band onstage, wailing the chorus. The reporter cut back to the studio.

There on the set, under the lights, in their makeup and cheap suits, the morning anchors shook their heads.

"That is over the top," a hair-sprayed woman complained.

"It sounds fun, but Detrick's twisted," a man said.

"Scary times," someone said. They called him sick. Called him dangerous. They pursed their lips.

He ground his teeth. He wanted to shout from the rooftops that he had *won*. He escaped from the courthouse. He outwitted the chickenshitting FBI.

Heat burned in his chest. A need. The anger.

He stood up. Aaron Gage's death hadn't hit the news yet. When it did, it would shut these clowns up. He clenched and unclenched his fists. He wanted to grab a knife. A life.

He stalked back and forth across the room.

Somebody had set the FBI on him. He knew that because the affidavit from Caitlin Hendrix supporting his felony arrest mentioned a confidential informant. A snitch.

Since landing in jail, he'd been trying to figure out who that snitch was. Somebody from work? From church? No. He'd been too careful. It couldn't be anyone from Austin. Which meant it was someone from his past.

When had he failed to be careful? In college. And who had glimpsed his weakness? Aaron Gage. Gage was the only person who knew about his thing for the white nightie. It had to be him. The drunken asshole had no concern for him, for his life, his needs. Nobody else could have so easily told the FBI about him.

After the home invasion at Gage's house, he felt sure.

Because he now had more information. He had the call history from Gage's cell phone. The phone was taken from Gage's pocket after he went down, and it told a fascinating tale. It told Detrick that Dahlia must be involved.

Detrick stopped, the heat pouring over him, though his skin was totally bare. He balled his fists, then spread his fingers, stretching them like talons. He headed into the bathroom and stared at himself in the mirror.

Dahlia.

In one way, he cared nothing about her. Even though Dahli was meant for him. He had seen this in the way she laughed at his witticisms. The way she couldn't take her eyes off him.

And the way she had succumbed to his seduction. It had been perfect.

But then she rejected him. Said it was a mistake. That he was immature and selfish and needed to leave her alone. Looked at him like he was a loser.

Him, immature?

He set the apartment on fire, and then he *rescued* her.

Him, selfish? He was a hero.

But she had wanted nothing more to do with him. So he'd sent cards and gifts that were subtle and ominous.

Him, a loser? When he'd tracked her so skillfully that

she never knew it was him. When he'd had the power. Screw that. Dahlia didn't mean shit to him.

Get me a knife.

In the bedroom his phone buzzed, the burner that had been smuggled to him in his jailhouse KFC lunch. Text coming in. He leaned on the bathroom counter, eyeing himself.

Yeah, he'd outfoxed them all.

He'd escaped from Crying Call with a fat roll of cash. He had withdrawn it from the safe-deposit box at his Austin bank before coming to Arizona. After his arrest, he had managed to convince Emma to sneak it to him, saying he needed it as jailhouse currency. She'd done it reluctantly and had been a nervous wreck. That was the straw that caused her to abandon him.

Never mind. Emma had been attentive, and little Ashley adored him, but Emma clearly wouldn't go to the mat for him. In the end, she was useless.

No loss. He had fresh help from a loyal fan. Somebody who wasn't weighed down by a kid and who was eager to do whatever he asked. A devotee who hated the law as much as he did and who saw in him something magnificent.

Somebody who would follow.

Turning sideways, he assessed his upper-body definition, then walked back to the bedside table and opened the phone message. *Well,* he thought, *what do you know.*

He turned off the TV. He showered and dressed and took the towel and wiped down all the surfaces in the room. He picked up the key that had been smuggled to him in jail along with the phone, and went out to the car. In Crying Call, it had been parked several blocks from the courthouse, ready for him. He fired up the ignition and headed south.

The text message read, Phoenix.

It was forty miles away.

49

The news wouldn't shut up. On the TV in the kitchen, and in the bedroom, and on Lia Fox's car radio as she hurried back from the 7-Eleven, where she'd gone when she ran out of smokes at six thirty A.M., it was wall-to-wall. *Detrick. Detrick. Detrick.*

The bozos in that Crying Call bar band thought Kyle was Billy the Kid. The Facebook groups were wetting themselves. Some commenters thought Kyle's jailbreak was the most exciting thing since O.J. Simpson's freeway chase. They posted photos of him. And drawings of themselves with him, generally locked in a seductive embrace. They posted slash fiction. Some of that featured Kyle kidnapping and exacting revenge on the FBI agent who arrested him, and who—at the end of the story—came around to the greatest orgasm of her life. Most stories starred the authors themselves, going on the run with the fugitive, to a life of endless sex on a beach. Anybody who expressed doubt about Kyle's innocence was shouted down as a heretic and a bitch.

What was wrong with people?

At ten A.M., after calling in sick to work, Lia finished her second pack of cigarettes and stubbed out a butt and broke from her jittering paralysis into frantic action. She pulled a suitcase from the hall closet and packed in a frenzy. After cramming in clothing and makeup and a shelf of her prescription medications, and panties to last two weeks, and a bottle of Chablis, she dragged the roller suitcase into the living room. She sent a text to her sister, Emily. Looked around. She didn't know how long she'd be gone. She unzipped the suitcase again and pulled photos from the wall and side table, fitting in as many as possible. The bag bulged when she zipped it back up.

She got the cat carrier from the hall closet and clicked her tongue until Zipper meowed and trotted out of the spare room. She shoved him inside, hissing, and loaded the carrier in the car before going back for her computer case and suitcase.

She bumped the roller case over the threshold. Standing on the front step, she looked around. Another sunny Phoenix day that looked sharp and dry and barren. She locked the apartment door, fumbling with her keys, and her phone rang.

580 area code. *Rincon, OK*.

It was Aaron.

Hand still on the keys in the door lock, she paused, both anxious and relieved. And, frankly, astonished at both those feelings.

Until two weeks ago, she could not have imagined speaking to Aaron again. She had fled from college because she thought he was a psycho stalker. She'd moved to Arizona. She had hidden from him. But the psycho stalker, the man she had feared for years, was not Aaron. Not at all.

Two weeks ago, when Kyle Detrick was arrested, her world shifted. Everything she thought she knew had been a lie. It felt like a massive scythe had swept over her past and cut it down, exposing a completely different landscape.

So she'd called Aaron. Cleared the air. Filled in the blanks.

Learning about the last seventeen years of his life— hearing about his years in the army, the awful story about how he'd lost his sight, finding out he had a wife— it had spun her around. She even had to admit that a part of her felt a pang when he told her he was happily married. His voice was the same. But sober, deeper, mature. She'd tried to convince herself to be pleased with what he told her. Learning the truth, and telling him she was sorry for suspecting him of something that wasn't his fault—doing that had lifted a dark cloud.

But now Kyle had escaped from jail. Aaron had to be as worried as she was. He had a little daughter . . . her heart caught in her chest.

She put the phone to her ear. "Aaron."

Nothing. The call was connected; she heard noise on his end. Traffic.

"Aaron? Hello?"

She pulled the phone from her ear and checked the screen. The call was connected.

As she studied the display, the phone vibrated and a

second call came in. 804 number this time. *Quantico, VA.* The FBI.

She said, "Aaron, hold on . . ."

A shadow fell across the back of her shoulders. The air behind her cooled. She turned and in a split second saw a tall silhouette. A man, arms spread wide, as if offering an embrace. But his right hand held a tire iron, and it was swinging toward her, fast. The blow came blunt and massive on the side of her head, smashing her into the closed apartment door.

50

Caitlin hung up. Voice mail again. She couldn't reach Lia Fox. At the counter in the diner on the Crying Call town square, coffee cups rattled. The waitress set down a bulging brown paper bag.

"Here you go, sugar."

Caitlin dug cash from the pocket of her jeans. The bag was hot: two fried egg sandwiches, two large coffees, and the last apples from the bowl by the cash register. Outside, the sky was an aching blue, as if apologizing for having inflicted the blizzard on the town. People were digging out.

The waitress stuck a pencil into her upswept ponytail. "You on your way out of town?"

Caitlin handed over the cash. She mumbled nonresponsively. She didn't need the locals to keep tabs on the comings and goings of the team. Detrick had already studied the area's law enforcement methods too well.

She did give the woman a smile. She needed coffee. She was sleep deprived. She didn't want to think about Michele having wine with Sean.

The waitress pinged open the register and whipped bills from the drawer. "You gonna find him?"

"That's the plan."

The waitress held out Caitlin's change. Her face was flat. "Good."

Caitlin grabbed the bag. "Keep the change."

She pushed through the door into blindingly white snow, the entire world burning blue and white. Her breath wreathed the air. Rainey waited in their Suburban at the curb, keeping the car warm. Caitlin hopped into the SUV and put their breakfast on the center console.

"Still no answer," she said. "Lia called in sick to work but isn't picking up at home. Hasn't answered my texts or e-mails either."

"Think she's deliberately gone dark?"

"Possibly. But it doesn't feel right."

Overhead, a state police helicopter buzzed across the square toward the peaks to the east. The Crying Call police and state troopers were combing the hills. They'd found no sign of Detrick. No vehicles had been reported stolen from the town. No homes had reported break-ins, though some far-flung mountain houses were vacation homes, empty during the week, and had yet to be searched.

If Detrick had bivouacked in the open during a two-day blizzard, in a tweed jacket and jeans, he was dead. But Caitlin didn't think he had bivouacked.

Rainey pulled out, the snow crunching beneath their tires. The pileup had finally been cleared, but much of the snow had not. They were bound for the FBI's Phoenix Field Office. Emmerich was at the Crying Call police station, helping coordinate the search for Detrick. He planned to meet her and Rainey in Phoenix. Caitlin figured he was resourceful and would get out of town via snowmobile, or by commandeering an elk.

"We have a path out of here?" she said.

Rainey crept up the street, the rear end of the SUV loose on the road surface. She nodded past the town square. "Them."

Ahead, a team of snowplows lined the shoulder of the highway, yellow hazard lights swirling. Rainey pulled up behind them and flashed the headlights. Caitlin smiled. An escort.

The plows led them out of Crying Call at twenty miles an hour, spraying snow onto the shoulders of the road in great white arcs. After twelve slow miles, Caitlin tried again to reach Lia Fox.

"Still no answer," she said.

Rainey had waited to eat until the road improved. Now she grabbed her cooling sandwich from the brown bag. "Call the Phoenix PD and ask for a drive-by."

It seemed an obsessive precaution, except it didn't. The highway descended a long slope and they finally reached a stretch where snow was already cleared. Flashing her lights again as a thank-you, Rainey pulled around the plows and gunned it. Pine trees heavy with snow flashed past. Caitlin made the phone call.

Twenty minutes after she'd put through the request, the Phoenix police phoned her back. She listened stonily. Ended the call.

"Patrol unit drove by Lia's apartment complex as requested. Her car was parked in its assigned parking slot outside her unit. She didn't answer the door."

Rainey shot her a look. "They go in?"

"Cat was in a carrier in the front seat of her car, moaning and clawing to get out. They found Lia's keys in a flower bed. Manager let the officer in. Nobody was there."

It was two hundred miles south to Phoenix. Rainey jammed the remains of her sandwich back in the brown bag and pushed the speedometer to eighty-five.

When Caitlin and Rainey pulled into the Phoenix apartment complex, it was seventy-five degrees and the sun burned gold overhead. The cops wore short sleeves. Two police cruisers and an unmarked detective's car were parked outside Lia Fox's unit.

Shedding their coats, Caitlin and Rainey strode up the sidewalk. Lia's unit faced away from the street. Caitlin's stomach was acid with anxiety.

Rainey eyed the complex. "It would have been easy to grab her late on a weekday morning, when the school run was over and most of her neighbors were at work."

They showed their credentials and the uniforms led them inside.

Rainey stopped inside the apartment door. "Yeah. She was about to bolt."

The hall closet was open, empty hangers on the rack. Photos on the walls were missing. Dust marks and hooks were the only things left. It seemed indisputable that Lia had been grabbed as she prepared to skip town.

Caitlin shook her head, frustrated. "Detrick got out of Crying Call on wheels. He didn't walk out."

"Hitchhiked, stole a vehicle from a vacation home, something."

Rainey went to a side table. A few photos remained, tipped facedown, as if knocked over in Lia's rush to get going.

"How the hell did he find her?" Caitlin said.

The Phoenix detective came in.

Caitlin said, "Witnesses?"

"We're canvassing the complex. And we'll pull video from surveillance cameras in the surrounding neighborhoods, see if we can find anything."

Rainey set the photos on the side table upright. "Hendrix."

She picked up one of the photos. It featured Lia and a lively teenage girl, hugging tightly, all smiles.

The frame said: *Happy Mother's Day. Love, Emily.*

"She has a daughter," Rainey said.

"Jesus." Caitlin's shoulders dropped. "I knew she was hiding something. Not this."

Rainey's chill dropped to subzero. "If Detrick finds out, he could go someplace primitive. We've got trouble."

51

Psychopaths exhibit primitive envy. They don't merely long for the object of their desire. They don't merely resent people who have the thing they yearn for. If a psychopath can't have what he wants, he'll destroy it.

Psychopaths, Caitlin had learned, devalued anything loving. Violent psychopaths killed what attracted them.

"*In Cold Blood*," Rainey said soberly, as they headed into the FBI's Phoenix Division. "The killers shotgunned four people, basically because the victims were a happy family. They couldn't stand the consuming envy they felt, so they exterminated them."

Detrick had been killing surrogates for Lia Fox, the object of his unbearable desire. For years, she'd been the primary target of his rage. But now, they had to presume he'd found out she had a daughter.

"His craving to destroy won't end with Lia," Caitlin said.

"He'll try to kill everything she loves."

The Phoenix Division occupied a modern stone and blue-glass building behind an iron fence. Caitlin took a free desk, with a view of saguaro cacti, gleaming traffic, and a horizon serrated by brown mountains. She coordinated with Nicholas Keyes in Quantico to find Lia Fox's daughter. Across the open-plan office, Rainey got on the phone with the Arizona State Police, reorienting the manhunt for Detrick. It had just significantly ramped up.

Statement kill. The thought went through Caitlin like a steel blade.

Emmerich arrived, still wearing his hiking boots. The sun, slanting through the windows, flashed against his eyes. "We just got two hits on earlier attacks Detrick may have carried out."

Rainey ended her phone call and walked over. Emmerich opened a screen.

"Detrick's DNA ties him to a sexual assault in Louisiana seven years ago. And to a Jane Doe found dead outside Laredo five years ago."

He brought up a morgue photo of the murdered woman. Young, Caucasian, drained of blood. Caitlin's fingers tingled. Rainey let out a slow, audible breath.

"She's in the Polaroids," Caitlin said.

Emmerich nodded. "We'll release that photo. Hopefully get an identification."

Confirmation—a link from physical evidence—should have been exciting. But with Detrick in the wind, a hollow silence settled over them.

Emmerich checked his watch. "I have two hours before I fly to Oklahoma. Where are we?"

Caitlin inhaled. "Lia Fox lives alone. She's rented her

unit for four years. The super says she's never had a roommate, much less a daughter living in the apartment."

She handed him the photo of Lia with the teenage
girl. "We'll find her, but . . ."

He studied the photo. It showed a rugged, windswept
beach, with fir trees on a cliff in the background. "This
was taken a long way from Phoenix. Maybe a vacation
shot. Or maybe this girl lives out of state."

Caitlin nodded, tight-lipped.

Emmerich handed the photo back. "Fox kept this
from us. She went to some lengths to do so."

Caitlin felt her cheeks flush. She was thinking: *Maybe
the woman had good reasons.*

"Lia was terrified," she said. "And I told her he wouldn't
find her."

"We're working to uncover how he discovered her
identity. Her name was not in any documents Detrick
could have accessed when preparing for his court hearing. Nobody in our unit so much as spoke her name in
Crying Call. We haven't had a data breach. Yet, somehow, he not only made the connection but uncovered her
home address."

"State police is in the loop," Rainey said. "And I just
had a quick call with Phoenix PD. One of Lia's neighbors
saw an unfamiliar car parked near Lia's unit this morning. Blue, 'Japanese make.' Cops are pulling video from
all CCTV cameras within a mile of the apartment complex."

"Good," Emmerich said.

That would all take time. Painstaking time. Caitlin
ran her fingers through her hair.

Emmerich turned to a large USGS topographical map
of Arizona on the wall. "Grabbing Fox so soon after
Aaron Gage was killed—but three states away?"

"Yeah," Rainey said. "How's Detrick doing this?"

Caitlin's laptop sang. She returned to the desk. On-
screen, from Quantico, was Nicholas Keyes.

He was leaning close to the screen. He pushed his
chunky frames up his nose.

"Found your girl," he said. "The daughter."

Caitlin's voice jumped up a notch. "Where?"

"Emily Erin Hart," Keyes said. "Age seventeen. She's
a freshman at Greenspring College in Portland, Oregon."
He clicked keys. "Sending you her vital statistics now."

Caitlin opened the file. She saw the teenager from the
Mother's Day photo. Wavy brown hair, lively eyes, attitude to spare. Her college ID photo showed a beaming
smile.

"Thank you. Keyes, I don't know how you did it, but
thank you."

"Magic." Keyes's eyes flicked up. "Quick thing, before
you go—remember the video from the Texas movie theater?"

"*Madden NFL.*"

"I told you the software was flagging strange artifacts
on the video? I don't know what to make of it, but I've
run the simulation ninety times, and I'm sure. While the
UNSUB was crossing the multiplex lobby, prepping to

intercept the victim, somebody else in the crowd was watching the UNSUB."

"What?" Caitlin said.

"There's another figure in the video, only visible intermittently—shorter, looks like a woman—who the software indicates was positioning herself so she could always see the UNSUB."

"She got a colorful circle beneath her feet?"

"Red. I'll see what I can make of it," Keyes said. "Hit me back when you need more." He tapped the keyboard with the eraser of a pencil and cut the connection.

Baffled but intrigued by Keyes's news, Caitlin picked up the phone to call Portland.

Emmerich said, "You'll provide a script for Emily to follow . . ."

"If Lia or Detrick contacts her. Absolutely."

Emmerich rapped the desk with his knuckles and headed across the room toward Rainey. Caitlin found the number for the Portland Police Bureau.

Caitlin spoke to the Portland police, then phoned Emily Hart. It took a few rings for the girl to pick up.

"Yeah," came a breathless teenage voice.

Caitlin put it on speaker. "Emily Hart?"

"Who's this?"

"Special Agent Caitlin Hendrix, FBI."

The shocked silence on Emily's end let Caitlin hear sports practice in the background. Something outdoors. A whistle blew.

"What? FBI? What?"

Caitlin had learned to break bad news in the most matter-of-fact way possible. Especially on the phone, when you didn't have the chance to physically hold someone's attention. Say it plain. Then shut up. Make sure the other person understood. Listen to their responses.

"Your mother is missing, Emily. We think she's been abducted."

Emily's voice turned sharp. "Oh, my God."

Shouts in the background. A cheer, and the sound of stampeding feet.

"You're sure?" Emily said.

"Positive," Caitlin said.

Emily was out of breath. "Lia texted she was getting out of town. She said she'd explain once she was on the road. She sounded so . . . oh, my God. *Afraid.*"

Another voice, a bright young soprano in the background, said, "Em? What's wrong?"

Emily covered the receiver. "Tell Coach I'll be . . . oh, God."

Caitlin said, "Emily?"

"This is not good," Emily said. "Omigod."

"You call your mom Lia?" Caitlin said.

"What? Lia. I do . . . oh, jeez." She seemed to take a breath. "I . . . sorry, yeah. Lia's my birth mom, I mean she's my mom, but I was adopted and raised by my grandparents. Lia's parents. I grew up thinking she was my older sister. I only found out Lia was my birth mother a couple years ago. High school."

That explained to Caitlin how Lia had managed to conceal a child from the FBI.

Emily said, "She was young, not ready for a kid. She'd had a rough time, her boyfriend was . . ." She gasped. "Omigod, is this him? That guy?"

Emmerich approached.

Emily's voice cracked. "I'm coming to Phoenix to help you. I can get there tomorrow."

Emmerich shook his head. On a notepad he wrote: *Detrick may be counting on that. Lying in wait.*

He spoke up. "Emily, this is Special Agent in Charge C.J. Emmerich. The FBI and Phoenix police are looking for your mother. But it's best you stay in Oregon."

"We've got to find her."

"That's our job. You need to stay put. The Portland police and campus public safety department will contact you about personal security."

"Personal security." Emily's voice abruptly sounded ten years older. "You think this guy would come after me too?"

Caitlin said, "It's possible. Right now, we have no evidence that he knows your whereabouts. But he's extremely dangerous. We want you to take every feasible precaution."

"Got it."

Another whistle blew.

Caitlin said, "Where are you, Emily?"

"Rugby practice."

Caitlin looked again at the girl's student ID photo.

She looked wiry—not big enough to throw a heavy tackle.

Caitlin said, "When practice ends—"

"I'll have Coach walk me to my bike . . ."

"No."

"Right. I'll get Coach and two teammates to accompany me home."

"That's it."

With every sentence, Emily seemed to be getting the idea. Though deeply shaken, she sounded grounded and steady.

"And once you're at home, don't open the door," Caitlin said.

"I assure you I won't open the door to anybody but the police, or walk a single step across campus without an escort."

"Good. We'll keep you updated whether we have new information or not."

"Just find Lia," Emily said.

"We're doing everything we can."

Caitlin hung up, relieved that the girl was safe and on alert. But they were scrambling to recapture Detrick. Every minute that passed felt like sand falling through an hourglass.

52

Saturday, the sun hung high above US 93, four miles east of the Colorado River. The freeway sliced a black line through the pale desert. The road was empty. Sagebrush twitched in the wind.

The Corolla sat on the shoulder of the highway with the hood raised. The driver leaned against the flank of the car, arms crossed, peering up and down the road. Finally, from the east, a pickup truck crested the hill. It was noon.

The young woman stuck out her thumb.

The pickup roared past her, raising dust. She threw her arms wide, like, *Dude, what the hell?*

But, in the end, it took only five more minutes before a blue Subaru Outback slowed, cruised past, and pulled over. She jogged toward it.

A bumper sticker read ASK ME ABOUT MY EAGLE SCOUT. The man at the wheel looked friendly and capable. He buzzed down the passenger window.

"Need me to look at the engine?"

She shook her head. "Fan belt's gone. A ride to the nearest gas station, that's enough."

The man glanced in the rearview mirror and turned to take a longer look at her car. Inside his Subaru, the radio was blaring. She caught a few words of a newscast. He hit the power button and silenced it.

The news report had been about that jailbreak in Crying Call.

The driver offered a wry look. "You're smart to worry, but it's not me. I'm an off-duty sheriff's deputy."

He wrestled his wallet from his back pocket and flipped it open to show her a badge.

It was shiny, and the star looked official.

She rested her hands on the windowsill. He seemed sincere. She straightened, eyeing the road east and west. A lone big rig blew past and vanished over the crest of a rise. There might not be another chance.

"Yeah, okay." She hopped in. "I'm grateful."

He signaled and pulled back onto the roadway. One of those pine-tree-shaped air fresheners swung back and forth from the rearview. The back seat was piled with camping gear.

"Excuse the mess," he said. "I'm on my way to Vegas but I can drop you in Boulder City. If you don't mind riding along until we hit the Nevada side."

"That's fine. I'm just glad for the warmth. That wind is cutting."

She tossed her blond hair over her shoulder. "I didn't get your name."

He accelerated and turned to look at her. She held out her hand to shake his.

A handcuff flashed into view and snapped shut.

◆   ◆   ◆

In Rincon, the storm had finally blown itself out. The Oklahoma plains were white, the trees glittering with ice. Emmerich drove up the wooded gravel drive to Aaron Gage's house. A police cruiser and a county crime lab van were parked outside it. He got out. A man wearing a Rincon PD jacket came out to greet him.

"Lieutenant Pacheco," Emmerich said.

The man pulled off latex gloves and shook Emmerich's hand. "The crime scene team is nearly done. Your eye will be welcome. And any suggestions to help us track the bastard who killed Aaron."

Emmerich took an aluminum briefcase from his car and followed Pacheco inside. The house was small but uncluttered, laid out with clear pathways that worked for a blind homeowner. Or had. On the kitchen floor, a heavy bloodstain marked the spot where the army veteran had died.

Emmerich oriented himself to the flow of the house. "What's been moved since the attack?"

"Nothing. From what Aaron told me, and from tracing the path of the blood, he confronted the killer in that hallway." Pacheco gestured.

Emmerich saw immediately: Gage had held the point. The attacker had not gotten past him to his daughter.

"Gage told you he cut the killer," he said.

"He felt the knife slice through flesh. He would know. He was trained in close combat." Pacheco eyed the stain in the kitchen. "Aaron fought. Damn hard."

Emmerich went to the hall. The blood on the

hardwood had dried into swirls and smears, evidence of Gage and the killer grappling on the floor. But on the wall, there was castoff—blood that had been flung either from a swinging knife or from a bleeding, swinging arm.

He saw how the battle had unfolded. Gage had engaged the killer in the hall. The fight had worked its way to the living room, where Gage was stabbed. After the killer fled, Gage dragged himself to the kitchen, trying to reach the phone.

A sliced forearm. Six stab wounds. Those penetrating wounds significantly distinguished this killing from Detrick's other murders. The fight could account for the difference in MO, but Emmerich didn't think it provided an explanation.

A crime tech came in.

Emmerich nodded at the hallway. "Have you collected blood samples to determine whether any of this impact spatter belongs to the killer?"

The young man said, "Yes. They'll be going to the lab."

"How long will it take to get results?"

The man shook his head. He didn't know. Not today.

Emmerich set his aluminum briefcase on the kitchen counter. He unlatched it. "Let me perform a couple of spot tests. I may be able to narrow the possibilities down."

It was nearly five P.M., the sun angling toward a burnished winter sunset, when the tourists strolling along the top of Hoover Dam stopped to admire its awesome height and scale. On the north side, Lake Mead sparkled. On the south side, below the dam—far, far below—the

Colorado River spilled out, an indigo snake sliding through stark canyon walls.

Jeremy Chung raised the camera that hung on a strap around his neck. He'd come from Saint Louis with his wife and kids, a winter break to grab some sunshine, see some shows in Las Vegas, maybe gamble a little, and eat—oh, the all-you-can-eat buffet at the Bellagio—and to visit the Hoover Dam. To a civil engineer like Jeremy Chung, the Hoover Dam was Mecca. He'd pined to see it all his life. Now, at forty-seven, he was finally here.

He raised his Nikon and snapped a dozen shots.

"It's an arch-gravity dam," he said to his teenage son. "Seven hundred twenty-six point four feet tall. Six-point-six *million* tons of concrete. At its base, the water pressure is forty-five thousand pounds per square foot."

The light was sinking—this was the start of the golden hour, and he was lucky to catch it.

Kelly and the kids strolled ahead of him. He lowered the camera.

"Guys. Turn around."

He wanted to compose the shot so the family was just off center, with the graceful curve of the dam at their backs, and beyond that the rugged hills of Black Canyon jabbing the blue sky, electricity pylons rising along its crest like sentinels.

They turned. They looked forgiving. Jeremy loved his camera. He was at best a middling photographer, but it was a hobby that got him outdoors. He waved them closer together.

He peered through the viewfinder and with two fingers

gestured his daughter to scoot in. Olivia sighed, but smiled.

"Perfect," Chung said.

While they posed, he checked the light settings. He got the camera halfway to his eye and paused, caught by motion in the distance.

Downstream, about fifteen hundred feet away, the O'Callaghan-Tillman Bridge carried US 93 across the gorge above the river—the border between Arizona and Nevada. Eight-hundred-eighty-foot clearance beneath the span—more than four times the height of the Golden Gate Bridge. Traffic was light. And something seemed off.

"Dad," Elliott said. "You've got the shot. Take it."

A car had stopped on the bridge. Road signs clearly forbade that. Stopping was plain dangerous. And this didn't look like a breakdown. The car door was open. Somebody was moving along the passenger side.

"Jeremy?" his wife said.

Chung felt his feet moving almost without volition. He walked toward the concrete abutment of the dam.

"No," he muttered. "What . . ."

Above him in the distance, a figure rolled over the railing of the bridge.

Chung yelled, "*No!*"

His family turned around to look at the bridge. Every tourist strolling along the dam did.

"Oh, *God,*" Chung cried.

But he was too far away. It was already too late.

The distant figure was wrapped in a white sheet. It

plunged from the span. Eight hundred eighty feet, straight down.

People around him screamed. Chung screamed. His daughter screamed. He grabbed her and pulled her head to his chest, covering her eyes.

Down and down and down the figure fell. The sheet streamed behind it like an angel's robes.

On the bridge, the car that had stopped pulled away.

Emmerich double-checked the two spot tests he'd performed. The results were incontrovertible. He pulled off his latex gloves and stepped onto the porch outside Aaron Gage's cabin.

He punched Brianne Rainey's cell number.

"Boss?" she said.

The view across the plains was white, cut by the serpentine red scar of the river. His breath frosted the air.

"It's not Detrick. The DNA and colorimetric assay tests are undisputable," he said. "Gage's killer is female."

A mile below the Hoover Dam, the white-shrouded figure that had plunged from the bridge washed up on the bank of the Colorado River. The Las Vegas Metropolitan Police Department Search and Rescue unit launched a boat, which swung along the rocky promontory where the victim had lodged. Two officers hopped into the knee-deep blue water and waded to the shore. They took their time. One of the officers signaled to the boat, and his colleague aboard began snapping photos.

It was clear that this was a recovery, not a rescue. But they had to check.

"Ready?" the officer said.

His partner nodded.

The sheet was tangled completely around the body, the ends floating like moss in the current. Getting their arms under it, they lifted it onto the shore. They grunted. It was heavier than they'd expected.

The sun had dipped below the rim of the canyon walls. In the shade, the temperature was dropping. The officer had an uneasy sensation that left him feeling even colder than the day.

He unwrapped the tangled sheet from the body.

His partner said, "Damn."

The victim's wrists and throat were slashed. The body had been stabbed and Tasered multiple times.

It was a man in a plaid shirt and jeans. When they pulled his wallet from his back pocket, they saw the badge.

"He's a sheriff's deputy," the search and rescue officer said. "What the hell?"

At the Hoover Dam, Jeremy Chung and his family milled, wretchedly, waiting for news. Finally, the cop who had responded to his 911 call—to all the 911 calls—replaced the radio in his patrol car and walked over. His face was hard.

"No chance, was there?" Chung said.

"No," the officer said. "May I see your camera?"

Chung pulled the strap over his head and turned the viewfinder so the officer could scroll through his shots.

When the body fell . . . was thrown . . . plunged . . . from the bridge, some instinct in Chung's mind had kicked in, and told him to *get some damned photos*.

"The person who fell . . . ," Chung said.

The deputy's jaw was tight. "He's dead."

"He?"

The deputy nodded.

Chung shook his head. "I'm sure the person I saw at the rail . . . the person had long blond hair. It was a woman. I'm positive."

The deputy clicked through the photos. Chung had managed to catch a streaky shot of the car pulling away on the bridge. The Subaru had driven west into Nevada, in the direction of Las Vegas.

In Phoenix, Caitlin's phone rang. Everybody's did.

53

At the FBI's Phoenix Division, Caitlin stood in front of the USGS topo map of Arizona. She was examining photos sent by the Las Vegas police.

They included crime scene photos from the bank of the Colorado River. And the victim's driver's license: David Nordlinger, age forty-three. And a streaked, out-of-focus picture, shot by a tourist who'd been atop the Hoover Dam—Nordlinger's car, being driven away.

The driver's license listed Nordlinger as five-seven, one forty-five. Welterweight. Still, the woman who dumped him over the rail had to be seriously strong. A photo of his body, laid out on the stony bank of the river beneath towering canyon walls, revealed cuts to his wrists and throat that were deep and showed no hesitation.

"Slashed and stabbed," she muttered. Like Aaron Gage. A woman involved. Like with Aaron Gage.

Across the floor, Rainey was on the phone. She was scribbling on a notepad. Her voice sounded—for her—unusually excited. "Thank you."

She hung up and strode over to Caitlin, holding a

tablet computer. "State troopers found a car abandoned with its hood up on US 93, four miles east of the Colorado River. A blue Toyota Corolla."

Caitlin's eyebrows went up. "Blue, Japanese make. Like Lia Fox's neighbor reported seeing at her apartment complex."

"A trucker phoned the cops when he saw the news about Deputy Nordlinger's murder—says he passed that broken-down car on US 93. Nordlinger's Subaru was stopped in front of it. A blond woman was standing at the window, talking to him." Rainey's eyes were bright.

"There's something else. What?"

Rainey turned the tablet to show Caitlin. "Phoenix PD got video from a gas station up the street from Fox's complex."

She hit PLAY. The video showed morning traffic on the street outside the gas station. And, in the distance, the driveway at Lia's apartment complex. A car was pulling out. A blue Corolla.

"It's the same car," Rainey said. "It's him. Detrick, this killing—it's all connected."

Caitlin eyed the topo map on the wall. Hoover Dam was two hundred seventy miles from Phoenix. Almost twelve hundred from Rincon, Oklahoma.

"What the hell is going on?" she said.

Jester, Nevada, was a faded mining town three hundred miles north of Las Vegas. In the high desert, the air floated thin and chill as the sunset emptied in the west. A billboard proclaimed JESTER—GATEWAY TO NEVADA'S

GHOST TOWNS. Scrubby sagebrush dotted the edges of the highway. The mountains were brown, rocky, and bleak. The horizon, glowing orange and pink, gave way to a sapphire sky. The stars were winking on overhead.

A car passed the city-limits sign and rolled along the main street, headlights bright in the deepening dusk.

Jester featured shuttered mines, twelve slot machines at the Silver Dollar Saloon, and two unadvertised local attractions. One was the old cemetery, a creepy spread of sand, rock-bounded graves, and tilted, weathered wooden crosses. Pioneer families were buried there from the late 1800s. Along with miners who'd been crushed, or died of thirst, or were shot in gunfights over cheating at cards at the Silver Dollar Saloon. The cemetery gate creaked, the wind howled, and sand was constantly scoured from the graves. It was a desolate place to lie for eternity.

The second attraction, next door, was the Circus Inn. On its sun-bleached sign, a whiteface clown leered at the highway.

The New York City tourists in the rental car slowed and pulled in, relieved to see VACANCY in the office window. To connoisseurs of tacky Americana, the Circus Inn was legendary.

Lissie and Xander Bailey parked and got out. They stretched and pulled their jackets tight in the chilly air. Jester was at six thousand feet elevation, and on winter nights like this, the desert turned freezing.

Xander sauntered across the parking lot, mouth open. "Unreal." He laughed.

Lissie clapped her hands. "Finally."

They'd planned their western road trip for months. Jester was a definite must on their itinerary. They'd seen the Circus Inn on friends' social media posts and thought they couldn't just snap a photo as they drove by. They *had* to stay here.

Their *Rough Guide* said all rooms at the motel featured black velvet clown paintings. They were hoping to get a room overlooking the cemetery, for the full creepazoid experience.

Heading for the office, they strolled past the empty swimming pool. Tumbleweeds filled the deep end, twitching in the breeze. There was only one other car in the parking lot. They couldn't see lights in any of the rooms.

"Guess we didn't need to worry about the place being sold out," Lissie said.

A washing machine sat on the porch outside the office. Through the front window, they could see a small television on the counter, showing a sitcom. Nearby, the cemetery gate banged under a gust of wind.

Xander opened the door for Lissie. A bell tinkled. They stepped inside, and stopped.

Lissie laced her fingers together and pressed her hands to her chin, breathless. It was real: The entire room was crowded with clown dolls, figurines, paintings, and masks. The shelves on the walls groaned with harlequin toys. On a bench in the corner, a quartet of garish tramp mannequins sat in tableau.

"Check it off the bucket list," Xander said.

The office was empty, the fluorescent lights buzzing. Despite the tinkling bell on the door, their entry brought nobody from the private office behind the counter. The TV gurgled, a laugh track adding false cheer.

Xander rang the bell on the counter. Nobody came. The overhead fluorescents flickered and continued to buzz.

"Hello?" Xander called.

Lissie approached the counter. "Where is everyone?"

Then she realized that the lights weren't the only thing that was buzzing.

Her voice came out as a whisper. "Xander."

He was frozen beside her.

Slowly they turned. In the corner, among the mannequins, flies were swarming.

Lissie tried to understand what she was seeing. Xander made a choked, gurgling sound. Like he was about to vomit.

The flies covered the eyes and mouth of a woman, gowned in white and heavily made up, propped among the clowns. She was dead.

The Baileys screamed.

54

The chartered Gulfstream swept into a bank and descended toward a narrow airstrip five miles outside Jester. The desert raced by below. Sharp hills cast long shadows across rocky ground in the morning light. From the air, Caitlin thought, the town looked like a collection of children's building blocks dropped along a black stripe of highway, in the middle of a thousand square miles of emptiness.

As the jet lined up on final approach, Emmerich's phone chirped. He glanced at it. "Homicide detective will meet us at the motel."

The jet flared and touched down, thrust reversers roaring. They taxied toward a hangar and single-wide trailer that served as the airstrip's operations base. A rental car was waiting, the rental company agent twirling a key ring nervously around his index finger.

The jet braked to a stop, the engines spooled down, and the first officer emerged from the cockpit to open the main door. Rainey grabbed her things. Caitlin jogged down the stairs behind her.

The morning sun was brilliant, the cold sky a flawless blue, but a black void seemed to eddy at the edges of her vision. She knew what was waiting for them in town.

Caucasian female, midthirties. Brown eyes, bleached blond hair. Well nourished, no identifying marks.

Emmerich took the car keys from the rental agent with a thank-you. They got in. Emmerich pulled onto the empty highway and sped toward town at seventy miles per hour.

Rainey checked her phone messages. She listened to voice mail with pursed lips.

"Message from the Crying Call police chief. We know how Detrick was communicating with the outside—and how he got out of town," she said. "Somebody smuggled a cell phone and a car key into the jail. A cashier at the local KFC ran his mouth to some friends—said a woman gave him a phone and key and asked him to plant it in a big-box meal."

The desert flashed past. Horse corrals. Trailer homes.

Caitlin said, "Detrick was being served KFC for lunch almost every day. I saw an empty box on the floor of his cell."

"An officer buys lunch for prisoners. One of Detrick's fans apparently followed the cop to the KFC. Convinced the cashier to slip the burner phone and key into the bottom of the box below the wax paper and greasy chicken. The cashier stuck the box in a plastic sack and handed it to the cop. The sack was heavy enough that the officer didn't notice the extra weight. Didn't search the box. At least not all the way to the bottom."

Emmerich said, "The clerk was paid?"

"A hundred dollars," Rainey said. "He's now under arrest."

"Description of the woman?"

"White, twenties, eager. She had black hair, but could have been a wig. She wore a hooded parka, ski hat, and sunglasses," Rainey said. "Crying Call PD is reviewing visitor logs and video to see if she visited Detrick in jail. But presume she wore a disguise and used a fake ID."

"Police artist?"

"They're bringing one in from the Flagstaff Resident Agency."

The car bottomed over a dip in the road. Emmerich's voice was dry. "Woman in Crying Call. Woman in Rincon. Woman at the Hoover Dam. Same one?"

They barreled down the highway, but Caitlin felt like they were running ten steps behind. Neither roadblocks nor a statewide BOLO had netted anything. Detrick was moving across the vast empty desert—maybe in stolen cars, maybe hitchhiking—but they couldn't corner him. Couldn't corner *them*.

They crested a hill and hit Jester's main street. Bleached-brick buildings. MONEY TO LOAN. WE BUY GOLD AND SILVER. LIQUOR. GUNS AND AMMUNITION. FAMILY MINE TOURS.

At the Circus Inn, the parking lot was blocked off with yellow tape. A forensic team was working the scene.

The local sheriff's department homicide detective had driven from the county seat, Coyote Pass, one hundred fifty miles away. The man climbed from an SUV, dressed in jeans and a ski jacket. His grim face was a startling contrast to the gaudy clown grinning down from the motel sign.

He introduced himself as Dave Perez and shook hands all around. "Victim's body's been transported to the local funeral home. Forensic pathologist is on his way from Carson City to perform the autopsy. Once he collects trace from her hands, he'll take fingerprints, and we can hopefully confirm ID." His eyes were narrow, his voice flat. "It was brutal."

Caitlin had seen photos of the body, taken before it was moved from the lobby of the motel. The victim had been beaten around the head and face, strangled, and her wrists were slit. The white nightgown she wore was soaked with blood.

Emmerich said, "He's devolving."

Not a dichotomy between organized and disorganized. A continuum. And Detrick was sliding along it.

"That mean he'll keep picking up steam?" Perez said.

"Yes," Emmerich said. "And he's gained at least one accomplice. A woman."

"How'd that happen?"

"She may be a groupie who became obsessed with him while he was in jail."

"Groupies don't usually join their idols in killing sprees."

"It's rare, but a recognized phenomenon—aggressive hybristophilia. Bonnie and Clyde syndrome."

Detrick's new sidekick was the most dangerous of fans—a collaborator. She didn't think he was innocent.

She wasn't after a vicarious kick from contact with a jailed killer. Fueled by lust, euphoria, and—possibly—fear of him, she was joining Detrick in committing crimes.

Caitlin said, "She's a thrill seeker."

"Looks like she got her chance," Perez said. "Armed and dangerous, I presume."

"A cop killer."

That chilled the conversation. Perez logged them into the scene, lifted the yellow tape, and led them across the motel parking lot.

Rainey looked around. "No sign of the motel clerk?"

"No." Perez's face was somber. "The manager's in Reno, long weekend. He left his nephew in charge of the front desk." He took a spiral notebook from his pocket. "Ezekiel Frye, age twenty. Hasn't been seen since six P.M. yesterday. We checked the rooms, the Dumpster, the pool. He's not on the property."

That wasn't good.

Caitlin absorbed the scene. "No cameras?"

"Nearest one's at the gas station half mile away." Perez nodded at the forensic techs. "They got here an hour ago from Coyote Pass. That's the nearest lab."

They passed the decrepit swimming pool. A chain-link fence surrounded it—maybe to pen the tumbleweeds that filled the deep end. On the far side of the parking lot was the bleakest cemetery Caitlin had ever seen.

Perez led them to the office door. He gave them a look and pulled it open.

Caitlin didn't often feel a spooky chill at crime scenes. Her job was to dissect and analyze the evidence, to help identify and prosecute offenders. And she didn't believe in ghosts. Not in demons or poltergeists or extradimensional forces that reached into this world to steal souls.

Then she stepped through the door into the lobby of the Circus Inn.

She stopped so hard that Rainey bumped into her from behind. She went cold. If she'd been a dog, she would have dug her paws in and laid her ears flat and backed out, growling.

Rainey stepped around her. "Lordy."

A hundred clowns stared at her, their manic eyes and skeletal grins seeming to X-ray the room. The sweet, putrid smell of decaying human flesh clung to the walls and floor and ceiling and furniture.

Under her breath, Caitlin said, "Oh, my hell."

Emmerich eyed her as he walked to the corner where the body had been found. The three adult-size harlequin dolls, which had been propped around it, had been removed from a bench.

Perez brought up photos on his phone, taken before the body was moved. "One thing. You can see it in this photo. The killer . . ."

His expression turned astringent. He handed the phone to Emmerich.

Emmerich zoomed in. "What did he do?"

"We think that's a bite mark, around the gash on her right wrist."

Caitlin felt light-headed. "You think he sucked her blood?"

"It seemed to be postmortem. But he may have inserted his tongue into the wound."

Emmerich looked up. "If so, there'll be DNA."

Perez nodded. "She'd been dead less than twenty-four hours. Rigor hadn't passed. And the flies were mature. They hadn't hatched from maggots."

He took the phone, scrolled, and raised it to show them a photo of the flies on the victim's face.

Caitlin shook her head. She'd seen it already. Seen all the photos. Despite the clown makeup, and the violence done to the woman's face, despite the need to obtain fingerprints for an official identification, she knew.

She was sure it was Lia Fox.

The black void swirled at the edges of her vision. It thickened and curled around her throat. She inhaled and forced herself to stay calm.

Her eye caught on three small clown dolls leaning against one another on a shelf above the harlequins.

"What's that?"

The three clowns had been rearranged to look like a human centipede, one behind the next. On each of their foreheads, a single letter was written in crimson lipstick. She stepped in to get a better look.

F-B-I.

"Not subtle."

The void receded. She saw the scene more clearly. She breathed through her nose, because that would eventually deaden the smell.

"This took exceptional audacity," she said. "And it's a

spectacle. Before now, Detrick hid his victims. In places where he could . . . *enjoy* them, privately." Anger edged into her voice. "But this is as public as it gets. It's reckless, but he doesn't care. He's beyond boundaries."

Emmerich said, "He's presenting this as a joke. But his fury's overwhelming."

"He's slapping us in the face," Caitlin said. "And using murder to do it."

Perez said, "You look a tad pale. You all right?"

"Fine." She clenched her hands in her pockets to stop them from shaking.

"It may be the altitude. You don't notice it because we're in a bowl on a high plain. But Jester's higher than Denver. Drink some water and get some breakfast."

She wanted to run outside and breathe uncorrupted air. Instead, she nodded. "Can we see the room where he did it?"

With a curt nod, perhaps reacting to her abruptness, Perez led them outside.

Defining the crime scene was always a deliberate decision, and homicide detectives had to get it right. Too small, and investigators could not only overlook evidence but leave it unprotected, open to contamination and destruction. Too large, and the search could become attenuated—resources spread too thin, with too little time, trying to cover too much ground.

Here, Detective Perez had defined the scene as the entire motel property, up to the street in front and the cemetery along the side. Caitlin thought that was probably right. But it meant they had two acres and a forty-two-room motel to search, inch by inch, for fingerprints, footprints, trace, fibers, DNA, and signs of disturbance.

Along the motel's back fence, a crime scene tech in white coveralls walked a grid, searching for evidence. Another tech searched the pool, pacing back and forth across the shallow end, working her way toward the tumbleweed-clogged deep end.

Perez led them across the parking lot to Room 4. The door was propped open, a tech working inside.

Perez took gloves and booties from a lab case outside the room. "Step inside the door but no farther."

Caitlin nodded, donned the booties and gloves, and crossed the threshold.

The bedroom looked dingy but clean. The bed hadn't been slept in. But the bedspread was rumpled, and the pillows had indentations. *Good*—lying on a pillow meant leaving hair, and if it was follicular, it would contain DNA. A sad clown grimaced from a painting on the wall.

She could smell the blood.

Hands hanging at her sides, Caitlin turned toward the bathroom. The door was open. The counter was smeared with garish makeup. The shower curtain had been pulled back.

From the riot of red streaks on the wall tile, the blood was spray from a severed carotid artery. Caitlin breathed in. Breathed out.

She stepped back outside. For a second, she couldn't think. She could only feel what the victim—what Lia, surely—must have felt as Kyle Detrick forced her into the bathtub and drew a knife. Her terror, her sorrow, her pain.

She turned away from the room. Perez said nothing.

Caitlin breathed in again. Out. Gold sunlight needled her eyes. Across the parking lot, the forensic tech paced the empty pool. On the highway, a gravel truck slowed as the driver gawked at the scene. Caitlin half saw Rainey walking toward her.

Beyond the pool, the cemetery sat dejected in the chilly sun. Crosses leaned at crazy angles, as if it were a Halloween haunted house. Dust scudded across the ground. At the cemetery's farthest edge, a tumbleweed was caught on the point of a cross, shivering in the wind.

Rainey approached. "What's that?"

Caitlin frowned. "Don't know."

The tumbleweed twisted, as though trying to break free. A ribbon—a silver stripe—was wound among its dry branches.

"Is that duct tape?" Rainey said.

She strode across the parking lot with Caitlin. They entered the cemetery and wound their way past the listing crosses and sun-bleached wooden grave markers.

"Damn. It *is* duct tape." Rainey jogged up to the tumbleweed. It was affixed to the tip of the listing cross so it couldn't blow away.

"Duct tape's part of Detrick's kidnap kit," Caitlin said. "It's a signal."

"To whom? Us?"

Caitlin scanned the scene, turning three-sixty. Panning the desert, she climbed over the cemetery's wrought iron fence and examined the ground. Behind her, Rainey whistled, high and loud.

"Emmerich," Rainey shouted.

A second later she hopped the fence and joined Caitlin. From the cemetery boundary, empty ground ran a mile or so to crinkled brown hills. Cautiously, surveying the sandy soil, Rainey walked forward. After a minute, she pointed.

"Tire tracks."

She crouched. Caitlin drew up beside her. They heard Emmerich loping toward them.

The tracks originated with twin divots, like the vehicle had accelerated sharply from a standstill. They ran straight across the sand toward the hills.

"I know what he did," Rainey said. "What *they* did." She stood and peered back at the motel parking lot. "They grabbed some tumbleweeds from the pool and duct taped them to the back bumper of the vehicle. The tumbleweeds dragged on the ground and covered their tracks when they drove onto the sand."

Caitlin knit her brow. "But they took them—or at least one—off and taped it to that cross."

"Yes. Because they wanted somebody to eventually come looking, and find out which way they went."

"Why?"

Emmerich jogged up.

"Tracks," Rainey said. "We need a photographer. And the techs should make molds ASAP, before the wind blows them away."

Emmerich's gaze followed the tire ruts across the desert. "They headed straight for the hills?"

On the hillside was a square opening, black against

the russet earth. Rocks and dirt trailed from its mouth down the slope.

Caitlin recalled the billboards leading into town. FAMILY MINE TOURS.

"Mine shaft," she said.

Emmerich spun and yelled at Perez to bring the techs and a four-by-four vehicle.

Rainey took off running, cross-country. "The missing clerk."

By the time they climbed the hillside, Rainey was wheezing and her face was slick with sweat. Her braids had fallen from her chignon and stuck to her face. Emmerich was wired and blowing hard. Caitlin's legs felt as wobbly as a foal's. The mine shaft was abandoned, its support beams split and rotted. The local officers approached the entrance with weapons drawn.

"Wait here," Detective Perez said.

He swept the beam of his Maglite across the mine tunnel and led a uniformed deputy inside. Caitlin tried to see beyond the intense sunlight into the shadows.

Perez turned to gray scale. His breathing and footsteps faded. After a minute, the deputy's voice echoed. "Detective. Over here."

Footsteps pounded deeper into the tunnel. Flashlight beams swung across the walls.

"Agents!" Perez called.

Emmerich ducked his head and charged in, with Caitlin and Rainey right behind.

Fifty yards into the tunnel, the motel clerk, Ezekiel

Frye, lay crumpled facedown on the ground. He was a young black man with dreads, his face dusty. His jeans and T-shirt were stiff with dried blood. Perez rolled him onto his back.

He went rigid. "Oh, Christ."

Emmerich's flashlight illuminated the clerk's body. Perez dropped to the young man's side. Frye was breathing.

55

In the abandoned hillside mine, Jester firefighter-paramedics slipped a cervical collar around Ezekiel Frye's neck and got an IV running. Frye had been stabbed in the abdomen, and one wrist had been hastily, shallowly slashed. He was hovering at the edge of consciousness. From the blood trail and drag marks on the dirt inside the tunnel, he had been dumped deep inside and tried to crawl back to the entrance, before collapsing.

Caitlin stood in the sharp sun on the slope outside the mine entrance. Fire trucks, an ambulance, and sheriff's SUVs were massed at the bottom of the hill. The medics brought Frye out, strapped to a stretcher, and used a rope pulley to lower him carefully down the slope to the valley floor. They lifted the stretcher into the ambulance.

Detective Perez came out of the shadowed mine entrance. "The kid's going to survive. Why'd Detrick do such a sloppy job?"

Emmerich turned. "I suspect that Detrick's groupie is the one who attacked Frye."

"Think they had to leave the scene in a hurry? Or did she think he was as good as dead?"

Below them, a paramedic jumped down from the back of the ambulance. He waved. "Detective."

Perez half jogged to the bottom of the slope, with the others sidestepping behind him on the crumbling dirt. Perez spoke to the paramedic and climbed into the ambulance. When Caitlin got there, Perez was leaning over Frye, hand on his shoulder, head turned to listen to the young man's whisper.

Perez nodded, squeezed Frye's shoulder, and climbed out. The paramedic slammed the doors. He got in the cab and the ambulance pulled away, lights spinning, jostling at speed over the sandy ground.

Perez's narrowed gaze was chilly. "There were two of them. A man tied him up. Woman stabbed him. Untied him when they dumped him in the mine."

Emmerich said, "They wanted him to escape."

Perez nodded. "Man gave him a message. 'She couldn't keep her mouth shut. So I shut it for her.'"

Emmerich flexed and opened his fists. He seemed to stare through the detective for a moment. "Where's the mortuary?"

Perez frowned. "Four blocks from the motel."

Emmerich jogged toward the detective's SUV. "Let's go."

Caitlin said, "I'm coming."

It took two minutes for Perez to drive them to their rental car, and two more for him to lead them in a convoy to the funeral home. Inside, they were directed to the prep room. When they came through the swinging double doors, the forensic pathologist and a mortuary assistant were gowned and gloved. The two men turned in surprise. On the stainless steel preparation table lay a black body bag, still zipped. The thick smell of embalming fluid permeated the air.

"Detective?" the pathologist said. "We're just about to start."

Emmerich strode up to the table. "May I unzip the bag?"

The doctor gestured for him to go ahead. Emmerich grasped the zipper ring and pulled.

The victim's face came into the light. Dead eyes open, lips parted, face flaccid under the thick layer of white pancake makeup. Her short hair was white-blond. It had been harshly and recently bleached. She was dressed in a see-through baby doll nightie. Against the black plastic of the body bag, she looked like a photo negative.

It was Lia Fox.

Her lips were open a centimeter. Emmerich leaned close.

"Something's stuffed in her mouth." He pulled on gloves. "Doctor?"

The pathologist handed him a pair of tweezers. Emmerich drew out a crumpled Polaroid.

He set it in a stainless steel tray and teased it open. It was old—very old. It showed a blond teenager on a sunny day, at a picnic on a Houston college campus.

Caitlin stared. She and Rainey had seen a nearly identical photo in the album at Aaron Gage's house.

The black vines swirled again, threatening to wrap Caitlin's throat and cut off her air. She put a hand to her neck. Breathed through her mouth.

Perez's phone rang. The detective stepped outside to answer it.

Emmerich thanked the pathologist for letting him intrude. He headed through the swinging double doors. Rainey followed.

Caitlin hesitated. She could do nothing for Lia Fox now. Couldn't comfort or reassure her. Couldn't even touch her, not without contaminating the body.

But she could find Detrick and stop him from doing this to anybody else. She reached out. With her fingertips, she brushed the exterior of the body bag. She blinked.

Nodding to the pathologist, she turned and left.

Outside, the low winter sun cast stiletto shadows. Emmerich, Rainey, and Detective Perez stood beside Perez's SUV. Perez had his laptop open on the hood.

Emmerich beckoned her. "The car belonging to the deputy who was killed at the Hoover Dam. It's been found."

On the computer screen were photos. The deputy's stolen Subaru, with the ASK ME ABOUT MY EAGLE SCOUT bumper sticker, had been abandoned at a trailer park north of Lake Tahoe. The victim's blood splashed the seats. Covering the dashboard, and taped inside the windows of the car, were Polaroids. Some showed the murdered man. Others showed Lia Fox, propped on the bench in the lobby of the Circus Inn. The rictus grins of clown dolls filled the screen.

Taped to the steering wheel was a single photo of Teri

Drinkall, the woman missing from the Dallas parking garage.

In the photo, Teri was alive, but Caitlin felt a draining sensation. She knew Teri was dead. And she felt certain that Detrick had posted it as a personal rebuke to her, for questioning him about Teri that day at the jail.

The truth broke through the frayed barrier of denial she had erected. Her eyes stung. For a second, the shields she tried to keep up seemed far too porous. She felt Rainey at her shoulder. She thought, *Rainey's wrong. I need stronger walls. Not more openness.* She took a breath.

Emmerich said, "It's a taunt."

No kidding, Caitlin thought. Detrick was telling them, *You lose. Victims will continue to die.* She heard his voice in her head. *Should have done yourself. Gonna wish you had.*

Static erupted from the radio in the SUV. Perez got in and grabbed the transmitter. A minute later he got out with a map in his hand.

"That trailer park where the deputy's Subaru was dumped? Another car's been reported stolen from there."

Perez unfolded the map on the hood. From Jester, Lake Tahoe was two hundred fifty miles north.

"Detrick could head in any direction from Tahoe," Perez said. "He could take I-80 into Reno. From there he could head to either Salt Lake City or San Francisco. Or he could head north. It's wild country in that direction, for a good three hundred miles."

Caitlin stuck her hands in her pockets. "We know which way he's heading."

Rainey nodded. "Agreed."

Caitlin stabbed the map. Crying Call. Phoenix. Hoover Dam. Jester. Lake Tahoe. With each abduction, every murder, each stop to kill and mock, Detrick was drawing closer to the Pacific Northwest.

"He's going to Portland," she said. "Detrick's going after Emily Hart."

Emmerich thought for a moment, his gaze sharpening. "He knows we'll come. Everything he did here in Jester after the murder has been deliberate. Leaving the clerk alive, showing us how to find his tracks, giving the young man a message that led us to the mortuary." He looked up. "He wanted to slow us down."

Caitlin pulled out her phone to call the Portland police. Emmerich managed to shake Perez's hand but was already rushing toward their car.

Only hours after they arrived in Jester, Emmerich, Rainey, and Caitlin raced back up to the airstrip. The door of the Gulfstream was open, pilots in the cockpit running through their preflight checklist.

As Emmerich squealed up outside the hangar at the edge of the tarmac, he got a text. He read it as he climbed out.

"The vehicle that was stolen from the trailer park in Lake Tahoe—it could have been taken as early as seven P.M. last night." He checked his watch. "Detrick could have been driving all night."

Caitlin said, "How far is it from Tahoe to Portland?"

"Five hundred seventy miles. He could do it in ten hours."

Detrick wasn't just ahead of them. He could already be there.

They grabbed their gear and strode across the chilly tarmac. Swinging a duffel over his shoulder, Emmerich jogged up the jet's stairs. As he ducked his head through the door, he called to the pilots.

"We're all here."

The first officer greeted Caitlin and Rainey as they climbed aboard. He raised the stairs and closed the door. He returned to the cockpit. As soon as he squeezed into the right-hand seat, the captain began engine start-up.

Emmerich took a forward-facing seat. "Flight plan's filed for seven hundred twenty miles."

Caitlin stowed her gear and took a seat across the aisle. She pulled her phone from her back pocket. On the way to the airport she had liaised with the Portland police as well as the cops at Greenspring College, arranging for uniformed officers to guard Emily Hart until the FBI team arrived. Now she had to make a more difficult call.

Emily picked up immediately. "Agent Hendrix. My mom? Have you found her? I heard . . ."

Outside, the twin engines of the jet hummed to life.

Caitlin inhaled, preparing to break the news of Lia's death, but pain flashed through her. *No*. A seventeen-year-old, alone—she couldn't tell Emily under these circumstances. Not over the phone. Not when Emily needed focus and calm and mental clarity. Caitlin needed to wait until she saw her in person.

"Sorry. I can't tell you anything yet," she said.

"Why are you calling?"

"Where are you?"

"Chem lab." Emily's voice took on a starker tone. "Why?"

"Is your professor there? Staff? Building security?"

"My TA. What's wrong?"

Rainey had already pulled up a satellite map. The Chemistry Department lab was in an annex at the butt-end of campus, down a dead-end road.

"Emily, this is urgent. I need you to stay in the lab and wait for the Portland police. They're on their way. Tell your TA. The officers will take you to a police station. You should wait there until I arrive."

"He's coming, isn't he?"

"We want to take no chances," Caitlin said.

The jet's engines spooled up. In the cockpit, the captain nudged the throttles. They swung around and began a slow roll to line up at the south end of the runway. Rainey was on the phone to the Portland police.

Emily's voice had a nervous edge. "He knows I go to Greenspring? He knows where I live?"

"We have to presume so."

"So—what about my sorority sisters?"

A cold light hit Caitlin's eyes. "Sorority?"

"I just pledged Xi Zeta. I'm moving in this week-end—I've already filled out a change of address for everything," Emily said. "If this guy figures that out, what happens to my sorority sisters?"

Caitlin ran her knuckles across her forehead.

"They need police protection too," Emily said. "Half the women in the house are on the rugby team with me. But backup would be good."

Caitlin almost laughed. Emily's confidence in her teammates was sweet and sisterly and empowering, and, in these circumstances, absurd. She thought about the sorority house. It would have staff on duty, and some security. But Emily was right: If Detrick managed to learn that she'd pledged Xi Zeta, that wouldn't be good enough. They needed police backup.

"We'll arrange it," Caitlin said.

"Good. Awesome. Thanks."

Across from her, Rainey confirmed the plan with the Portland cops.

"The police are on the way to the chem lab," Caitlin said. "When you get to the police station, sit tight and wait for the FBI."

"I will. Absolutely."

The jet taxied along the narrow airstrip. The landscape outside was still. No traffic, no other aircraft coming or going, seemingly no birds aloft. Just thin, empty blue air. And the barren land. So barren, Detrick had already skipped town.

"Keep your eyes and ears open, Emily. Hang tight. We're coming."

"I'll be waiting."

Caitlin ended the call. She looked out the cabin window. Scrub and sandy ground.

Detrick had gotten Lia. Caitlin was *not* going to let him get Lia's daughter.

The jet braked at the end of the runway and swung in a tight one-eighty, lining up for takeoff. The sun arced across the cabin interior. She buckled her seat belt.

Her phone pinged. She glanced at it: a text from Michele.

We okay, girl?

Caitlin's stomach was already churning. She swiped the screen to reply—but her thumb hovered over the keyboard.

The engines idled for a few seconds. In the cockpit, the pilots pushed the throttles forward. The power revved. The plane sat poised.

Caitlin reread the text. She shut off her phone.

Michele would know she had read the message and wonder if Caitlin was ignoring her.

The pilots released the brakes. The engines roared and the jet leaped down the runway, gaining speed.

Let Michele wonder. Caitlin couldn't deal with her own life right now. Detrick was still ahead of them. The jet accelerated and soared sharply into the air.

56

The descent into Portland was turbulent. The weather had turned dirty as they hit central Oregon, crossed the spine of the Cascades, and flew into the latest winter system blowing in off the Pacific. The small jet swept through patchy rain up the Willamette Valley. Below, the landscape was a deep forest green. Caitlin tightened her belt as they jolted through the air.

Rainey eyed the clouds to the west. "The day's going to get icy."

Wind buffeted the plane. Out the right-hand window, beyond the long spread of the city, the eastern view showed green farmland and, sixty miles away, the massive, snow-coated slopes of Mount Hood. The volcano dominated the horizon like a lonely god.

The plane yawed sharply. Caitlin gripped the armrests of her seat.

Rainey said, "You know what Keyes would say if he were here."

Rainey, former air force, had a cast-iron stomach and a casual disregard for the effects of even the strongest turbulence. Across the aisle, Emmerich was working on his laptop. He didn't look up.

Caitlin watched clouds flash by. Rain streaked the window. And ice crystals. "Keyes would tell us our landing velocity, the height of that mountain to the inch, and inform us of the last time it erupted."

"And how likely it is to erupt again."

Emmerich hit a few computer keys. "Mount Hood. Stratovolcano. Elevation eleven thousand two hundred fifty feet. Last eruption 1907."

Caitlin laughed under her breath. Rainey smirked. The jet banked, and Caitlin got a tilted view of downtown Portland. Forested hills to the west, skyscrapers packing the Willamette River. Bridges and ships. The jet made a sweeping turn. From the cockpit she could hear the pilots talking to air traffic control.

Emmerich closed his laptop. "Don't worry about Hood. Or about its sister there across the river. Not today."

They descended below the last shreds of the clouds, and the Columbia River came into view. It was the color of slate. Beyond it, on the Washington side, loomed Mount Saint Helens.

"I won't." Today, volcanoes were the least of their concerns.

They landed parallel to the river, spray blowing off the wings and tires, thrust reversers deafening as Caitlin was pressed forward against her seat belt. They turned and taxied past the airport's two commercial concourses, passing near the wings of jetliners bound for Seattle and Chicago and Tokyo. When they arrived at the general aviation terminal, two agents from the FBI's Portland field office were waiting with a pair of Suburbans.

The captain spooled down the engines and opened the door. A cold, wet wind greeted them.

An agent got out of one of the SUVs to greet them, shoulders straining the seams of his raincoat. Emmerich didn't slow.

"Update?"

The agent led them toward the vehicles. "Portland police notified us ten minutes ago. The car stolen from that Lake Tahoe trailer park has been sighted on the Greenspring College campus."

Caitlin's stomach tightened.

Emmerich gave a razor-sharp look. "'Sighted'?"

"It parked in a disabled space without a placard. Student called campus public safety to get it towed. Read the plate number to the campus dispatcher. It's the vehicle."

"But?"

"By the time the campus cops arrived, it was gone."

Caitlin's phone pinged. It was a text from Emily Hart.

> I'm at Xi Zeta.

Caitlin's jaw slackened. "Jesus hell."

> I know you wanted me to wait at the police station but I couldn't do that when my sorority sisters are still at the house. Cops were pissed but I'm an adult. Xi Zeta is on lockdown and two officers are here.

Emmerich turned. "Agent Hendrix?"

"It's Emily."

She explained the situation. Emmerich absorbed it, with the look of a father who had experienced his share of teenage surprises.

"I'll head to campus with these agents," he said. "You and Rainey go to the sorority house."

He climbed into one of the Suburbans. The Portland agent tossed Rainey the keys to the second vehicle. Then Emmerich was off, racing for campus. Caitlin and Rainey threw their things in the other Suburban.

Rainey jumped behind the wheel. Caitlin slammed the door and phoned Emily. No answer. She checked the GPS and sent a text.

> Leaving PDX. On our way to you. Stay on
> lockdown at the sorority house. ETA 45 min.

Rainey put the pedal down.

57

Under lowering clouds, the Oregon night closed in early. An icy rain blew down the Willamette Valley. At Greenspring College in northwest Portland, Emmerich and the two Portland FBI agents wound their way along twisting, narrow roads. They pulled into the parking lot where the car stolen by Detrick in Lake Tahoe had been sighted. Two campus police cars waited for them, lights flashing.

The campus was hilly, its buildings surrounded by tall stands of Douglas fir. Emmerich got out and sleet hit his face. He shook hands with the senior campus police officer.

Her name tag read LEWIS. "We're fanning out into quadrants to search for the stolen car."

The campus was designed around a series of pedestrian plazas. Under the streetlights, the parking lot was deserted—beyond what Emmerich would have expected from the weather alone.

"We've activated the campus emergency alert system. Texts, e-mails, and recorded calls went out to all students that a dangerous suspect is at large. Those messages include the description and tag number of the stolen car. The library, labs, and especially student resident assistants have been alerted and are instructing students to shelter in place."

"Good."

Emmerich was pleased that Greenspring had a well-organized campus emergency plan. However, the need for college lockdown procedures drove a corkscrew ache through his chest. His own daughter was a sophomore at the University of Virginia.

A police radio scratched to life in Lewis's patrol car. She leaned in, spoke, and replaced the transmitter. Her face was alert.

"Student just flagged down one of our units outside the science quad. Said he saw the stolen car pull into a parking lot."

"Is the car still there?" Emmerich said.

"The student said the driver got out and headed into the Biology Department. White guy, looked like a trucker."

Emmerich scanned the parking lot. "We'll need backup."

The Xi Zeta sorority house was on Greek Row, a mile off the Greenspring campus. As the rain turned to sleet, clouds snuffed the sunset and afternoon sank to charcoal darkness. Emily Hart paced near the living room windows, watching the street for headlights. On the hillside, the Douglas firs swept back and forth in the wind. Her packed bag sat by the door.

A Portland police cruiser was parked at the curb. An officer was at the wheel. His partner was in the kitchen, heating a cup of coffee.

The house was an old colonial where thirty-six sorority sisters lived. It was tall and sturdy and to Emily it felt like a fortress. Dinner was on hold. The cook had been told to stay home. A couple of girls were foraging in the fridge for snacks. They made small talk with the young police officer. Their voices were subdued. Upstairs, Adele vied with *SportsCenter*. In the dining room, somebody was memorizing the periodic table. Normally, the house buzzed with energy. Tonight, the buzz felt anxious.

Footsteps jogged down the front stairs. The housemother, Nina Grosjean, came into the room carrying her purse and coat. "What's the latest?"

Emily held up her phone. "The FBI agents are on their way." She watched as Ms. Grosjean put on her coat. "You going to pick up Gabrielle?"

"Yes. Triple A can't get to the spot her car broke down as fast as I can. I don't want her out there on the roadside." But Ms. Grosjean looked torn. "Emily, if this weren't an emergency . . ."

"Go. Gabrielle's out there alone. I'm fine," Emily said. "There's a cop in the kitchen, a police car parked fifty feet from the door, and the literal FBI is literally on its way to get me." She squeezed Ms. Grosjean's arm. "Thank you for letting me wait here."

Grosjean whipped a scarf around her neck. For a second, she softened. She was a no-nonsense person who regarded the house director job as equivalent to managing a small hotel for young adults. She patted Emily on the shoulder.

"You're a member of this sorority. Of course you're welcome here." She buttoned her coat. "Call me when the FBI arrives."

"Yes, ma'am," Emily said.

Grosjean hurried into the kitchen. Her car was parked in the lot out back.

The police officer set his coffee on the counter. "I'll walk you outside."

Frigid air blew through the hallway until he shut the back door. Emily exhaled. She returned to the front window. The sleet was coming down harder.

On campus, Emmerich and the local agents drove behind the two Greenspring marked units, following them along a slippery road past the main quad to a parking lot outside the biology building. There they met up with another unit. Silent approach: no lights, no sirens. Beads of icy rain turned the view through the headlights white.

The stolen vehicle was a nondescript gray Camry. It was the only car parked in the lot. Emmerich climbed out into the miserable sleet. Officer Lewis approached the Camry cautiously and shined her flashlight at it.

Nobody was inside. Emmerich peered in, swiveling his own flashlight. The interior of the car looked clean. No belongings. No blood.

"Key's in the ignition," he said.

Lewis gave him a look. "Any possible reason we need to wait and get a warrant?"

He shook his head. "Stolen car. Exigent circumstances."

Putting gloves on, he opened the door, removed the key, and walked back to the trunk. With apprehension, he opened it.

It was empty.

Lewis's shoulder-mounted radio came to life. She bent her head to it, spoke, and straightened. "Portland police tactical unit has arrived."

The biology building was a three-story brick edifice that fronted the science quad. Emmerich tented a hand over his eyes to block the sleet that was blowing in his face. The lights in the building's lobby were on, but only a couple of office windows were lit. The building looked dead.

"Layout?" he said.

Lewis pointed. "Lobby, branching hallways that lead all the way around the building and converge in the back. Elevators, stairs. At the rear exit there's a set of steps down to a path that leads to the back of the quad."

"What's behind the quad?"

"The back exit leads to dorms and off-campus Greek houses. The biology building provides cover, and a short-cut, for anybody heading toward student housing."

"You lead," Emmerich said.

Lewis spoke again into her shoulder-mounted radio. Then said, "Behind me."

The campus cops and FBI approached the building in single file. They entered silently. The Biology Department office door was closed and locked. They advanced through the building in stacked formation.

Office doors were shut. The officers' rubber-soled shoes were quiet on the tile floor. They reached a corner. Lewis signaled them to hold, and peered around. She pulled back.

She whispered. "He's halfway down the hallway, walking toward the back of the building."

She leaned around the corner again and gave the *Go* signal. They moved and caught sight of the man walking away from them. He wore a red flannel shirt and a baseball cap. He disappeared around the next corner, heading for the rear exit.

Lewis leaned again into her radio. "He's coming."

They moved quickly along the hall. Stopped at the far corner. They heard the bar on an exterior door open. Lewis checked and signaled for them to advance. At the rear of the building was a small back lobby with plate-glass doors. The man in flannel was outside, jogging down the steps toward the dorms.

Outside, positioned in the trees under cover of the night, the leader of the Portland police tactical unit yelled, "*Freeze.*"

58

Caitlin and Rainey wound their way through a hillside neighborhood outside campus. In the dimming evening, Rainey carefully navigated the slick road. The route to the sorority house took them up the back side of the hill from the college, along a series of switchbacks. The windshield wipers were collecting sloppy slush.

Caitlin's phone rang. As she pulled it from her pocket, she remembered with a pang that she hadn't replied to Michele's text message. Nicholas Keyes was calling from Quantico.

"News?" she said.

"Just got the artist's sketch of the woman who aided Detrick when he was in jail. The one who smuggled the phone to him in his KFC."

Caitlin put the call on speaker.

"With the hood, wig, and enormous sunglasses, she looks like the Unabomber," Keyes said. "Not much help. But. *But*—I suspect it's the same woman who's in the *Madden NFL*–style video. The one who follows Detrick around the lobby of the movie theater in Solace before he kidnaps his victim. And the more I run that video, the more the data convinces me Detrick does *not* know she's tailing him."

Caitlin and Rainey exchanged a glance. Rainey said, "Send the drawing."

"Thanks, Keyes."

"That's not the only reason I'm calling," he said. "Emily Hart's social media has photos with her new sorority sisters at Xi Zeta. Presume Detrick knows."

"Portland police are on scene." Caitlin checked the GPS. "We're half a mile away."

Rainey slowed to round another switchback. Tense, Caitlin scanned the road and the forested hillside above the Willamette River.

"Be careful," Keyes said.

"Police. *Don't move.*"

Behind the biology building, the man in the flannel shirt stopped dead at the bottom of the steps. Guns drawn, the Portland police rushed from the shadows. Emmerich, the local FBI agents, and the campus cops burst through the back door into the sleet, weapons raised. They ran down the steps. Two Portland TAC officers threw the man to the ground.

He landed facedown on the sidewalk with a dull thud. The beams of a dozen flashlights pinned him. The cops cuffed his wrists.

Emmerich holstered his weapon, reached down, and rolled the man onto his back.

Under the cold glare of the flashlights, the man's

pulse ticked in his neck. His eyes were shiny coins. Emmerich pulled off his baseball cap.

It wasn't Detrick.

The man was white, doughy—and no older than twenty-two. As he lay on his shackled hands, his mouth went wide. He peered back and forth between Emmerich and the cops.

"Don't hurt me."

Emmerich backed up and peered around at the drenched, dismal night. The wet wind snuck beneath the collar of his coat.

"What the hell's going on?" the man said.

Officer Lewis knelt at the man's side. "Who are you?"

"Kevin Reid."

"What are you doing here?"

"I didn't do anything wrong."

"Why were you in the biology building?"

"The guy."

Emmerich said, "What guy?"

"The guy gave me a hundred bucks to deliver an envelope to the biology office. I didn't do anything wrong. All I did was slide the envelope under the office door."

Lewis turned the man on his side and pulled a wallet from his back pocket. Inside was a crisp one-hundred-dollar bill. She pulled out the man's driver's license.

"Kevin Reid," she said.

On the sidewalk, Reid lay shuddering. "Delivering an envelope isn't a crime. Don't point your guns at me."

At Lewis's nod, the cops holstered their weapons. Lewis pulled Reid to his feet. Her officers took him by the elbows and led him away for questioning. Emmerich scanned the dim, forested campus.

Lewis's breath wreathed the air. "What's going on?"

Emmerich felt deeply chilled. "A diversion. In Arizona, our agents arrested Detrick by following him to his target. He learned from that lesson. He pulled us off track."

Lewis said it. "So where the hell is he?"

When the doorbell rang at Xi Zeta, Emily was in the kitchen, downing a glass of milk. Through the back window, she could see the parking lot. Ms. Grosjean's car was gone. The spot where it had been parked was a dark square of asphalt unmarked by the accumulating sleet. The cop hadn't come back in. His footprints led around the house, out of sight.

Emily set the glass in the sink and headed for the front door.

In the living room, two of her sorority sisters jumped up from a sofa. Three others ran down the stairs and ducked into the front hall. Emily moved toward the door but they waved her back.

"Nuh-unh," said Julia Chan. "Stay."

Several of the young women formed a protective barrier around Emily. She felt like a rugby ball in the center of a scrum. Julia and her roommate, Hannah, nervously approached the door. It was heavy, solid wood. Julia, fists tight, peered through the peephole.

"It's a woman in a black suit." She turned to Emily. "Holding up FBI credentials."

Relaxing, Emily said, "It's fine."

The barrier let her through and she unlocked the door. "Special Agent Hendrix."

The woman on the porch lowered the badge wallet and pocketed the credentials. "Miss Hart."

Emily stepped aside and let her in. The woman was young, with reams of blond hair. She eyed the other girls.

"I need to speak to Emily alone. Please go to your rooms and wait there. I'll be up to interview you individually in a few minutes."

Curious and reluctant, the girls backed away. The blond turned to the man who had followed her inside. "Along with Special Agent in Charge Emmerich."

The man had dark hair and gray eyes. He closed and bolted the door.

59

Sleet streaked the windshield of the Suburban. Climbing toward the crest of the hill, Rainey edged around the final switchback. Amid tall firs, house lights became visible, fuzzy through the icy rain. Parked cars lined the narrow street. Nobody was out.

Caitlin pointed up the block. "That's it."

Rainey slowed to a crawl and lowered her head to peer through the accumulation on the windshield. The Xi Zeta house was a weathered colonial. Under its porch light the lawn was white with slush. A Portland police cruiser sat at the curb.

At the house, the shades were up on the windows. Inside, in what looked like the living room, Emily was visible, wearing a dark blue hoodie, brown curls falling from a messy ponytail. Arms crossed, she spoke to somebody across the room, beyond their line of sight.

"They didn't pull down the blinds," Rainey said.

Whom was Emily was talking to? They drew closer to the house. A woman walked into view, her back to the window. Through the sleet, Caitlin could see that she had blond hair that fell below her shoulders. The house-mother? No—she was too formally dressed. She wore a black suit and white blouse. Like a catering manager or hospital insurance coordinator. Or an FBI agent.

"Hendrix," Rainey said.

She hit the high beams. Directly ahead, the parked police cruiser sat empty. The driver's window was down, icy rain blowing into the car.

Caitlin's stomach tightened. "Christ."

In the house, the woman shook her finger at Emily. Talking to the girl over her shoulder, she walked to the front window and pulled down the blinds. For a fraction of a second, her face was visible.

"Jesus, did you see her . . ."

The woman's shadow remained visible against the drawn blinds. She turned.

She grabbed Emily by the arm and twisted her elbow behind her back.

"They're here," Rainey said.

The lights in the house went out.

Caitlin jumped from the Suburban while it was still rolling.

Glock in hand, Caitlin ran across the front lawn in the icy rain. Behind her, the Suburban squealed to a stop. Its door slammed. Rainey's footsteps pounded behind her.

They rushed up the front steps of the sorority house and took positions on opposite sides of the door. Rainey grabbed the knob. Locked.

She pulled her phone from her back pocket. The screen was lit with an incoming call. She answered, scanning the dark house and lawn, her eyes shining and intense.

"Emmerich," she said. "Detrick's at the sorority house. No sign of the Portland police officers. We need backup."

Caitlin signaled that she would take the rear and raced around the side of the house. She ran into the shadows, sleet pricking her face. She heard Rainey smash a window to climb in the front.

She nearly tripped over the man lying on the ground.

It was a police officer. She crouched and put two fingers to his neck. Felt a pulse. He was breathing.

Her hand came away hot with blood. She wiped it on her jeans, grabbed her phone, and called the Portland police. Quietly, urgently, she gave her FBI badge number and location. "Officer down. Repeat, officer down."

Her own pulse hammering, she stood and crept to the rear of the house. She got a bare view that hinted at a patio, lawn, and bushes at the back of the property. She ran for the back door. It was wide-open.

Gun raised, Caitlin entered, clearing the doorway in vertical increments as she turned the corner. She found herself in the kitchen.

She stepped out of the doorway and swept her weapon from left to right across the kitchen. Her eyes had adjusted to the dark. Counters and sink under the windows. Large island in the center. Fridge and cabinets on the interior walls. She slid around, clearing the room in sectors, heart thudding.

She found the light switches. Flipped them. Nothing—Detrick or his partner had cut the power.

Edging farther into the kitchen, she slipped on something slick. She steadied herself and turned her flashlight on. To her horror, a pool of blood sprang into red view.

On the floor, around the corner of the island, a young woman in a Greenspring College sweatshirt lay motionless. The back of her head was wrecked from heavy blows. Caitlin crouched and put her fingers to the girl's carotid. No pulse.

Caitlin's breathing turned shallow. Bloody shoeprints led from the young woman's body to the kitchen stairs.

From the living room, Rainey called, "Clear."

Caitlin stood, stepped around the island, and swept the beam of her flashlight across the room. "Kitchen clear. Rainey—upstairs."

She turned off the flashlight and rushed up the kitchen staircase. Her boots thudded on the wood. Before she reached the top, she crouched, gun raised, heart pounding. Slowly she straightened, weapon aimed directly down the hall.

In the hallway at the top of the staircase, a second young woman lay sprawled. The bloody footprints continued along the hall.

Aghast, Caitlin thought, *Emily isn't Detrick's statement kill anymore.*

The sorority was too tempting a target for him to pass up. He was taking out the house like a redneck roaring along a highway smashing mailboxes with a baseball bat.

Rainey charged up the stairs. "No sign of Emily or that woman downstairs."

"The back door was wide-open."

She knew, with sickening clarity, what had happened. The blond in the black suit, Detrick's groupie, had already dragged Emily away.

"Detrick called an audible," she said. "Instead of grabbing Emily and fleeing with her, he stayed here."

From a bedroom at the end of the hall came moans, then a scream. Caitlin and Rainey raised their weapons. Rainey led, Caitlin immediately behind her, hand on Rainey's shoulder. They approached the door. Rainey took a position pressed against the wall to the left. Caitlin took the right.

Caitlin turned the knob. The door was locked.

She called, "*FBI.*"

Inside, a girl yelled for help. Caitlin stepped back. Rainey trained her weapon on the door to cover her. Centering her balance, Caitlin raised her leg and kicked the latch. The door didn't budge.

"Move away from the door," she shouted.

Scuffling sounds. A young voice. "Moved."

She adopted a sharp angle and emptied four shots into the frame around the latch. This time when she kicked, the door flew open.

Inside, a young woman sat on the floor, cradling her injured roommate.

Rainey poured through the doorway and swept her weapon to the right. "Right clear."

Caitlin was right behind her, angling left. "Left clear. All clear."

Icy rain was blowing through the room. The window was open, the screen kicked out.

The young woman on the floor looked up from under dark hair. She pointed at the window. "He jumped."

Rainey knelt at the injured girl's side. After a second, she called for paramedics and air support.

Caitlin leaned out the window. There was no sign of Detrick.

She phoned Emmerich. "He's running."

"I'm ten minutes out, with a Portland Police TAC team. Other units should be there in under five."

"Detrick's accomplice has Emily. She's probably going to rendezvous with him." Below the window was a concrete patio and broken patio chairs. "He hit the ground hard. He may be injured."

"Be careful," Emmerich said. "But find him."

Rainey knelt at the side of the injured young woman. The girl was unconscious.

"She's breathing. Her pulse is strong." Rainey turned to the girl's roommate. "What's your name?"

"Julia."

"Julia, how many other people are in the house?"

"Maybe . . . two dozen? All in their rooms; they told us to come upstairs . . ."

"Help's on the way. When we leave, close the door, push that dresser in front of it, and don't open it until you see uniformed police officers leading paramedics inside the house. Can you do that?"

"Yeah." The girl nodded vigorously.

Caitlin and Rainey ran back to the hall. Behind them the door shut and they heard the dresser scrape across the floor.

As they ran down the hall, doors opened a few inches. Rainey shouted, "Stay in your rooms with the doors locked. The police are on the way."

She and Caitlin bolted down the stairs. Outside, through the sleet, distant lights flashed blue and red. The police were coming from campus—a mile farther along the road, past the top of the hill. Rainey swept her flashlight across the lawn. Muddy footprints led unevenly toward the woods.

"He's limping," Caitlin said.

"The Remington." Rainey ran across the street to grab the shotgun from their Suburban.

Caitlin aimed her flashlight at the trees. Detrick's footprints disappeared into a tangle of rhododendrons.

From behind her, beneath the gusting sleet, came a sound. A muffled rumble. It swelled into the growl of a heavy engine. Headlights blared on.

A black SUV accelerated down the street toward the Suburban.

Caitlin was in motion toward it before she even formed the thought. "*Rainey.*"

The headlights illuminated Rainey in the street, near the Suburban. The black SUV sped straight at her. Rainey leaped, trying to dive out of the way. The SUV hit her.

She flew onto the hood of the vehicle and slammed

into the windshield, cracking it. Slid, raggedly, and fell to the pavement.

The SUV kept coming. It was a black Tahoe—practically the twin of the Suburban. It scraped the FBI vehicle. Then, swerving toward the sorority house, it mounted the curb and drove onto the lawn. Its headlights swelled, blinding Caitlin. She thought: *I'm fucked*.

She spun, and the Tahoe sideswiped her.

It was a glancing blow. But still it knocked her off her feet and sent her skidding facedown along the sidewalk.

The Tahoe lost traction, spun, and stopped on the lawn, driver's side facing Caitlin. The headlights cast stark beams and shadows up the street.

Stunned, shaky, Caitlin raised her head. Vaguely she saw faces in upstairs windows. A figure on a neighboring porch—who immediately ducked back inside. Blue and red lights flashed through the firs that lined the top of the hill. She heard distant sirens.

The driver's door of the Tahoe opened. The dome light came on. Emily was in the back seat, apparently bound—cuffed or zip-tied to the inside door handle. She was fighting futilely to break free.

The driver climbed out. It was the blond in the black business suit. She cast a glance at Rainey, who lay motionless in the road, and turned to Caitlin. The woman's eyes were cold. River stones, smooth, flat, eroded of empathy.

Even flat on the ground, Caitlin recognized that look. She'd seen it before—in Austin, on the street outside Detrick's office at Castle Bay Realty, when this woman had glared as if she wanted to gut Caitlin like a deer.

It was the receptionist. The woman who thought Detrick was amazing. Brandi Childers.

A knife gleamed in her hand.

Caitlin rolled, scrabbling for her Glock. Brandi charged.

A shotgun blast hit the woman in the chest.

The blare of the gun was cut by the wind, but nothing else looks like twelve-gauge buckshot hitting center mass. Brandi's white dress shirt, pale skin, and pale gleaming hair turned to a miasma of red. She toppled like her strings had been cut, and hit the lawn.

The slush turned scarlet beneath her. She lay still.

In the street, Rainey racked the action on the Remington. She held it, trained on Brandi, two seconds longer, making sure. Then she backed against the side of the Suburban and sagged to the asphalt.

Caitlin lurched to her feet. She kicked the knife from Brandi's hand, confirmed that she had no pulse, picked up the knife, and staggered toward Rainey.

Rainey was slumped against the Suburban, bloody and covered in glass spall. The shotgun shuddered in her grip. Caitlin dropped to one knee at her side.

Rainey said, "Fine, it's fine."

It wasn't, but Rainey's eyes were clear, her pulse strong when Caitlin grabbed her wrist. Rainey nodded: She could hold on. Caitlin handed her Brandi's knife and stood. The flashing lights were closer, sirens clearer.

She blinked. Up the road toward the college, a pickup truck sat crosswise in the narrow street, grille and tailgate nearly touching parked cars along either curb, blocking the road.

·Like the trash cans had blocked a lane on the highway in Crying Call after the courthouse escape.

She spun to look at the Tahoe. Through the icy downpour, she saw a shadow heave into the far side of the SUV. Emily screamed.

Detrick. Caitlin raised her gun and pitched toward the vehicle. Detrick jumped into the Tahoe's driver's seat, jammed it in gear, and floored it toward the street. Caitlin aimed, but Emily was in the line of fire. She had no shot.

The Tahoe slid into the slick road and hit a parked car. Detrick spun the wheel. He turned, eyes glinting, and took Caitlin in. Then he accelerated down the street, away from the approaching lights and sirens.

Caitlin took two steps toward the FBI Suburban. It was wrecked.

Rainey looked up. Her voice cut through the wind. *"Run."*

60

Caitlin took off after the Tahoe, running along the sidewalk. Her ribs ached. Her shoulder ached. Her left leg felt like bruised meat. The sleet hit her in the face.

Behind her, the sirens grew louder. She glanced back. Rainey remained crumpled against the Suburban. The spinning lights of the police cars had topped the hill. Soon, they would barrel down the narrow street and discover the pickup truck blocking their path. The truck wouldn't slow them long—a minute, tops—but that could be too long. Detrick was speeding out of this neighborhood toward main roads and Interstate 5. If Caitlin lost sight of him, he would disappear in the lowering storm.

If that happened, Emily was dead.

The Tahoe's taillights shrank in the icy downpour. Caitlin's throat tightened. She would never catch an SUV on foot. No way.

Then she thought: *I goddamn will.*

To get to the bottom of the hill, Detrick had to go around four switchbacks. She could cut him off.

Spinning, she ran back to the sorority house and into the backyard. At the rear of the property she pushed through the bushes.

She came out on a steep, wooded hillside. She heard the Tahoe in the distance, coming around the hairpin turn. She ran, off-balance, toward the road below to intersect him.

After a hundred yards' slippery sprint down the hillside, she glimpsed the asphalt through the trees, splashed white with sleet. Headlights were coming. She sped up.

Before she reached the road, the Tahoe rushed past.

"Shit."

She forcibly told herself: *Ignore it all.* Everything that ached from getting sideswiped. The bruises, the cuts. Ignore the cold ice hitting her in the face. Run harder. *Dig in, princess.* She dashed onto the road. The Tahoe's taillights were halfway to the next hairpin turn.

Her breathing came hard. She couldn't stop, couldn't slow. She had at least another half mile in her legs at this speed. And she had more speed. And what the hell was she saving it for?

She pummeled across the road and ran down the hill on the far side. Heard the Tahoe make the next turn. Arms in front of her face, she crashed past bushes and branches. Saw the road below her.

The Tahoe's headlights rose, and it passed in front of her again. She burst onto the pavement, only seconds behind it this time. It continued toward the next curve. Its brake lights came on—late. The Tahoe veered, scraped the guardrail, and barely negotiated the turn.

Detrick seemed impaired. Abandoning any last shred of caution, Caitlin crossed the road and leaped, pouring downhill in the dark. Behind her, back by the sorority house, the flashing lights dimmed in the storm. She listened for the Tahoe's engine.

Her foot snagged on a vine. She pitched forward.

She balled, tumbled, tried to roll, but hit with enough force to knock the wind out of her. Shouting in shock, she slid downhill through mud and grit and leaves. Rolled a second time, came up on her feet with off-balance momentum, and kept going. She heard the Tahoe's engine again. In the distance, the headlights swung around the switchback.

The SUV came around the turn. She was ahead of it.

She ran from the trees, stepped onto the roadway, and raised the Glock.

Detrick accelerated, directly at her. Icy fear sluiced through her. She held her finger against the trigger. Waited. She planned to fire multiple rounds into the radiator. She had a semiautomatic pistol. To hit the target, she had to be close.

The headlights screamed in her eyes. She aimed between them and squeezed the trigger.

Fired, heard the round ricochet. Squeezed again.

Dead trigger. The Glock didn't fire.

Christ.

The vehicle roared at her, bright, closing. She threw herself toward the side of the road. The Tahoe swept by. She spun, her heart jackrabbiting. Shined her Maglite on the Glock. God*dammit*. The extractor port was fouled with muck from her muddy slide. It had caused a double feed. The gun was jammed.

She'd missed. Detrick was past.

The Tahoe continued downhill. Ahead of it lay the final switchback. She had only one more chance to short-cut down the hillside to the road below and stop him.

She stuck the slim flashlight in her mouth. Locked the Glock's slide back and stripped the magazine. Racked the slide three times. Grabbed a fresh mag from her belt, inserted it, racked the slide again.

The round didn't seat. She tap-racked, but the gun still felt wrong. God knew what was in the springs, the chamber, the barrel. She had neither the time nor the tools to clear the gun. She holstered it.

She threw a look at the receding Tahoe. It was almost at the switchback. She turned toward the shortcut, watching for the brake lights to come on.

They didn't.

She blinked icy rain from her eyes. Under her ragged breath, she said, "Oh, Jesus."

The Tahoe's headlights caught the view ahead of it. Trees, a guardrail, yellow caution signs. It didn't slow.

Good Christ. It swerved on the sleet-slick pavement and missed the turn.

The noise was a shriek, a can opener slicing metal. The Tahoe cut a gash in the guardrail and plunged off the road.

Caitlin climbed around the torn section of the guardrail. Beyond it, the slope was plowed by the Tahoe's plunge. The

SUV had nose-dived down the hill, tearing through saplings and ferns. Below, in the dark, she heard rushing water.

She swept her flashlight along the fall line on the hill. Tire tracks ran in two trenches down the slope. After sixty yards, they went ragged and disappeared into the darkness. She gritted her teeth. The Tahoe had veered and rolled.

She picked her way down the hill. The sound of rushing water grew wilder. She slid the last ten feet on slick earth and scrambled to a stop.

The Tahoe lay wrecked in a concrete storm channel that was raging with runoff.

Under the beam of her flashlight, whitecaps frothed. The water was breaking against the grille of the SUV. The vehicle lay half submerged, driver's side down, the hood and roof facing her. One glaring headlight remained above water.

Caitlin breathed raggedly. Through the icy rain her breath wreathed her like smoke. The storm channel was twenty yards wide. Most days, water probably trickled along its center an inch deep. Tonight, a churning torrent splashed onto the channel's angled banks. She swept the flashlight around the scene. Ten yards downstream from the Tahoe, the channel dropped precipitously to the main river. She could hear the thunder of tons of water crashing below.

"Oh, my hell."

The SUV's front wheel was lodged on debris. A tree limb, rebar, something. It was keeping the Tahoe from being swept away.

For now. The water in the channel was rising.

Caitlin aimed her flashlight at the Tahoe's windshield. Water half filled the interior of the vehicle. Nobody was at the wheel.

Through the SUV's sunroof, Caitlin saw Emily. The girl was clearly zip-tied to the interior handle of the rear passenger door, directly behind the driver's seat. That door lay against the bottom of the storm channel. With the water at the midline of the vehicle, Emily could barely keep her face above the surface. She was fighting for air.

Caitlin pulled out her phone, called Emmerich, gave him the location. "We need fire and rescue. Now."

"Two minutes," Emmerich said.

The water was lapping over Emily's chin.

"She doesn't have two minutes." She couldn't wait for fire and rescue.

Dry mouthed, shivering, she put away the phone, stepped from the grassy hillside onto the sloping concrete bank of the storm channel, and inched down to the edge. Cold spray mixed with the sleet.

As a patrol officer, she'd seen vehicles swept away on flooded roads—when the water was two feet deep. This water looked deeper than that. It was a monster force.

From inside the Tahoe came a battering sound. Caitlin aimed her flashlight at the sunroof. Emily's forehead was bloody, streams of red running through her wet hair and across her cheeks. She had head butted the sunroof to get Caitlin's attention. Water splashed over the girl's face.

Caitlin flashed the beam on and off to signal back. "I'm coming."

She stuck the Maglite in her back pocket and scrambled upstream about forty yards. Blowing out a series of short, sharp breaths, she let out a harsh yell and stepped off the bank.

She dropped into water that was thigh deep.

"Holy God."

The cold didn't grab—it stunned like an electric shock. Her legs went stiff. A jolt of breathless pain shot all the way to the center of her brain.

Go.

She planted her feet wide to brace herself, held her hands out for balance, and worked her way toward the SUV. With every step, she fought against losing her footing. The cold, the power of the water, rent her with fear. If she lost control, even for a split second . . .

She thought of Sean. Thought of her father. *Jesus good Lord Jesus* she wished they were here with rescue equipment and ropes and a harness.

Emily was desperately tilting her head back, fighting to sip air. Christ, oh God—*screw it.* It was her. Her or nothing. *Go.*

Caitlin forded the churning water, legs burning with the cold. Forty feet, thirty, fifteen—she reached out and grabbed the grille of the Tahoe.

The force of the water pressed her against it. Slapping chilled hands against the SUV, she scrambled out of the water onto the front panel and right wheel of the vehicle.

She crawled to the front passenger door, teeth chattering. Couldn't get it open. It was crushed out of true. She kept crawling to the rear door.

With numb fingers, she clawed at the handle and pried the door up. She shoved it all the way open and peered down into the vehicle.

No sign of Detrick.

Had he been thrown out when it rolled? Been swept over the falls? Did the motherfucker *get away*? She couldn't see into the last row of seats or the Tahoe's far back.

Stop wondering. Move.

Directly below her in the back seat, Emily was submerged, floating limp.

Heart thundering, Caitlin worked her drop-point knife from her back pocket. Squeezed it until she was sure she had it solidly in her freezing hand. Telling her fingers, *Grip,* she dropped into the vehicle.

She landed again in icy thigh-high water. She took a breath, ducked under the surface, and fought not to gasp from the agonizing cold. She ran her hand down Emily's arm until she found the zip tie. She slipped the point of the knife under it and swiped. One sawing motion, and another, and she cut the plastic.

Emily floated free. Caitlin straightened out of the water, inhaled, and lifted the girl's head above the surface.

She wasn't breathing.

61

Emily's face was ghostly white, her lips charcoal. Her eyes were half open, whites showing. Caitlin's hands were bitter, but Emily's skin felt even colder. The girl was nearly frozen.

She couldn't put Emily in rescue position within the confines of the tipped-over Tahoe, much less lift her out and lay her on a flat surface. Caitlin hoisted the young woman in her arms.

She whispered through chattering teeth. "Come on, girl. Come on."

Rescue procedure was *ABC*—airway, breathing, circulation. She put a hand beneath the back of Emily's head, tilted her jaw up, and cleared her airway.

Nothing.

"Emily. Wake up."

Outside, the surging water battered the Tahoe. The SUV felt like a sinkhole within a roar. Water squeezed through every joint in the vehicle. As did fear.

Emily remained limp. Panic crept along Caitlin's nerves. How long had the girl gone without oxygen?

She got behind her, pulled Emily upright against her chest, and locked her own hands in a fist immediately below Emily's ribs. Bracing her legs, Caitlin popped her fists into Emily's diaphragm, giving her the Heimlich.

Water erupted from the girl's lips in a massive bolus. Emily coughed and inhaled.

Adrenaline jacked into Caitlin's veins. "Come *on*."

She held tight to the young woman. Emily took another breath and opened her eyes.

For a second, Emily stared unseeing at the darkness. Her wet breathing echoed inside the vehicle. Then she blinked, seemed to orient herself, and went stiff. Her hands came out of the water as fists. She bucked and tried to fight free.

"Emily." Caitlin held her tightly. "I'm Caitlin Hendrix."

The girl spat, "Prove it."

Shivering, Caitlin held tight. "Once we get out. Which is right now."

Emily held tense. Caitlin felt the girl's youthful strength flooding back. If it came down to fight or flight, this girl was going to battle.

"My creds are wet. I'll prove it when we get out of here," Caitlin said.

Emily clenched, ready to punch, for another second. Then she gave a small, frantic nod. "Yeah."

Caitlin braced the young woman until Emily fumbled her feet under herself. She was wobbly, coughing and shuddering. Caitlin doubted she could stand on her own.

"Reach up. Grab the doorframe. I'll boost you out," Caitlin said.

A sound came from the rear of the Tahoe. A splash. Inside the vehicle.

The air seemed to shift. Caitlin's skin shrank.

She leaned to see around the back bucket seats into the darkened rear of the SUV.

Shadow. Shape, black on black. A gleam.

Detrick crouched in the far back, staring at her.

She had an instant to take him in. Shining eyes, messenger bag slung over his shoulder. *Money,* she thought. *IDs. Getaway kit.*

She shoved Emily behind her. She was reaching for her knife when Detrick leaped at her.

He sharked between the back seats, hit her with a hard tackle, and slammed her all the way into the dashboard. He grabbed her by the neck.

Blood oozed from a heavy gash on his forehead. In the dim dashboard light, his gray eyes glowed silver. The look in them was unlike anything she'd ever experienced.

It was the look his victims saw in the seconds before he took them. It said, *Yes, this. You're mine. Believe, and die.*

He had a tire iron in his hand. He drew back his arm, preparing to hit her. She cupped a hand, swung, and slapped him hard in the side of the head.

He howled. His ears were full of water—she hoped she'd burst his eardrum. He dropped the tire iron and clapped that hand over his damaged ear. His eyes lit with rage.

Behind him, Emily gaped.

Caitlin wheezed, "Get out."

Emily didn't move. But Caitlin knew what would happen if the girl waited. Their only chance was for her to get out of the vehicle.

She shoved Emily with her foot. "*Go.*"

Emily's mouth opened. She raised her head to the open door above her.

Caitlin clawed in her back pocket for the knife. She pulled it free but her fingers were blocks of ice. Detrick slapped it from her hand. The silver rage filled his gaze. Indistinctly, other colors reflected from his face. Spinning, red and blue.

Caitlin went for his eyes.

She jabbed him and dragged her fingernails down his face. Recoiling, he roared and blindly punched her in the face. Her head snapped back against the windshield. Stars exploded in front of her.

For several buzzing seconds, she could see nothing else. Then the view turned black-and-yellow, etched with movement. Splashing. Shoving sounds.

The stars died out. She returned. In the back seat, Emily was reaching overhead. She had her hands on the doorframe and was struggling to brace a foot on a seatback so she could climb out the open passenger door.

Detrick grabbed the girl. He pulled her hands loose from the doorframe and hauled her down. Clenching her by the throat, he shoved her head underwater.

Unholy Christ. The car was awash with freezing water and still he wanted only to kill.

Caitlin didn't have the angle to kick him in the head. She curled to grab Detrick's belt.

Her right hand was handcuffed to the steering wheel. *Christ.* Getaway kit. Kidnap kit.

With her left hand, she grabbed the back of Detrick's shirt. It momentarily slowed him, but her fingers were too numb to hold on.

He swept his grip from Emily's neck to the girl's clawing hands, shoved her down, and stepped on her. Caitlin swiped at him again. Raising a knee, he kicked her. She tried to dodge and grab his leg, but his boot connected with her collarbone. Her entire body went numb.

Emily punched at him, trying to dislodge him and get air.

He paused. His face was battered, one eye swollen, but he looked darkly satisfied.

"Told you I was going to waltz away, and you'd have to swallow it."

Caitlin's breath came hard. No time. The cops were close, but Detrick knew that and wouldn't leave her and Emily alive for them to find. The primitive envy that ate at him wouldn't allow it.

One play left, she thought—that's all she had. And only seconds to pitch it right.

She inhaled. "You told me I was going to wish I'd killed myself."

It came out shaky. It came out shivering, through chattering teeth. Detrick eyed her with contempt.

Let go, Caitlin. Let everything go. It has to be real.

She forced her voice to a flat calm. "That's *your* wish. You want it?"

Bewilderment crossed his face. And she recited the words she'd spoken when she phoned him on the crisis hotline.

"I'll slip into floating darkness. It'll be like falling through a field of stars, into the black nowhere."

Detrick froze. For a moment he gaped, and she saw it click. He realized that Rose, the suicidal caller, was her. Uncertainty filled his eyes.

Caitlin reached down, grabbed the steering wheel, and turned it.

The front tire of the Tahoe was caught solidly against the debris in the channel, but Caitlin threw all her strength into it. If she turned the steering wheel hard enough, she might dislodge the vehicle.

Detrick's uncertainty turned to fear. Screaming, he let go of Emily and leaped for Caitlin, trying to stop her.

He tried to twist her hand off the wheel but she ratcheted her elbow around it—and when he pulled, she continued to exert lateral force. Abruptly focused on stopping her, he fought like a mad dog. Punching, clawing, trying to bite her face and neck. In the back seat, Emily rose, gasping.

With her left hand, Caitlin pawed beneath the water for her drop-point knife, but it was gone.

Emily lunged at Detrick, grabbing fistfuls of his shirt. "Stop it."

Caitlin looked past Detrick at her. "Go. *Now.*"

Emily's lips parted and her eyes went wide. She shook her head. Detrick continued trying to pry Caitlin's hands from the wheel. He didn't grab her gun. He'd seen it malfunction. And, focused on prying her hands loose, he apparently hadn't thought of using it to smash her fingers.

Caitlin screamed, "*Go.*"

Emily bolted, scrambling up and out of the door.

Caitlin yelled, "Shut it!"

Emily slammed the door. With her free hand Caitlin fumbled for the ignition—and the key fob. The Tahoe's headlights were still on, and the dash lights. The battery was still providing power. She hit LOCK.

A *thunk* ran through the vehicle. Detrick turned, blinking, at the sound. Letting go of Caitlin, he reached above his head and pawed the front-seat passenger-door handle. But that door was crushed shut.

Caitlin yanked the key from the ignition and jammed the fob in her jeans pocket. Detrick swiveled back to her, understanding.

The child safety locks had just engaged. He was trapped.

He lunged at her, but she wrenched both elbows around the steering wheel. It put her head just above the surface of the water.

Through the windshield she saw flashlights descending the slope of the storm channel. Above her, on the chassis of the Tahoe, Emily's footsteps thumped.

The girl yelled, "Here!"

Through the pelting sleet, the bobbing flashlights

reached the edge of the channel. Behind them, high-powered spotlights came down the hill. But the smaller lights didn't wait or stop at the water's edge. Amazingly, they began forming into a string. Bobbing, swaying, coming closer.

A group of young women was forming a human chain from the bank, fording the storm channel, to reach the Tahoe and pull Emily to safety.

Detrick tried again to open the door above him. He punched the window with a fist. Roared in anger and pain. Then he turned back to Caitlin.

Emily gingerly edged toward the grille of the SUV. The rear end of the Tahoe lifted with the current. A rope whipped out of the night and Emily caught it.

Detrick's hands clawed at Caitlin's forearms, but she had anchored them around the steering wheel. She threw all her weight to one side and turned the wheel hard, gaining maximum leverage.

She dug her feet against the seat to keep him from dislodging her. Emily's position was still precarious.

Voices, muffled by the roar of the water, shouted directions at Emily. She wrapped the rope around her waist and fumbled to tie a knot. Not the best, but all she could manage with frozen hands.

Arms reached out to her. Caitlin caught the flash of a high-visibility stripe on a helmet. A man in uniform. Motorcycle cop. Behind him she saw GREENSPRING RUGBY on another rescuer's sweatshirt.

Emily shouted, "Help the FBI agent inside."

The girl turned and looked through the windshield.

Her expression was taut. The rescuer locked wrists with her. She slid from the Tahoe's crumpled hood into the water.

The last thing Caitlin saw was Emily's desperate eyes. The chain of rescuers swept her toward the safety of the bank.

The hood of the Tahoe tilted up a few degrees.

A minute back, Caitlin had turned the wheel, to keep Detrick from pulling her free. She'd shifted the vector on which the car hung. Detrick hadn't noticed. In the cramped, freezing interior of the SUV, he was trying to dig the key fob from Caitlin's pocket. But it didn't matter.

Caitlin began taking fast, deep breaths. It wouldn't be long now. The back of the vehicle was slowly swinging toward the center of the storm channel.

She saw Emily reach the bank. The cop and her rugby teammate lifted her from the water, and she fell into the arms of her sorority sisters.

A tingling spark lit up the center of Caitlin's chest. *Safe*.

From beneath the Tahoe's trapped front wheel came a creaking, tearing sound. Emily's weight had been holding the vehicle down, just enough to keep it pinned to the rubble on which the SUV was lodged. Caitlin had known that when Emily climbed off the hood, the reduction in weight might make the difference. It had.

A wave hit the grille. The Tahoe lifted from the bed of the channel. With a lurch, the front tire slipped free of the anchoring debris.

The current grabbed the vehicle and swept it toward the lip of the drop-off.

Detrick shrieked, let go of Caitlin, and pounded on the windshield. Caitlin balled herself against the wheel, holding on with every ounce of strength, thinking: *Please. Emily's safe. Give me more time in the here and now.*

62

In the furious current, the Tahoe dipped, rose, and shot over the concrete lip of the waterfall into nothingness, with Caitlin fetal against the steering wheel, Detrick screaming.

The bottom literally fell out of the world. *Breathe, breathe, breathe.*

They dropped twenty feet. The back end hit first, hard, and they splashed into the river. The stop was jarring and they went all the way under before the Tahoe bobbed back to the surface and breached like a whale. The front end splashed back down and the SUV rolled upright.

The torrent poured down from above. The swollen Willamette River swiftly caught them. They were swept backward into the main flow of the river.

And, with the sound of cracking wood, they stopped.

They had lodged against the trunk of a downed tree. Freezing water washed over Caitlin, then subsided.

She breathed, stunned that she was conscious. Above, beyond the edge of the drop-off, the huge waterfall was eerily illuminated by spinning blue lights. Flashlights swept the slope.

In the front passenger seat, Detrick stirred. With her left hand, Caitlin reached across to her right hip and drew her gun.

Outside, flashlights, headlights, a helicopter spotlight, filled the air. Detrick opened his eyes.

His face was shadowed, but he straightened. Left-handed, she aimed at him.

"Kyle," she said. "You're under arrest."

He shook his head. "Thing won't fire."

"You're fucked. Sideways and twice on Sunday. Don't move."

His broad shoulders filled the car. His breathing seemed to steal the air. His self-assurance darkened the gap between them. He gathered himself.

Though her right hand was cuffed to the wheel, there was play in the chain. Caitlin smacked the butt of the Glock, racked the slide, and set her index finger against the trigger. *Please*.

As Detrick lunged, the light struck his eyes.

Caitlin shot him in the chest.

Portland Fire and Rescue launched an inflatable rescue boat and a Jet Ski into the swollen river. A police helicopter hovered overhead, its spotlight shimmering on the whitecapped water. The firefighters punched out the sunroof.

Caitlin tried to shout but merely hacked, "He's under arrest. I shot him, but he's still dangerous."

The water in the Tahoe was filled with Detrick's blood, the air with his labored gasps.

"I don't care if he vomits his heart onto his lap. Don't take him into the helo," she said.

He glanced at her, half aware, teeth bared. Another Jet Ski swung alongside, engine revving against the current. Behind the driver was a Portland tactical officer with a rifle. He aimed it at Detrick.

The firefighters hooked him into a harness. The helicopter winched him out of the Tahoe and carried him, dangling, to the riverbank, where a slew of police vehicles and a SWAT unit waited.

The firefighter turned to Caitlin, raising bolt cutters. "Your turn."

She remembered the sweet *ting* of the handcuff chain being cut, and the calm expertise of the firefighters who helped her into the inflatable. She recalled saying, *Thanks.* As the inflatable gunned its beautiful Evinrude against the swollen river, she noticed the headlights on the shore. Shadowed in front of them, she saw Emmerich's hard silhouette. Beside him stood Brianne Rainey.

She vaguely recalled a paramedic leading her to a warm ambulance and wrapping her in a silver thermal blanket. Eventually, when the shivering subsided, the night came back into focus.

Rainey sat across from her, bedraggled and bloody. Butterfly bandages closed a long gash across her cheek. She was still littered with glass spall. Under the harsh lights, it seemed as if a tiny galaxy was alight on her. Caitlin reached out and took her hand.

Rainey squeezed. "Emily's outside."

Caitlin stood, shivering, and climbed down from the ambulance.

Emmerich walked up. "Are you . . ."

"I'm fine. Where is she?"

He nodded past the vehicles. A group of young women stood at the edges of the light. They too were swaddled in thermal blankets, after carrying out their impromptu rescue. Emily was with them, speaking to a Portland police officer.

"Does she know?" Caitlin said.

"About Lia? No."

She shed the blanket and walked toward the young women, with Emmerich alongside.

Emily saw her, and though she was wet and hypothermic and had experienced a near drowning, she walked away from the policewoman and strode up to Caitlin and threw her arms around her. Caitlin let out a breath, let her shoulders drop, and held her tight.

"I thought . . . ," Emily choked out. "I saw the car go over, and I thought . . ."

"I know." Caitlin had seen Emily's face earlier, as the girl climbed out of the Tahoe. That meant more to her than anything. "You're okay."

Emily nodded tightly.

Caitlin held on to her. "We have other news."

They told her. Emily's head dropped. She cried for a rough minute. Then she straightened her shoulders.

"How soon can I fly to Nevada? I have to get out there to . . ." Her voice cracked. "To take care of Lia's body."

"Soon," Emmerich said. "Tomorrow or the next day."

Caitlin admired the young woman's grit. Emily was the polar opposite of Brandi Childers, who had latched on to a serial killer in a twisted grab at power and gratification.

Emily wiped her eyes. Her girlfriends walked over. Caitlin felt an ache, knowing that today alone Detrick had taken two young women, and maybe a police officer, within the space of a few minutes, and that nothing could bring them back.

Caitlin said, "You have amazing friends."

Emily nodded. The girls circled into a raw group hug.

Under the flashing lights, paramedics loaded a gurney into an ambulance. Detrick lay strapped down on it, unconscious, shackled hand and foot, guarded by two TAC officers with rifles. The doors slammed shut.

63

The next day the storm blew east and the sun rose gold in a porcelain sky. The streets, the hills, the trees, all gleamed under a brisk breeze. Caitlin rose with lingering exhaustion, her fingers tingling as if she were still immersed in cold water.

She stripped, cleaned, oiled, and reassembled her Glock, before spending time at the firing range in the basement at the Portland Police Bureau. The semiautomatic fired a magazine without jamming, clean and smooth. She felt calmer with it holstered on her hip. Centered.

After that, she, Rainey, and Emmerich spent the morning shuttling between the Detective Division at the police bureau downtown and the Xi Zeta house. They worked the crime scene alongside Portland homicide detectives—interviewing witnesses, outlining search warrant requests, and gathering evidence that would shape the prosecution against Kyle Detrick.

The police officers who had been on duty guarding the Xi Zeta house both had been badly injured. The driver of the patrol car had been found in its trunk with a head injury. Detrick and Brandi had driven up in an SUV that looked like an FBI vehicle and walked up to his car with their fake credentials out. When he lowered his window, Brandi tased him and Detrick beat him with a tire iron. He and his partner were both hospitalized. Their prognosis was guarded but hopeful.

The Portland police's cyberdivision coordinated with Nicholas Keyes in Quantico, tracing Detrick's path from Crying Call to Phoenix, Jester, Lake Tahoe, and Portland. The burner phone that had been in his pocket when he was arrested needed to be carefully dried before the crime lab could recover data. Brandi's burner contained texts she'd sent, coordinating Detrick's escape from the courthouse. One told him where she'd parked the car he would use as a getaway vehicle. Another said, Arrived Oklahoma. On way to Rincon.

They had Aaron Gage's cell phone, stolen when Brandi broke into his house and stabbed him. That was what had exposed Lia Fox's home address.

They were only beginning to excavate the link between Brandi and Detrick.

Her twisted attachment to him had been evident from the day Caitlin met her. In retrospect, so had her scorn for other women and her contempt for law enforcement. Brandi's passion for Detrick apparently grew from tangled psychological roots. She had an arrest record for attacking a love rival with a broken vodka bottle. She had an ex-husband who'd gone to jail for pistol-whipping another driver in a road rage incident. Brandi had married him at the courthouse while he was on trial. Violence had long aroused her.

She was the figure on the Solace multiplex theater CCTV video who surreptitiously tailed Detrick as he stalked his victim. She had known by then that Detrick was a kidnapper. Far from repelling her, his criminality—transgressive, cunning, risky—had drawn her to him.

After Detrick's arrest, Brandi threw herself into helping him escape. Freedom put him in her debt. Caitlin suspected that Brandi thought he'd be grateful. And that she had expected him to bond with her as his partner.

Maybe she'd thought they were outlaws. After all, Bonnie and Clyde had been from Texas too.

But Caitlin couldn't imagine that Detrick saw things that way. Brandi had made herself complicit in his crimes. Once she crossed that line, she was trapped. He owned her.

He wasn't grateful to her. He was a psychopath. He used her.

In the end, Detrick used her up. As she lay fallen from a shotgun blast, he didn't give her a second glance. He simply drove away.

The sorority house and street outside were cordoned off while forensics worked the scene. Caitlin's energy drained as she entered the kitchen and saw the outline where the first body had been found, blood spreading beyond it.

Primitive envy. If Detrick couldn't have it, he would destroy it.

At lunchtime she drove back downtown, to the bustling, green city center, and wrote a report on the confrontation with Brandi and Detrick. She got a burger at a café on Northwest Twenty-Third. Clean sunlight poured through the plate-glass window fronting the street, and she paused eating, to write. She breathed in the fresh air, took notice of the firs that carpeted the hills, let normal conversation, laughter, excitement, workaday purpose, wash past her in the café.

Her phone buzzed with texts and calls. Every time Caitlin scrolled through her messages, she saw Michele's unanswered text. We okay, girl?

Caitlin knew she needed to connect with both Michele and Sean, and that the longer she let this hang, the harder it would be. She finished her glass of iced tea, picked up the phone, and started to reply.

Hey, girl. Been crazy times. I

She deleted what she'd written.

Tried again. Didn't mean to leave you hanging. I've been on the run and

Backspaced. Her thumb hovered over a smiley face.

She heard a knock. Rainey was peering through the window, hands tented over her eyes. Caitlin waved her inside.

She came through the door tapping her watch. "Leaving for the airport in fifteen."

Caitlin stuck her phone in her back pocket. "I need to make one stop on the way."

The medical center was a tree-dotted complex near the Trail Blazers' basketball arena. It overlooked skyscrapers on the riverbank. When the Suburban pulled under the portico at the main entrance, Caitlin told Rainey and Emmerich, "I won't be long."

Upstairs, in the bustle and hush, the zone where technology met raw physical frailty, she showed her credentials to the nurse at the desk in the hospital's intensive care unit.

"No visitors," the nurse said. "No questions."

"I'm not going in."

She walked down the hall. Outside Detrick's room, a police officer was on guard.

Beyond the glass wall Detrick lay motionless, bristling with tubes and monitors, hands cuffed to the bed rails. She didn't even step to the doorway. She was fine keeping safety glass between them.

But she wanted him to see her. To see that she was standing, and he was not. She peered through the glass, waiting, until he turned his head.

He stilled, waxen. His chest rose and fell. He glared.

Caitlin lifted a hand. She waved. And, when she was confident she had his full attention, she smiled.

EPILOGUE

On Saturday night, the emergency room at Temescal Hospital in Oakland was getting slammed. It was seven forty-five P.M. when firefighter-paramedics brought in a raving woman. Not the first raving woman of the night, but the worst off.

She was strapped to a gurney, writhing. The paramedics wheeled her through the doors and greeted the triage nurse.

"Caucasian female, approximately forty years old. Found on the Berkeley campus, lying supine on the sidewalk, agitated and screaming incoherently," the senior paramedic said. "No wallet or ID."

They wheeled her along the hall. Her clothing was filthy. It didn't, however, smell like long-term street clothing. The woman arched her back and shrieked. Her eyes rolled and spittle flecked her lips. Her words were unintelligible.

She was covered in blood. Her wrists were bound with . . .

"Barbed wire?"

"She fought, trying to stop us touching her," the paramedic said. "We barely managed to lift her onto the stretcher. We started to open her jacket, but she lunged and tried to bite me."

The nurse directed them to an exam room. They parked the gurney beside the exam table as the emergency resident came in. He was pulling on latex gloves. His eyes were tired, his scrubs wrinkled. He'd been on call for twenty-six hours.

"On three."

Together, two nurses and the paramedics transferred the woman to the table. She thrashed and tried again to speak, but the sounds that emerged from her mouth were animalistic moans.

The paramedic said, "Vitals stable aside from a mild tachycardia. Heart rate one oh three. Gross neuro exam normal. Pupils equal, round, reactive. No sign of head trauma. Was conscious but disoriented when we found her—unable to tell us her name, date, or place."

He handed the RN a clipboard, she signed off, and they left.

With bandage scissors, the RN began cutting off the woman's jacket. Thinking: *Brain injury? Drugs?* The patient twisted. The nurse spoke calmingly, asking the woman her name, but the patient didn't respond. The resident examined the wire that bound her wrists. It ran up her arms beneath the sleeves of her jacket. The barbs dug into her flesh.

"Wire cutter," he said.

The RN snipped away the jacket and the woman's shirt. She stopped. "Doctor."

The other nurse handed the resident a cannulated pin-and-wire cutter. He braced the patient's wrist.

The RN stared in frozen horror at the patient's abdomen.

The woman was wrapped in duct tape. The resident slipped the jaws of the cutter around the barbed wire, preparing to snip it. The nurse leaned down and carefully turned the patient so she could get a view of her back.

The nurse leaped for the doctor, screaming, "*No—*"

At her apartment, sheltered by Virginia hickories and the winter night, Caitlin toweled her wet hair and pulled on jeans and a Warriors T-shirt. On the floor, clothes erupted from her open suitcase. Music rang from the stereo. Stevie Ray Vaughan, "Pride and Joy." Texas—the good stuff. She turned it up.

When she half danced into the kitchen, Shadow jumped to her feet, ears pricking.

Caitlin laughed. "Girl. Not another walk. We ran three miles before the sun went down."

She ruffed Shadow's fur and tossed her a dog biscuit from a box on the counter.

Caitlin should have been exhausted but felt weightless. She got a tub of fruit salad from the fridge. Thought again and pulled out a hunk of Parmesan cheese. And prosciutto. And a bottle of Pinot Grigio. The apartment felt warm. It wasn't exactly home yet, but with its French windows and built-in bookshelves, it worked for her. She heaped a plate, poured a glass of wine, and dropped onto the sofa. Muting the music, she turned on the TV. She cued up *Black Mirror*.

She sent Rainey a text. Dystopian satire it is.

A reply beeped. Hallelujah. Next: opera.

Smiling, Caitlin held on to the phone. She sighed. *No time like now.* Thumbing the screen, she sent Michele a message. Sorry I've been a brat. Then she called Sean.

His number rang. Shadow jumped onto the sofa. Her eyes pleaded, *Treat?* Caitlin nudged her back.

With a clatter, Sean picked up. Rushing air and engine noise obscured his voice. "I don't know anything yet. I'm on my way there. Nobody knows anything."

She froze. "Sean?"

"There's no reliable information. It's chaos. But, Cat—it looks bad."

A hot needle seemed to stab her between the eyes. She grabbed the remote and turned to a news channel.

On-screen was a blasted building. Flames were shooting from ground-floor windows. Fire trucks crowded the driveway. Beyond them, the sign above the building's entrance said, EMERGENCY.

Breaking: Explosion at Oakland Hospital.

"Jesus." It was Temescal.

Michele worked at Temescal.

Through the phone, Sean's truck engine gunned. "Phones at the hospital are down. Michele's not answering her cell. Fire crews can't even get inside." His voice had a fractured edge. "Caitlin, it's him."

Her own voice sounded distant. "The bomber."

The roar of the truck filled the phone. Orange flames filled the television screen.

Sean's voice was a rusty blade. "What if it's *him*?"

Caitlin's field of vision shuddered. She felt a sense of déjà vu. Seemed to see a visual echo. A shadow that wasn't there.

She stood. Her throat was tight.

"I'm booking a flight. Getting on a plane tonight." Her pulse thundered. "Sean. Hang on. I'm on my way."

ACKNOWLEDGMENTS

As always, I owe my thanks to a number of people whose skill, enthusiasm, and dedication have helped make this novel the best book it could be. In particular, I'm grateful to everyone at Dutton, especially John Parsley, Christine Ball, Cassidy Sachs, Jessica Renheim, and Jamie Knapp. For supporting me every step of the way, I want to thank the team at the Story Factory, especially David Koll and, above all, Shane Salerno. Thanks also to Carl Beverly, Sarah Timberman, Liz Friedman, and CBS; Joe Cohen and Tiffany Ward at CAA; and Richard Heller. For providing a sounding board, my thanks go to Ann Aubrey Hanson. For their support and encouragement, I'm grateful to Don Winslow and Steve Hamilton. For explaining how doctors talk, many thanks to Sara Gardiner, MD. For showing me how to disarm an attacker in the dark—and for believing in me from the day we met—my thanks go, forever, to Paul Shreve.

MEG GARDINER

"If you read Sue Grafton, Lee Child, Janet Evanovich, Michael Connelly, or Nelson DeMille, you're going to think Meg Gardiner is a gift from heaven."

—Stephen King

For a complete list of titles, please visit
prh.com/meggardiner